John 

LOOSE-LIMBED

David Barrie

www.looselimbed.com

Also by David Barrie:

Wasp-Waisted

Night-Scented

www.looselimbed.com

Visit the site dedicated to this book for:
Reading Group notes
Photos of all the key locations in Paris featured in the story
More about the author

www.davidbarrie.com

Visit the author's site for:
His blog
A short biography
Details of all his books

www.johnlawmedia.com

Visit the John Law Media site for:
Our editorial policy
Current catalogue of titles
Submissions guidelines

David Barrie

LOOSE-LIMBED

noir chic

John Law Media

Published by John Law Media Ltd.
P.O. Box 26515, Glasgow G74 9EF
www.johnlawmedia.com
contact@johnlawmedia.com
First published in Great Britain 2011.

ISBN 978 0 9562518 4 8

Printed in Scotland by Thomson Litho, East Kilbride.

Douter en amour est souvent un stimulant du cœur; douter en religion n'élève pas moins l'esprit au ciel; douter en politique est haute philosophie et grande sagesse; mais douter en art est une réelle calamité! Toute voie s'encombre; toute lumière s'éteint; toute vigueur s'affaisse; tout génie disparaît!

In love, doubt strengthens desire; in religion, doubt is a form of belief; in politics, doubt is the only wise path; but when it comes to art, doubt is disastrous! It will block your path; it will plunge you into darkness; it will sap your energy; it will banish inspiration!

Charles Garnier, *Le nouvel Opéra de Paris*

Although there are some French terms in this tale, most of them have long since been adopted into English. Here is a brief explanation of those which have not:

arrondissement	For administrative purposes Paris is divided into twenty arrondissements whose size and population vary widely (from 18 000 to 230 000 inhabitants). In the course of the city's history each one has evolved a distinct social character.
Brigade Criminelle	A special unit within the Parisian police force, the Brigade Criminelle investigates the city's murders and most serious crimes. It is based in the heart of Paris at 36 quai des Orfèvres on the Ile de la Cité.
commissariat	A police station.
DCRI *Direction Centrale du Renseignement Intérieur*	Officially created in July 2008, the DCRI brought together the two feuding arms of the French national security apparatus, the DST and the RG.
DST *Direction de la Surveillance du Territoire*	Created in 1944, the DST was a secretive organisation in charge of counter-espionage, counter-terrorism and protecting the French economy. It was merged into the DCRI in 2008.
flic	Widely used slang for "cop".
gardiens de la paix	The rank and file of the police force.
juge d'instruction	A magistrate whose job is to carry out preliminary investigations of crimes and misdeeds and judge whether they are ripe for prosecution. Once charged with an inquiry, a *juge* has complete autonomy to proceed as he wishes and is almost impossible to stop. The role of the *juges* is to handle very complex or sensitive cases deemed more suitable to elucidation by a powerful, independent and highly experienced judicial expert than by the normal police and bureaucratic process.
RG *Renseignements Généraux*	Created in 1911, the RG was a branch of the police charged with keeping an eye (some might say spying) on the citizens of the Republic and all others to be found within its frontiers. It was merged into the DCRI in 2008.

Monday, 11th May

Her feet were wrong.

She was svelte and elegant, without a hint of fragility. Her long legs and fine arms were shaped by tightly packed muscle, a promise of athletic grace were she to rise from her resting place. Despite her plain features and flat chest – barely swelling against her simple black cocktail dress – she could have claimed her place at a fashion shoot as an instance of flawless harmony.

Providing her feet were hidden, which they were not. Kitten-heeled shoes sat neatly aligned in front of an armchair across the room. She had not made it into them.

It was not the size of her feet – they were neither too big nor too small – it was the suffering they had seen. Their soles were thick and calloused. Several patches of skin, including a large area around one heel, bore the dark hue of recent, or repeated, bruising. The contour of the left foot was uneven, hinting at a past fracture. While the rest of her had been painstakingly shaped and groomed, they had been neglected, if not abused.

And then there were the toes. A hardy veteran dominated each foot, stocky and powerful, a survivor of constant attrition. The smaller ones, no less valiant, displayed kinks and bends, memories of the inherent frailty they had fought to cast off.

From the ankles up she told a tale of sculptural purity, but her feet were holding out for a different narrative.

They held Franck's gaze, despite the fact that his attention should have been elsewhere.

Georges Sternberg was quick to point this out.

"You'll have to look at her neck at some point," he said, fitting the lens cap back on his camera, having taken enough pictures of the corpse.

"I already have," said Franck. "Not much to see, though."

Whatever had been used to strangle her, it had been very thin and long enough to go round her neck three times. Pulled taut, it had not quite broken the surface of her skin while compressing her throat and denying her lungs the oxygen they needed, first to keep her conscious and then to keep her alive. Her face and throat were dark, purple having seeped in as her life ebbed out.

"The killer didn't do that to her feet," observed Sternberg. "They've been like that for years."

Franck nodded.

"Strange, though," he said. "Workman's feet on an angel's body. You'd think she'd have taken as good care of them as the rest of her."

"Think I should get a close-up of them?" asked Sternberg.

Franck shrugged.

"Like you said, none of the damage there is new. Our killer was too busy at the other end."

"All the same, a few photos could come in useful. I could show them to Annabelle. Might calm her down a little."

Sternberg palmed his lens cap, nudged Franck aside and squatted down, angling his camera at the victim's feet. While he snapped away, Franck searched his memory.

"Annabelle who?" he finally asked.

Sternberg got up, raised an eyebrow at Franck, and walked across the room to where he had left his two kit bags. He unzipped a side pouch and retrieved his wallet from it. Pulling one photo out from the many it contained was a bit tricky with his fingers in loose-fitting disposable plastic gloves, but he eventually managed it. He held it up in front of Franck's eyes.

It showed a girl, maybe thirteen, in a leotard. Her arms formed a pointed arch over her head while she stood on the tip of her toes in ballet shoes laced to her ankles. Her smile was determined but severe, her attention focused on her own posture rather than on the beholder.

"Ah, that Annabelle," said Franck. He had never actually met Georges Sternberg's daughter, but it was a safe bet that her father had mentioned her on countless occasions.

"Ballet-mad," said Sternberg. "Comes before everything else. A close look at the side-effects might give her back some sense of perspective."

Franck frowned at him. Clearly Sternberg knew something

he didn't.

"Gracious body. Misshapen feet," stated Sternberg.

"So?"

"We're dealing with a swan."

*

"Olivier Blanchard."

"Who?"

"Lieutenant Olivier Blanchard, formerly attached to the fifteenth arrondissement commissariat. Now working out of rue Chauchat in the ninth."

"Rings a bell," said Yves de Chaumont. "Very serious, cuts no corners, a stickler for detail? That's the one?"

"That's the one," confirmed Franck.

"So he's directing your caseload now? We *juges d'instruction* are certainly slipping in the hierarchy these days."

Yves was joking, but not entirely. The *juges d'instruction*, a time-honoured particularity of the nation's judicial system, a corps of buccaneering investigative magistrates elevated to elite status by their independence from the rest of the administrative machine, were indeed increasingly under threat. Rumours were rife about a forthcoming reform that would sweep away what influential voices in the current government were now insisting was an anomalous institution.

For the moment, however, Yves' title still conferred upon him substantial discretionary power. Had he wished to crush a simple lieutenant for presuming to steer an investigation towards a specific pair of hands within the Brigade Criminelle – and a very specific pair of hands at that, given that they did not really belong to the Brigade at all, but to Yves himself, under the conditions of an unwritten agreement with their real owner, the shadowy DCRI – a simple phone call would have sufficed.

But Yves' umbrage was feigned, as his smile indicated. Initiative was a rare enough occurrence within the sclerotic mechanism of the capital's police structure. It deserved a little encouragement. Moreover, Franck had nothing substantial on his plate at the moment – just some preparatory work on the Chantreau dossier, and a thief who specialised in second-rate religious artworks, although a pest Yves had been trying to stamp out for some time, was not quite as much a menace to society as a murderer.

"Any idea why he chose you?" continued Yves.

"Said he thought of me as soon as he saw the body."

"I suppose there's something strangely flattering in that, although I can't quite put my finger on it."

"There's also the fact that I'm probably the only person in the Brigade Criminelle he's ever had to deal with," Franck pointed out.

"In which case he's a fortunate man, although he probably doesn't know it yet. Anyhow," Yves laid his hands flat on the unencumbered surface of his desk, leaning forward above them to make an official pronouncement, "I have no objection to you taking on this case. What was her name?"

"Sophie Duval."

Yves closed his eyes, acknowledging the loss of one more life and paying momentary homage to the victim. He then nodded almost imperceptibly and snapped them open, a gesture Franck knew was not far removed from that of a hunter setting forth in the dawn, intent on returning with his prey.

"What do we know?"

"The victim was found this morning just after ten," explained Franck. "We have her alarm clock to thank for that. It had been ringing since eight thirty."

"Loud enough to be heard outside her apartment?"

Franck nodded. "Loud enough – and long enough – for her downstairs neighbour to complain to the concierge. Who had a spare set of keys. When she decided to use them, she discovered that the door was not locked. She found the victim on the floor of the main room of her apartment. That's when she called the local commissariat. They sent lieutenant Blanchard, who arrived on the premises at ten forty. He phoned me."

"So Sophie Duval was supposed to get up at eight thirty that morning, but didn't, having opened the door to the wrong person the night before?"

"Looks like it. She was dressed to go out – somewhere classy, judging by her hair, make-up, and dress. Her shoes were waiting for her to slip into them and her handbag was on a nearby table with her keys inside. Although she was strangled, there was no sign of a fight, other than the fact that she scraped her own skin trying to get at the cord around her neck. I'd say she was taken by surprise by someone already standing right next to her."

"To let someone get that close, you have to know them well."

"She won't be the first murder victim to have put her trust in the the wrong man."

Yves nodded.

"Sad but true. When was she last seen alive?"

"The concierge saw her around six the previous day. Coming in."

"How hard is it to get into the building?"

"There's a keypad on the outside door. A five digit code. To reach the stairs and the lift from the entrance hall you either have to have a key or use the intercom and be buzzed through."

"Anyone in the building mention anyone strange coming or going after the victim got home?"

"Not so far. The concierge's lodge shuts at seven. If the killer crossed anyone's path after that, no one seems to have taken any notice."

"No smoking guns, then, Franck. Time to start unpicking her life. Who was Sophie Duval?"

"Not a nobody."

"Nobody's a nobody," insisted Yves. "Not as far as this office is concerned."

"Sure, but it turns out that Sophie Duval was definitely not a nobody. I would have thought you might have heard of her."

Yves frowned and propped his chin on the fist of his left hand.

"Apart from Sophie Duval the dancer ..." he murmured.

"I'm afraid so," said Franck. "The one and the same."

Yves sighed.

Yet another case about artistic treasures.

*

Few buildings in Paris were as immodest in their intentions as the Opera House. Built for an Emperor, an entire neighbourhood had been ploughed under to provide a triumphal avenue over which it could hold sway. Its richly decorated facade announced that poetry, music, dance and song, embodied by vast allegorical statues, had at last found their true home within its walls. Every composer held in high esteem by the nineteenth century – Bach, Haydn, Mozart, Beethoven, and Rossini amongst them – had been recruited as a tutelary spirit, carved in stone on its facade. Excess was its very essence. The public areas it incorporated – a grandiose stairway feeding a pillared foyer and a series of salons designed to allow thousands to mill around in their finest, seeing and being seen – took up more space than the actual concert hall, which nonetheless boasted five levels of stalls and boxes above a vast semi-circle of velvet-draped seats. Its stage was wider and deeper than any of its European rivals and was equipped to allow the deployment of the most audacious and extravagant scenery that the creative imagination could conceive. Backstage, a warren of workshops, artists' lodges, offices and changing rooms ensured that the building functioned as a world unto itself.

It took fifteen years to build, in the course of which the Franco-Prussian war had been lost, Napoleon III toppled, the Paris Commune declared and crushed, and the Third Republic established. Throughout it all, its architect, Charles Garnier, calmly pursued his goal of erecting a temple to music and dance whose walls would enclose an enchanted realm, a refuge from whatever sordid acts reality happened to get up to outside.

Franck reckoned he had been inside maybe a dozen times,

which was probably about average for the relatively cultivated section of the capital's population. The true fanatics could cite five, ten, or even more times as many visits. Few, however, could claim to have been waved through the rear entrance, an unassuming archway on boulevard Haussmann topped by two dwarf-like obelisks and a stone lintel, ignored by the hordes of shoppers drawn to the nearby Galeries Lafayette and Printemps. Far more modest than the principal facade which crowned the avenue de l'Opéra, this was nonetheless the most exclusive of the entrances to the building. Money could not get you through it; only talent could.

The first was just as well, since Franck was as impecunious as an honest servant of the state should be. As for the second, within the past twelve months a weighty official report had cast severe doubt upon his professional abilities and judgement. Luckily for him, he had a card up his sleeve – an appointment with Anne-Laure Favennec, Dance Director of the Opera Ballet.

Forty-five minutes later Franck was still waiting, perched on a seat in a corner of a small office. Favennec's assistant, whose desk took up most of the available space, threw apologetic glances at him whenever the constantly chirping phone on her desk gave her a little respite. Her embarrassment was understandable – she knew why he was there. The ninth arrondissement commissariat had informed the Opera Ballet of Sophie Duval's death while Franck went back to the quai des Orfèvres to see Yves de Chaumont. He had then phoned from his office to set up an appointment with the Dance Director. Given that a dead ballerina was the reason for his visit, Franck had expected Anne-Laure Favennec to be waiting anxiously for him. Not so. Apparently she had other priorities. The show had to go on, and presumably she was making sure it did so.

It seemed that every incoming call was a supplication to meet or talk with Favennec. Her assistant kept the exchanges brief. Her fingers moved constantly over her keyboard as she nodded sympathetically, a light headset linking her ears and providing her with a microphone into which she uttered countless assurances that Favennec would get back to whoever was on the line. Maybe Franck was more privileged than he thought, given that he had obtained an interview with no more than an hour's notice. Assuming that it actually came to pass.

He eventually got to his feet.

"Is there a coffee machine handy?" he asked.

"Would you like me to get you one?" asked the assistant, pushing back her chair and reaching up to free herself from her headset.

"No, no," insisted Franck. "Stay where you are. You're a lot busier than me."

"Go right out the door and take the first corridor on your left," he was told. "Half-way down you'll find the coffee room. Just follow the noise."

"Would you like me to get you something?"

"I'm fine," smiled the assistant.

"I'll be back," promised Franck as he turned to leave.

"I hate to say it, but you can probably take your time."

Franck followed the directions he had been given. If the public half of the Opera building was a series of stately spaces designed to hold multitudes who came seeking pomp and ceremony, its rear quarters were sober and utilitarian, with offices, workshops and rehearsal rooms crammed into whatever space was available. Not that his surroundings could be mistaken for the tired corridors of the capital's innumerable administrative buildings. After all, two teenagers, a girl in a tutu and a boy in crotch-hugging tights, had just sprinted past him.

He ran into an obstacle just short of his destination. A young girl sat in the middle of the corridor, both legs before her, her left one stretched out on the floor and her right one held up as an offering. She wore a black leotard under an oversized sweatshirt. Her hair was caught in a tight band, keeping it out of her eyes, which were focused on a pair of hands busy looping the ribbons of her ballet shoe around her heel.

"Firm, not tight," she was told. "You feel the difference?"

The young dancer nodded. The woman from whom she was taking instruction knelt before her in a grey t-shirt with matching slacks. She gathered the ends of the ribbons, knotted them together, tucked them neatly under one of the bands which circled the girl's ankle, and leant backwards, gently lowering the dancer's foot to the ground.

"Your turn now," she said.

The dancer pulled her left leg up towards herself and set to work on the other set of ribbons. She carefully reproduced the cross-hatched pattern borne by her right foot. When she had finished, the woman tugged gently at her handiwork.

"Perfect," she said. "Never choke your ankles, Claire. They've got enough to put up with as it is."

She shifted her weight from her knees to her feet, straightened her legs and stood up, revealing herself to be as tall as Franck. She extended a hand to the girl, who took it but did not even tug lightly upon it as she too rose to a vertical position.

"Get back to your class," she was told, although it came out more as a piece of advice than a command. The dancer turned and scampered away, flowing around Franck without altering her pace.

"Sorry if we held you up," said the woman.

"That's OK," said Franck. "I wasn't in a hurry."

Her eyes swept over him.

"You wouldn't be my three o'clock appointment, would you?"

"Captain Franck Guerin," he said, extending a hand. "Brigade Criminelle."

"Anne-Laure Favennec," she offered in return. "Opera Ballet."

She closed her hand around his, holding it softly.

"I've kept you waiting a long time, captain. I strive to be punctual, but I always fail." She smiled, uncurling her fingers and releasing him. "Actually, to tell the truth, I don't strive that hard."

"My time's not been wasted. I've now got a better idea how to tie a ballet shoe."

"Yes, but could you actually do it? If seeing it done once was enough, I wouldn't spend so much time running after my girls just to make sure their blood is still circulating."

With that she glanced down at Franck's feet. He followed her example, wondering if his own laces were undone.

"Of course, a shoe can be too loose as well as too tight," she observed.

Franck shrugged.

"I've got wide feet. It's hard to get shoes that fit just right, so I tend to take the next size up."

"Must slow you down, though. Isn't that a problem in your line of work?"

"There's a lot more sitting around than you might think," said Franck.

"Waiting for people like me, I suppose. Well, you have done so most patiently, Franck – I can call you Franck?"

He nodded. He had expected the woman in charge of one of the world's major ballet companies to prove a little more formal, but she could call him anything she liked.

"Because you must call me Anne-Laure," she continued. "Everyone does."

He had also expected her to be a little more sombre.

"What do you need to know about Sophie Duval?" she asked, once they were seated in her office.

Although substantially larger than that of her assistant, it still seemed cramped. With a table hemmed in by six chairs, a three-seater sofa and a large desk whose surface held several piles of papers, there was little room to manoeuvre. They sat at the table at an angle to each other. Her eyebrows were slightly raised, signalling that her attention was all his. Although Franck wasn't averse to avoiding the spectacle of another's grief, he was thrown by her businesslike air.

"Did you know her well?" he asked.

Anne-Laure gasped, and she stared at Franck, her mouth

agape.

"Did I know her well?" she repeated, incredulously.

"Well, you must have, what, over a hundred dancers?"

"A hundred and fifty-four. At least until yesterday. But I know them all, captain. They are my charges – I watch over, I encourage, I perfect, I train, I push, I counsel, I groom, and I console each and every one of them. But even were that not true, your question would still be absurd. Sophie was an *étoile*. You are aware of what that signifies?"

"Like a starlet?" offered Franck.

Anne-Laure snorted contemptuously. "It doesn't take much to be a starlet. The right figure, the right director, the right publicist – sometimes even the right parents are enough. To become an *étoile* in the Opera Ballet takes exceptional talent, unstinting dedication, and a lifetime of work."

"A lifetime?" repeated Franck. Sophie Duval had been twenty-nine when she died. In the Middle Ages that might have counted as a lifetime, but by contemporary standards she had been robbed of two-thirds of her allotted span.

"A lifetime," insisted Anne-Laure. "Most of our *étoiles* come from our own ballet school. We take pupils from the age of eight. From that moment on they live and breathe ballet every day for the rest of their childhood. And adolescence. They won't actually join the *corps de ballet* – assuming they make it – until they're seventeen. So by the time you become a *quadrille*, you've spent more of your life in the Ballet than out of it. And even then, you've only got a precarious grip on the lowest rung of the ladder. You'll spend at least a year there before we let you near the *coryphées*."

"The what?" Franck had let *quadrille* go, as it at least sounded French.

"*Coryphée*. I believe it has its origins in Greek tragedy – one of the ranking members of the choir. Don't forget, ours is a very old institution – true, we don't quite stretch back to Athens and Socrates, but we can claim Louis XIV as our founder – so our vocabulary is a little specific. The *coryphées* form the second rank in the *corps de ballet*, or the fourth in the

Ballet as a whole."

"OK." This was a little more detail than he had counted on. He had already grasped the point of their exchange – Sophie Duval's dance career had lasted something like twenty-one years before she was killed. Not far short of a lifetime after all. Still, he could sense that Anne-Laure had not finished with her explanations. "So I'm eighteen and I'm a *coryphée*. What next?"

"If your technical prowess is unquestionable and your sense of artistry blossoming, two or three years later you may be named a *sujet*. If you have given your soul to your art and you deserve to be counted amongst the best in the world, at twenty-four or twenty-five you may be called to the rank of *première danseuse*. But you become an *étoile* only if the gods of ballet throw their mantle upon you, revealing you to be one of their chosen few."

"How few?"

"As of this afternoon, there are seventeen *étoiles* in the company." She sounded like a general surveying the ranks after a battle, not so much counting casualties as evaluating the remaining strength of his forces. "I know every one of my dancers, but my knowledge of my *étoiles* goes beyond that – it's intimate. With very few exceptions, I made them. I saw their potential and allowed them to realise it. Had I moulded Sophie Duval out of clay and breathed life into her, I couldn't have known her better."

"In which case," said Franck, slowly, "her death must have been a terrible shock."

Anne-Laure shot him a sideways glance. One of irritation. "I must disappoint you, captain. I am insufficiently grief-stricken. Is that what you're thinking? A young woman I have carefully tended for years is dead and I offer you not a single tear to prove the depth of my attachment to her."

"You describe your dancers as your family, the *étoiles* as your most gifted children, ..."

"No." Anne-Laure cut across him. "I did not say they were my family. I said they were my charges. My flock. My disciples. In all, nearly three hundred people work for the Opera Ballet – dancers, ballet masters, teachers, musicians, physical therapists, seamstresses, support staff – and they all look to me for guidance. Things go wrong every day – dancers are injured, costumes are lost, budgets are overspent, choreographers fail to deliver, critics are cruel, dreams are shattered, tempers flare, individuals lose heart, but through it all we put on a hundred and seventy performances, year in, year out. And not just any old performance. The best ballet in the world – the most beautiful, the most flawlessly executed, the most heartfelt, the most musical, the most breathtaking. Bar none. You think that would be possible without an iron grip on the helm? It is not my job to weep, captain. It is my job to lead. Don't presume to know my heart."

Franck raised both hands in apology.

"I'm sorry. I didn't mean to offend." It was time to start again, with the only question that really mattered. "What can you tell me about Sophie Duval?"

Anne-Laure waved Franck's contrition aside. Before she could speak the door into her office opened slightly, allowing her assistant to angle her head around it.

"Van Roon on the phone," she said. "Very insistent."

Anne-Laure shook her head. Her assistant withdrew.

"Where to start? Like any *étoile*, Sophie's entire life revolved around her art and this company. She joined the Ballet school as soon as she was eligible. When I became Director she was a *sujet*, and a precocious one at that. It didn't take me long to work out that she would be an *étoile* one day, and it fell to me to hand her that honour at the end of our last season."

"Which was?"

"July last year."

"So she was at her peak, professionally?"

"The first peak, yes. The ultimate summit comes a few years later, when a dancer has taken possession of the repertoire and made it her own."

"Was this a busy time for her?"

"If it's not August, it's a busy time in the Opera Ballet. Particularly for an *étoile*. Sophie is currently dancing Myrtha in *Giselle*. She was due on tonight. She was also the female lead in a new ballet we are to *première* at the end of this month."

"Was she having any problems?"

"Myrtha is a delight to dance. As for *Diana and Acteon, ...*"

Franck raised an enquiring finger. She had lost him. *Giselle* he had heard of, but not this *Diana* thing.

"*Diana and Acteon* is the new ballet. It's a special commission from a – what can I say? – somewhat challenging choreographer. It's been hard for everyone involved, and particularly so for Sophie, but it's probably the most important contemporary project underway in the ballet world, so that's only to be expected."

"What about her personal life?"

"What personal life? Being an *étoile* is not a nine-to-five job, it's a passion, a whirlwind affair that absorbs you entirely. You give it every minute of your existence because you know it won't last forever. Retirement comes early to dancers. After that, you seek what solace you can. Only then do you really have time for what you would call a personal life, captain."

"She was single? No steady relationship? No known lovers?"

"Lovers? No doubt. Who exactly, I could only hazard a guess. There are things I choose not to know – that I have no right and no need to know. But no steady relationship – that would have come to my attention."

They were interrupted again.

"Ministry of Culture," said Favennec's assistant. "Permanent Secretary."

All she got in return was another curt shake of the head. She closed the door as quietly as she had opened it.

"Was she here yesterday?" asked Franck.

"Yes. She was working on *Diana and Acteon* for most of the afternoon. We were expecting to see her in the evening too."

"She was to dance?"

"No. The house was dark yesterday. But we were hosting an evening for the American Friends. Sophie was supposed to be there."

"The American friends?" echoed Franck.

"The North American Friends of the Paris Opera House. American Friends for short. Most of them are simply opera buffs, but there's an active minority of ballet fanatics and we cultivate them assiduously. Once or twice a year a group of them come over – thirty or forty at a time – and spend four or five days in the city. They're very well looked after – the most coveted seats in the house, backstage visits, encounters with our best and brightest. Last night there was a reception in their honour in the Grand Foyer of the Opera and we – the Ballet – were doing the honours. I'd arranged for eight *étoiles* to be there."

"And Sophie Duval never turned up?"

"No."

"What time was this event?"

"It started at seven, with dinner at nine. I knew Sophie might be late, but I expected her to be there by the time the food was served."

"The rehearsal hadn't just run over?"

"No, they finished just before six. The *étoile* who partners her in *Diana* got to the reception on time."

"There was no word from her?"

"Nothing. I told several people to phone her, but none of them got through."

"You could have sent someone round to her place," suggested Franck. "It's not that far away."

Duval had been found in her apartment on rue Notre-Dame de Lorette. It was less than ten minutes from the Opera House.

"I could have," admitted Anne-Laure, "but I didn't. I assumed that if Sophie wasn't there, she had a very good reason. She knows how important the Americans are to our funding. She wouldn't have stood them up lightly."

"So as far as you were concerned, all was normal in Sophie Duval's life?"

"I'm not quite sure the notion of 'normal' applies to a world-class ballerina. She had her challenges, her crises, her highs and lows, but there was nothing unusual in that. As far as I'm aware, the past few days or weeks in her life were no different from the months which preceded them."

Franck tried another tack.

"What does her death mean?"

"What does it mean? It's a great loss for the world of ballet. It's a source of shock and sorrow for all the members of the company. It's thrown the program for the end of the season into upheaval. It threatens the quality of what we do. It's a challenge we have to rise to and overcome ..."

They were once more interrupted, but this time it was not Favennec's assistant who popped a head in.

"Sorry for the intrusion. Piet's on his way. On the warpath."

And then the head was gone. An appealing face with a strong chin, stately nose, and serene blue eyes. A man somewhere in his forties with short-cut but vigorous greying hair.

"Serge!" said Anne-Laure, summoning him back.

This time he stepped fully into her office.

"I'm very sorry," he said, addressing himself to Franck. "I'm not usually this ill-mannered."

"Serge, this is captain Franck Guerin," explained Anne-Laure. "He's from the Brigade Criminelle. He's investigating Sophie's death."

He closed the distance between himself and Franck, took his hand and squeezed it firmly, looking intently into his eyes.

"Help us understand what happened, captain," he said. "You can't imagine what Sophie meant to us. We're all walking about numb out there. It's as if our hearts have stopped beating."

"This is Serge Morin," explained Anne-Laure. "Serge is one of the rocks on which this company rests. He may be of more use to you than I can, Franck."

"Anything. Anything at all I can do to help, I will," declared Morin.

Franck got to his feet. If he had understood correctly, Anne-Laure had just dismissed him, passing him on to another. He would go with the flow. There did not seem to be much else he could gain from the Dance Director.

"Maybe we can talk in your office?" he suggested.

Serge shook his head with good humour. "I look like I have an office?"

He was dressed in khaki trousers with a red shirt unbuttoned at the collar. He had scuffed espadrilles on his feet.

"Serge will be dancing Albrecht in tonight's production," said Anne-Laure. "He's our longest-serving *étoile*."

Franck bit his lip. "Sorry. I don't know that much about ..."

"Never mind, captain," said Serge, smiling broadly to put Franck at ease. "I don't know much about the police."

Serge offered to take Franck to his lodge, but they found a small empty meeting room some distance down the corridor – a slightly unsteady table, five chairs, and a paperboard covered with indecipherable scrawling and figures. Serge made sure Franck was seated before he took his place beside him.

"You've been to the scene?" he asked, hesitatingly. "Sophie's apartment, I mean. You saw her?"

Franck nodded, waiting to see what Morin would ask. Morbid curiosity was not a characteristic he appreciated.

"It must be hard. Even when it's your job. I don't think I'd have the strength, captain."

He laid a hand on Franck's shoulder, commiserating with him, and then sat back.

"Thanks for your concern," said Franck, hesitatingly. "But, like you say, it's my job." He was about to say that he had seen worse – because he had seen worse, much worse – but he restrained himself. Strangling might be a relatively clean way to kill, but it could not be said to provide a pretty death. Indeed, there was probably no such thing as a pretty death, with the possible exception of old age's exhausted surrender to slumber.

"Anne-Laure Favennec implied that you knew Sophie Duval well," Franck prompted, changing the subject.

"How could I not? I've been here longer than anyone, at least as far as the performing half of the company is concerned. I was already an *étoile* when Sophie joined the *corps de ballet*. As she came up through the ranks, we began to dance together. We did a *pas de deux* in *La Bayadère* the evening she was named an *étoile*. We were supposed to take to the stage together tonight."

"So you saw her frequently?"

"Sure. Particularly over the past months, because of van Roon's new piece."

"That's the ballet she was rehearsing yesterday?"

"I wouldn't call it a ballet – not quite yet. It's a new piece we've commissioned – or, more accurately, a private sponsor has helped us to commission, since van Roon doesn't come cheap. Let's say it's a work in progress – most of it is there, but we're still working out the details and some crucial passages are still missing."

"You're directly involved?"

Serge inclined his upper body forward, bowing slightly even though he was sitting down. "I don't have my bow and I left my dogs at home, but I am nonetheless Acteon. Sophie is – was – Diana. Van Roon never works out his choreography on his own. He does it directly with his performers. He has a reputation as a slave-driver. It's wholly merited, believe me."

"In which case, you may be one of the last ones to have seen her alive," stated Franck. "Can you run me through the time you spent together yesterday?"

"We started at three, finished at half five or thereabouts. We had all drifted away by six. She was supposed to come back that evening. There was a reception for ..."

"Yes," Franck cut in. "I know about that. Did you see Sophie leave? Was she alone?"

"I walked with her to the rear entrance, had a chat, then she went off on her own."

"On foot?"

"Yes. She doesn't live far."

"Rue Notre-Dame de Lorette."

"That's right. She was going to clean up, rest a little, and then come back to the Opera."

"Had anything particular happened during the rehearsal? How was her mood? Did she seem worried? Was she in any way apprehensive about going home?"

"If anything," said Serge, "she was probably looking forward to a bath and some time on her own. Van Roon had been treating us like shit – which is what he usually does. Demanding the impossible and screaming at us for not being able to supply it. She was certainly tired, probably a bit dispirited, but that's how we've all felt since we started on *Diana*."

"It's not going well?" demanded Franck.

"Oh, it's going well. It'll be an astonishing piece when it's finished. It's a van Roon, after all. But it's a punishing process – although we knew from the outset that's how it was going to be."

"But the pair of you volunteered anyway."

Serge shook his head, momentarily drumming his fingers on the tabletop.

"This is the Opera Ballet, captain. We have hundreds of years of discipline and rigour behind us. We don't volunteer – we do what we're told."

"By whom?"

"By Anne-Laure. The Dance Director does just that – she directs the dancers. In every way. This is an autocratic institution."

"Napoleon III would have been pleased," commented Franck. "So Sophie was tired, maybe stressed, but nothing out of the ordinary?"

"That's right."

"And over the past days and weeks – nothing strange, nothing new, nothing that now seems significant?"

Serge thought for a moment and then shook his head. "The season's in full swing. It's been full steam ahead, as ever. Sophie was dancing as well as she always does. Did."

"Can you tell me anything about her personal life?"

"I'm not a gossip, captain."

"And I'm not a columnist. I'm a captain with the Brigade Criminelle and I have a murder victim on my hands."

Serge held up a hand, conceding the point.

"OK. Sorry. But there's not much to say about Sophie. She had her friends, she had her relationships, but what she had most of all was this place."

"Was she in a relationship at the moment?"

"Not that I'm aware of."

"Would you have known?"

"Not necessarily. Sophie was pretty discreet."

"Who would know?"

"Her best friend, I imagine."

"You know who that was? How I can get in touch with her?"

"I'll take you to her, if you like."

He was lucky to have a guide, as he would never have found her on his own.

Franck followed Serge Morin back along the corridor, past the Director's office, up a narrow circular stairwell, down another corridor, along a passage which overlooked a complex network of steel ropes and suspended walkways in the vast, cavernous space high above the Opera stage, along yet another corridor which offered occasional glimpses out over the city, and finally up a short flight of stairs.

"Where are we?" asked Franck, who was under the impression that they must have traversed the entire Opera building.

He was not far wrong.

"This is the entrance to the Chauviré studio," explained Serge. "It's the uppermost level of the Subscribers' Rotunda, right inside the dome."

The Opera House originally boasted three separate entrances. The one currently in use – the imposing pillared entrance that rose above avenue de l'Opéra – was originally the least prestigious as it was the only one destined for those who arrived on foot. About a third of the way down each side of the building stood rotundas accessible by horse-drawn carriage. The one on the eastern side was reserved for those holding subscriptions, who could descend from their vehicles directly underneath it, safe from the wind and rain, and enter the Opera through a sculpted grotto overseen by a huge bronze representing a priestess of Apollo. The one on the western side was intended for the Emperor and his court, complete with a horseshoe ramp which allowed them to be deposited directly at the level of the salons reserved for them – thereby putting the subscribers in their place, as reaching the auditorium from their special entrance meant climbing more, rather than less, stairs than the general public.

Franck and Serge were on the third level of the Subscribers' Rotunda, which had been converted into a rehearsal studio.

"This is where I leave you."

Serge opened the door before them and ushered Franck through. He did not follow him.

The studio turned out to be anything but ornate. The walls were white, as were the curving iron beams which supported them, leaning inwards to meet under the now-invisible dome, which was hidden by a false ceiling with polystyrene tiles and strip-lighting reminiscent of the vast workspaces of modern office buildings. The floor, covered in a form of black vinyl marked with countless scuff marks, albeit not a single tear, cut across the bottom of the cupola's eight oval windows. It was a far cry from the rich splendour of the building's public rooms.

A solitary figure stood in the centre of the room, side-on, her arms raised and twisted so that her palms faced behind her. She wore a leotard over which a short diaphanous skirt had been slipped. Her knees were slightly bent, alerting Franck to the fact that she was not frozen in place but was evolving at a glacial pace through a series of movements. She descended slowly towards the floor, one leg tucking itself behind the other as they folded beneath her. Her arms descended at the same time, her palms turning. They then rose in front of her until each hand clutched its opposite shoulder. She now had one knee on the floor while her other leg formed a sharp angle before her, towards which she bowed her head, trusting her brow to its unwavering support.

The movement stopped. She was still.

Franck waited for her to raise her head and acknowledge his presence. She must have glimpsed him as he entered. Unless her eyes were closed. Or elsewhere, contemplating an irretrievable absence.

He soon had his answer. She took a deep breath, released it slowly, and pulled her head up. Even from across the room, Franck could see that her eyes were red and swollen, her cheeks moist, and her face drained. Here at least Sophie Duval was being mourned as she no doubt deserved.

"Lisa Roux?" asked Franck. That was the name Serge Morin had uttered to him before ushering him, alone, into the rehearsal room.

For a while she looked at him blankly, as if unable to believe that anyone had dared to disturb her, to violate her sanctuary. She then rose in a single movement, simultaneously straightening the leg she had bent before her and unfolding the other. She pivoted on the ball of her left foot and fixed him with a stare.

"I'm captain Franck Guerin from the Brigade Criminelle. I'm sorry to have disturbed you. If you'd like me to come back when you've finished practising, I will."

"I wasn't practising, captain," she said. Her voice was steady but hoarse, as if parched. "I was thinking about Sophie. You're here for Sophie, correct?"

"Yes. I'm told you were close."

Franck had not moved from the doorway, nor had Lisa relinquished the dead centre of the room.

She looked down at her hands, which she held in a heart shape at the level of her lower abdomen.

"My little sister," she stated.

It was not hard to believe. They shared the same physical type – sparely built, strong and supple, elongated faces, modest breasts and thin waists. Lisa was probably a year or so older, her hair auburn rather than black, and a good deal longer. Her face bespoke more character, with a prominent nose and cheekbones and vivid brown eyes, although the latter were currently the worse for wear. Overall, Franck would have judged her the more striking of the two. But the comparison was unfair. He had never seen her little sister alive.

"Not genetically, of course," she continued, "but here, inside the Ballet, we had grown together. Intertwined. I led the way and made sure it was safe for Sophie to follow."

"Then you're the person I need to talk to. Can I ask you some questions? Here? Now?"

Lisa took a deep breath.

"Of course," she said, uprooting herself and coming over to him, extending a hand for him to shake. "It's too late now, but I'll still do what I can for her."

A cotton jumper was draped over the wooden bar that ran all the way round the studio. She picked it up and slipped it over her head. She then retrieved a water bottle that had been sitting underneath it, took a long draught, and lowered herself to the floor with her back against the wall. She patted the floor alongside her, inviting Franck to do the same.

He did so, but with far less grace.

"The rumour is that she was strangled," she said, looking straight ahead. "Is that true?"

"Yes."

Lisa's hand brushed against her throat, apparently of its own volition.

"Who could have done such a thing?" she asked, her voice quavering. "Sophie never harmed anyone in her life. All she lived for was to dance."

"That's what I'm trying to find out," said Franck very quietly, deliberately not turning his face towards her. "Everything suggests Sophie died quickly and unexpectedly."

Lisa swallowed, clutched her hands tightly together and pressed them against her mouth. Franck was close enough to have put his arm around her. He did not. It was not his place. It would have felt like an intrusion.

It took her a few minutes to speak again. When she did so it was to repeat something he had said.

"Unexpectedly."

"Yes," confirmed Franck. "She was taken by surprise. She was at home. She was getting ready to come to a reception here."

Lisa nodded. "The American Friends. I know."

"Were you there?"

"Yes, but only to keep Sophie company. She was the one who really had to be there, since she was working with van Roon – everyone wanted to hear about the new ballet."

She stopped.

"Unexpectedly?" prompted Franck, fearing she was about to lapse back into silence. They were still not looking at each other. "You think it wasn't?"

"Something was different about Sophie this past week," she eventually said, albeit tentatively.

"How?"

"She seemed anxious. Or troubled."

"Frightened?"

Lisa thought about it, then shook her head. She finally turned to face Franck.

"No, not frightened. More like she had something on her conscience. Something to confess."

"Something she'd done? Something someone had done to her?"

"How can I say? She didn't say anything specific to me. But from time to time I got the feeling she was on the verge of telling me something, only to pull back."

"You said this past week. This was definitely a recent thing?"

"Yes. Normally we don't hide things from each other." Franck did not correct her tense. "Well, not for long, anyway."

"How often did you see her over the past seven days?"

"Every day. It's not as big as it seems, the Opera House. When both of us are here, we always run into each other."

"And outside? Like over the weekend?"

Lisa allowed herself a brief smile. "Weekends don't always exist for us, not during the performing season. And certainly not for Sophie, given she was working on *Diana*."

"The new ballet?"

"Yes."

"You're sure that wasn't what was making her anxious?" asked Franck.

"It made her other things, but not anxious. Sophie could do anything van Roon could come up with. And if she couldn't, then nobody could."

"What other things, then, if she wasn't anxious?"

"Tired, of course. Unhappy, for sure. And a little self-pity, perhaps, since she found herself trapped in a situation she hadn't expected."

"Why do you say that?"

"Van Roon didn't want Sophie, but Anne-Laure forced him to take her. He got everything else he wanted – the money, the time, the freedom to what he liked, the rehearsal space – but not even he could take a casting decision out of Anne-Laure's hands. Famous as he is, in the end of the day he's only a choreographer. Even he had to bow to the Opera Ballet's traditions."

"So Sophie dragged her feet to rehearsals?"

Lisa frowned at him. "Of course not. Van Roon didn't want Sophie, but she wanted the role. She gave her all, as she always did. But van Roon gave her hell in return. He criticised her. He belittled her. He constantly reminded her she had been imposed upon him. But," – she pointed a proud, triumphant finger in the air – "he couldn't break her. Not Sophie. And she had Serge. He tried to protect her."

"Serge Morin?"

"Yes. The last of the true gentlemen. Serge is dancing Acteon. Apparently he took van Roon to task several times. I doubt it did any good, but at least that way Sophie felt she wasn't all alone."

"I've talked with Serge Morin. He didn't say they were close."

Lisa nodded, unsurprised. "Who's not close to Serge? You know how long he's been an *étoile*? Twenty years. I said Sophie and I were like sisters. Well, Serge is everybody's favourite uncle. The aging, unmarried uncle – the loveable rake with an unending series of girlfriends who never quite realise that he gave his heart away a long time ago."

"To whom?"

Sophie swept her hand in the air – an effortless gesture for her, but a hypnotic one for Franck.

"To all this."

Tuesday, 12th May

"Well, at least she wasn't strangled with the ribbons of her ballet shoes."

Franck was reading the autopsy report over Sternberg's shoulder. This was the source of a certain amount of frustration for Sternberg, a more experienced reader of such documents. Knowing when to skim and when to stop, he had to wait for Franck to catch up with him at the bottom of each page. He filled the time with comments on what he had just read.

"Standard signs of asphyxiation," he continued. "Tiny red spots all over her face from broken blood vessels, more and more visible after death as the skin dries and becomes less opaque. Not all the classic strangulation symptoms, though. Her hyoid bone made it through intact."

"Whatever the hyoid bone might be," observed Franck.

Sternberg turned in his seat and touched Franck's Adam's apple with a fingertip. He then pushed his finger slightly up his throat and outlined a ridge than ran in horseshoe fashion under the skin.

"That's your hyoid bone. Hangs under your jawbone. Exactly where people put their hands to throttle each other, which soon snaps it. Not in our case, though."

"Because?"

"Because of the path taken by the cord around her neck. Skin abrasion shows three circles which spiral into each other. Two of the loops passed underneath the hyoid and the third one above. Since whatever was used was very thin, no direct pressure was applied to the bone. It might have been squeezed, but it didn't break."

Thin was the operative word: the report insisted that Duval had been garrotted with a length of robust, highly flexible material no more than three millimetres thick – which, as Sternberg had observed, effectively eliminated the ribbons on her shoes as a potential murder weapon.

"Why use something so thin?" asked Franck.

"Lots of advantages. Easy to carry and conceal. Easy to

loop round the neck. Hard for the victim to get her fingers under and try to loosen. But the real plus is that the thinner the ligature, the less force you have to apply."

"Why's that?"

"The whole point of strangling is to obstruct the larynx, the jugular vein or the carotid artery. Hit the vein or the artery and you take out the brain directly. Without a constant flow of blood, brain cells quickly start shutting down until you go effectively brain-dead, with the rest of the body soon following suit. Hit the larynx and you starve the lungs of oxygen. It's an indirect path – the lungs can't oxygenate the blood, the blood can't oxygenate the brain – but the larynx is an easier target as it's bigger and softer. The jugular and the carotid are harder to find and require more force to close – a lot more in the case of the carotid. All in all, it's hard work strangling someone. If using a cord, the force you apply is spread out across its entire surface. The wider it is, the less pressure it brings to bear. If you doubt your strength, go for something skinny."

"But if it's too skinny, it'll just break."

"Not necessarily. Look at fishing line."

"A possibility here?" asked Franck.

"I doubt it. Even the toughest fishing line is never more than a millimetre thick. Otherwise it's too obvious. Fish are not that smart, but even they know that it's a bad idea to bite something visibly attached to a string that runs through the ceiling and out into the world of strange shadows on the other side of the water. There's also the fact that one of the things which makes fishing line tough is its ability to stretch. That's not a plus point if strangling's your game. Stretching dissipates the force, meaning you have to pull all the tighter."

"OK, so skinny doesn't exclude sturdy. But a thin cord must still pose problems. What about handling? The thinner a piece of string is, the faster it gets tangled up. You don't want to slip behind your victim, pull your weapon out your pocket, and spend the next five minutes unknotting it."

"You could carry it looped round the palm of your hand, ready to spool it off. If it's thin it's unobtrusive. Could even have been transparent or flesh-coloured for all we know."

"Not that unobtrusive," objected Franck. "It was at least a metre long." This was an estimate based on the diameter of Duval's neck, plus some extra for the murderer to grasp and pull upon. "By the time you've wrapped a cord that long round your hand, it's got to be five or six times thicker than it originally was."

"Fair point," conceded Sternberg. "But the really interesting bit is the bulge."

He pointed to a paragraph towards the bottom of the page. In the middle of the second loop around Duval's neck the coroner had noted that the depression left by the ligature in the surface of the skin had widened, if only by a few millimetres, for a three and a half centimetre stretch.

"No," countered Franck. "The really interesting thing is that the apartment had all sorts of things that could have done the job – from her ballet ribbons to the power cord on her MacBook ..."

"Not as well," objected Sternberg, ready to repeat all he had just said about the superior performance of a narrow ligature.

"But well enough," continued Franck. "But he didn't use them. And we found nothing at the scene which would fit the imprint on her neck."

"So?"

"So that means he walked in with the murder weapon and he walked out with it afterwards."

"So it's still in its pocket?"

"Until he feels inclined to pull it out again."

*

Not for the first time, he wished that something could be done about the coffee machine.

"It's not very good, but it's warm and sweet."

Both of them had asked for extra sugar. Delayed shock, perhaps, except that Franck was unsure whether shock could be delayed for twenty-four hours.

They sat uneasily on a pair of uncomfortable chairs in his office in the quai des Orfèvres. Liliane and François Duval, once proud parents to an *étoile*, now slowly adjusting to the horror-struck bereavement that haunted those whose child had become a murder victim.

They lived in Saint-Germain-en-Laye, less than an hour from the centre of Paris by the suburban train network. They had taken it to come in and formally identify their daughter's body the previous afternoon, before the coroner set to work. They had then returned home, no doubt to sit numbly and contemplate their loss, having accepted Franck's request to come and talk with him today.

The offer of coffee was just an awkward preliminary, to give an illusion of normality to the whole proceedings. Just a friendly chat with a police officer in the course of his enquiries. Not a dissection of their daughter's brutally terminated life.

"It's confirmed? About her neck?" asked her father. They had been told yesterday that in all likelihood Sophie had been strangled.

"Yes," said Franck. "I've seen the official report. Asphyxiation through strangulation. No other wounds. No other marks. Nothing else was done to her."

They knew what he meant.

"Is it ... Will she have suffered greatly?" asked her mother.

Some equated being strangled with drowning, which sailors said was a gentle death – that the mind floated off in a dream as the oxygen ran out. Although poor science, based on the observation that the faces of drowning victims rarely expressed any anguish, it was a persistent myth. But it was a myth all the same. Choking to death on water could scarcely count as a calm surrender to the embrace of the sea. As for being strangled, Franck was unwilling even to try to imagine how it might feel.

He offered what little he had.

"We think it was very quick. There were no signs of a struggle. We don't think she saw it coming."

They said nothing. Everything that they had been told over

the past twenty-four hours had been difficult to process. Franck's words would sit undigested for a long time until distance and resignation wore away their harsh contour.

"I'm going to ask you some questions about Sophie. I'm asking them now because time is of the essence in a murder enquiry. The more we know, the faster we move, and the quicker justice is done."

He deliberately spoke as if the latter was inevitable. Statistically, it almost was – the most recent document he had seen on the subject gave the national murder clear-up rate as eighty-seven percent. It was, of course, the thirteen percent left over that worried him.

"Go ahead," said François Duval. "We'll do our best." He reached out and closed his hand around his wife's.

"How often did you see Sophie?"

"Not very. Not during the ballet season, anyway. She had too much to do to come down to Saint-Germain. She phoned from time to time. Not so much in the evenings – not with all the performances. Once a week, or so. Most weeks. When she could."

His wife proved more direct.

"We lost Sophie to the Opera Ballet when she was eight. Since then, she never really had much need of us. It became her family, her world."

François Duval winced, but he did not contradict her. Franck did not blame him for having wanted to paint a different picture. All they would have now were memories, and memories could be shaped if the will to do so was strong enough.

"When did you last see her?"

"In March," said Liliane. "She came for lunch. Ate nothing, as ever. Talked non-stop about the new ballet that was being commissioned."

"From Piet van Roon?"

"That's right. She really wanted to be in it."

"She got it – the leading role," said Franck.

"Eventually, yes," said her father. "But when we saw her

that hadn't been decided yet, and she was worried it would slip through her fingers."

"Not worried – angry," corrected her mother.

"Angry with the choreographer?" prompted Franck. "Piet van Roon?"

"No. With Lisa Roux."

"Lisa Roux?" echoed Franck. "Weren't they close friends?"

"Oh, closer than friends," said her father. "Lisa was the sister Sophie never had. They'd grown up together in the Ballet school."

"Not just a sister – a big sister," clarified Liliane Duval. "Lisa always thought she knew what was best for Sophie. She'd already been at the Ballet school two years when Sophie arrived. She took her under her wing and from that day on Sophie always let her have her way."

"Lisa's always looked after Sophie," said François, anxious to repair any bad impression his wife's words might have left. "She did what we couldn't do, or weren't in a position to do."

"She shut us out," insisted Liliane. "Oh, I'm not saying she did it deliberately." She moved her hand on top of her husband's and gave it a squeeze. "And François is right, she definitely watched over our little girl. But she was part and parcel of the whole process, the way the Ballet absorbed Sophie, took her for its own."

"So what about this dispute?" asked Franck.

"Apparently the van Roon commission was a big deal," explained Liliane. "The eyes of the ballet world would be focused on whoever danced in it. Sophie wanted it. She felt it would confirm her status as an *étoile* – she'd only been promoted last year, you know."

"And Lisa was the first to congratulate her," interjected François, still intent on rendering Sophie's protector her due.

"As she could well afford to," said his wife, turning to address him, "given that she'd been one for three years by then, but you're not going to tell me that Lisa was a better dancer than our Sophie?"

"They weren't rivals," he insisted. "They were allies. A

team."

"Maybe so, but in whose interest? Lisa made sure that Sophie held back and didn't try to push herself into the limelight before her, which she could well have done."

"So what about the new ballet?" asked Franck, drawing their attention back to him.

"Lisa wanted to do it. So did Sophie."

"Wasn't it up to the Dance Director to decide?"

"In the end of the day," said Liliane. "But that was the first time they both lobbied separately for a part. I think it sent a minor shockwave through the company."

"So Anne-Laure Favennec chose Sophie over Lisa."

"Yes. But not before they'd tussled for weeks."

"They'd patched things up since then?"

"We imagine so." Her father had taken up the story, steering it back to less contentious ground. "Sophie called a few times over the past few months. I got the impression things weren't working out as she'd hoped with the new piece. She had a lot of complaints about the choreographer. Apparently he hadn't even wanted an *étoile*." His tone indicated incredulity. "I suppose that's the risk you run when you bring people in from outside – they don't quite understand what they're dealing with. Anyhow, the problems with the new ballet probably helped to reconcile Sophie and Lisa. You don't toss aside twenty years for a single part."

Franck turned to Liliane. She nodded slowly, almost reluctantly.

"I'm sure they patched things up. But I hope Sophie learned something from it. That if she stood her ground, she could have what she deserved."

"Anything else out of the ordinary over the past few months?" asked Franck.

The question did not inspire any immediate reaction.

"What about her personal life? A relationship? A new boyfriend? A lot of dates?"

Her father took the lead.

"We got the impression things were pretty quiet on that

front. I'm sure she had lots of admirers, but I doubt she had much time for them."

"She was happy just dancing?"

"Yes." Their replies fused.

On this point, at least, there was neither doubt nor divergence.

Wednesday, 13th May

The body was gone, but Sophie Duval was everywhere he looked.

Working his way through her apartment in rue Notre-Dame de Lorette for the second time, Franck's eyes kept snagging on details he had ignored on his previous visit. The walls of the salon bore large framed black-and-white photos of dancers frozen in movement. He only recognised one image – the predatory young Rudolf Nureyev – but assumed the others were as celebrated by aficionados. The kitchen was stocked with fruit and tiny portions of white meat and fish, typical favourites of those who sought to be both strong and slim. Her freezer cabinet was jammed with ice packs, ready to be applied to strained tendons and aching joints. Her bathroom contained an oversized tub in which to float and attain the weightlessness so determinedly pursued onstage. But it was one of the wardrobes in her bedroom that proved the most telling. It revealed a collection of worn but well-preserved tutus which evolved in size from child to adult, and in colour from eye-straining fuchsia to virginal white. Preserved in boxes beneath them were the corresponding ballet slippers, scuffed and twisted, many with cracked soles, looped together in inseparable pairs by the ribbons sewn into them.

Nonetheless it was her recent, not distant, past that interested him, and it seemed to have left few traces of itself. There were the abandoned towels in the bathroom, where mascara and lipstick teetered precariously on the edge of a small shelf above the hand basin. There was a decaying banana skin in the otherwise empty trash can in the kitchen. There were the clothes stuffed half-in, half-out a laundry basket, a pair of leggings and an unadorned cotton top, both no longer damp but bearing the scent of intensive exercise. There was the shoulder bag whose contents had been emptied out onto the bed, presumably to allow a select few to be transferred to the small Dior evening clutch that lay on a sofa in the main room. The few hours which had passed between Sophie's returning home in the early evening and her death may have been busy, but they betrayed no signs of the frantic activity of someone who knew a killer was drawing close.

In search of information about the days leading up to her death, Franck sat down at a desk in the apartment's spare room, which held a single bed, a chest of drawers, another wardrobe and a low table with a printer, an external hard disk drive and a winking router. An ultra-slim MacBook sat on an antique writing desk. Franck opened it and turned it on. In the absence of any password protection he quickly found his way into her mailbox. There was not a lot of correspondence from the past seven days: some innocent-looking messages from what he took to be friends or colleagues and a number of exchanges with what seemed to be her financial advisor, mentioning sums that were way out of Franck's league. The few emails which had arrived on Sunday were unread. He moved on to her web-browsing history. Once more there was nothing for Sunday, but she had been using her MacBook intensively over a couple of days in the previous week. He followed her tracks, most of which led to ballet sites which provided images and accounts of individual dancers and their performances. Time and again, she had returned to the same subject: Serge Morin, from his early days as an *étoile* in the late 1980s to his most recent appearances at the Opera House. From his faun-like youth to his solid, athletic forties, Morin cut a fine figure in every photo.

The writing desk had a single drawer, which was locked. Franck delved into the battered leather briefcase he had brought with him and rooted about inside it until he found a lonely paperclip. He straightened it out, bent it down about a centimetre from one end and made a loop at the other to give himself some leverage. After a couple of tries, plus some extra bending to thicken the end that was doing all the work, he succeeded in disengaging the lock. The drawer held a chequebook, just under three hundred euros in notes, a couple of expensive-looking pens and a large scrapbook. He folded the computer shut and laid the scrapbook on top of it, slowly turning the pages.

He was looking at a chronological record of Serge Morin's career. Some of the images, printed with the colour inkjet that sat in a corner of the room, he had just seen on the internet. Others were clipped from magazines or newspapers. Many were quality black-and-white or colour prints on thick photographic paper. In not a single shot was Serge at rest. He was seen spinning in place; leaping through the air, his limbs angled with precision; stretching while maintaining a seemingly impossible equilibrium; supporting the weight of a ballerina with one or both arms, sometimes over his head. One – an old monochrome shot in which he seemed to be in his late teens – captured him pirouetting in near-perfect synchronisation with the ageing Rudolf Nureyev, presumably from the latter's days as Dance Director at the Opera Ballet.

Franck counted the pages. There were fifty-seven pictures in all, each of them dated with the month and the year in what he took to be Sophie Duval's careful script. Alongside each of them she had sketched a stick figure mimicking Morin's stance. The drawings were annotated with coloured arrows indicating specific points of his anatomy and arcs estimating the angles created by his limbs. It looked as if Sophie had been obsessed with Morin's technique. Added to what he had already been told about her, the scrapbook seemed to confirm that she was a fanatical, perfectionist dancer.

However, there was the question of the final photo. Surely the most recent, it showed Morin dressed in breeches and a waistcoat, either catching or holding a ballerina in mid-air. Morin had but one foot on the ground, the other stretched out behind him, a toe pointing to, but not quite touching, the stage. His back was ramrod straight. His partner was Sophie Duval. Draped in a simplified version of a long eighteenth-century dress, her hands were clasped by the side of her head as Morin held her by the waist, her face hovering above his. Their eyes were locked and a complicit smile illuminated both faces – a smile that would have been imperceptible even for those in the best seats in the Opera House; a smile that had not been staged.

Franck studied the look that passed between them.

It might have been innocent in a legal sense, but not in any other.

*

"You sure you didn't leave something out last time we talked?"

Franck had tracked Serge Morin down in one of the backstage corridors of the Opera House. He was chatting with a blonde dancer in her mid-twenties. She was dressed in jeans and a short-sleeved blouse, but her profession was revealed by the ballet shoes casually slung over a shoulder, their ribbons grasped lightly in her left hand. She had been leaning against the wall, allowing Serge to occupy the width of the corridor, shifting from one foot to the other as he told her an animated tale. Although she offered a smile and bobbed her head as she listened, sometimes playing distractedly with her hair, Franck got the feeling Serge was investing more in the exchange than she was.

Franck's question caught Morin in mid-gesture, his arms raised and parted, palms flat, ready to clap together. Serge glanced over his left shoulder, raised his eyebrows when he saw who it was, and redeployed his hands in order to direct the young dancer's gaze towards Franck.

"Clara, this is captain Franck Guerin. He's investigating Sophie's death."

She caught her lower lip in her teeth and looked at him with open curiosity, as if he belonged to some exotic, rarely glimpsed species. Which, in these corridors, was probably true. Franck thought about sidling around Morin to offer his hand, but settled on a simple nod instead.

"I need to borrow Serge," he explained. "May I?"

"Don't keep him too long," she said. "He's very much in demand."

"Looks like I'm all yours, captain," said Serge, stepping back to allow Clara past.

She stopped in front of Franck and extended her hand.

"Clara Santoni, *première danseuse*."

"Franck Guerin, Brigade Criminelle."

"My pleasure, captain Guerin," she said, releasing his hand and proceeding down the corridor away from them.

Serge observed Franck as he watched her go.

"Beware of Clara's Mediterranean charms," he said. "Many pine after her, but few get close."

"I'll keep it in mind," said Franck, turning to face him. "We really need to talk."

"This way, then."

Within five minutes they had travelled up a flight of stairs, down a heavily populated corridor where Serge fielded constant greetings, raising a hand and firing off a few words each time, and up some more stairs. Having rounded a narrow corner and unbolted a heavy door, they stepped out into a wide passage that provided access to the first level of stalls and boxes which circled the Opera's auditorium. Serge led Franck past five doors and chose the sixth. It led into a narrow box containing six chairs, lined up in pairs.

"How about this?" asked Serge. "We can't have you stuck backstage all the time."

"It's not quite as private as I had hoped for," observed Franck, looking diagonally down towards the stage where a crew was moving pieces of scenery about.

"The acoustics carry the sound outwards from the stage. Nobody's going to hear us. Have a seat, captain, although these are not the best in the house – probably only about seventy euros. If we hop down one box that way –" He pointed towards the back of the auditorium. "– we'll have to pay twenty euros more. Keep going another three or four and we'll need an extra forty."

"This'll do," said Franck, sitting down on a red upholstered chair. Even though it was at the very front of the box it would have offered a rather awkward angle if a performance had been underway. Serge perched on the edge of the chair next to him, turning towards Franck and giving him all his attention.

"Explain to me again to what extent you and Sophie Duval were close," said Franck.

Serge tipped his head slightly to one side, as if he was studying Franck's expression.

"You said I left something out," he eventually said. "Something about Sophie?"

"For instance."

"You've found something?"

"What might I have found?"

"Not letters," mused Serge. "No emails either, or at least none that would seem strange. Text messages – that's it, isn't it? I read and delete. Sophie too, as far as I was aware, but maybe the phone company keeps them on record for a while." Serge shook his head, as if at his own naivety. "We weren't such great conspirators after all."

Franck let him talk. Of course the mobile network operators kept a record of customers' texts, but getting your hands on them took time and a convincing display of probable cause. Not in his old days with national security, of course, but two years on the outside were threatening to turn those into a distant memory.

"So, yes, you're right – I did leave something out – but that's what Sophie and I agreed on. That's how she wanted it."

"Why?" asked Franck, confident that the 'what' would come on its own.

"There are a hundred and fifty dancers in the Opera Ballet. We live on top of each other, day in, day out. It's a small world, and an incestuous one at that. Gossip moves fast, particularly if an *étoile* is involved. When Sophie and I started, we didn't know where we were going, we didn't know how long it might last, but we did know that the Opera Ballet was where we wanted to spend the rest of our professional lives, whatever became of us. So we decided to keep it a secret. Office romances are always a delicate affair. Even inside the police, I imagine."

"How long had you been involved?" asked Franck, ignoring Morin's attempt to draw him into complicity.

"Two months? Maybe a little less. Depends on how you define 'involved'."

"How about when the flirting stopped and the sex began."

Serge shook his head, somewhat ruefully. "Not the flirting. The hand-holding. The tear-wiping. The propping back up. I didn't start it, and Sophie didn't either. I doubt we'd ever have become lovers if it wasn't for van Roon."

"The pressures of working on his new ballet?"

"We sought refuge in each other. Metaphorically and then ..." Serge backed away from his own phrase, frowning slightly at what might have been construed as a lapse of taste.

"So when did you switch from partners in adversity to lovers?" insisted Franck.

"Six weeks ago, more or less."

"And nobody knew? Not Lisa Roux, who watched out for Sophie? Not this van Roon, who was stuck in a room with the pair of you for hours at a time, day after day?"

"Dancers are also actors, captain. We are above all else creatures of discipline. We made sure it was invisible, and only met up when we could do so secretly."

"So you've been to Sophie Duval's apartment?"

"Yes. More than once."

"Do you have a set of keys?"

"Yes."

"You'd better have a good alibi for Sunday evening."

He did.

The North American Friends of the Paris Opera House were a privileged caste – affluent, cosmopolitan, well-connected – and they made sure that their comings and goings were committed to record speedily and efficiently. That, after all, was why they had an institutional web site. Only two days had elapsed since the reception in their honour at the Opera House, and already an extended report of the event was available on-line, complete with several photos of the occasion.

The first few images concentrated on the venue. As the reception had been held in the Opera House's Grand Foyer, this was understandable. A colonnaded hall as long as the Opera was wide, the Grand Foyer stood at the front of the building, separated from the auditorium by a ceremonial staircase which allowed the Opera's patrons to shrug off all memory of the city's streets as they rose into the magical world in which they would pass their evening. Strictly speaking, the Grand Foyer had nothing to do with the building's role as host to operas and ballets, as it provided neither additional performance nor viewing space. In reality, though, it reflected the Opera's architect's solid grasp of the fact that what happened on stage was but part of an evening's entertainment. If the Grand Foyer had the dimensions of a parade ground it was because it served the same purpose – to allow a crowd draped in the uniform of opulence to manoeuvre amongst itself, observing and being observed, exchanging words and glances, luxuriating in the sense of being exactly where it belonged. For the Grand Foyer was all gilded and fluted columns, low-hanging chandeliers, allegorical frescos and polished marble. It declared the wealth of the age in which it had been built and extended a complicit invitation to all those who felt entitled to such surroundings.

The American Friends, having flown first class across the Atlantic and poured substantial donations into the Ballet's coffers, were no doubt convinced that they deserved no less.

Franck spent little time on the images of the venue's architectural extravagance. The photo that Serge wished him to see featured three men standing arm-in-arm and beaming at the camera. He had to squint to read the accompanying caption, which identified two of them as John E. Fielding and Charles Hance. Looking plump and prosperous in suits and ties, they stood proudly on either side of the company's longest-serving *étoile*, whose smile seemed full and fresh, even though it was surely but one of many offered up in the course of the evening.

"It was a big night," explained Serge. "I was there at seven as part of the welcoming committee – Anne-Laure's orders. Since I've been around for a while, I've got to know a fair number of the Friends, so I'm a bit of a fixture at this kind of event. Everyone else had to fall in by nine at the latest. Things didn't wind down until midnight."

"A good evening?" asked Franck, handing Serge back his

iPhone, which had loaded the page faster than Franck's desktop in the quai des Orfèvres would have managed.

"Yes, it was actually. They're not just rich groupies, the Friends. They're real enthusiasts and some are genuine ballet connoisseurs. So although you could say it's just work – you have to mix and mingle, making sure every guest gets a chance to talk to you – at least you're performing for an appreciative audience. And their support is really important. They're direct sponsors of *Diana and Acteon*. I doubt they're picking up the full tab – van Roon is very expensive – but they're the ones who stepped up and finally made it possible."

"Was van Roon in attendance?"

"Our contrarian genius? Of course not. There's nothing he despises more than his paymasters."

"What about before it started?"

"Before?"

"The rehearsal finished at half five. Sophie left the Opera at six. What about you?"

"I showered and changed here, then hung about waiting for Anne-Laure Favennec to get off the phone and out of her office."

"You arrived at the reception together?"

"Yes."

"Anyone see you while you were getting ready for the evening?"

"Sure. I must have bumped into half-a-dozen folk."

"Could you give me their names?"

Serge blew the air from his cheeks in a low whistle. "Not off the top of my head. But if you let me think about it ... I remember running across Anne-Laure's assistant in the corridor – she warned me not to be late, which is a bit of a running joke here, given Anne-Laure's record on that front. And there were certainly others."

"When you can, give me a list. Just to make sure."

"OK. But if you don't mind me saying so, captain, your reasoning escapes me. You seem to have forgotten that I've just admitted to being Sophie's lover. Surely that would eliminate me as a suspect?"

"Love stories don't always go smoothly in my world," explained Franck. "Or in yours either, if *Swan Lake*'s anything to go by."

Franck had one more thing to do before leaving the Opera House.

Anne-Laure Favennec's assistant had called him that morning to inform him that Sophie Duval's lodge would be cleared out that day so that its contents could be sent to her parents. He had asked to be present.

Each *étoile* had a lodge at the very rear of the Opera House. Sophie's was a narrow room with windows looking out over rue Scribe. It had a dressing table under a long strip of mirror, a two-seater sofa pushed under the window, a disused fireplace at one end, a couple of chairs, a narrow wardrobe and a chest of drawers. The floor was oak parquet, but little of it could be seen. Aside from the space taken up by the few items of furniture, a carefully arranged pyramid of ballet shoes had been constructed in front of the fireplace. Franck guessed there were at least fifty pairs piled up there, one shoe slipped neatly inside the other.

"They go through a lot of shoes," explained Favennec's assistant. "An awful lot of shoes – sometimes two pairs in the course of a single performance."

She laid the key she had used to open the door on top of the dressing table.

Franck picked it up and looked at it. It was probably as old as the Opera itself, boasting a single prong. He could have made its equivalent out of a paperclip in under a minute.

"I think you should invest in new locks," he commented. "Not unless the *étoiles* never leave anything of value behind them."

"You'd be surprised at what you might find in one of these," said Favennec's assistant, gesturing around the room. "The girls may have taken a vow of obedience, but not chastity and poverty."

"They earn a lot?" asked Franck. The Opera was a state-funded enterprise, which ought to have placed some limit on salaries, but his slight knowledge of Sophie Duval's finances suggested otherwise.

"A hundred thousand a year, or thereabouts." Around three times what he earned. "That's from the Opera. If they do any extra performances outside on their own account, they can charge up to ten thousand a time."

"That's not bad," observed Franck. "So there might well be things worth stealing in a lodge."

She frowned at him. "The girls might steal the odd lover from each other, but not jewellery or a silk scarf. There is such a thing as *l'esprit du corps*."

Franck said nothing. People assumed the same thing about the police, but it did not always prove to be the case.

"Did you see a lot of Sophie?" he asked her.

"Often enough. The *étoiles* are always popping in and out to speak to Anne-Laure."

"I thought Anne-Laure was always too busy for anyone."

"Not for them. Few things in this company are more important than an *étoile*. I've seen her keep a government minister waiting so that she could listen to an *étoile* complain about her roles or a choreographer."

"Was Sophie much of a complainer?"

"No, not at all. If Sophie had a grievance, you could be pretty sure Lisa Roux would intervene and sort it out. Lisa's always looked out for her."

"Except when it came to deciding who would be Diana in the new ballet," insisted Franck.

"True, but that was a one-off. On every other issue she let Lisa fight her battles for her."

"So you saw more of Lisa than of Sophie?"

"Yes. Strange thing is, though, Sophie had made an appointment with Anne-Laure for Monday – the day she was found dead. You almost never see an *étoile* make an appointment. They just grab Anne-Laure as and when they can. Making appointments is the Director's prerogative."

"Only to turn up half an hour late. At the very least."

Favennec's assistant smiled, but defended her boss.

"You can't blame her. You have no idea of the workload she's carrying."

"And you have no idea why Sophie wanted to see her? Particularly in such a formal fashion, rather than just turning up unannounced?"

"None whatsoever."

He could always ask Serge, now that he had come clean about his relationship with the victim. He might know what Sophie had been planning to discuss with Anne-Laure.

Favennec's assistant put a large empty cardboard box down on the dressing table and began lifting things off its surface to place them inside it.

"I'll do the wardrobe," said Franck, opening its single door.

Two collapsible umbrellas lay at the bottom of it, along with a pair of scuffed ankle boots and yet more ballet shoes – five pairs, neatly bundled in their ribbons. Eight wooden hangers hung unsolicited alongside a black gabardine raincoat. A series of sparsely populated wooden cubby-holes ran up the right hand side of the interior. They yielded a few dance-related magazines, assorted lightweight tops and a few leotards, all folded in orderly fashion, a clean towel, two bras and matching panties, some toiletries aligned in ordered ranks on a separate shelf, a pile of make-up and a monogrammed Louis Vuitton cosmetic pouch.

Franck put the umbrellas, the footwear and the clothes into the box first. He ruffled the pages of each magazine to make sure there was nothing inside, before dropping them in too. Favennec's assistant came over to help him and was reaching in to gather up the disorderly pile of lipstick, mascara, blusher, eyeliner, and the like when Franck caught her arm.

"Wait," he said.

She turned to him, puzzled.

"Look at the toiletries," he said, pointing them out. Four bottles of shampoo, three different moisturising creams, one shower gel, a conditioner and four cleansing lotions stood equally spaced, two lines deep. The rear line was staggered to ensure that each product could be seen through the gaps in the front rank.

"Now look at the make-up." It lay in a heap, from which some items had escaped, rolling towards the back of the wardrobe.

Franck opened his briefcase and extracted a pair of transparent throwaway plastic gloves. He picked up the cosmetic pouch and shook it lightly. It made a sound reminiscent of a wave troubling a pebbly beach. He unzipped the top and peered inside. It was full of pills – three different colours of elongated tablets – and glass vials containing transparent liquids.

"Did Sophie Duval have any medical conditions?" he asked.

"I don't think so. Bruised feet and strained muscles, I imagine, but you can't dance if you're not in good shape."

"Well, if these were for recreational use, she was quite the party girl."

Thursday, 14th May

Sophie Duval's pharmaceutical collection was anything but recreational.

Georges Sternberg had placed a single representative of each drug from her make-up pouch in a round open-topped plastic dish on a workbench. There were eight samples in all.

"We'll start at this end," he said, pulling a pair of tweezers from amongst the many pens and pencils in the breast pocket of his lab coat. Franck placed himself dutifully alongside him.

Sternberg tapped the first dish.

"This is benzedrine – a good old amphetamine. The stuff that kept the bomber pilots awake on long-haul missions in the Second World War. Take an amphetamine and fatigue becomes a thing of the past – you're alert, confident, and up for any challenge. It's a con – amphetamines change nothing at a physiological level. Your body is tired and your energy is low, you just don't notice it. Amphetamines trick the brain into thinking all is well."

"Downside?"

"Why do we feel pain, Franck? So that we pull our hand out of the fire. When we feel tired, it's time to take a rest. If you don't see the warning signs, you just keep going until you collapse."

"OK. Next?"

Sternberg moved the point of his tweezers along.

"This is an anabolic steroid. Promotes muscular growth."

"That's for weightlifters," objected Franck, "not dancers. You saw Sophie Duval – she was a greyhound, not a pitbull."

"Take steroids with a low protein, low fat diet, the fat you're carrying gets changed into muscle. You stay the same shape, but you're a lot tougher. Well, actually, you don't stay exactly the same shape – not if you're a woman. This is basically made from testosterone, which means that if you take too much of it you'll begin to look like a man. Your breasts will shrink, you'll stop having periods, you'll get greasy hair and skin. Not pretty."

“That’s not a good description of Sophie,” Franck pointed out, although he now wished he had paid more attention to the labels of the numerous bottles of shampoo and skin cleanser in her lodge.

“Maybe she took just enough. Doping’s all about dosing. You get it right, you get away with it. Anyhow, she had something better.”

He picked up a round pill from the third dish and flourished it before Franck’s eyes.

“This is a beta-agonist.”

“You don’t mean beta-blocker?”

“No. A blocker deadens – this stimulates.”

“Stimulates what?”

“Ever met someone with asthma? His inhaler is throwing a beta-agonist at his lungs, relaxing the muscles and letting him take in more oxygen.”

“But these are pills, not a spray.”

“That’s because they’re packed with the stuff. Take the right beta-agonist, like salbutamol, at a high enough dosage, and it stimulates muscle production. Without endangering your *décolleté* this time.”

“If this does the same thing as the anabolic steroid, why use both?”

“Performance enhancement is a shady science,” explained Sternberg. “You don’t get a lot of published studies in peer-reviewed scientific journals. It’s practised by people who have stepped outside the respectable bounds of their profession – not so much doctors as mad scientists. They’re all great believers in cocktails – in the magical combination that maximises the gains and minimises the costs. Here’s a good example.”

He moved on, this time to a small vial of transparent liquid.

“This is somatropin – human growth hormone. At first glance it looks like it does the same thing as its predecessors, improving the fat/muscle ratio, but in actual fact it doesn’t make you stronger, it just siphons the fat off. However, although it doesn’t increase muscle mass *per se*, it helps maintain it, repairing any tears in connective tissue, which means you can bounce back from injury faster."

"Makes sense if you stretch yourself to your limit several times a week. Do you drink it?"

"No, you inject it," said Sternberg.

"There wasn't a syringe in the pouch."

"No, and I don't recall seeing any in her apartment either."

"So that's a problem. Does the same thing apply to this one too?" asked Franck, pointing to the next sample, which was also a vial.

Sternberg nodded.

"This is EPO – a big, fat and unstable protein. Nobody's yet succeeded in packing it into a pill to release its contents through the stomach lining. You have to inject it."

"And what's EPO when it's at home?"

"EPO is the stuff that regulates the production of red blood cells. You take this, your hematocrit levels shoot up beyond fifty percent and your blood is super-charged with oxygen, which means you can keep on going long after everyone else."

The next dish took them back to the pills.

"This is an iron supplement. Contains 350 milligrams of ferrous fumarate. It's easy enough to get, particularly if you have chronic anaemia, heavy periods, or you're pregnant. You can't make red blood cells without iron. If you're churning them out with EPO, you need a lot more iron than usual. Unfortunately, we're not very good at absorbing iron – there's a lot of waste. So you either start eating red meat by the kilo, or you take supplements and put up with the side-effects."

"Which are?"

"Turns your stools black as night. Cirrhosis of the liver if you really go overboard."

He moved on. Another vial with thin glass walls.

"This is PFC, which goes where EPO can't. Think of EPO as a factory churning out red cells and plugged into your bloodstream – PFC is more like synthetic blood. Most of the oxygen that flows through you is carried by your red blood cells, but a tiny proportion is dissolved in the very liquid of the blood. Inject PFC and that proportion goes up, which is good news for your muscles, since they can draw on it directly."

He had reached the last dish. It contained an oblong pill rounded at both ends.

"So what do you think this one is?" asked Sternberg.

"What's left? This'll be the one that makes you more beautiful and more intelligent."

"Let's hope so," said Sternberg, who picked it up with his tweezers, deposited it on his tongue, and swallowed it dry.

Franck waited for a minute or so before observing, "It's not working."

Sternberg swivelled to grab a bottle of water on a nearby table and took a swig.

"I hope it does soon. Explaining all this to you has given me the beginnings of a headache."

"So what was it?"

"An anti-inflammatory. Ibuprofen. Fights swelling – be it in the head or the ankles."

Franck ran a finger along the workbench, parallel to the line of samples.

"This one – more focus. These three – more muscle. These two – more energy. This one – less pain."

"Not quite as impressive as my explanations, Franck, but a fair summary," conceded Sternberg.

"So which ones are illegal substances?"

"Well, unless you're an Olympic athlete, none of them are. Every sporting body has regulations against using performance-enhancing drugs, but as far as the Ministry of Justice is concerned, neither the possession nor the consumption of these substances is an offence."

Franck moved to a nearby stool and sat down.

"What on earth was she doing with all this? Wasn't a lifetime of training enough?"

"She might have been planning on trying her hand at the Tour de France," suggested Sternberg.

"Sweating litres crouched over a bike with your legs pumping away? Nowhere near graceful enough."

"So you might think," said Sternberg, smiling to himself,

"but there's definitely a connection."

Franck folded his arms and looked at him warily.

"Tell me."

"I managed to pull some prints off the drugs in the make-up bag, particularly the glass vials. Not many, and all of them partial, but I succeeded in knitting some of them together and producing almost-complete thumb and index prints."

"Sophie's?"

"Yes, Sophie's, but not just Sophie's."

"Who then?"

"Léon Abkarian."

Franck had to think about it for a few minutes, during which time Sternberg watched him expectantly.

Then it came to him.

The Tour de France. Of course.

*

"What's the Opera Ballet's policy on performance-enhancing drugs?"

Anne-Laure Favennec looked at him uncomprehendingly.

"We don't have a policy. Why should we? Dancers aren't athletes, out to get gold medals and sponsorship deals whatever the cost. Dancers are artists. They're not going to soil themselves – both body and soul – with drugs."

"There's no penalty for their use? You don't carry out drug tests at any point in a season, or at any stage in a dancer's career?"

"I don't think you're listening to me, Franck. Steroids and blood transfusions and whatever other dirty tricks get you first past the post on the sporting field have no place in ballet."

"Aren't dancers fitter than most football players? Aren't they stronger than most tennis pros? Can't they keep going longer than a marathon runner? Dancers are athletes, and the hardest working of all – they don't compete once a month, they do it several times a week."

"They don't compete," insisted Anne-Laure. "Not ever. You

can't beat a choreographer's steps or another dancer. They perform. They do what they've dreamed of doing all their lives."

"They push their bodies to the limit, seeking perfection onstage and working feverishly towards it when off. They dance through strains and blisters and hairline fractures, for all I know. They probably absorb as much physical punishment in a week as a boxer does in a single bout."

"That's not true," she said, bluntly. "No choreographer has ever sought to hurt or punish a dancer. They may work at the limit of what is possible, but never beyond it. You might be able to pull off the impossible once, but not night after night. And our ideal is effortless grace – not strenuous achievement. An Olympic sprinter arrives doused in sweat, bent double and grimacing. We exit as we entered – tall, loose-limbed and ethereal."

"Maybe you don't know what really goes on," suggested Franck. "Maybe you're out of touch."

She scoffed.

"It may be over twenty years since I danced, but I was an *étoile* for eight years in this very company and what I danced is still in the repertoire today. I know the steps. I know what they take. As for the notion that things go on behind my back, you forget that I've been moulding this company since I took over in 2001. The younger dancers confide in me. The older ones are an open book to me, I've studied them so long."

"You can't know everything."

"Can't I? Hervé Quévillon is in the middle of secret discussions with American Ballet Theatre, since he suspects we'll never make him an *étoile*. He's right. Mélanie Lorieux is eight weeks pregnant and is still dithering over whether to have an abortion. She hasn't told the father, Francesco Massari, who blithely continues to two-time her with Marie-Isabelle Bertaud, no doubt inspired by his idol, Serge Morin, who at last reckoning had charmed his way into the beds of a fifth of the *corps de ballet*. I could go on, Franck, but I'll spare both them and you. I know their secrets, their foibles, their aspirations, and, most importantly, what they're capable of. I wouldn't be doing my job if I didn't."

"When you calculated Morin's twenty percent, did you include Sophie Duval?"

Anne-Laure breathed out slowly, fixing Franck with a narrow gaze. She seemed unwilling to believe he could have bested her on her own terrain.

"No I didn't," she admitted, cautiously. "But by forcing her on van Roon, I may have thrown them together. You are sure about this?"

"Yes, but it doesn't worry me as much as this."

He lay his briefcase flat on the table that sat between them, flipped it open, and tugged out a sealed plastic bag containing samples from Sophie's cosmetic pouch. He slid it across the table. It stopped just short of Anne-Laure's left elbow. Her fingers were linked, propping up her chin. She glanced down diagonally at the bag, making no attempt to touch it.

"What is that?"

"Steroids, amphetamine, growth hormone, oxygen boosters. A do-it-yourself kit for a leaner, stronger, more resilient body. To take a gifted dancer and make her superhuman."

"This has nothing to do with the Ballet," she insisted, looking again at the bag, this time with evident distaste.

"It was in Sophie Duval's lodge."

"Not possible," she stated, with steely conviction. "Not Sophie. Someone else must have put it there."

"She left partial fingerprints on some of the drugs. She handled them. There's no doubt about it."

Anne-Laure closed her eyes, her breathing shallow.

When she opened them again they were hard, flinty and vengeful.

"Then she betrayed me. She betrayed the Ballet."

So they did have a policy on performance-enhancing drugs after all.

*

"No injection marks."

They had agreed that Sternberg would get the medical examiner to take another look at the body. The first time round, her neck had been the centre of attention. An autopsy was always supposed to be comprehensive, but the general rule that you find what you're looking for – and its corollary, that you don't find what you're not looking for – applied in this domain as in many others. Particularly if what you're not looking for is as small as a pinprick.

Franck stepped off the pavement into a doorway, turning his back on the traffic noise, his phone pressed against his ear.

"Is that definitive?"

"It means she didn't inject herself over the past four or five days. And if she was previously in the habit of doing so, she changed location every time."

"Would that have worked?"

"Maybe. We're not dealing with substances you take every day. If she was following a strict, carefully planned protocol, it could be compatible with the absence of any trace marks."

"What's your feeling?" asked Franck.

"Hang on. There's more. Data first, then conclusions."

Sternberg would have done well in the RG, thought Franck, a reflexion worthy of Catherine Vautrin, his old boss. He kept it kept to himself.

"I'm listening."

"We double-checked the serology and toxicology. Ferritin 160. Hemoglobin 17. Hematocrit 51."

"Which means?"

"A good stock of iron and lots of oxygen in her blood."

"When you say 'good' do you mean 'not abnormal'?"

"Correct."

"And no strange substances floating around?"

"We found the ibuprofen, but that's it."

"So she was clean?"

"Not necessarily. These drugs are notoriously hard to spot. Once again, it's all about when she last took them, and that we don't know."

"Any more data?"
"Nothing significant."
"Can I ask you now?"
"Sure, go ahead," invited Sternberg.
"What's your feeling?"
"I'd guess that what she had in that pouch wouldn't have covered her needs for more than a month. So maybe she knew she was running low and had gone clean for a while, stretching things out until she took delivery of her next batch."
They had worked together long enough now for Franck to be able to decipher Sternberg's tone. He was describing a theoretical possibility. Which meant there were others.
"Or?" he asked.
"You've got to be disciplined if you're going to dope yourself effectively and discreetly."
"Dance is all about discipline," Franck reminded him.
"Sure, but disciplined people don't run out. They keep a check on their stocks and order in advance."
"Good point. So what does that leave us with?"
"Well, what if this was a starter pack?"
"There'd be no injections yet, and no murky blood work," said Franck, tracing Sternberg's mental footsteps.
"Right, but there'd also be instructions. What to take, and when, and in what combinations. At some point I'll go back through Duval's apartment, see if I can find them."
"OK. If you do, let me know."
Franck ended the call and slipped the mobile into his jacket.
There was, perhaps, an easier way.
He could ask the instructor.

*

If the appearance of respectability was what you were after, then the boulevard de Malesherbes would not let you down. It ran across two arrondissements, from place de la Madeleine in the eighth to place de Wagram in the seventeenth. Another of baron Haussmann's wide-spaced arteries piercing the heart of

Paris, it provided an endless series of stately stone-cut facades which confidently announced their wealth, standing and moral rectitude. Léon Abkarian M.D. had chosen well.

Franck emerged from the metro at the edge of a large open space where boulevard de Malesherbes and avenue de Villiers met. He was heading a little further north, to number 116, but he took the time to wander over to an enclosed grassy patch at one end of the square where a plinth supported a group of statues paying homage to one of the nation's literary giants. Alexandre Dumas, a man who never wrote one word when three would do, and never wrote them himself if he could pay someone else to pen them for him, sat stolidly in a low armchair, quill in hand. Perched below him, visibly at ease but ready to slip off his stone support and raise his sword if need be, was d'Artagnan. With his floppy boots and feathered hat, tasselled cloak and elaborate buttonholes, finely curved moustache and elegantly crimped hair, he exemplified the adventurer as fearless dandy, whose firm gaze belied his dainty lace collar.

Three generations of the Dumas family reigned over the square. Alexandre's son had a monument near at hand, his muse not a flamboyant musketeer but a weeping woman, as befitted someone who had rejected the heroic epic in favour of the archly sentimental. Not so Alexandre's father, who would have found a welcome place in d'Artagnan's company. A general of the revolutionary era, a rival of the young Napoleon, the original statue erected in his honour had not survived the Nazi occupation. The Vichy regime had toppled it, unable to come to terms with the fact that one of the nation's military heroes was born a slave in Haiti, and chose to bear his black mother's family name over that of his French-born father. His victorious exploits during the revolutionary wars were too much of an embarrassment to those who fantasised about the existence of a master race. The vanished statue had taken almost seventy years to replace, a new monument celebrating general Dumas having been inaugurated a month previously. It represented a massive pair of broken slave irons.

A large photo of the inauguration hung in Abkarian's waiting room. It showed the Mayor of Paris shaking hands with a group of officials from UNESCO, on the edge of which stood doctor Abkarian, looking solemn and dignified. How he had conspired to slip into the group, Franck had no idea, for no respectable institution would ever have willingly let him anywhere near one of its delegations. Léon Abkarian had a sulphurous reputation, and he delighted in it.

The waiting room was empty, which came as no surprise. Those who consulted doctor Abkarian rarely advertised the fact, and appointments were no doubt carefully spaced out to ensure confidentiality.

Not that Franck had an appointment, but when he had announced at the intercom at the entrance to the building that he was from the Brigade Criminelle, he had been ushered up without a murmur of protest. Abkarian was used to unannounced calls from officialdom, although they normally came from various sporting bodies. He always welcomed them in. After all, as he always insisted, he had nothing to hide.

He worked out of an apartment on the second floor. No assistant came forward to greet Franck when he arrived at the front door. A sign invited callers to ring the bell and enter, which he duly did. In the small entrance hall another sign suggested he take a seat in the waiting room, which was large, comfortably furnished, and full of framed photos of the good doctor. Franck only had time to study a few of them, including the one featuring general Dumas' new monument, before he was taken in hand.

Léon Abkarian entered with a neutral expression. In his early fifties, he was short and rotund, dressed in a dark suit, white shirt and unpatterned tie. His face was square-shaped, his hair a sparse collection of curls, his eyes hooded, brown and alert. He tugged a squashed packet of Gitanes from the breast pocket of his shirt, extracted a cigarette, lit it and inhaled slowly, not once taking his eyes from Franck, who had turned to face him.

"I wouldn't have thought briefcases were standard

equipment in the Brigade Criminelle," he eventually commented.

"It's a personal idiosyncrasy," offered Franck.

"Good for you. I like the idiosyncratic. Those who are not afraid to determine their own path. Who care little what others think."

"Sort of sums up your career, doesn't it?"

Abkarian smiled, held his cigarette in the air between two stubby fingers, and bowed slightly.

"Doctor Léon Abkarian at your service. Whatever you've heard about me, it's probably true."

"Captain Franck Guerin."

"I have to confess I've never heard of you."

"No reason you should have."

"Well, you are welcome, captain Guerin," said Abkarian, moving towards him. He switched his cigarette to his left hand so that they could shake hands. "Please follow me into my office."

They returned to the entrance hall and took another door. Abkarian's office was as large as his waiting room, which had allowed him to install an imposing dark wooden desk at one end and a clump of low armchairs around a coffee table at the other. He steered Franck to the desk, waiting for him to sit down before he took his own place opposite him, with his back to the wall.

"Is this, by any chance, a personal call?" he asked.

"No."

"You're quite happy with your performance, captain? You wouldn't like to move faster, to think clearer, to keep going longer? Yours is surely a punishing line of work. Given what is at stake – dealing out justice, righting wrongs – why be any less good at it than you could be? I could help."

Franck held up an open palm.

"Spare me the pitch. I'll stick with the body I've got."

"But I'm not just talking about your body," continued Abkarian. "There's your mind. The brain is an organ like any other. It has to be irrigated, stimulated, kept in top condition.

There are techniques – some of them very old, some of them cutting-edge – whose effects would astonish you. Personally, I would be honoured to help someone in law enforcement rise to the top of his profession. Don't short-change yourself, captain. You are capable of greater things than you suspect. I have helped many other clients achieve their full potential, I can certainly ..."

Franck waved his still-erect palm.

"Full marks for persistence, doctor, but you're wasting your breath."

Abkarian shook his head and gestured as if he was tossing something over his shoulder.

"It's your loss, but so be it. In which case, if this is not a personal visit, perhaps you'd like to enlighten me as to the reason why you're here?"

"Of course."

Franck fished about in his briefcase and brought out the same plastic bag he had shown Anne-Laure Favennec. He handed it across the desk. Abkarian took it, turned in his revolving chair and held it up to the light coming through the windows, tipping the bag from right to left so as to separate the pills and vials which had gathered at the bottom.

"EPO, growth hormone, a standard testosterone-based steroid, PFC, looks like benzedrine, an iron pill perhaps, and some other stuff. An interesting collection, captain. If you leave them with me, I could probably identify them all authoritatively for tomorrow. Are you looking for an expert witness?"

"I've already got one, thanks. He's also a fingerprint expert. He found yours on the haul I took these from."

"Well, these are all excellent products, if used intelligently. Given my field of expertise, I'm sure you weren't surprised to learn that I'd come into contact with them."

Performance enhancement – that was Abkarian's field of expertise, as proudly declared on the plaque on his office door, the nameplate on the intercom, and his very professional-looking website. Others – particularly the sports journalists who had covered his career – called it doping instead.

For many years he had been one of the shady figures to be found on the fringes of the Tour de France, as medical advisor either to individual cyclists or entire teams. He became notorious through his association with Gino Finetto, a young Italian racer who came from nowhere to win day stages and threaten the leaders in the Italian, Spanish and French tours. Having watched over Gino's health – his own phrase – for five years, he was as shocked and saddened as millions of television viewers to see the cyclist topple from his bike four hundred metres short of the Beille plateau in the Pyrenees on the 22nd of July 1998. Gino had been one and half minutes ahead of his nearest rival, Marco Pantani. Eleven days later Pantani was crowned champion of the Tour de France on the Champs Elysées while Gino was buried in his home town in Umbria. He died at the side of the road of heart failure brought on by exhaustion and dehydration. Abkarian's only public remark on the event was to the effect that the human body, although capable of mighty deeds, was not above sudden acts of treachery.

Finetto's death attracted less attention that it might otherwise have done thanks to the Festina affair, in which an entire team of cyclists was barred from that year's Tour after one of their medical specialists was caught in possession of a vast quantity of EPO, growth hormone, amphetamines and testosterone. In any case, it had no adverse effect on Abkarian's career. Within the profession, Finetto's rapid ascension from mediocre cyclist to world-class racer was what people remembered, not his unfortunate end. It was said that Lance Armstrong's total domination of the Tour de France from 1999 onwards led a number of gifted cyclists to enter into a Faustian pact with Abkarian. He never delivered the Tour's famous yellow jersey, but he made sure they were able to keep breathing down Armstrong's neck.

In 2006 Abkarian grabbed a few headlines by declaring that cycling would no longer be his primary focus. Denouncing the sporting world's lack of interest in seeking to surpass the limits of what convention held to be organically possible, he announced that he would turn his attention to performance improvement in areas such as business and the arts which were not under the thumb of – in his own words – the regulatory cartels of mediocrity. Rumour had it, however, that the frequent trips he had made to the USA in recent years were not without links to the peculiar sports which that nation was alone in practising.

Abkarian pushed the plastic bag back across the desk towards Franck.

"Have you come to charge me with something? None of these substances are, in and of themselves, illegal. Using them may breach the rules assorted associations have been sufficiently misguided to apply to activities they claim to oversee, but I wouldn't have thought that would be of any interest to the Brigade Criminelle."

"No, I'm not here to arrest you," stated Franck. "I just want to talk to you about the person you – as you would say – prescribed these to."

Abkarian tutted and waved a premonitory finger.

"You're going to ask me about a patient? You're forgetting my obligation of secrecy and discretion. I took an oath when I became a doctor, and I am forbidden to reveal any information concerning the health of a patient. Only the patient himself can authorise me to do so. Otherwise – I think it's article 226 of the Criminal Code, but I'm sure you can check – I'm liable to a fine of fifteen thousand euros and a year in prison. You're not about to ask me to break the law are you?"

"I thought you had clients – not patients," countered Franck.

"The term is elastic," said Abkarian, a smile tugging at the corner of his mouth, indicating the pleasure he took in jousting with authority.

"Let's try another approach," suggested Franck. "Does the name Sophie Duval mean anything to you?"

Abkarian's expression did not change.

"Denying that someone is a client – or patient, if you prefer – amounts to much the same as admitting that someone is.

Every week I get calls from the papers or television asking me to confirm or deny that so-and-so has been seeking to enhance his or her performance. I just hang up. Some day they'll get the message and stop wasting their time. It's amazing how everyone has forgotten what discretion actually means. There's just me and the Swiss bankers – and I hear even they're thinking of succumbing to pressure these days."

"Sophie Duval was a dancer – an *étoile* – at the Opera Ballet. I say 'was', because she's dead."

"I'm sorry to hear it. I'm not much of a ballet fan, but I'm sure she was a very nice young woman."

"She didn't die of natural causes. She didn't die of unnatural causes, either, unlike Gino Finetto."

Abkarian tutted again.

"That remark is in very poor taste, captain. You should know better. So what did she die of?"

"She was strangled."

Abkarian raised an eyebrow, but said nothing.

"Sophie Duval is a murder victim and to find out who did it, I have to know everything about her life. These" – he tapped the plastic bag that lay on the desktop before him – "were found in her possessions. They have her fingerprints and your fingerprints. So I'll ask you again – was Sophie Duval one of your clients?"

"Given the circumstances, I can understand how frustrating my answer must be, but principles are principles – I don't talk about my clients."

Franck pushed back from the desk, stuffed the samples back in his briefcase, and stood up.

"Know this. I too have my principles. You won't like being on the wrong side of them."

"So which d'Artagnan do you think this is?"

Franck had stopped by the statue of Alexandre Dumas, conscious that he was walking too fast, that his mind was needlessly churning, and that his frustration at Abkarian's refusal to cooperate would poison the rest of his evening if he failed to master it. He forced himself to calm down, control his breathing, and think about something else.

He was having some success, until Léon Abkarian's voice intruded upon him. Franck pivoted to face him. Abkarian stood a couple of metres away from him, his chest heaving inside his unbuttoned jacket, his breath troubled, his face red. He looked as if he had just run from his office, which he undoubtedly had. Franck wondered if he had accidentally left something behind, obliging Abkarian to try to catch up with him and hand it back.

"I'm sorry, what did you say?" he asked.

"Which d'Artagnan do you think this is?" repeated Abkarian, placing his hands on his upper thighs and leaning forward, making Franck wonder whether he should offer to prop him up.

"How many are there supposed to be?" asked Franck. There were other musketeers – Athos, Porthos, and Aramis – but there was only one d'Artagnan. He was, after all, one of the very few French literary heroes whose fame had spread around the world.

"Is it the mature but slightly melancholy d'Artagnan of *Twenty Years Later*?" A deep breath. "The fatalistic veteran of *The Viscount of Bragelonne*?" Another. "Or is it the young and reckless d'Artagnan of *The Three Musketeers*, unaware of how age and experience will change him?"

Franck had to smile. He had devoured the three tomes of d'Artagnan's life in his early teens and had returned to them in his twenties, seeking out the reassuring company of an old friend. He knew his experience was far from unique – only those who were allergic to the written word were immune to the call of Dumas' hero – and this was probably true of every generation born since the 1840s when *The Three Musketeers* had first appeared as a newspaper serial. The purpose of Abkarian's interrogation was clear – he was demonstrating that they had something in common in the hope of extending an olive branch.

"It's a good question," Franck conceded. "He's rather too well dressed for the penniless Gascon of *The Three*

Musketeers. I'd guess it's how he was in *Twenty Years Later*."

"In which case he's a very well-preserved thirty-eight year old," observed Abkarian. "Particularly for the seventeenth century."

"You think he was an adept of performance enhancement?"

"Ah, not even I would have anything to add to the valiant heart and *panache* of a d'Artagnan," admitted Abkarian. Definitely an olive branch.

"Are you OK?" asked Franck. Abkarian was still bent forward, dragging air into his lungs.

"I'll be fine. I didn't warm up, you see. You should never exercise without warming up first. Ask any doctor." He retrieved his packet of cigarettes from inside his jacket, placed one between his lips, and lit it with a disposable lighter. "This'll help."

"That I doubt."

"So you're the one giving me medical advice, captain Guerin? How would you like me to tell you how to solve the odd crime?"

"I'd be all ears," insisted Franck. "Particularly if it happened to be the murder of Sophie Duval."

Abkarian rolled his eyes. Contrary to all logic, he did indeed seem to be breathing more easily now that he had a cigarette in his hand.

"You don't give up easily, do you?"

"You reckon that's dangerous for my health?"

"It could well be," counselled Abkarian. "Depends on who's on the other end of your stubbornness."

"Today it's you."

"I noticed. Would you care to join me for a drink? I think we got off on the wrong foot. But I have to warn you in advance – I can't promise you any revelations."

"I'll take what I can get," said Franck. "Starting with that drink."

Franck was not much of a drinker, particularly when he was carrying his service revolver. Léon Abkarian, on the other hand, seemed to regard alcohol as a tastier version of water. He had steered Franck towards a brasserie which stood at the junction of boulevard Malesherbes and rue de Monceau. Having been greeted with the raised hands and curt nods that were reserved for regular customers, he proceeded to knock back two whiskies at the speed with which Franck normally despatched an espresso.

They did not talk about Sophie Duval. They talked about bodysnatching. Or at least, Abkarian did.

"Without the Saints-Innocents cemetery, would we have had *De humani corporis fabrica*?"

"You've lost me," signalled Franck. Not with the Saint-Innocents, which he knew had once stood in the Halles neighbourhood, and was to this day commemorated by an elaborately carved sixteenth-century fountain, a rallying point for local skateboarders and idle teens. It was the string of Latin which meant nothing to him.

"I can see you didn't go to medical school," observed Abkarian. "Andreas Vesalius. One of the great explorers of human anatomy. With *De humani corporis fabrica* he produced the first really useful atlas of the skeletal and muscular systems. But how did he do it? How could he see what was hidden, the secret mechanism of man, made in God's image, whose body even in death was a temple not to be despoiled? He plundered graveyards, starting with the Saint-Innocents when he came to study in Paris in the 1530s. He took corpses and hung them from the ceiling, peeling off the skin, turning and repositioning them, paying artists to draw what he revealed."

"He must have had a strong stomach."

Franck, for one, did not. He avoided autopsies whenever possible. It was easier to read a coroner's notes and conclusions than to stand by his side as he cut into a murder victim with a power tool.

"Mastering your stomach is easy. Having the will and force of character to do what others condemn is the hard bit. Vesalius ended up court physician to the Holy Roman Emperor, but he still had to keep glancing over his shoulder to keep clear of the Inquisition."

"OK," said Franck. "I see where you're going."

"Progress in medicine has always come from doctors confronting the prejudices of their time. How else could we have come up with vaccination – deliberately infecting a healthy organism in order to train it to resist a dangerous disease? How else could we have discovered the potential of stem cells – a human repair kit recovered from embryos?"

"Look," declared Franck, holding up a hand to stop Abkarian, "I'm not a scientist. I don't have any firmly held opinions on what you do."

Abkarian smiled and shook his head.

"If only you had. Then we could dissect them, confront them with the facts, and talk about them like reasonable men. The problem is that your opinions on what I do are loosely held – indeed you're probably not aware of holding them at all. They're instinctive. They're your gut reaction. They're your sense of what's right and what's wrong."

"If I didn't have a moral compass, I wouldn't be much of a policeman," Franck pointed out.

"Not everyone would agree with you. As a public servant, all that should concern you are the laws of the Republic. Your personal morality is neither here nor there. It's the corpus of criminal and civil law, as written and amended down the years by the relevant institutions, that should determine your actions."

"Fortunately, the two tend to converge. I am, after all, a product of my time."

"Of course you are. But we both know that from time to time your personal sense of what is right or wrong steps forward and takes the upper hand."

Franck nodded. He was not about to explain to Abkarian that in his time with national security he had bent some laws way beyond their breaking point. Nor that he was no longer entirely sure that the end had always justified the means.

"So, tell me this, are you a man for the horses?"

For the moment perplexed by the shift in direction, Franck shook his head.

"Any particular reason why not?" continued Abkarian.

"I'm not a gambler, but like everyone else I think a horse in full flight is a magnificent spectacle."

"Do you own a dog then?"

"Definitely not."

Franck had soiled too many shoes to have any patience for dogs in Paris.

"But you watch with admiration as a guide dog helps its master onto the metro?"

"Sure."

"And you think a thoroughbred stallion, or a docile golden retriever, are what Nature intended them to be – rather than a short and stocky wild horse, or a scavenging wolf running in a pack? Human history is an endless tale of tinkering with what the planet had to offer. But whereas we feel at ease with the animals and the landscapes we have created, we're strangely loath to do it to ourselves. Now, were you to tell me we were God's handiwork and that to tamper with it would be blasphemous, I'd respectfully back off and leave you with your delusions. But we're living in Europe's only truly secular state, which means that public policy should be on my side."

Abkarian's eyes were twinkling. He was not lecturing Franck, he was teasing him, hoping he would come up with a counter-argument with which he could engage. Like the young d'Artagnan, doctor Abkarian was not averse to crossing swords.

"*Touché*," Franck conceded. "I don't feel comfortable with what you do, but I don't really know why."

"Good! Recognising your prejudices is the first step to overcoming them. We should drink to your stumbling progress on the path to enlightenment."

Abkarian held up his empty glass and waved it at a nearby waiter. Franck still had a largely untouched beer in front of him.

"Don't forget," continued Abkarian, "that I work with

consenting adults. Louis Pasteur, on the other hand, thought nothing of injecting young children with experimental vaccines, but he's a national hero while I'm the favourite villain of the sporting pages."

A new glass of whiskey was carefully deposited on their table and its predecessor whisked away. Abkarian raised it and waited for Franck to do the same with his beer.

"Like yourself, I'm a man of principle, captain. Learn to work with mine and you might find they're not incompatible with yours."

Franck could feel himself beginning to like Léon Abkarian. Not for nothing was he known as the Witch Doctor.

Friday, 15th May

The phone hit the floor just as the doors closed. She had sensed something and turned immediately, looking back through the carriage window as the metro began to shudder forward. Her face was twisted in frustration and anger – perhaps at her bad luck, perhaps at her own carelessness.

Objectively, it ought to have been the latter. Franck had watched it all happen. She had been sitting opposite him, on the fold-down seat right next to the double doors which let each station's load of passengers on and off. She had been texting furiously, her right thumb dodging rapidly across the mobile's keypad, and had looked up almost too late to realise the metro was at her stop. An insistent buzzing noise warned that the doors were about to shut, leaving Saint-Germain-des-Prés for Odéon. She leapt to her feet and stepped down onto the platform, folding her phone shut as she did so, transferring it to her left hand, dropping it into her open shoulder bag, and missing.

Franck slid off his seat, which sprung up behind him, and scooped it up. He held it up to the window as the metro advanced, pointing to it with his other hand, and silently voiced the words, "Call it". Although she was now some metres away, he was still in her field of vision. She nodded slowly, her eyes on his face rather than on her phone.

Franck regained his place, lowered the seat down, and flipped open the phone. It was a basic black slimline Motorola. The battery indicator showed three bars. She would not have to rush. He opened his briefcase and placed it inside.

"Nice looking girl," said the young man sitting beside him, dressed for an office that still required suits but had abandoned ties. "I'll look after it if you like," he offered.

"Try being faster on the draw next time," suggested Franck.

*

"Nothing better to do than play computer games?"

Sternberg had a portable computer folded open on his workbench. A MacBook. Sophie Duval's MacBook.

"Guess what she'd been looking at on the web over the past month," invited Sternberg.

Franck did not tell him that he had already checked the past few weeks. Chances were that Sternberg had been more thorough. For a start, he was already talking about an entire month.

"Pictures of tutus?"

"A lot of pictures with tutus in them, that's for sure. But we're not going to start blaming a ballerina for looking at photos of dancers."

"Just as I wouldn't blame you for browsing sites dedicated to gruesome corpses."

"Those? There're not too many of them about," observed Sternberg. "And almost all of them are fake."

"You've checked?"

"Professional curiosity. You know how it is."

Franck made a non-committal sound. This was not a conversation he wanted to pursue.

"So what exactly is it that caught your eye in Sophie's browsing history?"

Franck knew she had been looking at photos of Serge Morin, but he also knew why. He hoped Sternberg had found something different, something new.

"She was studying the uses of performance-enhancing drugs and their long-term consequences. Remember the little *exposé* I gave you yesterday? I'm pretty sure she could have done it just as well."

"Now that is interesting."

"Sits well with the notion of a starter pack," said Sternberg. "Why bother reading up on drugs if you've been taking them for years?"

"Unless you're suddenly worried about side-effects."

"Come on, Franck. Nothing in her blood, no injection marks on the body, a limited quantity of drugs in her possession, and now this – a recent interest in the subject. Sounds like a novice to me."

"I see your point. But I talked with Léon Abkarian yesterday ..."

"The Witch Doctor himself?"

L'Equipe, the sporting daily, had been the first to come up with the nickname. It had stuck. Indeed, Abkarian probably looked upon it as his own personal *légion d'honneur*.

"Yes. He refused to say anything about Sophie, citing doctor-patient confidentiality."

"That's remarkably convenient," scoffed Sternberg.

"It is. But here's the thing about Abkarian – once you've talked to him a little, you get the feeling he's not as shady as his reputation suggests. It could be he really does refuse to name names through a sense of principle."

"So there's no chance of him telling us if Sophie had just started, or had been on this stuff for years?"

"I doubt it."

"Well then, we'll just have to wait for the investigating officer to come up with more information to confirm or deny the hypothesis."

"The investigating officer is doing his best. Didn't he bring you a MacBook with a disk drive of – how many gigabytes?"

"A hundred and twenty."

"And that's all you got from it?"

"Actually, no. We've been through her emails, which she was old-fashioned enough to continue to stock on her drive."

"And?"

"It looks like she was thinking of leaving the company."

"You sure?" demanded Franck.

"The email exchange concerns the New York City Ballet. Most of it took place in March. It's a bit patchy – for a start, it's in English, which is not my strong suit – and it's pretty obvious there were phone calls going on in parallel. However, it seems they were all set to recruit Sophie as a principal dancer."

Franck remained sceptical.

"You don't spend your entire life training to be a member of the Opera Ballet, only to walk away when you've just been named an *étoile*."

"That was my reaction too, so I roped in an expert and asked her advice."

"That would be ..." He concentrated for a few seconds, searching for the name of Sternberg's daughter. "Annabelle?"

"Exactly. Well, according to Annabelle, the New York City Ballet has one thing that no other company can claim – it was founded by George Balanchine."

"Should I be impressed?"

"If you're going to get anywhere with this case, you really have to spend some time with my daughter. According to her, Balanchine was one of the great twentieth-century choreographers, famous for carrying classical technique into contemporary dance. The New York City Ballet is dedicated to defending his legacy."

"And that makes it more appealing than the Opera Ballet?"

He doubted very much that Anne-Laure Favennec would think so.

"Maybe Sophie had personal reasons for wanting a change," suggested Sternberg. "Live inside an institution your entire life, you're bound to get itchy feet."

Live under someone's benevolent dominion your entire life, it could have the same effect.

*

She threw a shoe at him.

Since it was a ballet shoe, and weighed next to nothing, Franck didn't even flinch when it hit his cheek. He concentrated on keeping his eye out for the next one, which arrived in quick succession. He caught it in mid-air, bent down to pick up the first one, and offered them both back to Lisa Roux.

She swung her foot up and knocked them from his hands.

"You have no idea what you've done," she stated, the words coming rapidly, her voice low. She closed the gap between them, her eyes menacing.

He felt the sting of the slap before he actually registered the fact that her arm had moved. That she was agile was no surprise, but he would never have imagined she was so strong. Instinctively he stepped backwards and brought up his hands to defend his face. The only thing he gained from the move was her contempt, to judge by the look she gave him.

He was beginning to regret having stepped into her lodge, where she had been sitting alone, massaging her feet.

"Anne-Laure summoned me," she hissed. "She ordered me to tell her if I knew anything about Sophie taking drugs. I thought she was talking about cannabis or ecstasy, or something like that. I actually laughed, and reminded her that she too had been a dancer in the company. She too had known the parties after a successful *première*, or to celebrate a promotion, or someone's birthday. She cut me off. She said Sophie had been doping herself to gain strength and speed. She said you had proven it and she had to know how far the cancer had spread. That's the word she used – cancer – like Sophie was some kind of tumour that had infected her precious company."

"There were drugs in Sophie's lodge. We don't know yet what they mean. I have to talk to you about it."

"They had nothing to do with her," said Lisa, speaking slowly and clearly, as if to an idiot. "I don't know what they were doing there, but I can assure you they had nothing to do with her."

Franck shook his head, albeit almost with regret, since Lisa's conviction seemed absolute.

"She had handled them. Her fingerprints are on them. They definitely had something to do with her. Just what that something was, I'm trying to find out."

"No," insisted Lisa, one arm with a blade-like palm descending in a chopping motion only to freeze at a perfect right angle to her erect and indignant body. "That's not what you're doing. You're destroying all that's left of her – her reputation, our memories, our affection. You're speculating without regard for the consequences. You're torturing Sophie – even though she's dead – and if you continue –" She stepped up to him again. Franck steeled himself for another blow. She raised her right hand and clawed at the air in front of his face. "– I'll choke the last breath out of you."

With which she froze, aghast, her mouth open, her eyes widening with the shock of what she had just heard. What she had just said.

Suddenly her cheeks were overwhelmed with a flood of tears and she collapsed forward into Franck's arms.

"What am I saying?" she whispered.

Franck hushed her and guided her back to the chaise longue she had occupied when he first entered the room. He placed her upon it and sat alongside her, allowing her to lean her weight against him. Lisa regained control of her breathing. Franck dug a tissue out of a jacket pocket and she took it, blowing her nose. They sat in silence for a while.

"Go ahead," Lisa finally said, in a tired voice. "Ask your questions."

"Did you ever see Sophie with a syringe? Doesn't matter where it was or why she might have been carrying one. Did you ever see a syringe anywhere near her?"

"No," said Lisa, instantaneously.

"Think!" urged Franck.

Some seconds passed.

"No," repeated Lisa. "Never."

"Did she frequently take pills?"

"Sure – we all do. Aspirin, paracetamol, ibuprofen – this place runs on them."

"But apart from those, nothing else?"

"Not that I can recall. Sophie took really good care of herself. She was almost never ill."

"Did she ever mention a doctor Abkarian? Léon Abkarian."

"Abkarian? The Witch Doctor from all those sporting scandals?"

"Yes, that Abkarian."

"Never. Definitely not. He has something to do with this?"

"The pills and vials found in Sophie's lodge had gone through his hands at some stage."

"Something is seriously wrong here, captain," insisted Lisa. "Abkarian's a Frankenstein figure. He creates monsters out of human beings. Sophie wouldn't have gone within a thousand metres of anyone like that. She wasn't at war with her body, she was at one with it. She willed a gesture, a movement and it came into being. Doping herself would have destroyed that harmony."

"So what was she doing with those drugs?"

"There's got to be another explanation. And you've got to find it – and fast, or Anne-Laure's going to tear this place apart."

"I thought she was going to be very discreet," said Franck. "She has nothing to gain by creating a public scandal."

"You don't know Anne-Laure. If she thought that burning the Opera House down would cleanse and purify the Ballet's soul, she would strike the match without a moment's hesitation."

*

"Kill them all. God will recognise his own."

Franck had not been around when Arnaud Amalric had uttered these words, condemning the entire population of the town of Béziers in the south of France. Since Amalric, a Papal legate and crusader against heresy, had been active in the early thirteenth century this was scarcely surprising. However, he imagined that Amalric had spoken with the same steely calm as Anne-Laure Favennec.

"I will protect this institution come what may," she stated, hammering the tabletop before her with a rigid finger. "Against each and every dancer within it, if need be."

"This is all premature," countered Franck. "We don't know what Sophie Duval was doing with those drugs. We don't know if she ever used them."

"They were within these walls. That's sacrilege enough.

The Opera Ballet isn't just another dance company. The Bolshoi was stultified by Stalinism. New York's soul was lost to publicists and celebrity. Paris alone has maintained its cohesion, its traditions, its loyalty to the repertoire. This is the temple of dance, and our *étoiles* are no more than its most dedicated acolytes. They have no right to seek to remake themselves, to go beyond the boundaries that Nature has established. Self-abnegation is at the heart of what we do – a dancer must lose herself in the dance, not seek to outshine it. We are mere mortals in the presence of something divine. Not gods in the making."

Franck sat silently, his hands in his lap. He was watching the fire in her eyes. Waiting for it to consume itself.

"I danced, Franck," she resumed. Her voice was no longer strident. "*La Bayadère. Giselle. Sylvia. Swan Lake. Coppelia.* They were the headiest days of my life. I have never felt such exultation since. But I stopped. I stopped when I was thirty-six. I stopped when my technique was flawless, my strength and energy undiminished, my emotional grasp of the roles at its most mature. I stopped at my peak – because I would not inflict my decline upon an art that I worshipped. I knew to step aside, to accept my fate. Humility, dedication, and discipline – the three pillars on which this institution stands. They will not be swept aside or insidiously undermined. Not while I'm here."

"I understand," said Franck, not because he did – not entirely, anyway – but because he had to rein her in. "But given what's at stake, there's nothing to be gained by moving too quickly. If you start interrogating all the dancers, rifling every lodge, opening every locker, denouncing drug use as an abomination, then a scandal is born and the Ballet will have to live with it forever. You'll end up with urine tests and random searches and a cloud of suspicion that can only thicken. And maybe – because we still don't know – all for nothing."

Anne-Laure took a deep breath and laid her hands flat on the table. It was the first time they had lain still since the opening of their exchange.

"What do you propose?"

“Who have you talked to? Who knows about Sophie Duval’s cosmetic pouch?”

“My assistant. Lisa Roux. Serge Morin.”

“What did Serge say?”

“He seemed bewildered. Said he’d never seen Sophie take anything suspicious. Said she’d never dream of such a thing.”

“Well, we know he’d seen a lot of her recently,” said Franck. “Maybe you should take what he says at face value.”

“Sophie’s fingerprints were on the drugs,” Anne-Laure reminded him.

“I know. I just don’t know why. I need more time. Let’s keep the whole drugs thing quiet for the moment. Lisa won’t mention it – she’s too protective of Sophie’s memory. What about your assistant?”

“Nothing to worry about there.”

“And Serge?”

“Serge is a gossip, but he entered the Ballet school when he was nine. He has lived inside these walls for forty years. If they crumble, he’ll have nowhere to go. He’ll keep it to himself.”

“Good,” said Franck. “I’ve got another question for you. Did you know Sophie was planning on leaving the company? She had made an appointment with you for the day after her death. That may well be why.”

“I take it you’re talking about the New York City Ballet?”

“So you did know?”

“I’m impressed that you do. She kept it very quiet. I’m pretty sure she never talked to Lisa Roux about it, for instance.”

“You think it had something to do with her death?” asked Franck.

It was a loaded question. If anyone would have wanted to stop Sophie leaving, after all the company had invested in her, it was the woman sitting right across from him.

Anne-Laure shook her head at him. Almost pityingly.

“I know for certain it did not,” she stated. “Sophie never seriously sought to leave us. The City Ballet’s a decent company, but at the end of the day, they’re just Balanchine’s orphans, worshipping at the altar of their long-lost father. They don't have the depth of tradition we have, nor, quite frankly, the technical excellence we take for granted. Sophie was just stringing them along."

"Why?"

"So that she would have some leverage with me to get what she wanted."

"Which was?"

"Diana."

"That's why you gave it to her rather than Lisa?"

"In a sense, yes. Not because I believed the threat of her leaving was real, but because I was impressed that she was threatening me at all. And that she was prepared to cross swords with Lisa."

"You were happy to see her enter into conflict with her closest friend?"

"Personally, not at all. But for the company's sake, yes, it could only be a good thing."

Franck did not know how to respond. It seemed that Anne-Laure could switch at will between her personal and her institutional identity. It was impressive. And slightly worrying.

*

"Did Sophie explain to you how she fought with Lisa for the role of Diana?"

Serge laid down the banana he had been about to peel. Franck had knocked on the door of his lodge, expecting to find him in. There was a performance of *Giselle* that evening. Serge was already in costume, wearing tight breeches, a billowing shirt and a rustic coat – prince Albrecht in his peasant garb.

"Ah, it's the troublesome captain Guerin," he said, waving Franck in.

Franck made sure to close the door behind himself.

Serge's lodge was larger than Lisa's or Sophie's. Long service clearly had its advantages. Aside from the standard dressing table and wardrobe, it featured four leather armchairs pulled in a semi-circle around a decommissioned fireplace filled with brightly coloured flowers. Close inspection would reveal them to be made of fabric, a convincing demonstration of the props department's many skills.

"First of all you find all those strange substances in Sophie's lodge," continued Serge. "Now you want to rake up the story of Sophie and Lisa's catfight over *Diana and Acteon*."

"Anne-Laure tells me you never saw Sophie taking anything suspicious."

"I didn't."

"You're not just covering for her?"

"You think I would have stood by while Sophie put her future in danger by fiddling about with drugs? In a company run by Anne-Laure Favennec who would have cast her to the dogs if she caught the slightest hint of it?"

"And you never saw any strange marks on her? Pinpricks on veins, that kind of thing?"

"Never. And, believe me, if there had been any such thing, I would have seen it. If anyone pored over her in the course of the past weeks, it was me." He stopped, perhaps troubled about having referred to their recent intimacy in a way that could be deemed flippant. "You know what I mean."

Franck nodded.

"So you're convinced that the pills and stuff I found had nothing to do with her?"

"Absolutely."

"Despite the fact that they were found in her lodge?"

"Look at the door behind you. How often do you think it gets locked?"

"You tell me."

"In the evening when I leave – if I'm not too tired to remember, which is often the case after a performance – and whenever the cleaners come through, since they're under strict instructions to lock up afterwards. But that's it. And I don't expect many of the other *étoiles* take greater pains than me. Nothing gets pilfered in the Opera. It's a world apart. A better world."

"Except that you're implying it's a world in which someone might plant drugs in Sophie's lodge."

"It's the only possible explanation for their presence. Tell me this – how hard were they to find?"

"Zipped into a make-up pouch sitting on a shelf."

"Doesn't sound like a very good hiding place to me. Sounds more like a place where you'd put something you wanted to come easily to light."

"Sometimes the best spot to hide something is in plain view," said Franck. "But, if you're right, who'd you suggest was out to besmirch Sophie's good name? Who would want to imply a connection with Léon Abkarian?"

"With whom?"

"Léon Abkarian, also known as the Witch Doctor. You're not a cycling fan, I take it?"

"Can't say I am."

"Abkarian is a notorious practitioner of so-called performance enhancement. He supplied the drugs found in Sophie's lodge."

"You know this for sure?"

"Fingerprints rarely lie."

"Then ..." Serge spoke hesitantly, peering cautiously at Franck as he did so, as if unsure of his intelligence, "why don't you ask him about them?"

"I have, but he refuses to speak about his clients."

"Can't you force him?"

"We don't waterboard on this side of the Atlantic. Given time, though, I might get something out of him. Despite everything, he might turn out to be a reasonable man. In the meantime, though, if you can think of anyone who might have wanted to set Sophie up, I'm all ears."

Serge tipped his head back to stare for a moment at the ceiling of his lodge. It proved an ineffectual source of inspiration.

"I have no idea."

"Makes it a rather implausible hypothesis then, doesn't it?"

"Not as implausible as Sophie using performance-enhancing drugs. She was twenty-nine. She was as fit as any dancer in this company."

"Maybe she'd decided to reach beyond the other dancers in the company. Look at the way she fought to get the part in *Diana and Acteon*. Against her best friend, no less."

"That's different. She wasn't trying to get ahead of Lisa, she was just standing up for herself. There's no rule that says the more experienced *étoile* gets first choice of new roles. It's down to Anne-Laure every time, and Sophie made the more convincing candidate. To tell the truth, more than a few of us were rather pleased to see Sophie stepping out of Lisa's shadow."

"There was something unhealthy about their relationship?"

"Unhealthy? No, that would be melodramatic. Lisa and Sophie were a formidable pair. They'd been close so long they almost shared the same thoughts. If you'd ever seen them dance together, you would have been amazed. Perfect, effortless synchronisation. But, as in most dances, there's one who leads and one who follows. Sophie had always followed Lisa's lead. And I think that's how Lisa liked it. She has a domineering streak she doesn't like to own up to."

"You speak from experience?"

Serge fidgeted a little, as if debating something internally.

"There's something I should know about you and Lisa?" pursued Franck.

"It was a long time ago," Serge confessed. "Five years. When she was still a *première danseuse*. It didn't last very long. It was a dance thing. You know how it is."

"No," insisted Franck, wondering if Anne-Laure Favennec had not underestimated the extent of Serge's conquests within the company. "I don't."

"We found ourselves dancing *pas de deux* in two major productions, back to back. When you go out on stage and pull off something both gracious and difficult night after night, then you begin to feel there's some kind of connection. It spills over."

"Was it common knowledge? Your ... whatever you called it."

"No. Lisa was married at the time, although that was well on the way to breaking down before we started. Sophie knew, though. She provided Lisa with an alibi as and when required. But, like I said, it didn't last."

"Because?"

"We moved on to other roles, danced with other people, found new connections."

"No hard feelings?"

"No. It's not a subject we like to bring up, so I'd prefer it if you didn't cross-examine Lisa about it. But, no, I think it's safe to say we both moved on."

Serge, of course, had moved on several times, finally reaching Sophie.

"Did Lisa know about you and Sophie?"

"I doubt it. I certainly didn't tell her. I doubt Sophie did."

*

"I'm so sorry to have put you out like this."

Franck waved her apologies aside.

"That's OK. I'm sure you'd have done the same if it'd been my phone."

She had risen to wave at him when he entered Le Drouot, demonstrating a good memory for faces. Franck was pretty sure she had ignored him from the moment she got on the metro that morning till the moment she got off, catching but a glimpse of him gesturing with her phone as the train pulled away. His level of certitude was due to the fact that he had not done the same.

It was her handbag that had first caught his eye. It was a Louis Vuitton, a wide bag made of panels of textured and smooth leather with sturdy straps tethered to brass fixtures. Franck was scarcely a connoisseur of handbags, but Isabelle Arbaud, the woman at the centre of the Night-Scented case, had possessed exactly the same model. Its image was unlikely ever to leave him.

His attention snared, he had then observed her – early to mid-twenties, a grey hussar-style jacket over a black-and-white striped top, black trousers with wide, high cuffs over dainty-looking open-topped shoes, chestnut hair, gathered together as it fell to the nape of her neck, no earrings, brown eyes, small nose, lips which she had a tendency to press together while she peered at the tiny screen of her phone.

He would have recognised her at the back of the café, wave or no wave.

She invited him to sit beside her and raised a finger to an attentive waiter, who immediately came over. Franck ordered a coffee. There were two empty espresso cups on the table. A kindred spirit. A Blackberry lay alongside them.

"My name's Noémie," she said, taking the phone Franck held out to her. "Noémie Berger."

"Franck Guerin."

"I felt so stupid this morning. I just got that phone yesterday. I decided it was time I had separate phones for business and for personal use – I've been using this for both." She tapped the screen of her Blackberry. "Which basically means that I've been at work twenty-four hours a day, even when I'm out at a restaurant or at the cinema. I'd just started sending out messages to friends with my new number when ... well, you saw what happened. Makes me wonder, now. Two phones – twice as many things to lose."

"Can't give you much advice on that front. I've only got the one."

"So you're not worried about mixing up the personal and the professional?" she asked.

He was not quite sure how to reply. His vocation was personal. It always had been, ever since the day he had been accepted into the DST and had been introduced to the high-stakes world of national security. It was no less so now that he was on the outside, relegated to the Brigade Criminelle. That was why, after all, he knew before she told him that the mobile she had dropped was new. Only four numbers had been put into its directory – her mother, a certain Gaelle, a Pauline, and a Susan – the latter two with Swiss prefixes. Four text messages had been sent, all of which simply stated the fact she had a new phone and provided the number. No calls had been made. He could have dismissed the quick check he had made as idle curiosity, but was well aware that his training lay behind it.

"I've got used to it."

His coffee arrived. He emptied the cup.

"So what is it you do, Franck? Apart from gather up orphaned phones in the metro."

"I'm with the police," he admitted.

"You're not!" she exclaimed.

He shrugged. It was a profession that rarely elicited a neutral response. There was a fifty-fifty chance she would now ask about his gun. He hoped not, though. It always made his heart sink.

"It's funny," she continued. "I'm less impressed now by you bringing me back my phone. Like you were duty-bound to do so. Isn't that strange?"

"Actually, it's quite reassuring. That means you don't have too dim a view of us. It's not that common."

"Yes, but it is rather ungrateful, isn't it? So, just so that you know," – she laid her hand on his forearm – "I really do appreciate what you've done."

"So what is it you do, professionally speaking?" he asked in return.

She recovered her hand and pointed across the interior of the café to a window that looked out upon the Hôtel Drouot, since 1852 the site of the capital's principal auction house.

"Antiques. I source them, evaluate them, and from time to time buy and sell them."

"What does 'sourcing' mean in this context?"

"I find them. I look through old estates, I visit private collections, I go to sales in the provinces, I keep my ear to the ground."

"And when you find something?"

"I generally act as a go-between for a dealer or a collector, but sometimes, if it's a real steal, I'll invest in an item myself, mark it up and sell it on, or bring it to Drouot and let the bidders get carried away."

"You've been at this a long time?" asked Franck.

She laughed.

"I didn't start as a toddler, if that's what you're asking."

"It's just," whispered Franck, gesturing discreetly at the other customers in the café, most of whom had probably nipped in from the auction rooms across the street, and all of whom were well into middle age, if not beyond. "Your hair's the wrong colour."

"There's no rule that says you have to be an antique to deal in them. I've been at it for two years full-time. I dabbled a bit while I was writing my thesis, and figured it might be fun to try to go it alone, rather than get a job as a staff evaluator for one of the big boys."

"Is it?"

"What?"

"Fun."

"It is, actually. I travel a lot. I'm based in Basel, but I rent a tiny apartment near here too since Drouot's one of the centres of my universe. I meet a lot of very interesting people. Present company included."

"You don't know if I'm interesting," Franck pointed out.

"True, I don't know – but I've got a hunch, and you don't survive very long in my profession if you're not good at hunches."

"Mine too. So if you're only an occasional visitor to the capital, what brings you here this time?"

"I have a collection of frames up for auction in four days' time."

"Frames? Not pictures, just frames?"

"That's right. Nine assorted Louis XVI gilded wood frames."

"With no Louis XVI paintings inside them?"

"Unfortunately, no. But original frames are worth quite a bit on their own."

"Where did you find them?"

"Here and there."

"That's pretty vague."

"I can't reveal my sources – I'd soon be out of business if I did. But I've got receipts for them all, if that's what you're asking."

"Art theft's not my field," said Franck. Or at least, not yet, given Yves de Chaumont's regular attempts to involve him in the Chantreau dossier.

"I don't imagine lost property is either," she observed.

"Lost lives, actually. I'm with the Brigade Criminelle."

She took a sharp intake of breath and inched back slightly, looking at him as if from a new angle.

"I don't know what to say now," she admitted. "I can scarcely ask you if it's fun. Are you working a case right now?"

He nodded.

"Sophie Duval. The dancer." It had been in the press. There was no blackout on the case itself, only on its salient details.

"I saw her last December. In *The Nutcracker*. I'm not a big ballet fan, but a guy invited me."

"A good evening?"

"The show was great. The guy," – she bobbed her head slowly from side to side – "not so much."

"I'm sorry to hear it," said Franck. Although he knew how to sound sincere, she looked at him with evident amusement.

"They say the seas are teeming with fish, so I cast a line from time to time. You get the strangest catches though. How about you, Franck? You've hooked your special fish?"

"I'm not much of an angler."

"Too busy running after the bad guys?"

"Something like that."

She glanced at her watch and looked up at him with a frown.

"I actually have to go. I have a meeting with a dealer down the road in about three minutes. Here ..." She started digging in her handbag.

"I'll get these, don't worry," said Franck, pointing to the three empty coffee cups.

But she wasn't looking for her purse. She pulled out a tiny leather wallet that held her business cards and slipped him one, having taken a pen and added another number to it.

"Since you don't have the time to come running after me, just call. I'll come to you."

Saturday, 16th May

"Is it you I have to thank for sending that banshee after me?"

Franck was at a loss. He had been surprised to see Léon Abkarian's name flash up on the screen of his mobile phone when it rang. Even though he knew better – Abkarian was not the type to have a sudden crisis of conscience – he was unable to stop himself hoping that he was calling to come clean about whether or not he been involved with Sophie Duval. All he got instead was a question that left him perplexed.

"I didn't send anyone after you, and I can't say I know many banshees," he replied, the first half of which, at least, was true.

"So Jung was right. Just think, captain – in the space of two days two completely unrelated people turn up in my office to talk to me about a certain Sophie Duval. It seems synchronicity is a universal phenomenon after all."

"Who are we talking about?"

"Sophie Duval, a gifted ballerina with the Opera Ballet," said Abkarian, being deliberately obtuse.

"Funny," countered Franck. "I thought her name meant nothing to you."

"Were I ignorant then, I've had ample opportunity to make up for it, now that one of her colleagues has sung her praises to me."

"Who are we talking about – and no games this time."

"You have heard of a young woman called Lisa Roux? Turns out she's an *étoile* too. Turns out that she heard I had some kind of involvement with drugs found in the possession of Sophie Duval. Turns out that she is prepared to kill me if I prove responsible, directly or indirectly, for blackening Duval's name."

"She said that? Explicitly?" Franck had no difficulty imagining Lisa Roux doing so, but was surprised that she had made the connection with Abkarian. Until he remembered that he was the one who had mentioned the doctor's name to her.

"Words spoken in anger, captain," said Abkarian, choosing

now to sound forgiving. "I'm sure she has no intention of carrying them out. Particularly as I have no intention of ever speaking ill of mademoiselle Duval and the abilities she possessed – which it seems were quite remarkable. Were they indeed acquired with a little professional, scientific help, she would have made a good advert for performance enhancement."

It sounded like Abkarian would still neither confirm nor deny any involvement with Sophie, but was tempted to try floating a rumour linking the two of them. Viral marketing, as some would call it, and just as sickening as its name implied.

"When did she arrive in your office?" asked Franck.

"Yesterday late afternoon, out of the blue. A bit like yourself."

"I'll talk with Lisa Roux and tell her to stay away" said Franck. "But I'd advise you to talk to no one about Duval, except with me."

"It seems you feel very possessive about this young woman, captain. Is that healthy?"

Franck hung up.

He wasn't about to take medical advice from Léon Abkarian.

*

"Remember – you are hunters! Play with her, then kill her!"

When Franck had asked where he could find the dancers working on *Diana and Acteon* he had been told to try the Lifar studio. And warned not to go in.

The first challenge, as ever, was simply finding it.

Two shapes dominated the roof of the Opera House. One was the cliff-like slab that rose just behind the building's centre point, its towering height dictated by the need to accommodate the machines required to raise and lower lights and backdrops over the stage. Topped with a triangular pediment, it provided a perch for Apollo himself, raising his lyre as a priest would a consecrated host. Right in front of him lay the building's other key feature – the cupola which hovered above the auditorium. A crown of green and gilded copper, it sat upon a ring of stone pierced with circular windows, each inset with the outline of a lyre in homage to the god whose benevolent gaze looked down upon it. Just as Apollo's eyrie sat atop a mass of ropes and pulleys, so the cupola's proud outline originally hid the Opera's heating and ventilation system, not to mention the space necessary to haul up and clean the eight ton bronze and crystal chandelier that hung in majesty above the audience. However, unlike the area above the stage, which was still crammed with weight-lifting machinery, the advance of technology since the nineteenth century had allowed the inside of the cupola to be cleared out and rehearsal rooms installed.

The Lifar studio took up half of the stone circle supporting the copper crown. Inside the semi-circular room the original iron beams supporting the dome above were still visible, as were the round windows barred with the profile of Apollo's preferred instrument. The floor was dark vinyl and ever-so-slightly spongy underfoot. One wall was completely mirrored. Wooden bars had been installed all the way round the perimeter of the room. A grand piano sat in a corner by the door.

In the centre of the studio Lisa Roux stood on her left foot, one leg straight, the other one crossed behind it at knee-height, toe pointed. Her left arm was extended downwards at a thirty degree angle to her torso to where her hand grasped the mid-point of a longbow. Her right arm shot up alongside her head, where she clutched the shaft of an arrow, whose point reached towards the ceiling of the rehearsal room. Her eyes looked straight ahead, her lips tightly shut.

Six metres from her Serge Morin held exactly the same position.

Six metres from both of them, the third corner of a perfect equilateral triangle, stood a dancer in her mid-twenties. She had placed her right leg in front of her left, with her leading foot turned to the side. Both arms were raised and curved above her head. Unlike the two others, she had no props. She looked familiar, but Franck could not recall her name.

"No prettiness. No pity," instructed the figure in a corner of the room. He was well on his way to being two metres tall and was perched on a high stool that lifted him even further off the ground, his back as straight as the dancers. Indeed, in physical terms, there was not much difference between them. His arms, revealed by a tight black t-shirt, were thin but muscular, as were his legs, encased in thigh-hugging leather trousers. His hair had been shaved close to the skull, uncovering a low forehead and a thick ridge of bone above his eyes. The harsh accent with which he spoke French, hardening sounds which ought to have been soft and yielding, did not make his appearance seem any more reassuring. Nor did the fact that he issued his instructions in staccato fashion. "Pursue her. Pierce her. Watch the life die in her eyes. On three. One. Two. Three."

Lisa and Serge surged forward in perfect synchronisation, evolving over the next few minutes as perfect mirror images. Between them and around them flowed the third dancer, caught and thrown by their surging arms, entangled and then freed by their insinuating legs, blocked and driven back by their twirling bows, until she broke for a distant corner of the room while Lisa and Serge raised their bows, arrows nocked. As she leapt with outstretched legs they loosed their arrows which flew by on either side of her. She landed on the ball of her right foot and then instantly crumpled, twisting as she fell to the floor. Lisa and Serge launched themselves into the air at the same moment, landing on either side of her and gazing down with what looked to Franck like triumphant disdain.

A single handclap punctured the silence of the room.

Lisa relaxed. Serge extended a hand, bending his knee, and helped the third dancer to her feet.

"Not so wide!" yelled the figure in the corner. He slid off his stool and snatched a longbow that stood propped alongside it. He knelt and grabbed two arrows from a pile on the floor. He fitted one to the string, pulled back and released it in a single movement. The arrow crossed the room behind Lisa, causing her to instinctively jerk her head forwards, and clattered against the mirror of the distant wall. “One metre wide. No more. Learn from Serge.”

Lisa’s eyes were easy to read, but she gave no voice to her anger. Franck did not give her a chance.

“Isn’t that dangerous?” he asked.

All eyes in the room, which up to that point had ignored his quiet entrance, turned towards him.

“Dangerous?” repeated the figure in black. “I hope so.”

He retrieved another arrow, drew his bow, and pointed it at Franck.

“Hey!” Franck was raising his right hand, fingers spread, in an official injunction to stop when the arrow struck his left shoulder. It stung, like a hard punch made with the knuckles, and then toppled over him, hitting the wall and falling to the floor.

Franck knelt and picked it up, ignoring the reverberating pain in his shoulder. The arrow was blunt, its tip simply silver paint on the shaft.

“Perhaps that will teach you not to interrupt our rehearsals,” he was told. “You three take a break. Clara, get me a coffee.”

“I’ll give you a hand,” said Serge, skipping alongside the third dancer as she moved towards the door, getting there before her and opening it with a flourish.

Before the door could close behind them Lisa caught it, having cast her eyes in the air as she strode past Franck. She left the room.

“You want me to shoot you again?” the figure in black asked him.

“Not really. I’d have to arrest you. Violence against a police officer, that sort of thing.”

“You are a police officer? Show me your gun, then.”

“No, but I will show you my ID.” He pulled it out, crossed the rehearsal room, and held it at eye level. “Captain Franck Guerin, Brigade Criminelle.”

“Piet van Roon.”

He set aside his bow and offered his hand. Franck shook it.

“You are too late, captain. You should have protected

Sophie when she was alive. That way, I wouldn't find myself having to start all over with that Lisa Roux."

"So you were happier working with Sophie?"

Van Roon looked askance at Franck. He dug a hand into the pocket of his trousers and pulled something out. Without glancing at it he nestled it in his right hand, slid a finger along the top of it, and let it fall. It was a yo-yo. A bright orange yo-yo, hurtling downwards until it almost touched the vinyl-clad floor, at which point a jerk of his wrist brought it rushing back up.

"If you ask that question, you already know the answer. I didn't want Sophie Duval, but I put up with her."

"She wasn't good enough?" asked Franck. The yo-yo was still ascending and descending. Van Roon had still not deigned to look at it.

"She was too good. Not too good a dancer. Too good a person. I wanted someone wild, half-tamed, someone who chafes under ballet's yoke."

"Sure you were looking in the right place? As I understand it, that's not what the Opera Ballet is famous for."

A smile crept across van Roon's face. His fingers closed upon the yo-yo as it reached the top of its climb.

"You're not wrong, captain Guerin. In a sense, the Opera Ballet is not ideal for what I'm seeking to do, given the way it shapes its dancers. But it offers a very prestigious platform. Not to mention a very generous commission. And anyway, constraints and obstacles bring out the best in me."

"Are you happier with Lisa Roux, then?"

Van Roon grimaced. The yo-yo released itself from his grasp and set off once more down its string.

"If anything, Lisa is worse than Sophie Duval. Sophie tried to please me – tried to become what I wanted. Lisa is too proud to make such an effort. It's a pity, as I had the perfect solution to hand, but madame Favennec would not listen to me."

"Well, if you were looking to bring someone in from outside, it's scarcely surprising she turned you down."

"Nothing of the sort. From the outset I wanted Clara

Santoni to be my Diana, foolishly forgetting she was a mere *première danseuse*. Hierarchy, captain – never underestimate it. Clara has been present at every rehearsal of this piece since I arrived in Paris – when madame Favennec granted me that, I assumed she recognised Clara's place as understudy. But no. When Sophie died, all that Clara was allowed to do was to teach the steps to Lisa Roux."

"Sophie didn't die," stated Franck. "She was murdered."

The yo-yo did not stop.

"I don't wish to sound callous, but it is the fact of her death that matters to me – not the manner of it."

"That does sound callous."

"I'm as much a victim of the event as she was," said van Roon, shrugging.

"She's dead. You're having to train a new ballerina. It's not quite the same."

"You're right – it's not the same. Sophie's struggle is over. Mine is still underway."

"You're lucky Lisa Roux isn't in the room," observed Franck.

"I'm not afraid of Lisa," said van Roon, very calmly.

"Mind if I talk to her before she comes back?"

"Be my guest."

Franck walked over to the door, watching van Roon in the mirrored wall as he did so. The choreographer hopped back onto his stool, crossing his legs and leaning over them. The yo-yo continued to bob up and down unnoticed by his side.

Franck found himself trying to gauge the length of its string.

Serge, Lisa and Clara were coming back down the corridor outside the studio.

"You're a brave man, captain," cried Serge. "Confronting the dragon in his den. This, by the way, is Clara – Clara Santoni."

"We've already met," declared Clara, who held a full cup of coffee in the air at shoulder height.

"That's right," said Franck, remembering their encounter in

a corridor a few days previously.

"Get what you wanted from him?" asked Serge.

"A bruised shoulder, that's about it. Anyhow, I wasn't looking for him. Can I talk to you, Lisa, before you go back in?"

"Sure," she said. "Anything that might annoy Piet."

Serge and Clara walked on. Lisa and Franck sat down side by side on a narrow stairwell which she assured him was infrequently used.

"So what do you think of Piet van Roon, the nearest thing choreography currently has to a superstar?" she asked him.

"I think he needs to be dragged before a health and safety inspector. You could knock out an eye with one of those arrows."

"Danger focuses the mind," she quoted. "That's one of his dictums. The archery adds an extra challenge to the piece. Piet worships difficulty."

"Why on earth did Anne-Laure commission him?"

"Well, unfortunately, Piet produces dances of extraordinary beauty. Despite the gimmicks he loads them with. But you don't get one without the other. And critics love what he does – everything about it. They say he is tugging ballet closer to the notion of total performance."

"Whatever that is." Franck had sensed Lisa's scepticism, so he borrowed it.

Lisa chuckled. "Well, whatever it is, it sells tickets and attracts wealthy sponsors. Anne-Laure wanted a new signature ballet for the company, and so she bought van Roon. I hate to admit it, but it will probably prove an excellent investment. Even though it's not finished yet – and even though I'm still struggling to absorb it – and even though he hates me for taking the principal role – *Diana and Acteon* is shaping up to be an extraordinary piece."

"Would you have let Clara Santoni dance your part?"

"Maybe. She's very good – you saw how she dances the hind? She's holding nothing back from this project. And she has a *rapport* with Piet that neither I nor Serge have."

"Does she have a yo-yo too?"

Lisa burst out laughing.

"You saw it then? It never stays in his pocket very long. It has a life of its own, that thing. I don't think even Piet's aware of it."

"So what's it for?"

"His version of prayer beads, I suppose. Helps him concentrate. Keeps him calm. It's part of his image too. Everyone knows about Piet's yo-yo. It keeps him a step ahead of the other personalities in the contemporary dance scene, where being at least a little weird is *de rigueur*."

"You couldn't get it for me, could you?"

"What?"

"His yo-yo. Does he ever leave it lying around?"

"Never. It's either looped around his finger or in his pocket. Why the interest? Want to kidnap it to take revenge for him shooting you?"

"Something like that," said Franck, changing the subject. "Anyhow, I have something more important to tell you."

"Go ahead."

"Stay away from Léon Abkarian."

"Ah," said Lisa, nodding to herself, "you heard about that."

"He phoned me. You're not helping by harassing him."

"And he's helping?" she threw back at him, indignantly. "He refuses to clear Sophie's name when it would be so easy for him."

"You don't understand a character like Abkarian. His real source of power lies in remaining silent and cultivating his *mystique*. Leave him to me. In fact," – he slid down one step so that he could turn and look her directly in the face – "leave the whole investigation to me. Answer my questions when I come to see you, but don't take any more initiatives."

"Only if you promise me you'll protect Sophie's memory."

"I'll do what I can. Anne-Laure will say nothing about her and the drugs. Not for the moment, anyhow."

"That's not a promise," objected Lisa.

"I don't make promises I can't keep," said Franck. "But if

you want her killer found, just stay out of things."

"I don't make promises I can't keep," echoed Lisa, getting to her feet and walking away from him.

*

"It's just as well we have the American Friends."

Yves de Chaumont broke the silence with which he had listened to the update on the case.

Franck would have preferred to be with him, in order to watch his reaction to the information he had just provided. He was acutely aware that it did not amount to much. Not enough, in any case, to justify interrupting Yves' weekend retreat in his eighteenth-century manor in the countryside outside of Chartres. However, the *juge d'instruction* had been too busy all week to see him, and the telephone briefing had been his idea, not Franck's.

"Because?" prompted Franck, leaning forward in his chair. He was in his office in the quai des Orfèvres.

"Thanks to them, we can set aside the hypothesis of an inside job – at least as far as Duval's closest colleagues are concerned. Favennec, Morin, Roux, and a handful of the other *étoiles* were all at the Friends' reception when Duval was killed in her apartment. Helps to eliminate professional jealousy as a motive."

"Van Roon wasn't there, though."

"You think he was busy playing with his yo-yo? My childhood is long past, Franck, but I don't recall the string on any of my yo-yos being a metre long."

"Yours was a children's toy. He's a grown man. And he's Dutch – the giants of Europe. Maybe he has them custom-made."

"The towering Dutchmen – you think anyone has ever worked out why they're so tall? I'd have given a lot for their secret when I was a child. I was small for my age. If someone had offered me magical pills that would have made me shoot up, I don't think I'd have hesitated."

"Even if the someone had been as shady as Léon Abkarian?"

"Probably," mused Yves. "I hope I wouldn't have accepted any sweets from him, but magical pills, who's to say? Don't get too distracted by the yo-yo – stay with the drugs. They're the one thing that sticks out. Everybody says that they should never have been in Duval's lodge, and yet there they were. Everything suggests that she would never have frequented someone like Abkarian, and yet their fingerprints are found together."

"Strictly speaking, the fingerprints don't put them in the same place at the same time. They just mean they touched the same collection of pills and vials, but maybe days or weeks apart. Sophie might not have known where they came from. We need something more to really link the two of them."

"Is he the charitable type, the good doctor?" asked Yves.

"I doubt that very much."

"In which case, if Duval had turned to him, then money must have changed hands. You won't be able to get your hands on his financial records, but I'm sure hers are accessible."

"Someone like Abkarian isn't going to accept payments by cheque or card, or any other means that might leave a trace."

"True, so look for significant or regular withdrawals of cash from Duval's bank accounts. Thanks to plastic, good old-fashioned money has become an endangered species. It stands out like a sore thumb."

"It would be even easier if we knew how much Abkarian charges."

"A lot, I imagine. I doubt that growth hormone, powdered unicorn horn, and whatever else he serves up, comes cheap."

"Assuming she purchased them," observed Franck. "Which we shouldn't just be assuming. We don't know if she actually took the drugs, or was planning to take them, or was hiding them for someone else. And so long as Abkarian refuses to talk about it, we'll be none the wiser."

"Not necessarily," said Yves. "He won't talk about Sophie Duval, but he might talk about the drugs and how they should be used, were they to be used."

"He's not the cooperative type," objected Franck. "Not on the basis of what I've seen. He loves to talk, but he doesn't like to give anything away."

"That's not entirely true. He invited you out for a drink, after all. Maybe he was offering you an opening, but you didn't see it. Did you try anything other than simply appealing to his better side?"

"Rather than what? Wiring him up to a generator with some jump leads?"

"That wouldn't be your DST training coming to the surface, would it?" asked Yves, archly. "Why not try this – rather than questioning him in the context of a criminal investigation, try flattering his professional ego."

"I don't think his ego needs any more flattering."

"You're probably wrong on that front – a susceptible ego requires constant care and attention. All I'm suggesting is that you consult him."

"Consult him?" repeated Franck, unwilling to contemplate returning cap in hand to Abkarian's office.

"He's a doctor. Consult him. That's how he makes his living, after all. And it'll have the advantage of revealing how much he charges."

"I doubt he's covered by Social Security."

"Of course he isn't. Just put it on expenses, Franck."

So he was going to take medical advice from doctor Abkarian after all.

Franck had one more call to make before leaving the quai des Orfèvres. He was not looking forward to it. He decided to make a visit to the coffee machine first, but that scarcely lasted five minutes.

It was François Duval who answered, which he supposed was a small blessing.

"This is captain Franck Guerin from the Brigade Criminelle."

"There's news?" The question came instantaneously,

probably slipping out before Sophie's father was aware what his tongue was up to, revealing his hunger for some kind of resolution.

"Nothing definitive," said Franck – a polite way of confessing that they had no serious suspect. "But our enquiries are certainly making progress. I have a difficult question for you, though."

"Difficult?" echoed François, his voice suddenly weary. "It was difficult for us just to make it through this week. I doubt your question can be worse than that."

"To the best of your knowledge, did Sophie ever use any drugs?"

"What? No!" Outrage suddenly animated his voice.

"I'm not referring to recreational drugs. I'm talking about products that might have helped her training – give her more energy, fight off fatigue, that kind of thing. Magic potions."

"She was very careful about what she ate, and she was always exercising, but nothing other than that."

"You're sure? You never saw any syringes in a toilet bag, or anything like that?"

"No. Never. Why are you asking me this?"

"There are things I have to ask in order to eliminate certain lines of enquiry."

"So it was a random question? Some kind of checklist you have to go through?"

"No, there's no checklist. It's just that we found some substances which might have been linked to Sophie. I wanted to know if you could help us to confirm or deny it."

"Deny. If you're talking about drugs, you can be sure they had nothing to do with our Sophie."

"OK." There was no point in insisting. Maybe, given a little time, a memory would come to the surface which he might suddenly view in a different light. "On a different topic – you said you didn't think Sophie was involved in any relationships."

"She was?" This time the question was almost eager.

"It seems so. You've heard of Serge Morin, the *étoile*?"

"Of course."

"Well, Serge and Sophie became quite close over recent weeks. In fact, they seem to have spent quite a bit of time together."

"We didn't know that."

"She never talked about him?"

"Not in that way, no. She's been talking about Serge Morin for years, first as an idol, then as a colleague, but never as a ..." He trailed off, perhaps realising that talking – about Serge, or anything else – was something Sophie would never be doing again. "Do you think we could call him?"

"Serge?"

"Yes."

"I'm sure he'd be delighted if you did," said Franck.

He looked up Serge's number in the directory of his mobile phone and dictated it to Sophie's father. In the absence of a culprit, he could at least provide a shoulder to cry on.

One more absorbent than his own.

Sunday, 17th May

"Two thousand euros!"

Léon Abkarian nodded, his eyes creased as if puzzled at Franck's reaction.

"That only covers the initial consultation – and I would like to point out that I'm not charging extra for coming in on a Sunday."

"My regular doctor takes twenty-two euros."

"And I'm sure he gives you twenty-two euros' worth of expertise in return. I, however, am in the fortunate position of being able to offer about a hundred times that."

"In the course of an initial consultation?"

"I know it sounds immodest, but yes. Should we decide upon a programme of treatment, then I will of course have to ask for a lot more later on. However, I am one of the very few practitioners in my field open to the notion of success fees based on achievement of jointly agreed goals, so you won't necessarily have to pay for it all upfront."

"Right now, we're just having an exploratory chat."

"In the course of which I will no doubt dip into my vast pool of knowledge and understanding, acquired at great cost and inconvenience to myself. But if you're unwilling to pay, captain, we can stop the discussion here and now."

"You'll take a cheque?"

"It's not my preferred means of payment, but if you insist."

Franck took his chequebook from his briefcase and wrote out a cheque for two thousand euros. He passed it across to Abkarian.

"I'll need a receipt," he said.

Abkarian took a prescription pad from a drawer in his desk, scribbled rapidly upon it, and tendered the result to Franck, who checked that the sum mentioned was correct. He pushed aside all thought of the fun he was going to have explaining his expenses report when he handed it in. Yves de Chaumont's sway did not extend to the back office staff of the quai des Orfèvres.

"So tell me about your ambitions and frustrations, captain," invited Abkarian. "And I'll open your eyes to what can be done about them."

"I'm not here for myself," declared Franck. "I've come for a friend."

"If you're about to talk to me about Sophie Duval, I'm going to have to give you this back," warned Abkarian, nudging the cheque with his forefinger.

"Don't worry, it's not about Sophie. Let's just say I have a friend who's female, 29 years old, 49 kilos, a professional dancer at the highest level, has done all she can with conventional methods – exercise, training, nutrition – but wants to be even better. Can you help her?"

Abkarian chuckled, shaking his head and casting an appreciative glance at Franck. It looked as if he was willing to play along.

"Depends what you mean by even better," said Abkarian. "If she wants to leap higher or stand on points for longer, then I can strengthen her legs without fattening them. If she wants to heal faster when she tears or strains ligaments, I can do that too. If she wants to have a sharper focus when she's on stage, that should be possible. If she wants the energy to rehearse eight hours a day and then dance for three, that's easy."

"She's already done some shopping," said Franck, lifting several evidence bags from his briefcase. He had brought the entire contents of Duval's cosmetic pouch. "Could you work with this?"

He pushed them across to Abkarian, who did not even bother looking at them.

"I could. But you tell her from me that if word gets out she's using any of this stuff, then she'll be in big trouble. There's no International Olympic Committee or International Cycling Union for dance, but the public like their princesses to be pure and innocent. Ballerinas are there for little girls to worship. She'll be burned at the stake if she's caught."

"She's prepared to take the risk. She wants to be the best, come what may."

"A sentiment I can only applaud."

"She's sufficiently solvent too."

"I should hope so. She's looking at an initial investment of twenty thousand euros minimum."

"But she's already got all these," insisted Franck in mock protest. "That should save her some money."

Abkarian picked up each evidence bag in turn, glancing at the pills or vials it contained.

"She's got three week's worth of amphetamine. For boosting oxygen levels, given her age and overall fitness, there's a greater marginal gain to be had with PFC than EPO. She's got the same quantity of both here, so she should ask her supplier if he'll take some of the EPO back and give her PFC in its stead. I'm not sure I'd counsel intensive use of these testosterone-based anabolic steroids – think East German women shot-putters – you wouldn't want to see that in a tutu. The beta-agonists should work fine though. But I'm glad to see she's got so much somatropin. If she's dancing over a hundred times a year, she can use as much as she can get."

"You're saying her shopping list was wrong?"

"Oh, the basic ingredients are fine, but quantity-wise she's a bit off-kilter. A cocktail has to be carefully composed and delicately shaken. But I'll soon put her right. We'll have to do some tests first, to get the dosage spot on."

"I'll let her know," said Franck, gathering up the evidence bags.

"You do that."

Franck stood up and extended his hand across the desk.

"Thank you for your time, doctor."

"Thank you for asking better questions this time around," replied Abkarian, shaking Franck's hand and watching him leave his office.

The two thousand euros still smarted, but they had not been wasted.

If Franck had understood correctly, the contents of Sophie Duval's cosmetic pouch were telling him one of two things:

Either they were a randomly extracted sample from a larger

stash which had yet to come to light.

Or they were never destined for her.

*

Lisa Roux would not sit down.

She stood by the window overlooking rue Notre-Dame de Lorette, as if anxious to regain the street outside. She made no attempt to hide her unease at finding herself in Sophie's salon, the very room in which she had been killed.

Serge Morin threw a sympathetic glance towards her from time to time. He had taken up position on a sofa opposite Franck, who stood leaning against the back of an armchair.

"Both of you have been here before," he said. "Lisa, many times, I imagine."

She nodded.

"Serge?"

Morin winced. Presumably he felt this was a delicate subject to broach in Lisa's company. As far as Franck was concerned, there was a time and a place for such considerations. This was neither.

"Serge?" he repeated.

"Maybe a dozen times over the past few months. Very occasionally before then."

Lisa did not react to the news. Indeed, she seemed not to have heard Serge's words.

"Sophie kept this place very much to herself," she explained. "It was her refuge. She wasn't one for inviting bunches of people over. It's a high-pressure lifestyle being an *étoile*. You need somewhere to decompress."

"She felt safe here," suggested Franck.

A bleak and involuntary sigh escaped from Lisa. Serge glared at Franck disapprovingly.

"What I mean," he hastily continued, "is that she could hide away here. She could even hide things away here. Nobody was likely to disturb her. Although the concierge had a copy of her keys, Sophie didn't have a cleaner, so it was very unlikely anyone ever entered in her absence. You had a set of keys, Serge, but that's a relatively recent phenomenon." Serge frowned, his eyes darting towards Lisa, and then gave a short, curt nod. "Lisa?"

Again, she did not seem to have been paying attention. It was almost as if, for her, she and Franck were the only people in the apartment. Or maybe, given the time she took to answer his question, she thought she was alone.

"Lisa?" he prompted again.

"I have keys, but I don't carry them around with me. They're locked in a jewellery box in my apartment. Sophie gave me them just in case she lost her own."

"You still have them?" asked Franck.

"Of course."

"You checked recently?"

"No, but I'd have noticed if my box had gone missing."

"Check next time you're home, OK?"

"Sure."

"So what's your point, captain?" asked Serge. "Why bring us here?"

"I can talk to you two about this because you're the only people in the company to know about Sophie's stash of drugs."

"About the drugs found in Sophie's lodge," Lisa corrected him. "I could have put them there. So could anyone. It's not that difficult to get into an *étoile*'s lodge."

"You're forgetting the fingerprints," Franck reminded her. "But actually I'm not far from sharing your opinion. The drug collection found in her cosmetic pouch doesn't make sense."

"We know that," said Serge. "Like Lisa keeps saying – Sophie would be the last person to dope herself."

"It doesn't make sense," continued Franck, "because the quantities are wrong. Wrong for her."

"What do you mean?" asked Serge.

"I went back to see Léon Abkarian. This time he was more cooperative – probably because no threats were involved." He tipped his head towards Lisa. She scowled in return. Now she was listening. "He made it clear that he wouldn't have prescribed the precise mixture of drugs found in the pouch for Sophie."

"So she's in the clear," declared Lisa.

"You're forgetting the fingerprints," Franck repeated.

This time it was Serge who spoke. He did so slowly, as if voicing thoughts as they formed in his head. "You think they were for someone else? That she was transporting them or storing them? That she was dealing in them?"

"This is absurd!" protested Lisa, leaving the window and striding over to Franck, stabbing a finger at his chest. "You accept that she wouldn't poison herself, but think she'd do it to others? You think she needed the money?"

"You think it's why she was killed?" asked Serge quietly from where he sat. "Some kind of drug-dealing dispute?"

Franck glanced down at Lisa's finger and then looked up at her, one eyebrow raised. She recovered her hand and threw herself down on the sofa alongside Serge, who placed a calming hand on her knee. She ignored it. He squeezed gently, succeeding in drawing her eyes to him. She half-smiled, apologetically. Franck was impressed. Little wonder Serge Morin had become such an avuncular figure in the company.

"I have no idea," Franck confessed. "But what I need to know is whether anything is missing from here – a box, a file, a piece of furniture, a small safe, anything. You two are probably the only ones who were here often enough to notice if something has changed."

Serge shifted forward to the edge of the sofa and cast an eye around the room.

"It doesn't look any different to me," he said.

"This is the kind of thing you have to do slowly," advised Franck. "I'd like the pair of you to go from room to room – here, the two bedrooms, the kitchen, the bathroom, the entrance – and spend at least five minutes in each of them. Think back to your recent visits here – what was going on, who was where, who touched what. Reconstruct the scenes in your imagination and check that the backdrop is still the same."

"OK," said Serge, standing up. He turned and offered a

hand to Lisa. She took it and rose to his side.

"OK," she conceded.

"I'll stay out of your way," advised Franck. "If something strikes you, call me in."

"Maybe you could make us some tea while you're at it," suggested Serge. "Sophie had a great collection of teas and tisanes. You want some?"

"Why not," acquiesced Lisa. "Use the Japanese green tea, if you can find it."

"Sure," said Franck.

Tea was not his strong suit. He found a packet in the kitchen covered in indecipherable characters and extracted a few spoonfuls of what looked like crushed leaves and stems. He dumped them in a small, heavy cast iron teapot, filled it under the tap, and placed it on a gas ring. While he waited for it to boil he checked every one of the three dozen or so varieties of tea Sophie had collected. None of the tins, boxes or packets contained any pills or vials.

When he ferried two cups to Lisa and Serge they were standing against the wall of the main bedroom, saying nothing, no doubt plunged in radically different memories.

Twenty minutes later they returned to the salon, depositing their cups on the coffee table. Neither had been touched.

"Nothing?" asked Franck.

"Nothing," confirmed Lisa while Serge nodded.

"What now?" she asked.

The doorbell rang. Franck went into the entrance area and opened the front door. Georges Sternberg stepped in, followed by a pair of crime scene technicians and their gear. Franck was impressed that Sternberg had managed to get two of them to come in on a Sunday. It said a lot for the esteem in which he was held by his troops. Or the power of a promise of overtime.

"It's all yours," declared Franck.

"It's a shame. It's a nice apartment," observed Sternberg.

"Take it to pieces."

*

This time he remembered her name.

"Clara!" shouted Franck, hoping she would hear him above the noise of the traffic.

He had spotted her turning into rue Lamartine, which started where rue Notre-Dame de Lorette came to an end. She was walking quickly in jeans, running shoes, and a knitted jumper. A long silk scarf had been wrapped once around her neck and thrown over her shoulder. That was what had initially caught his eye – until his gaze moved on to the quiver on her back and the vertical shaft of a longbow in her right hand. Clara Santoni – an Amazon in the streets of Paris.

She glanced over her shoulder, failed to see him, and carried on. Franck waited to allow a few cars to go past, crossed a road, and began jogging up Lamartine behind her.

"Clara!" he tried again.

This time she stopped dead and made a smooth 180 degree turn on the ball of her left foot. She smiled when she recognised him.

"Captain Guerin. The only man capable of kidnapping two *étoiles* and spiriting them away from the Opera when they're desperately needed to finish an end-of-season ballet."

"Van Roon's been complaining? It's a Sunday – weren't they due a break?"

"Let's just say he's been using your name in vain."

"Well, I've released them now."

"Too late, I'm afraid. He's stormed off to the Theatre de la Ville. He's got a gala performance there tomorrow. Told me to go and get some archery practice."

"Which explains this," said Franck, reaching out to tap the longbow which she held across her body. Unstrung, it was taller than her. "If I get any reports of Parisians pierced with arrows, I'll know who to come after."

"I wouldn't want you on my tail, captain. I doubt you give up easily."

Franck shrugged off her comment with his best attempt at becoming modesty.

"Yes, but you're a fleet-footed hind. You'd soon outpace me. So where do you go to practice?"

"The Paul Gauguin gym. First on the left here. Rue Milton."

It had to be a municipal facility – a private gym would have had a snappier name.

"They have an archery setup?"

"Want to come along and see it?"

"Why not? So long as you don't ask me to stand with an apple on my head."

"You're lucky I'm not van Roon – that's the kind of remark you quickly regret making when he's around."

They started walking together up the street, side by side.

"Personally, I just regret being there when van Roon's around," said Franck.

"His reputation as a bad-tempered ogre is not entirely justified, you know," said Clara, coming to his defence. "Sure, he's been hard on me, but he's given me a lot of encouragement too."

"Don't take this personally, but isn't that because you're his favourite?"

She threw an amused glance at him.

"How exactly am I supposed not to take that personally?"

"Because it's an objective fact. Van Roon wanted you to take the lead in his new ballet. Anne-Laure Favennec blocked it, but he's still not got over it. He made sure you were in it all the same, in what I imagine is an important role."

"That's true. The hind symbolises all the creatures of the forest. It comes back in every act."

"And when Sophie died," Franck continued, "he tried again to make you Diana."

"He's a stubborn man. And too Dutch to understand that the *ancien régime* still holds sway in the Opera Ballet – that the prerogatives of the *étoiles* cannot be ignored."

They turned into rue Milton and started heading north.

"Is that a hint of bitterness?"

"A temporary hint. The day I'm an *étoile*, I won't be complaining."

"Well, at least you're lucid. So what do you have to do to make it?"

"Train myself to exhaustion. Dance myself to tears. Do whatever is asked of me. And wait for an *étoile* to disappear."

"There's a quota?"

"Not in theory, but in practice of course there is. For a start, there're only so many lodges backstage in the Opera House and I don't think they'll be extending the building anytime soon."

"So not every *première danseuse* can become an *étoile*?"

"That's for sure."

"How do you rate your chances?"

"I'm a pretty good dancer. I was raised to believe that anything is possible. I am Corsican, after all. We sent a nobody called Bonaparte to the mainland and next thing you know he'd crowned himself Emperor and put Europe at his feet. I've got it in my sights, let's put it that way. But it's not an obsession. Life's too short for that. Particularly a dancer's life."

"Too short and too busy," observed Franck. "If you're not onstage, you're rehearsing. If you're not rehearsing, you're taking archery lessons. If you're not taking archery lessons, you're drafted into public relations exercises to exchange chit-chat with the American Friends and their like."

"There's less call for that if you're just a *première danseuse*. The sponsors want to meet the real stars. The more money they give, the pickier they are. That's one of the qualifications for being an *étoile* – you've got to know how to behave yourself at receptions and galas. Serge is the king of that. He's shaken more hands and kissed more dowagers' cheeks for the company than anyone else."

"I've not seen him in action, but I can well believe it. Did you get dragged along to the American Friends reception? They're the ones underwriting the new ballet – you didn't have to go and pay your respects?"

"Are you kidding? I doubt any of them even know I exist. But that'll change. Give me a little time."

"So what did you do?"

"When?"

"The evening of the reception."

She stopped, twisting her right hand to bring the long staff of her bow down in front of Franck and force him to pull up too.

"Is this an interrogation?" she demanded.

"If it was an interrogation you'd be in a basement room at the quai des Orfèvres. It's a question. Sophie's dead, Clara. I need to know everything about her immediate circle in her last days."

She twisted her lips, as if turning something over in her mind, and then removed her bow, switching it back to the vertical.

"Fair enough." She started walking away. Franck fell in alongside her. "That was last Sunday, wasn't it, a week ago today? There wasn't a performance. I was at home. I phoned a few people, watched a DVD, then went to bed. Not my most exciting evening."

"Where's home?"

"In the eighteenth. Rue Marcadet."

"You were alone?"

"Yes. Is that bad?"

"No, it's not bad." Now that he knew she did not have an alibi, he did not insist on the point. After all, she was not a suspect. Not yet, anyway. He brushed the subject aside. "This is Paris – over half the households are single-person. Mine included. Doesn't make either of us a criminal."

"I'm glad to hear it."

They had reached the gym.

"You coming in?"

It stung.

And left an angry-looking vertical stamp on the inside of his wrist.

And he had missed the target. By a wide margin.

He handed the bow sheepishly back to Clara.

"What did I do wrong?"

"Just about everything," she commented, although not

unkindly. She reached out to touch the spot where the bowstring had slapped against his wrist. “I can ask if they’ve got some ointment here, if you like.”

“I’ll be OK,” said Franck.

“Adding to your collection of scars?”

“Something like that.”

He stepped back and allowed her to take her position. Her feet were aligned at ninety degrees to the target, which stood eighteen metres distant. One arm was extended directly towards it, holding the bow dead-centre. She fitted an arrow to the string and pulled it back, her elbow only slightly above the level of her shoulder. Her head remained erect and aloof, as if unaware of the bowstring grazing her cheek.

She hit the second inner circle. Franck nodded appreciatively, even though he had no idea what she had done right and he had done wrong.

“Of course, that’s the easy bit. The hard bit is doing it while jumping across the stage.”

“Had you done this before van Roon came along?” asked Franck.

“No.”

“You’ve learned fast.”

“Not really – I’ve been working on *Diana and Acteon* for months.”

“But why’s it so important you learn how to do this. Is the hind going to start shooting back?”

“Just in case I have to step into the main role. Piet’s got to have a backup.”

“He’s already lost one *étoile*,” objected Franck. “He’s scarcely going to lose another.”

“You know how they say that lightening never strikes the same place twice? It’s completely untrue.”

*

She waved at him with her right hand, her left one being too busy holding a cigarette to her lips.

Franck had just emerged from a pharmacy at the corner of rue Réamur and rue Montmartre. She was sitting at an outside table of a café across the road. Waiting for him.

Franck crossed over.

"Fancy meeting you here," he said, taking a seat alongside her.

She wore a plain top, a pair of narrow-cut trousers, flat shoes, and a long coat. All were black – a colour normally prized for its ability to make the wearer look slimmer, but completely superfluous in her case. She lived on nicotine alone, which meant that any curves she might once have possessed had disappeared a long time ago.

"Isn't life full of interesting surprises. How are you, Franck?"

"I'm fine."

He did not return the question, since it was one she notoriously held in contempt.

Strictly speaking, he still belonged to Catherine Vautrin. All his time in section C3 of the Direction de la Surveillance du Territoire had been spent under her unforgiving gaze. His secondment to the Brigade Criminelle in the aftermath of the Corsican affair had been pushed through with her complicity. She could take him back whenever she liked. Given his tarnished reputation inside the hermetically sealed circles of national security, she had shown herself in no hurry to do so.

"How's the DCRI shaping up?" he asked.

The DST, his *alma mater*, had been merged with the Renseignements Généraux in June 2008 in the hope of bringing to a close a long tradition of infighting between the two services of the Ministry of the Interior dedicated to keeping French soil safe from nefarious interlopers or home-grown threats. The name of the newly-born service created from these feuding twins was the Direction Centrale du Renseignement Intérieur.

"As you would imagine. The shoot-first-and-ask-questions-later brigade are still trying to disentangle themselves from the new internal procedures, while the ask-questions-first-type-up-the-answers-then-file-the-results-in-triplicate brigade feel very uneasy about the disreputable company they now have to keep."

Franck knew where Catherine stood on this divide. Her handbag lay casually on the small round table in front of them, two cigarette packets spilling from it and the stock of her revolver within easy reach.

A waiter appeared. Franck ordered an espresso. An untouched one sat beside Catherine's bag.

"You can have that one too, if you like," she said.

Franck picked it up with his left hand and touched its contents against his upper lip. No longer as hot as he preferred, but not too cold. He hated to see coffee go to waste. He knocked it back.

"Been in some trouble?" she asked.

His sleeve had slipped downwards as he drank the coffee, revealing the ugly red mark on his wrist.

"Just got it. Shooting accident."

"I take it that means Clara Santoni let you play with her bow and arrows. What's that all about?"

At least he now had an inkling as to why she was here.

"It's for a new ballet she's involved in. *Diana and Acteon* – a fanatical hunter meets the goddess of his reigning passion. The choreographer wants the dancers to shoot blunt arrows at each other. Thinks it'll make things more interesting."

"If he wants to make things truly interesting, he should give them real arrows," said Catherine. "That would up the stakes a little, keep everyone on their toes."

"If he could, I suspect he would. You should meet him."

"Piet van Roon? I'll speak to a Dutchman the day they finally do something about the Islamic networks running through Amsterdam."

"Piet van Roon and Clara Santoni," observed Franck. "You seem very well-informed about what I'm up to."

"Being well-informed is my job. All the more so now I've got a pack of useless RG types to keep busy."

"They gave you some?"

She nodded.

"Behold the head of section 121 – a multidisciplinary team pioneering real-time collection, processing and exploitation of actionable intelligence. Look it up in the organisation chart – except of course you can't, since you no longer have clearance."

"Section C3 sounded better."

"You have to choose your battles, Franck. Even I know that."

Franck's coffee arrived. He drained it.

"So why's section 121 so interested in Clara Santoni. Or is it van Roon?"

"Who wouldn't be interested in Clara? She's young, she's cute, she's talented, she's Corsican. In actual fact, she's from Sartène – a child of the mountains rather than of the sea. She's the only daughter of Jean-Pierre and Nicole Santoni – both of whom are dark-haired, by the way, which makes me think that Clara's a bottle-blonde. Not that we should hold that against her. Nor indeed the fact that her mother, Nicole, is the little sister of Jeannine Agostini. Which makes Clara ...?"

Franck's heart sank. Of course, this changed nothing – Clara could not be held responsible for a member of her extended family. But whenever Catherine Vautrin poked her nose into his work with the Brigade Criminelle, it was bad news. And whenever the name Agostini came up, it was really bad news.

"Gabriel Agostini's cousin," he said.

"I'm surprised it took me to remind you. You used to know the Agostini dossier inside out."

"A few years have passed." Two, to be exact. "What I do remember is that we checked the entire family at the time. None of them had anything to do with Appoghui. We were even pretty sure he rebuffed his younger brother when he tried to get involved."

Appoghui Terra – originally known as Appoghui Terra Corsu, when it limited its activities to its founder's island birthplace – was a pioneering ecoterrorist organisation.

Although its profile was low, its reputation was burgeoning, particularly amongst corporations whose profits came at the planet's expense. It had sent their personnel security budgets and insurance premiums through the roof. Gabriel Agostini had set himself up as the earth's avenging angel, and now had several kills to his account to prove it.

"Well, I just thought you'd like to know. You wouldn't want to be getting too involved with an Agostini."

"She's not an Agostini."

"She's half an Agostini. That should be enough to make you particularly cautious."

"Anyhow, I don't get too involved with parties of interest in a criminal case."

Catherine broke into a grin and rolled her eyes upwards. If it had not been her, Franck would have sworn she was on the edge of genuine laughter.

"You're priceless, Franck. Just tread warily, that's all I'm saying."

"Do you have Clara under surveillance?" he asked.

"No," she announced briskly, pushing the cigarette packets back inside her bag and getting to her feet. "Section 121 has bigger fish to fry. Good luck with your strangler."

There had to be more to it than that. Gratuitous advice did not exist in the world Catherine Vautrin inhabited.

"Know anything about performance-enhancing drugs?" asked Franck.

"A blight on countless sports which would otherwise be a fine example for the nation's youth."

She winked at him and stalked off. Within two minutes a large car with tinted windows pulled up alongside her and she slipped into it.

Franck started digging around for some coins with which to pay for the two coffees. Having found more than expected he decided he could delay his departure for the quai des Orfèvres another five minutes or so. He raised a hand to catch the attention of the waiter.

"Another espresso please."

To each his own performance-enhancing drug.

*

"Nothing."

"Nothing?" repeated Franck, a little disappointed but not really surprised. He was in his office, rubbing antiseptic cream onto the welt on his forearm while listening to Georges Sternberg.

"No removable sections of parquet, no false-backed wardrobes, no watertight containers in the cistern, no hideaways in the ceiling, no hollowed-out music speakers, no additional plumbing where water never goes – nothing."

Sternberg was famously thorough. As far as Franck was concerned, his verdict was definitive. Sophie's apartment was clean.

"Any luck with the bank?" asked Sternberg.

Fortunately, Sophie Duval's bank was French, not Swiss. Franck had been able to go through the past three years of her financial history with her branch manager, having persuaded him to give up his Sunday lunch and come into his office at midday. It had kept Franck busy between his appointment with Abkarian and his rendezvous with Lisa and Serge in Sophie's apartment.

"Nothing unusual. No significant inflows aside from her salary from the Opera Ballet and payments for one-off galas and appearances. Took out two hundred euros at a time through ATMs once or twice a week, and never drew cash from a branch. Had standing orders for her taxes, mortgage and bills, used her card for the rest. Infrequent cheques, all of them traceable."

"So she's either got a shadow banking operation on the go we know nothing about ..."

"Or her finances, like her apartment, are clean."

"You beginning to think the drugs are a false trail?" asked Sternberg.

If they were, they had nothing.

Except the marks around Sophie Duval's neck.

Franck was crouched underneath his desk when his phone rang again. He was looking for the cap from the tube of antiseptic cream. It had run for cover in the course of his exchange with Sternberg. He could see no trace of it on the scuffed parquet floor. For a moment he considered ignoring the phone's strident claim to his attention. He hated an uncapped tube. He would be obliged to throw it out, despite having used next to nothing of its contents.

He sent one of his arms up around the edge of the desk to blindly grab the phone.

"Guerin," he announced curtly, as his gaze continued to sweep the floor.

An instant of silence followed before his caller finally spoke.

"Doesn't sound like the courteous captain Franck Guerin I met a couple of days ago," she said.

"It's not," he said, recognising the voice. "It's the irritable captain Guerin who's lost something and can't seem to find it again."

"Need a hand? I told you that if you called me I'd come running."

"You wouldn't want to be where I am right now. Too much dust and decay."

"Sounds grim. Is this homicide-related?"

"Not exactly. Hang on." He carefully pulled himself out from underneath the desk and regained his seat. His free hand reached out to the tube and tossed it into a nearby wastepaper basket. He could live without it. "That's better. How are you, Noémie?"

"I'm fine, although I do feel a bit out on a limb here. Since I hadn't heard from you, I thought I might give you a call – but, of course, you hadn't given me your number. If you hadn't told me you were with the Brigade Criminelle, I'd never have been able to track you down."

"I'm sorry," said Franck, although not quite sure why he

was apologising. "I've been busy. I was meaning to call." Not a statement that would stand up in a court of law. Right now, though, it was almost true.

"Look, I don't want to impose, but you brought me my phone back and I didn't even buy you a coffee. How about if I take you out for dinner?"

"Hmm, sure."

He could hear her laughing.

"I'll ignore the first half of that statement and concentrate on the positive bit. What about this evening?"

"OK," said Franck, slowly. He had no plans, other than mulling pointlessly over the lack of progress in the case.

"How about nine? Can you meet me at Strasbourg-Saint-Denis."

"OK. Which exit?"

"Under the arch."

"Which arch?"

But she had gone.

As he hung up, Franck noticed a spot of white at the foot of a coat stand that stood next to his office door. He dug the tube of cream from the basket and reunited it with its cap.

Order had been restored.

*

There were two massive stone arches near the Strasbourg-Saint-Denis metro, and Franck was standing under the wrong one.

Both had been erected in the 1670s to commemorate Louis XIV's victorious campaigns to push back the kingdom's north-eastern frontiers. With hostile neighbours further away, Paris could henceforth be entered through sculpted triumphal arches rather than heavily guarded gates embedded in centuries-old fortifications. Standing at the northern limit of the second and third arrondissements, ignored by the traffic that surged past them and the bustle of those entering and leaving the metro, they were a reminder of how small the city's footprint had been during the reign of the Sun King. Not to mention a neglected monument to the countless troops slaughtered in his determined efforts to place France at the centre of Europe's balance of power.

Franck had posted himself in front of the more elaborate of the two, which sat at the foot of rue du Faubourg Saint-Denis. At ten past nine he pulled out his mobile, called Noémie, and discovered she was under the other one, at the bottom of rue du Faubourg Saint-Martin. He walked over to join her.

"I'm sorry," she said, leaning towards him and kissing his cheeks. "I had forgotten there were two."

"Napoleon has two," observed Franck, thinking of the Arc de Triumph at the top of the Champs-Elysées and its smaller forebear in the gardens of the Louvre. "Louis XIV couldn't let an upstart lieutenant of artillery outdo him – even if he hadn't been born yet."

"And a Corsican to boot," she added. "Not even one of his subjects."

Corsica had not been added to the kingdom until fifty years after Louis' death, an event the churlish isle had still not digested. Franck's administratively ambiguous presence in the Brigade Criminelle was a tiny part of this troubled legacy. Not that he was about to explain that to Noémie.

She led him to a wedge-shaped bistrot squeezed between the main boulevard and a side street.

"Been here before?"

Franck shook his head.

"You'll like it," she announced. "Not the slightest trace of pretension. It'll suit you down to the ground."

Franck hoped this was a compliment, although she scarcely knew him well enough to make it. The other possibility was that it was a comment on the way he was dressed. Since he had not known in advance he would find himself in company that evening, an excuse did not seem to be in order. After all, Noémie was not dressed to the nines – under a short-cut khaki trenchcoat she wore a tiny rust-coloured skirt combined with a thickly woven light brown shirt left loose at the neck to accommodate a gauzy amber scarf. Enumerating all this, and noting that her heeled pumps were exactly the same shade as her skirt, made Franck change his mind.

"Sorry I'm a bit worn at the edges," he said, gesturing towards his erratically ironed shirt and crumpled jacket.

"You look fine," she reassured him, as a waiter came up to steer them to a free table.

In the course of the next hour and a half, Franck learned a lot about changes in framing styles and techniques down the ages, about how to spot a bargain at an auction sale, and about why Basel was not as dull a place to live as you might think. He was called upon to provide little in return. Noémie spoke freely and endlessly, taking the occasional questions he asked as springboards for entertaining, if rambling, monologues.

By the time the waiter had spirited away the remnants of dessert and brought their coffees, Franck was feeling quite content with the way the evening had turned out.

"You must think I'm utterly self-obsessed," she observed. "It's been me, me, me non-stop."

"Not at all. I'd rather listen to you talking about your profession than me talking about mine."

"So how's it going with the ballerina case?" she asked, demonstrating that she had not forgotten their brief exchange at their last encounter.

"Slowly."

"What does that mean?"

"We've got the where and the when. We know a bit about the how, but the why and the who are complete unknowns."

"No clue at all as to the why?"

Franck shrugged. He had said as much as he could.

"If there's no obvious reason why, isn't that a bit worrying?" she persisted. "Doesn't that mean it could be something completely irrational, like a serial killer targeting dancers?"

"Let's hope not," said Franck.

He was deadly serious.

Monday, 18th May

How Serge managed not to drop her was beyond Franck.

He moved swiftly behind Lisa, his steps matching hers except at the moments when she leapt into the air, sometimes soaring, sometimes twisting, but always landing in his arms. Each time he caught her he spun in a full circle, shifting her so that when they were once more facing forwards she was in a vertical position, her feet extended. He then placed her on her points and stepped back. She glanced languorously around at him and then launched herself forward again. They repeated the cycle six times in under three minutes.

When they stopped, Lisa moved over to the wooden bar that ran along the mirrored wall at the base of the semi-circular rehearsal studio and tipped her head backwards, taking deep breaths. Serge stayed where he was, going back through his last few steps, trying different angles with his arms.

"Morning captain," he said when he had finished, turning towards Franck.

"Morning Serge, Lisa," – she gave a small wave – "where's the big bad choreographer?"

"He's given us the day off," said Serge.

"Doesn't look like it."

"The day off from him," Serge explained. "Not the day off from rehearsing."

"Do you know where I can find him?"

"At the Theatre de la Ville. He's got a gala there tonight."

"Probably giving his dancers hell as we speak," added Lisa.

"You two aren't part of it?"

"No, no. It's a Dutch contemporary dance troupe. His home team, if you like."

"Poor souls," commented Lisa.

"I'll take a walk over," said Franck.

"I'd save my breath, if I were you," said Serge. "You'll never get to see him – not today. He'll be in one of his moods."

"Two of the pieces they're to dance haven't been staged for years," said Lisa. "He'll spend all day tweaking them. He's difficult enough at the best of times, but when he's working against the clock he's insufferable. Try him tomorrow. After a triumph he might prove more charitable with mere mortals like you and us."

"I don't suppose he's left his pet yo-yo here by any chance?" asked Franck, looking towards the empty stool in the corner of the room from where van Roon habitually brooded over his dancers.

"His constant companion? Never leaves his side. Probably just as well. If he didn't have it to absorb his tension, I suspect there would be a few less dancers alive by the end of the day."

Serge winced, realising what he had just said, and shot a glance at Lisa. She waved a hand, dismissing his concern.

"He's even done a yo-yo piece," Serge continued. "Ten dancers, each with an orange yo-yo. They first use them to beat time vertically, then to extend their arm gestures, then to catch and bind each other."

"How?"

"Like a bola. You know, the gaucho thing – you throw it at a cow, balls wrap a rope round its legs, and down it falls. In van Roon's piece the dancers don't actually throw the yo-yos, but they loop them around each other's limbs, pull close, then break away with the yo-yos going once again. I've only seen it once, and it's a bit gimmicky, ..."

"It's more than a bit gimmicky," interjected Lisa. "It's a circus act. It's his vulgar side – his uncontrollable urge to show off. Piling difficulty upon difficulty."

"Like the archery in *Diana and Acteon*?" suggested Franck.

"Exactly!" cried Lisa. "There's a crossbow in *Swan Lake*, but no one's ever complained about the fact that it doesn't actually shoot any bolts."

"It's the shock of the new, Lisa," said Serge. "Come on, I'm forty-nine and I appreciate what he's trying to do. It should be easy for you."

"Well, at least the arrows are blunt," said Franck.

"For the moment," observed Serge.

*

"I think we can safely assume he's ignoring my calls."

She put down the receiver and shrugged.

It was not an encouraging sign. If van Roon did not pick up for Anne-Laure Favennec, who had assembled millions of euros in order to lure him to Paris, he was unlikely to do so for a mere captain temporarily assigned to the Brigade Criminelle.

On the positive side, Anne-Laure had tried to help him. She seemed less fiery today than at their last encounter. Maybe it was the simple fact that the walls of the Opera House had not, after all, crumbled around her in the wake of Sophie's death. Perhaps she was beginning to believe that there was no drug scandal – that, at worst, Sophie had been alone in dabbling with Abkarian's wares, and that her dark secret would accompany her to the grave. Or rather the furnace, since Sophie's body was to be cremated the next day.

"Why the hurry?" she asked. "He'll be back tomorrow. We're ten days short of the *première* of *Diana and Acteon*. There's a lot left to be done. He'll probably be here night and day."

"Scents go cold," said Franck. "It's a week since Sophie was killed."

"And I'm still waiting for you to clear up all the unknowns about those drugs," she reminded him.

"There's some good news on that front – whatever Sophie was doing with the drugs, I don't think she was using them."

"She still brought them into the Opera," insisted Anne-Laure. "I can't forgive her for that."

"Give me time," insisted Franck. "It may turn out that their presence in her lodge had nothing to do with her either."

"Give you time? I thought the scent was going cold."

He sighed, unwilling to admit that the investigation was running out of steam. That his pursuit of van Roon was little more than an attempt to stir things up in the hope that something floated to the surface.

"How about the gala tonight? Won't he have to mix with

the public after it? Could you get me in?"

"The gala has nothing to do with the Opera Ballet. It's a corporate event, paid for by a private sponsor. I only have a ticket because Piet insisted that I be given one."

"There're no strings you can pull?"

"I doubt it. I'm told it's a very select event – the *gratin* of the financial sector. Unless you have a very good friend inside Lasry Frères, there's no way you'll get across the threshold."

"Lasry Frères are the sponsors?"

"Yes."

Anne-Laure gazed quizzically at Franck.

"Why the big smile?"

*

When it comes to extending your social circle, nothing beats an arrest.

Five years after having hauled Sylvie Thomas in on suspicion of money laundering, Franck knew her office number, her home number, her mobile number, the code to her building in rue Franklin, her favourite restaurants, her fondness for the theatre, her unblemished neck and strangely attractive ears, and her unbridled passion for all things financial. Over the same period Sylvie had proven her acumen and aggressiveness as a deal-maker and risen to become a senior partner in Lasry Frères.

As such, she was not always easy to get on the phone.

Franck had been on hold for over ten minutes, and was beginning to wish he had called from a landline, when her assistant's voice rematerialised.

"I'm sorry to have kept you so long, captain. Mademoiselle Thomas will be delighted to talk to you now." She patched him through.

"Apparently you're delighted to talk to me," Franck informed her.

"Who on earth told you such a thing?" she demanded.

"Your assistant."

"My brand new assistant, you mean, whom I've yet to break in. I'll be having a word with her."

"Be nice, Sylvie," he remonstrated.

"Being nice did you a lot of good in the DST," she observed. "Is it working any better in the world of criminal justice?"

"Actually, it probably is, and I think you should follow my example."

"What do you want, Franck?"

"An invitation to the van Roon gala you're sponsoring at the Theatre de la Ville."

"You've got to be worth at least ten million to us on an annual basis to get invited to that," she pointed out. "It's cost us a lot of money, and we're going to make sure it was worth it. Anyhow, there won't be any spare seats, not this late."

"Someone might have cancelled – got a better invitation," he suggested.

"There is no better invitation," insisted Sylvie. "Not tonight. Not in Paris. Believe me – we don't screw up on timing for an event like this."

"People fall ill."

"Only the poor fall ill. The rich inject a little money and bounce straight back."

"Can you at least check?"

"It's not an evening for you, Franck. It's van Roon's ultra-contemporary work – not his commissions for the big ballet companies. It's deliberately obscure and utterly unattractive to watch."

"So why did everyone accept the invitation?"

"Because it's exclusive. Van Roon's a star, and his profile's got even higher since he signed on to do a new piece for the Opera Ballet. This is a one-off show and the only way you can get in is if Lasry Frères thinks you're worth our while. Being there's the best proof you can offer of your net worth. There are a handful of people who will be noticeably absent tonight, and I suspect they'll find it harder to rollover their leveraged debt tomorrow morning. You'd hate it. I'm doing you a favour."

"It's for an investigation."

"You're arresting someone? If it's me, tell me now, and I'll wear comfortable shoes."

"There'll be no arrests – I promise. But it really would help. I'll be very discreet."

"In which case, promise me that you will not come in comfortable shoes. Nor in whatever else you happen to be slouching about in right now. This is a classy event."

"I'll make an effort. Get me two seats and I'll even make a splash. In a good sense."

"That's intriguing," murmured Sylvie. "How?"

"An invitation for two," repeated Franck. "You won't regret it."

"I'd better not."

*

The Theatre de la Ville had sprung up in the 1860s as baron Haussmann was remaking Paris in his own image – orderly, imposing, self-assured and destined to incarnate for eternity the virtues of the nineteenth century's upper orders. Ten years later it was burnt to the ground as the ragtag army of the Commune briefly defended an alternative vision of the capital. It was rebuilt shortly afterwards, despite the fact that the city was scarcely lacking in theatres. By the end of the century it had fallen into the hands of Sarah Bernhardt, whose name it then adopted and proudly bore for sixty years, despite the Nazis' determined efforts to rebaptize it during the Occupation. Its current name dated from 1968. As befitted a year in which dreams of a radical break with the past briefly took hold of the nation, the theatre's orchestra, upper circle, balconies, and private boxes were ripped out to be replaced by an egalitarian slope upon which a thousand seats were marshalled in unvarying ranks. Its new configuration was accompanied by a new vocation – championing the cause of contemporary dance – from which it had never since wavered.

Seen from the place du Châtelet it had a certain Romanesque flair with five wide arches running most of the way up its facade, filled with glass to allow light into the interior. Round and square pillars completed the decorative schema along with sculpted medallions and cornices, giving it a demurely classical public face, as if unaware of the metamorphosis which had occurred inside its walls. Despite its deliberately sparse and utilitarian auditorium, the building still furnished a fitting backdrop for ceremonial entrances and exits. Although not a vast temple to a religion deemed universal, as the Opera House claimed to be, the Theatre de la Ville was nonetheless the gathering place of a cult.

Tonight, though, the worshippers belonged to a different sect than the usual one. No bedraggled arts students, no bespectacled teachers committed to the pursuit of all things alternative, no black-on-black leather-clad addicts of existential angst. None of the customary aficionados of contemporary dance were to be seen. In their place taxis and high-end cars – Mercedes, Audis, BMWs – deposited men in suits and women in cocktail dresses. Since most had come straight from an office sombre tones dominated, with the exception of the patterns on the men's ties and the discreet flashing of the women's jewellery. Ushers in black long-sleeved polo shirts and straight-legged trousers stood at the doors checking invitations. The Lasry Frères logo was nowhere to be seen, but its presence was unnecessary, as the heady scent of money was in the air.

For once, Franck almost looked the part. Although it was not really cold enough to justify it, he had brought along his Marco Chiriotti overcoat, which he wore open over a dark suit. He tried not to look impatient, despite the fact that it was now only two minutes before curtain up.

Heels clattered to a stop behind him. He swivelled around to find Sonia Delemazure beaming at him.

"I took the metro!" she proclaimed. "Why everyone says it's crowded and uncomfortable, I don't understand. People are so polite – they give you so much room!"

Little wonder they had stood back. Sonia wore a burgundy red bodice under a short-cut jacket. Below lay a thick wad of stiff, semi-transparent tulle in layers of varying shades of grey. It shot out horizontally a good half metre from her hips, curving down slightly at its outer rim. Beneath it she wore black stockings whose embroidered tops could be glimpsed through the shifting screen of her tutu. Red varnished pumps with elevated heels kept her legs tensed and alert.

"You're looking very smart, captain," she said, leaning over to kiss his cheeks. "If I'd known I'd have got dressed up myself."

Franck shook his head with a wry smile and offered Sonia his arm. The circumstances in which he had made Sonia's acquaintance two years previously had scarcely been propitious – the murder of one of her friends and fellow *haute couture* models – but she had taken a curious liking to him and had popped up in his life at irregular intervals ever since. She had cried out in delight when he called her that afternoon with an invitation to the gala. She had also promised him she would rise to the occasion. Thus far, Franck reckoned she had kept her word.

They headed towards the nearest usher, who accepted the oblong card Franck tendered him and waved them through.

Inside the foyer the affluent and influential were being deferentially herded into the auditorium. Franck spotted Sylvie Thomas standing at the top of a small rise of stairs, exchanging brief words and nods with the guests who moved past her. She lifted her head and raised an eyebrow in his direction before returning to her task.

Their journey across the foyer and up through the rising banks of seats to their place did not go unnoticed. Few gazes did not swivel in their direction, and many a voice dropped suddenly to comment on their passage. Sonia kept her sparkling eyes straight ahead. She bounced slightly with each step in order to keep the fabric of her tutu quivering constantly around her. Franck's extended arm acted as a shock absorber to ensure that she remained stable while doing so. He could not even be sure she was doing it deliberately. For Sonia, life was an endless catwalk. Her professional instincts were deeply ingrained.

Darkness descended just after they took their seats. Three vertical cylinders of yellow-tinged light appeared on the stage, each ending in a male dancer crouched in a loincloth. Another three columns, this time pale-blue, manifested themselves, containing female dancers in what looked like one-piece bathing suits. Mechanical chirping, like a hundred synchronised typewriters, issued from the sound system. The gala had begun.

There was no interval. Sonia shared with Franck her suspicion that this was to make it impossible for anyone in the audience to bail out without being noticed. An hour and fifty minutes later, after five separate works, including a lengthy extract from his celebrated ballet *Casanova*, van Roon strode onstage. He had chosen a suit, dark grey with a narrow pinstripe, an open-collared cream shirt and gleaming black pointed shoes, as if he had deliberately sought to reassure the audience that he was no different from them. Except that tethered to his right hand an orange yo-yo was ascending and descending with mechanical precision.

The applause was fulsome, but did not go on too long. The evening's guests were demonstrating that, while cultivated, they were also busy people, and now had other affairs to attend to. Like champagne and finger food and deal-making in the foyer. Van Roon bowed twice and exited stage left just as the hand-clapping began to ebb.

As the lights came on Sonia leapt to her feet and stumbled down their row of seats, uttering apologies as she went, the tulle of her dress brushing faces and backs of heads. A few vicious glares followed her, but appreciative smiles were more numerous. When she reached the aisle she called back to Franck who sat, abandoned, where she had left him.

"Champagne – pink, preferably. Ten minutes."

He then lost sight of her as the thousand or so guests followed her example.

Twenty-five minutes went past before she returned.

Franck had dutifully sought out a glass of pink champagne in the meantime, but he had not managed to hold onto it. Sylvie Thomas had appeared at his side and plucked it delicately from his grasp. She wore a one-piece satin dress, midnight blue, with an oriental cut that hid her collarbone and imprisoned her legs, allowing her no more than the daintiest of steps. Her hair was bound in a tight chignon, her feet demure in dark leather pumps with kitten heels. She was playing the unassuming hostess, despite the fact that she had designs on the wealth of all of those present.

"That was quite an entrance, Franck."

"Sonia is a model," he offered, in apology. "She can't help it."

"The poor thing. So," – she bumped her shoulder lightly against him – "are you going to tell me why it was so important you be here?"

Even if he had intended to do so, he did not get a chance. Sonia parted the crowd and planted herself in front of them.

"Sonia, this is Sylvie Thomas, who was kind enough to invite us."

Sylvie nodded and smiled at Sonia who, refusing to keep her distance, stepped forward and provoked an exchange of pecks on the cheek.

"That's a remarkable dress, Sonia," observed Sylvie.

"It's a Jeanne Michaud. Nobody's ever heard of her. She's just started. She's got a workshop in the twentieth. I can give you her card."

"I couldn't pull it off," said Sylvie, her right hand tracing the contour of Sonia's dress. "And even if I could, it's not what's expected of me – not on a night like this, anyway."

"Well, keep her in mind for the nights that are a little less dull," suggested Sonia.

"Leave her card with Franck – he owes me a present," suggested Sylvie. She stepped back, winked at both of them, and slipped away.

"Are you two ...?" asked Sonia.

"No," said Franck, very quickly.

"Are you sure?"

"Yes."

"Well, so long as you're sure," mused Sonia, glancing over at Sylvie as she worked her way slowly through the crowd, shaking hands, exchanging words, laughing and smiling. "But she looks like quite a catch."

Franck did not rise to the bait, but asked about her own fishing expedition, although he could see that her hands were empty, which was not an encouraging sign.

"It didn't work?"

"First things first," declared Sonia. "Where's my champagne?"

All of the waiters circulating in the crowd were carrying trays of clear champagne, so Franck had to squeeze his way to the nearest open bar. When he returned, a tall glass in hand, a young man was backing away from Sonia with a broad smile, restoring his pen to an inside pocket while waving his invitation in the air.

"You gave him your real number?" Franck asked her.

"Never you mind," she replied and took the glass from him, sipping it avidly.

"Well?"

Her left hand descended behind her back and delved into the multiple layers of her tutu. It emerged seconds later bearing an orange yo-yo.

"The things you can hide in there!" she declared cheerfully. "You'd be amazed."

Franck nodded appreciatively, took the yo-yo and slid it into a jacket pocket.

"Go on – say it," prompted Sonia. "You know you want to."

"Good girl."

She curtsied, her palms held flat at opposite extremities of her tutu.

"You really are an unreconstructed patriarchal oppressor, you do know that?" she observed.

"Probably," conceded Franck.
"Well, are you taking me to dinner then?"

Tuesday, 19th May

"Hold still, will you?"

Franck had every confidence in Georges Sternberg. They had worked several cases together and he knew him to be highly competent, diligent, and creative, not to mention good company. Nonetheless, he was unable to stop himself flinching as Sternberg wound the string tightly round his neck.

"There we are," announced Sternberg. "Three times round."

"There's still enough to pull?" asked Franck.

"Sure. What's more, the fact that I can hold onto the yo-yo itself makes it easier to get a good grip and apply pressure. If I keep my finger slipped through the loop at the other end, that gives me good leverage too. And to think we let children run around with these things."

"Wouldn't you break the knot that's holding the string to the yo-yo if you pulled too tight?"

He asked the question against his better judgement, as he didn't want to encourage Sternberg to push the demonstration any further.

"Ah, no. This is not the kind of yo-yo you're used to. The string isn't attached to the axle of the yo-yo. It ends in a loop that runs around it. You want to know why?"

He did not wait for an answer, but unwound the string from Franck's neck and fed it back inside the yo-yo. He then stepped to one side and launched it downwards, crouching as he did so. The spinning orange circle hurtled down the string, hit the laboratory floor, and rolled forward until the string was completely extended. Sternberg then jerked his hand into the air and the yo-yo responded by climbing back up towards his palm.

Franck gave him a brief round of applause.

"That's called taking it for a walk," Sternberg explained. "Can't do it without a loop around the axle. That's how you distinguish a stunt yo-yo from a simple toy."

"And for your next trick?" prompted Franck.

"For my next trick I will require a volunteer with a soft and yielding neck."

Reluctantly Franck raised his chin.

Sternberg grazed it with the fingertips of his left hand.

"I did say soft and yielding, not leathery and half-shaven. Ah, but I see that mademoiselle here is willing to help."

A few metres away stood a female shop dummy. Dressed in a long t-shirt for modesty's sake, its neck was covered in a layer of bright green plasticine at least a centimetre thick.

"Will you do the honours?" he asked Franck, handing him the yo-yo.

Franck unravelled the string, walked behind the dummy, and slowly encircled its neck three times, trying to reproduce the pattern he recalled from Duval's autopsy notes. Once he was ready, he looked round at Sternberg.

"Tug the two ends slowly and steadily. Don't cut all the way through the plasticine."

He did as requested. Sternberg then took his place and carefully pulled the string out from where it had embedded itself. He switched on a nearby lamp and busied himself with a magnifying glass and a ruler.

"Three millimetres," he announced.

"But no strange bulge," observed Franck.

"Not yet."

Sternberg laid the yo-yo out on a bench and placed the tip of his finger on the mid-point of the string. He wound the string around it and then fed the end furthest from the yo-yo through the loop he had created, pulling it tight. He repeated this several times, creating a series of knots. He then returned to the dummy, smoothed down the plasticine, and strangled it for a second time. Once he had measured the results he turned to Franck.

"Five millimetres wide over a short stretch right at the front of her neck," he announced. "Just like the distinctive ligature mark on Duval. It showed slight ridge marks too, just like these knots, whereas on the rest of the neck it was smooth."

"Why would anyone put knots in the middle of a yo-yo?" asked Franck. "Wouldn't that stop it working?"

"Ask van Roon. He's the expert."

*

Six male *étoiles* shouldered the coffin once it had been extracted from the hearse, with Serge Morin at the front on the right.

Every one of them had lifted her, carried her, caught her, and steadied her time and again on the stage of the Opera. Today they were sharing the burden, their grief lending weight to a body they had borne with ease and elegance in the exercise of their art.

Luckily, the heavy wood of the coffin hid the fact that the corpse inside was lighter than it had ever been. Sophie's parents had insisted that her funeral take place as quickly as possible, despite the fact that the investigation was far from over. As a result their daughter was entering the Père Lachaise crematorium without her internal organs or her brain. Although she had been sewn back together before leaving the morgue, it was as well that her casket had not been opened since.

Franck took his place at the back of the group of mourners. Sophie's parents had vetoed the idea of a formal funeral, so Anne-Laure Favennec had told the bulk of the company to stay at the Opera and take a moment to think of their former colleague at ten thirty that morning. She was present, as were Serge Morin, Lisa Roux, and all the other *étoiles*, most of whom Franck could not name. A handful of more elderly figures hovered near Sophie's parents. Family and friends, no doubt. The only person to shuttle between both groups was Serge, who seemed to have a word for everybody.

The service was short. A priest went through the motions, conjuring up the prospect of eternal life in a better world. When he had finished he stepped aside, the lights dimmed, and a projector hidden somewhere in the ceiling came to life. A grainy film of Sophie, probably eight or nine, illuminated the darkness. She wore a white tutu. With a little help from Tchaikovsky she danced with great seriousness and no little grace for about three minutes. When she had finished she curtseyed and then broke out in a huge smile. The film stopped. The lights came on. The coffin was no longer there, having silently descended below their feet while their thoughts were with its occupant's carefree youth.

Franck was the last to offer his condolences to the grieving parents. Liliane Duval was unable to speak and closed her eyes repeatedly as she stifled silent sobs. François Duval shook Franck's hand and thanked him for coming. There was no talk of justice or of revenge. They knew their loss was irreparable.

When Franck emerged the other mourners were converging towards the nearest exit. Those from the Opera Ballet were clustered tightly around Lisa Roux. Throughout the proceedings she had been the object of careful attention on their part – murmured words, gently supportive touches of the hand, solicitous gazes. Lisa had borne herself with quiet dignity and had spent a short moment with Liliane and François Duval. They had spoken in low voices and made all the right gestures. From his vantage point, however, Franck felt sure there was a hint of frost in the air. Sophie's mother was holding out for full ownership of her daughter, even in death. Franck could not blame her, although he suspected that Liliane's jealous ire was misdirected – the world of ballet had stolen her daughter from her; Lisa was just an accomplice.

Franck started walking through the cemetery. He maintained a slow pace. He had no intention of catching up with the others.

He was not the only one hanging back. Serge stood in what seemed to be a melancholy daze, contemplating a freshly flowered grave. Franck moved over to him.

"You OK?"

"That was hard," he admitted. "I didn't sleep at all last night. I spent the evening looking at photos of her, watching performances on DVDs, trying to recall how she was when she was alive – but I wasn't prepared for that film of her as a child. I know today's supposed to be a day of remembrance and letting go. Of forgiveness, even. But I can't. Everything's going on as if she never existed. *Diana and Acteon* will still be staged, all the other *étoiles* are filling in for her in the regular repertoire, and I understand all that – the Ballet's bigger than any one of us. We know that when we join. I'm part of it too. I'm coaching Lisa in *Diana*. I stood opposite Aurélie Dupont rather than Sophie in *Giselle* the day her body was found. Life is going on, and taking me with it. But, just for a moment, I wish it wouldn't. Does that make sense?"

"It's about the only thing that does, Serge. You want to go for a drink?"

"Absolutely."

*

The call was anonymous. A man's voice. It came in just before ten that morning, giving the address and the victim's name.

The local commissariat sent round a lieutenant and a *gardien de la paix*. They found the outer door of the apartment open and soon encountered the body. They called for a forensic squad and contacted the Brigade Criminelle.

Franck was tackling his second espresso when his phone rang. He apologised to Serge Morin, who was sipping at a cognac – his second too – and answered. After a brief exchange he hung up and grimaced.

"Bad news?" asked Serge.

"Very bad news for one person in particular," answered Franck. "I have to go. I'm really sorry, Serge."

Before he could say anything else his phone rang again. Franck answered. It was Georges Sternberg.

"I'm in the van. Tell me where you are and I'll pick you up."

"Rue des Pyrénées, behind Père Lachaise. A café called l'Ange Gardien."

"OK. Be outside in fifteen minutes."

Serge was laying some money on the table.

"I've got fifteen minutes," Franck told him as he stood up. "You don't have to hurry away. I can have you dropped off at the Opera if you like."

"I don't think I can take any more bad news. Not today."

He squeezed Franck's shoulder and left.

*

Finding nowhere to park the van, Sternberg simply forced it up onto the wide pavement before 116 boulevard de Malesherbes. He invited Franck to go on ahead while he and another technician unloaded their gear. Franck took the stairs and showed his ID to the policeman on the second floor landing. He pointed to an open door and switched his attention back to his cigarette. He had a packet of Gitanes. Franck hoped he had not stolen them from the victim.

Franck slipped off his shoes, replaced them with elasticated plastic bags, put transparent gloves on his hands, and wandered in.

Léon Abkarian was comfortably installed in his office, dressed much as he had been when Franck had last seen him. His arms hung by his side as he leant back in his chair behind his desk. He was staring at the ceiling. Or would have been, had his eyes not been lifeless.

Franck inched alongside him, studying his neck.

Only two loops this time.

*

Tracking down the anonymous caller was easy. He had used his mobile phone.

In and of itself, this was a good indicator of his probable innocence – or culpable stupidity. The former was confirmed when he produced an alibi for the previous evening, the coroner having placed Abkarian's death at between nine and fourteen hours before the discovery of the body.

As for his intelligence, that remained to be determined. His anxiety, however, had been patently clear from the moment he arrived at the quai des Orfèvres. His name was Jean-Pierre

Pelletier and he was a young, ambitious professional cyclist, although perhaps not for much longer.

"It was just a preliminary meeting," he insisted. "I'm not a patient. I've never actually taken anything."

"In which case, why didn't you give your name when you called?" asked Franck.

"I was in shock. I wasn't thinking clearly."

"It wasn't that you were worried about your name being associated with Abkarian's?"

"Well, of course. If word got out that I'd had an appointment with him, people would just assume ... well, you know."

"You could always have explained that it was just a – what was it? – preliminary meeting."

"Even so. You know how sensitive this is. There's a good chance one of the top teams will soon sign me. This kind of news could scare them away. That's why you've got to keep my identity secret, captain. I'm happy to help with enquiries, but I need some kind of guarantee in return."

"Did you know Abkarian had a safe in his office?"

Pelletier shook his head.

"Of course not – you'd never been there before. So you wouldn't know that he kept the key to the safe in the inside pocket of his jacket?"

Pelletier kept shaking his head.

"So you didn't know that this was inside it?"

Franck pulled out a tabloid-sized see-through ziplock bag. It contained several smaller bags, all sealed in the same fashion. Most of them contained narrow glass vials. One held a dozen capped syringes. The rest held pills. A large sticker had been smoothed onto the outer bag. It had been marked 'JPP' in large letters with a black felt-tip pen.

"And you have no idea who JPP might be?"

Pelletier stopped shaking his head.

"You didn't happen to be carrying a lot of cash this morning?"

Pelletier said nothing.

"Look, I happen to know Jean Beaufort, who happens to be photo editor of *Exposé*. I wouldn't say he's a friend – in fact, he's anything but. However, I have his number and if I phone him, he'll listen to me. And unless you start talking, that's exactly what I'm going to do."

Franck had no intention of doing any such thing, but his hard-set face said otherwise.

"I haven't committed any crimes," Pelletier objected.

"I'm inclined to believe you. Using this stuff," – Franck tapped on the plastic bag – "may be frowned upon by the International Cycling Union, but it's not something I need to arrest you for. So if you answer my questions to my satisfaction, you can count on my discretion. Do we have an agreement?"

Pelletier nodded.

"Try articulating," Franck suggested. "The nodding and shaking won't get us very far."

"Yes."

"How long have you been using doctor Abkarian's services?"

"A year, a year and a half. I first saw him just before Christmas. Not last Christmas, the one before."

"December 2007?"

"Yes."

"How did it start? Who approached whom?"

"I called him. He's a legend in cycling circles."

"One of the darker legends, I'd have said."

"That's unfair. He's done tremendous things. There've been accidents, maybe folk who weren't as tough as they thought, but he's worked miracles. There're riders at the front of the pack today who would've been stuck at the rear without him."

"Didn't he once say he'd given up on cycling?"

Pelletier looked puzzled.

"Never mind," continued Franck. "How easy was it to get in touch?"

"His number's in the Yellow Pages. All you have to do is make sure no one sees you dialling it."

"You ever meet any of his other patients?"

"No. I mean, there're riders I'm sure are using him, but it's the kind of thing you don't talk about."

"But when you came to his offices in boulevard Malesherbes, you never saw anyone in the waiting room, or going in or out?"

"No. He spaces out appointments, and most of the time they don't take place there. The address is too well known."

"So where then?"

"He comes to you. Or you meet in a park, or a metro station, or a hotel."

"So what about this?" Franck patted the ziplock bag. "How long would this lot last?"

"That's two months. It's a training pack."

"Rather than?"

"A race pack. When I've got a competition, I take more stuff, in different doses."

"Is this the standard packaging?"

"What do you mean?"

"Is it always like this? A separate bag for each product. No bottles, no boxes. One big bag with all the smaller ones inside."

"Yes. Always."

"Always ziplocks, not open bags or completely sealed ones you have to tear into?"

"Yes."

"Where are the instructions?"

"The what?"

"There're no bits of paper in this. How do you know what to take and when?"

"I've already got that. He doesn't put one in each time. Not unless something has changed."

"And what do you do when you get one of these? You empty it out? Mix it in with whatever's left over from the last one?"

"No. Abkarian always said to leave everything in the bags. That way you were less likely to mix things up – take the wrong thing or the wrong dose."

"So you were supposed to take what you needed every day, or every whenever, and rezip the bags when you were finished?"

"That's right."

"OK. Did you ever need to get supplies from anyone else?"

"No. He made sure I never ran out. That's what people don't understand – doctor Abkarian's really serious about what he does. He's not a drug dealer. He's a real doctor who wants to help you ..."

"Achieve your potential," Franck cut in. "Reach beyond your limits, maximise your performance – I've already heard the speech, thanks. You were never threatened or blackmailed because of your involvement with him?"

Pelletier looked at Franck blankly.

"Nobody knew about it. How could anyone threaten me?"

"There's no poaching of clients between rival witch doctors?"

"Look, he was a real doctor, right?"

"OK. There's no poaching of clients between rival practitioners of performance enhancement?"

"No, not that I've heard of. Maybe sometimes people change if they hear someone else's getting better results."

"But there's no violence, no intimidation?"

"No."

"It's a perfectly functioning free market then?"

The blank look was back again. Time to stop.

"Fair enough," said Franck. "I've got enough for the moment, Jean-Pierre. You can go now. I'll keep my side of the bargain."

Pelletier gestured towards the plastic bag.

"Can I have that? I really need it. I've got the money – cash – if you like."

The question of his intelligence was no longer in suspense.

*

"I'm kicking my heels near Drouot. I've got a client dinner in two hours. Want to go for a drink in the meantime? It'll keep me out of mischief and we can celebrate the sale of my frames."

It was Noémie Berger. When he had walked her home on Sunday evening, she had extracted his mobile number from him just before pecking him on the cheek at the entrance to her apartment building. Franck fleetingly wondered if his had been the first number she had dialled in her search for a little distraction before business called once more.

"I can't. Sorry. I've got something this evening."

"Another girl?" she asked, playfully.

"If you think I have the time to chase after multiple women, you should take a look at my caseload."

"What's up? Another murder?"

"Actually, yes."

"Two cases at once? Is that fair? Is the Brigade Criminelle that short-staffed?"

"Same case, just an extra corpse."

"Not another dancer?" Her voice tightened as she asked the question. The flippancy had gone.

"No, not another dancer."

"That's a relief." She sounded sincere. "Who is it then?"

He saw no reason not to tell her. Abkarian was almost a public figure, and the press were sure to have a field day with his death.

"Léon Abkarian."

"Sounds familiar."

"The man behind Gino Finetto."

"Sounds sort of familiar," she said, more tentatively this time.

"Finetto was a cyclist. He was on track to win the Tour de France in 98 until he dropped off his bike stone dead. Or maybe just stoned. Whatever it was, Léon Abkarian was probably behind it."

"I remember!" she exclaimed. "The master of potions. The man behind the muscles. No – the Witch Doctor – that's it! What's he got to do with your ballerina?"

“That’s what I’m planning on spending the evening trying to find out.”

“I’d better leave you to it, then.”

“Some other time,” said Franck.

“Next time you phone me. I feel like I’m harassing you.”

“I will.”

“Promise?”

“Promise,” he said.

His promise was sincere, even though he had lied to her in the course of their exchange.

He was meeting another girl that evening.

*

Franck had finally taken Georges Sternberg’s advice.

He was in his daughter’s bedroom.

The Sternbergs had a two-bed apartment on rue du Poteau in the eighteenth arrondissement at the foot of the northern slopes of Montmartre. Annabelle’s room looked out onto an inner courtyard and did not get much light. This was probably just as well, for otherwise the pink wallpaper and furnishings would have been all the more glaring, and possibly slightly nauseating.

Annabelle, however, was unapologetic about her chosen colour scheme. The door to her room bore a sign proclaiming ‘La vie en rose’. In any case, the pink was not the backdrop for a mawkish enclave of soft toys and posters of well-groomed ponies. Not for nothing had her father described her to Franck as a ballet geek.

Posters of dancers were everywhere. A tutu hung in front of the room’s only window, presumably in lieu of gauze curtains. Shelves of dance DVDs were bolted to the walls, interspersed with ring binders crammed with articles and photos. Several pairs of worn ballet shoes dangled from the ceiling. They hung by their ribbons from pink-wrapped wire arms hooked through a ring where a light fitting should have been.

As there was only one chair in the place, she made Franck

sit on her narrow bed and pulled over the desk which served as a perch to her computer. It had a seventeen inch screen kept scrupulously free of dust and fingerprints.

"What do you need to know?" she had asked him.

"Just the basics," he explained. "So that I don't seem a complete idiot."

"Hope you've got the entire evening free, then."

They started with the positions – first, second, third, fourth, and fifth. She showed him a short video on the web, then demonstrated herself, then forced him to try.

First position was not too difficult – heels together, feet splayed to the side, arms bent out to the front. Aside from the fact that Annabelle kept kicking his feet in an attempt to increase the angle between them, she did not seem too critical of his attempt. Second position involved sliding his feet apart and raising his arms to a horizontal line. It was from the third onwards that things got trickier. Placing the heel of his right foot at the mid-point of his left one while straining to keep the two as parallel as possible robbed him of his sense of balance. Raising one arm above his head and curving the other out in front of him did not help. He moved quickly to fourth in the hope that it would help him stay upright, pushing his right foot forward to create a gap between it and his left one, both still pointing in opposite directions. He forgot about his arms, and Annabelle had to intervene to pull one down and tug the other out horizontally from his left shoulder. As for fifth, where the heel of his right foot was supposed to touch the big toe of his left one while they aligned themselves perfectly alongside each other, he tried twice but never got anywhere near it. He could do the arms, though, holding them in a round arch above his head. Although he pointed this out, Annabelle gave him no credit for it at all.

"Until you can do the positions instantly, without thinking, there's not much else I can teach you," she warned him.

"I'll keep practising," he promised her. "Maybe we should just work with my eyes, not my feet, for the moment."

She took him through a few more terms of vocabulary, with

videos to help. They made a brief visit to the corridor that ran the length of the apartment so that she could reproduce a short *chassé*. She skipped forward, her leading leg pursued by the one trailing behind, rebounding off it each time it caught up.

For a pirouette, they had to move to the salon, as the corridor was not wide enough. Annabelle pushed back a sofa that sat facing the television and took up position in the centre of the room. She stepped forward to place her left foot flat on the floor, her back straight, her right leg bent behind her, resting on the ball of her foot, right arm curved in front, the other thrown out to the side. What followed was too quick for Franck to really grasp. Her right arm uncurled itself and she followed its motion, turning away from him. As she did so she raised her right leg, bending it to jut out above her left knee. She turned, maybe three, maybe four times, her arms first outstretched and then curving in towards each other. As she slowed she returned her right foot to the ground, this time flat down and angled at ninety degrees to her left one. Franck applauded and she offered a deep curtsey in return.

She moved on to the *arabesque*, the ball of her left foot on the floor, her body levered forward, her head chin up, her right leg raised behind her, hovering somewhere short of ninety degrees, her left arm floating above it, her right one raised before her.

Then it was back to the corridor, where she posted him at one end and returned to him from the other in a series of *tours chaînés*. She moved forward with her right leg, then placed her left leg in front of it, heel raised, and used it as a pivot to turn, before extending her right leg once more, repeating the manoeuvre until she bumped into him.

"I should be doing all this in points, of course," she told him.

"It's impressive enough," he assured her.

"You should be ready for the real pros now," she decided.

So it was back to the bedroom. Annabelle plundered a selection of boxes from her DVD collection and sat herself alongside Franck on her pink bedspread.

"We'll just do Petipa, OK?"

The next hour and a half involved lots of loading and unloading of DVDs, fast-forwarding and -backwarding, pausing and slow-motioning. He got to see a selection of ensembles, *pas de deux*, and solos from *La Bayadère*, *Sleeping Beauty*, *The Nutcracker*, and *Don Quixote*. Annabelle apologised for the fact that only one was an Opera Ballet production. Apparently the Americans and Russians were better at commercialising their performances on video.

Watching with Annabelle was not a relaxing affair. She provided a non-stop commentary, and her hand was constantly shooting forward to grab the mouse to ensure that Franck had not missed any of the technical mastery on show. If her father had not finally interrupted proceedings, he might never have escaped.

"She's really jealous of you, you know," Sternberg informed him. "Getting backstage at the Opera House is one of her dreams."

"Don't they have tours?" asked Franck.

"Front of house only," Annabelle informed him.

"I'll see what I can do."

"Not until the case is closed," Sternberg insisted. "I don't want my daughter in there with a murderer roaming about."

Annabelle rolled her eyes.

"You can't imagine what it's like having such a drama queen for a father. How dangerous can it be?"

Sternberg reached out and patted her on the head.

"You poor thing."

She had no idea what her father had seen in his years on the force.

And he had no intention of ever telling her.

"Thank you. I was wondering if I'd ever see it again."

Piet van Roon rolled the orange yo-yo from the palm of one hand to the other.

"So you caught the dastardly yo-yo thief – that fearless young woman with the distracting tutu – found this in her stash of booty and realised it had to be mine?"

"Something like that," said Franck.

Van Roon looped the yo-yo's string around his index finger and sent it sailing downwards.

"Care to explain yourself, captain?"

"I wanted to check whether your yo-yo could have been used to kill Sophie Duval."

Van Roon forgot to tug on the string at the critical moment. The yo-yo spun fruitlessly at the end of its tether, a few centimetres above the floor.

"You're joking," he said slowly.

"I'm not known for my sense of humour. And as it turns out, it could have."

"What? It's a yo-yo, captain. It's a toy."

"No, it's a thin, strong piece of cord firmly attached to a handy knob which is easy to grasp while the other end of it is anchored to a finger. It's the right length to be twisted round a neck three times and it's exactly the width of whatever was used to strangle your first Diana."

Van Roon jerked his forearm upwards, causing the yo-yo to leap into the air, where his hand closed around it. He proceeded to wind the string back into place. When he had finished he handed it to Franck.

"You'd better take it back, then. I imagine it'll be a prime exhibit at the trial. I'll be interested to hear what you have to say about my motive, though."

"You didn't want her in *Diana and Acteon*. She was forced upon you. So you got rid of her."

"And I did this a few weeks before the *première*, so as to put the entire creation in jeopardy?"

"You had a replacement to hand. You'd wanted Clara Santoni all along, so you made sure she followed the rehearsals and knew all the steps."

Van Roon snorted and shook his head, walking a few paces away from Franck.

"In which case," he announced, pivoting back to face him, his voice thick with irony, "I'll need my yo-yo back, since I have to kill Lisa Roux now. Not that there's any hurry. If I wait another week or so then Clara will be the only solution. It'll be too late for another *étoile* to step in and learn the role. My ballet will at last be seen as I intended. Two dead ballerinas – not too high a price, I think you'll agree?"

Franck tossed the yo-yo to him. Van Roon swept his left hand up to catch it.

"Be my guest," said Franck.

"You're hoping to catch me red-handed?"

"You're no longer a viable suspect. On Monday evening someone else was killed in exactly the same fashion as Sophie Duval. You were at the Theatre de la Ville."

Van Roon did not ask who had died. Presumably he felt that if it was someone of concern to him, he would already have been informed. His reaction to the fact that a murder had been committed on the night of his gala was coldly egocentric.

"So I should be grateful that your charming friend with the tutu disarmed me, since that way you know I didn't sneak out after the performance and do the dirty deed."

"You didn't leave before midnight."

"Are you sure? I don't recall seeing you there."

"I was long gone, but I've talked with the sponsors. They assured me that you did your duty – you let everyone shake your hand and pour inanities into your ear."

Van Roon nodded, grimacing. "And all that without the solace of my yo-yo. But patrons must be fawned upon, or else they'll take their money elsewhere."

"You could always work for nothing," suggested Franck.

"I could." Van Roon pretended to be giving the suggestion serious thought. "But I would be an idiot to do so. If you buy a pair of shoes for forty euros, captain, you won't be too concerned if they get scuffed or stolen or permanently soiled – you know you can always just get another pair."

Franck thought about interrupting him by holding up his briefcase. He was particularly fond of it, despite the fact that he had acquired it at a modest price from a workshop in Annecy many years ago. However, given its stained leather, unpolished brass fittings, and torn seams, he realised he might end up confirming whatever point van Roon was in the process of making.

"If you buy a pair for five hundred euros," continued van Roon, "you'll polish them carefully, make sure they're dry before you store them away, and walk attentively when they're on your feet. We prize what costs us dearly. If I worked for nothing, I wouldn't have the Paris Opera Ballet at my disposal – I'd have a youth group from an Amsterdam suburb. If I want to make works like *Diana and Acteon*, then I need the resources to do so. The more expensive I am, the more resources I'm given. It's one of the paradoxes of the world I live in. I don't know why it works that way, but I know it does."

Franck made no comment. Although he had a direct line to a senior partner in Lasry Frères, money and its mysterious logic was a mystery to him too.

"How long had you been thinking about *Diana and Acteon* before the Opera commission came along?" he asked.

"Years. But I didn't want to do it until conditions were perfect."

"As in?"

"My reputation at its zenith. The money to rehearse as long as I liked. And the Opera Ballet at my disposal – since, despite my occasional dispute with its esteemed Dance Director, I happen to share Anne-Laure's opinion that it is the best company in the world."

"So this should be your *chef d'oeuvre*?"

"If it's not, I won't get a second chance to do anything like it."

Franck was working his way towards a new hypothesis. If van Roon could not be the killer, and his desire to have total control over his new ballet was not the motive behind the deaths, then maybe the unknown murderer sought a completely opposite goal – to prevent *Diana and Acteon* from coming to fruition.

"Does it mean anything in particular?" he asked.

Van Roon's grasp of French momentarily left him. He uttered something – some kind of harsh expletive – in Dutch. Not for the first time, Franck found himself being scrutinised as if he was retarded in some way.

"*Diana and Acteon*," Franck carried on, blithely unconcerned. Playing the idiot to provoke others into displaying their intelligence was a trick he had learned a long time ago. It rarely failed. "Does it have some kind of message?"

"Rather than just a random collection of physical movements loosely set to some music? Rather than an inchoate expression of barely comprehended emotions?"

"Yes," said Franck, as ingenuously as he could.

A smile stole across Van Roon's face and he started to chuckle, abandoning his tone of indignant mockery.

"You are either a holy fool or a very intelligent man, captain. Which is it, exactly?"

"Does it matter?"

"Probably not – although I expect it's a source of some concern to your employers. What exactly are you getting at?"

"I'd like you to explain *Diana and Acteon* to me."

"As if you knew nothing? Had never heard of the goddess of the hunt or her unfortunate admirer?"

"Yes."

"Right here and now?"

"If it's convenient."

"It's not. I'm in the middle of a rehearsal. What about tomorrow? We could make a brief visit to the Louvre – it would be easier with visual aids."

"OK," said Franck. "But if this is a rehearsal, where are the dancers?"

They were in the Lifar studio inside the Opera's central dome, but there were only the two of them.

"Drinking coffee. It's the drug of choice of the Opera Ballet."

Franck did not contradict him, since he ardently hoped he was right.

The door to the room swung open. In stepped Serge Morin, Lisa Roux and Clara Santoni – a picture of good-humoured complicity as they chatted between themselves and nonchalantly reeled their orange yo-yos in and out.

They were surprised by the sudden frown with which Franck greeted them. He turned to interrogate van Roon with his gaze. All he got in return was a shrug.

"I have a box full of them, captain. Would you like one?"

*

"He won't be missed."

"That's a little harsh," admonished Franck. He was in Anne-Laure Favennec's office, updating her on the latest development, biding his time until the *Diana and Acteon* rehearsal finished. "He had a family, friends, patients, ..."

Thus far they had contacted Léon Abkarian's ex-wife and his brother. The ex-wife had proved either remarkably stoical or completely unconcerned. She received the news in silence, thanked Franck for informing her of her former husband's death and assured him that she had been at home with her new one in their house in Nice on the Monday evening. When he offered to keep her up-to-date on any progress in the investigation she had told him not to bother. She would content herself with whatever the newspapers had to say. Abkarian's brother, himself a doctor, had just muttered something about playing with fire and burning your fingers.

As for patients, the nearest thing they had to a list were the initials on the four bags of drugs found in his safe. Franck had put in a call to *L'Equipe* in the hope that its journalists could fill in the spaces with some educated conjecture.

"His junkies – that's what he had. No doubt one of them finally took revenge for his chemical slavery." Anne-Laure had an air of righteous satisfaction. The diabolical doctor Abkarian had cast a menacing shadow over the Opera Ballet and had paid the price. "I imagine this means you'll be spending less time within our walls now, captain?"

"Because?"

"Because Abkarian was not of our world."

"And yet he had some kind of link to Sophie Duval."

"Maybe, despite appearances, Sophie Duval was not of our world either."

This from the woman who had led her *étoiles* in mourning at Sophie's funeral the previous day.

"Twenty-one years in the company's orbit, and she wasn't a part of it?" objected Franck.

Anne-Laure made a fist of her right hand and cupped it in her left.

"Every religion has its apostates."

"Who are to be cast out and burnt, along with those who led them astray?"

"I am the Dance Director of this institution, captain, not a Grand Inquisitor."

Franck scrutinised her. Somewhere in the vast costume collection of the Ballet there was surely a hooded black cape in which she would appear ideal for the role.

"Ever received a present from Piet van Roon?" he asked.

She frowned at him, surprised by the change of tack.

"I gave van Roon an inestimable treasure – a place in this company's repertoire. All I want in return is a masterpiece. He's not going to waste his time trying to curry my favour by showering me with gifts."

"So you've never received a present from van Roon?" Franck repeated. "Big or small."

"This is a strange line of enquiry. Have you decided to sniff around for corrupt practices within the Ballet?"

"So he's given you nothing?" Franck insisted.

She sighed in exasperation and pulled open one of her desk drawers.

"In the interests of full disclosure, captain Guerin, here is the only token of appreciation I've had from Piet van Roon."

She dumped it on the desk.

Yet another orange yo-yo.

Not that it helped, since she too had been at the van Roon gala while someone had been choking the life out of Léon Abkarian.

*

"I'm going to need your fingerprints."

Lisa Roux looked at him as if he was insane, and pushed open the door to her lodge. He had been standing beside it, waiting for her. Along with a well-stuffed shoulder bag she was carrying a bow and a quiver.

"Been told to get some extra practice?" Franck asked her. "Off to the Paul Gauguin gym?"

"Later. I've got some work to do on *Giselle* first. What's this nonsense about fingerprints?"

"Did van Roon tell you?"

"He told me I had no idea how to mix violence and sensuality, and had the cheek to ask Clara to show me how. I don't recall anything else – well, aside from the fact that I'm still reluctant to shoot at my colleagues rather than away from them."

"Nothing about Léon Abkarian?"

Lisa's face clouded.

"What's he been up to? Slandering Sophie again?"

"He's been killed. His body was found in his office yesterday morning."

She raised her eyebrows and sank into a chaise longue. Franck took the chair that sat at her dressing table, turning it round to face her.

"Is this a coincidence, or something to do with Sophie's murder?"

“They were both killed in exactly the same fashion.”

“I suppose that’s sort of good news then,” she commented.

“Because?”

“It’ll provide more clues – make it easier to identify who attacked Sophie.”

Strictly speaking, this was true. In a murder investigation, two corpses were always better than one. Except from the point of view of their previous inhabitants.

“I must seem callous,” said Lisa, taking Franck’s momentary pause for thought as a silent rebuke, “but the only thing I know about Abkarian is that he was a pusher of poison and may somehow have attempted to lure Sophie into his web. You can’t expect me to feel sorry for him.”

“People are murdered every day, Lisa. Nobody asks you to feel anything for them. The thing is, though, you met Abkarian.”

“For all of – what – fifteen minutes? We had a shouting match, not a conversation. It’s not like we got to know each other.”

“From what I heard it was a rather one-sided shouting match. You were the only one doing the yelling. More importantly, you were the only one doing the threatening.”

Her eyes narrowed.

“That’s why you want my fingerprints? You think I killed him?”

“We’ve lifted prints all over his office. We know you were there five days ago. If we have yours on record we can eliminate them and concentrate on the others.”

She subsided.

“Ah, that makes sense.”

“Can you call into the ninth arrondissement commissariat today? After your archery practice, say? Ask for lieutenant Blanchard. He’ll make sure you’re processed and out of there in no time.”

“OK.”

“I’ll get out of your hair then.”

“Before you go, can I ask you a question for a change?” she

asked.

"Sure."

"Have you had a lot of contact with Sophie's parents – François and Liliane?"

"Not a lot, no."

"But you must have talked to them."

"Of course. I was with them when they identified Sophie's body and I interviewed them for some background information."

"Did they talk about me?"

Franck hesitated just a split-second too long.

"They did, didn't they?" she continued. "Something's wrong. I could tell at Sophie's funeral. They were a lot warmer with Serge than they were with me, and yet I've been Sophie's closest friend since she was eight." She paused, reluctantly correcting herself. "Was her closest friend."

"I'm sure they recognise that," said Franck. "But their world has just crumbled around them. You can't expect people to behave normally when they've lost their only child."

"Don't tell me what you think – tell me what you know. They've talked to you. Has Liliane gone back to believing I stole Sophie's soul, seduced her to be my handmaid inside the Ballet? I was twelve when I first heard her say something like that. Sophie was really upset. Luckily for us all, her father was a lot more sensible than her mother. He always appreciated the fact that Sophie had someone she could count on unconditionally within the Ballet."

"Let them grieve. Talk to them in a week or a month. Things will be different."

"Maybe I should ask Serge to intercede. All of a sudden, they seem very fond of him. Funny, isn't it? Everyone loves our resident rake, but everyone doubts the motives of someone like me who really cared for Sophie."

"Look, it's not my place to tell you this, but it'll filter out sooner or later – Serge and Sophie were closer than you think."

"Don't get me wrong, captain. I'm not saying that Serge didn't care for Sophie. He stood up for her when van Roon was sniping at her, and I'm grateful to him for that. More to the point, I'm sure he did it out of the goodness of his heart."

"Rather than?"

"Rather than as a ploy to get her into his bed. Don't forget Serge's reputation. As we tell the young dancers who've just joined the *corps de ballet* – if you let him wipe away your tears, you may soon find him slipping you out of your underwear. Not that the warnings ever have much effect. He has too much charm for his own good, that man."

"You speak from experience."

"Was that a question?" She seemed intrigued, not irritated, by his observation.

"Not really."

"You've heard about me and Serge?"

Franck nodded.

"Well, it's true. It was a long time ago, though."

"And there are no lingering hard feelings?"

"No. Not at all. After all, I've been chasing him around with a bow for almost a week, but I don't think he's ever felt in danger."

"He knows the arrows are blunt," Franck pointed out.

"They still hurt, though. The point is, that's all in the distant past. Both of us are happy to leave it there. I'm fond of Serge. I just don't have any illusions about him. But I'm not going to deny that he was kind to Sophie."

"More than kind. They were lovers."

"What?" she suddenly leant forward, peering intently at him.

"So it seems."

"How do you know this?"

"Serge told me."

Lisa clamped her hand over her mouth and her eyes narrowed, as if she was looking for a flaw in what she had just been told.

"I can't see him making something like that up – not given the circumstances – but ..."

"He didn't make it up. She had his keys. He had hers. Why

do you think I asked him to come and inspect her apartment with you?"

"I thought that was odd," she admitted, "but I figured you just thought that two pairs of eyes would be better than one."

Lisa blew the air from her lungs and slumped against the back of the chaise longue.

"Serge and Sophie. She didn't breathe a word of it."

She sounded not just surprised, but perplexed, and more than a little hurt.

"I imagine she thought it might upset you. After all, she knew Serge was an old flame. Maybe she thought ..."

Lisa waved a hand distractedly. Franck let his words tail off.

"You don't have to cushion the blow, captain. I know what it means. Sophie was drifting away. First there was our little tussle over who would be Diana. Then a secret affair. Who's to say what would have been next?" There was no anger in her tone, just regret. "Liliane and François know about this?"

"Yes. But she hadn't told them. I did."

She seemed to take a little comfort from this fact.

"They always did worry about her being alone. I'm sure her mother blamed me for that as well. So that's why they were so nice to Serge at the funeral. They didn't see him as the most unsuitable partner imaginable for their daughter – they saw him as the last one to have held her tight."

"Probably," affirmed Franck.

Lisa reached out and squeezed his arm.

"Thanks for telling me. Better hearing it from you than through the grapevine."

Franck waited till she had released him and got to his feet.

"I'll leave you to yourself now," he said. "Don't forget ..."

She nodded.

"The fingerprints. I won't."

Franck moved to the door and pulled it open. He turned back to her just before he left.

"By the way, how do you get van Roon to give you a yo-yo?"

"You just have to put up with him long enough."

"So when did you earn yours?"

"Two days ago. That was our reward for promising to work really hard while he was away at his gala."

"Been practising?"

"With the yo-yo?"

"Yes."

"A little. It's kind of addictive."

*

"Can I walk with you a bit?"

She had been waiting in the Opera House's rear courtyard, near the entrance gate, sitting on the bonnet of a somewhat battered white van which bore the Opera's logo. She had been chatting with two other dancers, one of whom had borrowed her yo-yo and was demonstrating remarkably little skill with it.

When Franck left the main building she slid down to her feet, said a quick farewell to her companions, and walked towards him. She turned when one of the dancers called her name, and cupped her hands to catch the yo-yo as he tossed it to her.

"I'm heading towards Saint Lazare," said Franck. "That suit you?"

"It'll do."

They exited through the gate and stopped at the edge of boulevard Haussmann, waiting for a red light to tame the wide stream of traffic that poured down it.

"I don't want to pry, captain, but Piet told me there's been another murder."

"It's true."

"But he didn't say who."

"That's not surprising – I didn't tell him, and he didn't ask me. He didn't seem too concerned."

"Well I am."

The traffic had stopped and the group of people who had bunched around them as they waited surged forward. Clara did not. Nor did Franck, since she had her hand on his sleeve.

"Was it someone linked to the company?"

"Have you heard any rumours?" asked Franck in return.

"No. The only person who seems to know anything is Piet. But that's kind of scary in itself. How can a death go unnoticed?"

He ought to keep her in the dark. The fewer the people who knew about the connection between Sophie Duval and Abkarian, the better. But, unwittingly, Clara had become part of the inner circle. And she had almost benefitted from Sophie's death, which cast a shadow on her status as an innocent bystander. Telling her could be a means of questioning her.

"It's not someone from the company. And it's not a secret either. Buy a copy of *L'Equipe* on your way home, or listen to *France Info* or turn on the news once you get there. It's bound to come up, although I doubt anyone will talk of a possible link to the death of Sophie Duval."

"So who is it?"

"Léon Abkarian."

"Never heard of him."

"I take it you're not a big cycling fan?"

"No. Who was he."

"A doctor. A witch doctor, to be more precise. Follow his prescriptions and you had your chance at the yellow jersey."

"So what's the connection with us?"

"Officially, there isn't one. And if you want to stay in the Dance Director's good books, it's not a subject you should bring up. With anyone."

"When did it happen?"

"Monday evening," he said, adding inconsequentially, "I was at the van Roon gala at the Theatre de la Ville."

"Wow. You must have good connections."

"You'd have liked to have gone?"

"Loved to."

"You should have told me. I had two tickets and had a hard job finding anyone who wanted to go." This was scarcely true – Sonia Delemazure had jumped at the chance – but right now

Franck was not interested in the truth. Or at least, not in the truth as concerned what he had done that evening. "You could have accompanied me – that way I'd have had someone capable of explaining what was going on."

"Come on, captain, Piet's work's not that obscure. But I couldn't have come anyway – I wasn't free that night."

"Boyfriend? Bunch of girls out on the town?"

"No, nothing like that."

"Like what, then?"

The traffic stopped once more. Clara hopped forward onto the road. Franck kept up with her.

"You don't want to say?" he persisted.

"I'd rather not. It's ... personal."

This time he was the one who grabbed her sleeve.

"I'm investigating a double homicide. I don't have time for personal issues."

"Look, I can't tell you. But it had nothing to do with this guy Abkarian, OK? After all, I'd never heard of him until now."

"You can't tell me? Not even if I take you into the local commissariat and sit you down in an interview room?"

"Even then. I'm sorry. It's just not possible."

Horns blared to their right. The lights had changed and a car had leapt forward, only to brake about a metre short of them. They hurried to the kerb.

"I have to go this way," she said, pointing down rue La Fayette, which just happened to lead away from Saint Lazare.

"Clara, why not try trusting me?"

"Oh I do trust you," she said, already walking away. "That's not the problem."

*

"Onion soup, *steak tartare* with *frites*, cooked apple with some kind of pastry – probably a *tarte tatin*."

They were discussing the contents of Léon Abkarian's stomach. The undigested contents of his stomach, to be precise, a fact which helped to narrow the window for the time of death. He had eaten a substantial dinner and was killed very shortly afterwards. Assuming he was not an unfashionably early eater, it was unlikely he had been strangled before ten in the evening. Canvassing local restaurants would probably bear this out.

"You can tell it was a *tarte tatin*?" asked Franck. Forensic science had long ago won his grudging admiration, but he had never heard that an autopsy was capable of identifying specific recipes.

"A hypothesis based on two things," explained Georges Sternberg. "First of all, there were traces of cream, and I don't know a single restaurant which serves *tatin* without fresh cream, whereas a simple apple tart generally comes on its own. Secondly, it's what I would have chosen."

"After a *tartare* with *frites*? You wouldn't be tempted by something lighter?"

"I would have avoided eating all the *frites*, thereby leaving room for dessert. I'm a far-sighted man. Who wants to round off a good meal with a sorbet or a *crème brûlée*? You want a dessert you'll notice, not one you'll have forgotten by the time the coffee arrives."

"Well, if the *tatin* hypothesis leads us straight to the murderer, I'll make sure you get the credit."

"If you like I could have them look at the apple mush again – see if there's any trace of caramel," suggested Sternberg.

"For the moment, let's just rest with the conclusion that Abkarian liked his food."

"That's something of an understatement," observed Sternberg, flicking back to the opening page of the coroner's report. "He was a metre sixty-four and weighed in at 94 kilos. That's borderline obese. Kind of ironic for someone who claimed to be the athlete's best friend."

"He smoked too."

"I could have told you that. Want to hear the description of his lungs?"

"Spare me," said Franck. "Just tell me about the neck."

"Double loop ligature this time."

"His neck was too fat to go round a third time?"

"I doubt it. He certainly had a thicker neck than Duval, but with a metre-long cord the killer could have done a third loop if he wanted."

"Maybe he was using something different this time."

"Doesn't look like it. The trace on the neck is three millimetres wide throughout, except for a three and a half centimetre stretch."

"The bulge?"

"The very same. Approximately double the normal width of the cord. On the left-hand side of the throat this time."

"Is that significant?" asked Franck.

"Could be a different angle of attack. Last time he attacked his victim from behind, placing the mid-point of his cord, where we're assuming the thick bit is, right at the front of her throat. This time he came more from the side, or Abkarian tried to turn towards him at the critical moment."

"He was sitting on a swivelling chair. A single push of the foot could change the angle."

"That would make sense."

"The bulge is the signature, isn't it?" said Franck. "It's the one thing that indisputably links the two killings."

"That, and the fact that Abkarian didn't seem to feel threatened by his killer. First of all he let him into his office late at night. Then he let him come round his desk and stand next to him."

"You still sticking with your knots-in-the-string theory?"

"No, I've got a better one," declared Sternberg.

He put a hand into each of the side pockets of his lab coat and pulled out two yo-yos.

"Wrong colour," declared Franck.

They were smaller than van Roon's model and were decorated with cartoon characters whom Franck did not recognise.

"Same thickness of string, though," said Sternberg, unspooling both of them and laying them on a nearby workbench, their heads distant and their tails touching. He tugged one of the strings until it overlapped the other, pushed it underneath it, and braided them together, tying the loop at the end in a knot to keep it in place. He then did the same thing with the loose end of the other string, braiding it into place until the tails of the two yo-yos were linked.

"You sure that'll hold?" asked Franck.

Sternberg placed a hand at either end of the now-joined strings and pulled them tight. The braiding did not unravel.

"What's the point? Sure, the string's now twice as long, but van Roon's yo-yo was long enough to begin with."

"Come here."

Sternberg beckoned Franck over to the shop dummy, whose neck was once more a smooth expanse of plasticine.

"Ever heard of the thuggees?" he asked.

Franck shook his head.

"Indian bandits. One of the banes of the British Empire, known for killing and robbing travellers out of the blue. Since stealth was their trademark, they were keen stranglers – one, because it makes no noise, and two, because it means you don't have to carry any obvious weapons. They used their headscarves, tying a stone or piece of lead into one end and throwing it around their victim's neck. Thanks to the weighted end the scarf would loop round on its own until it was caught by the thuggee's free hand, cutting off the victim's respiration before he could defend himself. Simple and effective. Now watch."

He grasped one of the yo-yos in his right hand and let the other fall to the ground, dangling from the braided cord. He moved to the side of the dummy, swinging his right arm round as he did so. The second yo-yo took flight, pulling the string tight. It passed behind the dummy and then, when the string encountered its neck, swung round back towards Sternberg. He caught it with his left hand and took a step forward, looping the string around the dummy's neck to encircle it once more. He then pulled hard with both hands.

"All I have to do now is keep up the pressure."

He released the two yo-yos and turned back to Franck.

"If you really know what you're doing you can get the yo-yo to swing round the neck twice first time. I've been practising."

"Isn't this all a bit complicated?" asked Franck. Operational experience with the DST had taught him that any plan which could go wrong would go wrong. A smart killer would know this too.

Sternberg shrugged.

"It's a stylish way to do it, if you get it right. All it takes is a little dexterity. So if you think our killer's a cack-handed fumbler then, sure, I'm way off track."

Franck deliberately did not reply, so Sternberg continued.

"I forgot – it's not like we have any potential suspects who are quick on their toes with excellent coordination."

*

"He was killed for who he was, not for what he had."

Yves de Chaumont was inclined to agree.

"Since it took you all of five minutes to find the key to his safe, and it was chockfull of doctor Abkarian's medicinal marvels, he certainly wasn't killed for his wares."

"There was also about five thousand euros in cash in there," added Franck. "Although it's safe to assume the drugs were worth a lot more."

"What about the unhappy patient hypothesis? Some musclebound monster who used to be a promising sportsman, or someone recently banned from competing because Abkarian's undetectable doses proved not to be so?"

"Well, we'd have to know who his patients were first, and that's proving tricky. According to the journalists at *L'Equipe*, Abkarian had two apparently contradictory gifts – that of attracting as much personal publicity as was possible and that of maintaining near-total confidentiality over who he was treating."

"Near-total?" echoed Yves.

"They gave me some names, but warned me not to repeat them."

"Any of them deformed mutants or sporting outlaws, adrift and penniless?"

"I'm afraid not. They're all very successful and probably a little worried about maintaining their past record now that the good doctor has gone."

"So there's no way around it – Abkarian's death has to have something to do with your dead dancer?"

"That's what the marks on the necks say."

"Don't get too carried away with your yo-yo hypothesis," warned Yves. "I know you and Sternberg are having a lot of fun with it, but I can think of better things with which to strangle someone."

"You're right – it could even be deliberate misdirection. But if someone is trying to focus our minds on Piet van Roon or the dancers working with him, they have to know all about van Roon's personal quirks, which means they're at the very least aficionados of the dancing world."

"They weren't that well-informed – they missed the fact that van Roon was tied up at a gala on the night of the murder."

"Not all night, though, and they couldn't have known that I was going to deprive him of his yo-yo, putting a damper on any post-performance misbehaving."

"One of his yo-yos," insisted Yves. "I doubt your friend Sonia managed to frisk all his pockets."

"I'll never know. She wouldn't tell me how she managed to get it from him."

"Well, since you seem to like the idea that our most gifted ballerinas have a homicidal streak, how's Lisa Roux looking?"

"Her fingerprints are on Abkarian's desk and, more worryingly, on the back of his office chair, but we know she was there before."

"So an initial visit to threaten the future victim serves as cover for the actual deed? She has an alibi for the night in question?"

"A partial one," said Franck. "She had dinner with some

friends, but that was all over by eleven thirty. In theory, she could have gone to boulevard Malesherbes afterwards."

"In theory?"

"Abkarian's death was signed in the same way as Sophie's. Lisa didn't kill her little sister."

"Let's hope not."

"She was at the American Friends reception," Franck reminded him.

"So what does that leave us? Any other interesting prints?"

"Most can't be matched, but we do have Bertrand Pech, thanks to the fact that he hit his girlfriend six months ago."

Pech was a middleweight boxer, a rare French contender in a sport where the nation scarcely figured. Assuming sport was the right word.

"He really hit her?" asked Yves.

"Apparently so, but in the end she refused to press charges."

Yves snorted.

"Pity we can't ..."

"Indeed it is," agreed Franck. Leaking the information would cast enough of a cloud over Pech to keep him out of the limelight in his chosen profession. But, as Yves had said, they could not do such a thing. There were rules, and they played by them.

"So where do we go from here?"

"To La Défense." The city's business district, where towering pillars of glass and concrete held the offices of some 1500 firms.

"Because?"

"There was one more thing in Abkarian's safe. It was a fax from his bank confirming that two hundred thousand euros had been transferred to his account on the seventeenth of this month. Last Sunday. I called them up about it and asked where it had come from."

"Not a Swiss account, then," observed Yves.

"No. Don't forget Abkarian's schizophrenic character – living half his life in the sun and half in the shadows. This was a transaction that he felt he didn't have to hide."

“Not from one of his clients, then?”

“Not unless he was able to boost the performance of investment bankers.”

“Because it came from ...?”

“Lasry Frères.”

*

“What can you tell me about Lasry Frères’ dealings with Léon Abkarian?”

“Nothing, I imagine,” said Sylvie Thomas, as imperturbable as ever. “We’re not in the habit of discussing our dealings with anyone, let alone the Brigade Criminelle. Now, if you were asking on behalf of the DST, or whatever it is they’re calling themselves these days, that might be different. National security is very close to our heart, as well as being about as resistible as a steamroller. But criminal investigations – well, it’s all so petty and sordid, isn’t it? Not the kind of thing we like to get involved with.”

Franck scowled at her. She was grandstanding, despite the fact that she knew her audience would prove anything but receptive. She could not help herself – a provocative gene featured prominently in her DNA.

“Let me try again,” he said. “Tell me about Lasry Frères’ dealings with Léon Abkarian.”

“Léon who?”

“Léon Abkarian, known as the Witch Doctor, one of our fine nation’s most notorious practitioners of what is euphemistically termed performance enhancement. The man who made legs go faster, arms push further, blood turn brighter, and lungs pump better. The man who was killed in his office two days ago.”

“Oh, that Léon,” she said impishly. “I was wondering how long you’d take to knock on my door about him. You traced the transfer?”

“It wasn’t very hard. You’d done nothing to hide it.”

“No reason to. It was a straightforward transaction. All

above-board. I organised it myself."

"He was a client, an investor?"

Sylvie laughed, shaking her head.

"We were way out of his league, Franck."

"So how did you end up wiring two hundred thousand euros to him?"

"A favour for a client. One who is very much in our league."

"A business favour or a personal favour?" asked Franck.

She rolled her eyes.

"You want to explain the difference to me?" she demanded. "I've always found it very difficult to understand."

"Why was it done, particularly since it appears that you were the one who did it?"

"I know why I did it – Charles Hance asked me and I jumped at the chance to be of service to him. Why he wanted it done, I have no idea. It never occurred to me to ask."

"Someone asks you to pay out two hundred thousand euros for him, and you don't wonder why?"

Sylvie looked at him with what Franck took to be affectionate scorn.

"Only you could deliver that line so incredulously," she observed. "It was only two hundred thousand. It was scarcely worth making a big fuss about."

"So who is Charles Hance?"

"Charles Hance is a billionaire. A real billionaire – not a single-digit one who just scraped in around 2006 only to tumble back into the anonymous ranks of the millionaires a year or so later. He's a property developer, although we should say real estate, since he's from New York."

"And why did he ask you?"

"Because we're both Friends."

Franck's brow creased. Either his hearing was awry or Sylvie's grasp on grammar was slipping.

"You're friends?"

"If only we were," sighed Sylvie. "But I'm working on it. I managed to lure him to dinner the last time he was over, but it wasn't quite a tête-à-tête. I took along two other Lasry partners, including our commercial property specialist. So for the moment, we're just both Friends, but not of each other."

"Friends of whom, then?" asked Franck, still lost.

"Friends of the Opera."

"You mean the North American Friends of the Paris Opera House? The ones who were in Paris ten days ago?"

"The very same," confirmed Sylvie.

"And you're a member?"

Sylvie leant forward and pretended to admonish him.

"Why is that such a surprise? I love opera. And you can't doubt how passionate I am about ballet, given that I too sat through van Roon's gala."

"You're not North American, Sylvie."

"Well," she said airily, "that's a moot point. Money's American. In twenty years' time it might be Chinese, but for the foreseeable future it's American. So, given how fond I am of money, I think I qualify as American, don't you?"

Franck was too busy shaking his head to reply.

"Much to their credit," she continued, "the North American Friends of the Paris Opera House are a lot less parochial than you. They don't ask to see your passport. They just ask to see your donation. Anyhow, when I joined I used the Lasry Frères' address in Liberty Street." She paused. "New York."

"Why?" It slipped out before he could stop it. He knew what her answer would be.

"If you'd ever seen the membership list, you wouldn't be asking such a question. The fact that Charles Hance was on it would have been reason enough, but he's just one of many."

"And you have no idea why this Hance wanted to slip two hundred thousand to Abkarian? You think he mistook him for an impecunious tenor, or a *sujet* from the *corps de ballet* having trouble paying the rent?"

She folded her arms and leant back in her seat.

"Don't know. Don't care."

"You think Hance knows Abkarian was murdered?"

"Probably not. He's back on the other side of the Atlantic

now, and no doubt has many other things on his mind. His property portfolio took a forty percent hit over the past two years. He's keeping it on life support while he preys on those who took a fifty plus hit."

"Maybe you should tell him. You're both Friends, after all. You could also tell him there's a criminal investigation into Abkarian's death and that the officer in charge wants to know what was behind their transaction."

"Were I to say that, Franck, you'd find yourself face to face with an army of stonewalling lawyers in a matter of seconds. I'll try it my way."

"Which is?"

She winked at him.

"Irresistible."

Thursday, 21st May

"I've talked to Charles Hance."

"What did he have to say for himself?" demanded Franck into the phone, satisfied to find that Sylvie had moved so fast.

"Well, we had a most interesting chat, very little of which had anything to do with you. However, he assured me that he had no idea who Léon Abkarian was."

"So why was he so keen on giving him two hundred thousand euros?"

"Because he was asked to do so. As a favour to the Opera Ballet."

"He didn't ask why?"

"No. He was told it was important for the company's future, and that it had to be done through an indirect channel. He was happy to oblige. He's a man who knows how much a favour can be worth in the long run. Speaking of which, you can note this down as one of mine."

"Will do," said Franck. "Who was doing the soliciting?"

"The only person who can truly speak in the Ballet's name."

"Anne-Laure Favennec?"

"The very same."

*

Anne-Laure Favennec seemed not in the slightest perturbed, despite Franck's best efforts to back her into a corner. She showed no indication of guilt at having failed to inform him of her dealings with Abkarian.

"The only regret I have is that in the end the money was wasted – unless you know of some way we can get it back?"

"I don't see how – it wasn't the Ballet's money after all. You made sure of that. And I'm curious to know why you bothered going through a third party if you were so sure you were doing nothing wrong."

She shook her head and looked at him as if he was a naive child.

"Come now, Franck. Over sixty percent of our budget is underwritten by the state. That means that a hundred percent of it is pored over every year by inspectors and accountants who delight in the slightest irregularity. When I spend this institution's money, I always make sure I get an invoice in return, and I could scarcely ask doctor Abkarian for that. So I turned to one of our Friends instead, who doesn't have the same constraints."

"If Abkarian had given you an invoice, what would he have written on it? For services rendered?"

"For keeping his mouth shut," she said.

"He was blackmailing you?"

"That's not the term he used, but that's certainly how I saw it."

"What did he call it then?"

"A mutually advantageous agreement. He kept what he knew to himself, and I didn't have to worry about the company's reputation."

"When did he get in touch?"

"The sixteenth."

The day after Lisa Roux had stormed indignantly into Abkarian's office. Unwittingly, by demonstrating how sensitive the whole issue was, she may have inspired his next move.

It also happened to be the day before Franck had his own so-called consultation with Abkarian. In the course of the same weekend, the Witch Doctor had decided to give him a helping hand while stealing from the Opera Ballet with the other. He was nothing if not flexible in the application of his much-heralded principles.

"He phoned you? You met him?"

"We met."

"Here? At his office?"

"On neutral ground. A café near Saint Lazare."

"He came straight out with his proposal – two hundred thousand for a promise of silence?"

"No," said Anne-Laure, nestling her head in the palm of her

left hand. "First of all he explained to me how together we could engineer a generation of dancers who would surpass all those who had gone before. How we could free them from anxiety about whether they could execute a movement properly, whether they could stay on points until the end of their solo, and so on. How the two of us, working hand in hand, could take ballet to the next level."

"I take it you weren't convinced?" asked Franck, even though her tone made his question superfluous.

"The next level? What did he think ballet was – some kind of video game? I told him the only way he'd get access to my company was over my dead body."

Or his. Not that the thought managed to slip past Franck's lips. He had another, more pressing, question.

"Did he offer any proof to back up his claims? Did he name any names? Did he talk about Sophie Duval?"

"No. But he was clearly convinced of what he was saying. Either that, or he was an excellent salesman."

"Except that you weren't buying, were you? Not his potions, anyway. All you wanted was his promise to keep quiet."

"That's correct. I made sure he understood the contempt I felt for his grandiose schemes, his Promethean madness, his tinkering with Nature. I told him no sorcerer's apprentice could contribute to the great art of ballet."

"How did he take it?"

"He was very business-like. He told me he both regretted and respected my decision. He assured me he appreciated the institution's need to police its reputation, and that he was willing to do his part. He then gave me the details of his bank account."

"I don't suppose there was a contract? Any signing of documents?"

She frowned at him.

"Of course not," he continued. "You just trusted him to keep his word after he got the money."

"What option did I have?"

"You really thought he wouldn't ask for more?"

"I was prepared to take the risk. If he didn't, then the two hundred thousand would have been well spent. It was worth trying."

"And if he did?"

"He didn't," she stated flatly.

"But if he had?" pursued Franck. "What was your plan then?"

She changed her posture, shifting her weight to the rear of her chair and tipping her head backwards, as if to relax her neck.

"I didn't have a plan, Franck. I was fire-fighting. Doing whatever I could to smother a scandal before it got out of hand."

"So you're saying the transaction worked? As far as you were concerned, Abkarian was going to keep his promise."

"It worked to a certain extent. But after the money had been transferred I called him again."

"Why?"

"To make sure that he'd got it. To remind him of his undertaking. And to clarify something that we hadn't touched on in our first meeting."

"Which was?"

"He was to have nothing to do with any of my dancers in the future. He was not to approach them, and was to refuse to work with them if any of them ever approached him."

"I would have thought that was implicit from the start."

She tipped her head forward, locking eyes with him.

"I'm glad to hear it. So did I. So you can imagine my surprise when ..."

"He wouldn't agree?"

"No. He said he was duty-bound to treat anyone who called upon his services. Some nonsense about the Hippocratic oath."

"What then?"

"We had an argument. He wouldn't budge. I hung up on him."

"And then?"

"The next day he was dead. The problem had gone away."

*

"Are you going to arrest me?"

"Should I?"

Their paths had crossed as Franck walked down a corridor away from Favennec's office. Lisa Roux was in a leotard, leggings and a sweatshirt. She was carrying a longbow, unstrung, and a quiver of arrows.

"With my fingerprints on the door handle to Abkarian's office and my notorious dislike of the man, do you have any choice?"

"Except that the same person murdered both Abkarian and Sophie. And if there's one person who didn't kill Sophie Duval, it was you, Lisa. Fancy a coffee, or is van Roon waiting for you?"

"He can wait."

They walked together to the nearest coffee room. Its high tables were littered with empty cups, but there were no dancers or backstage staff. While Franck dug around for some change for the machine Lisa cleared a table. She laid her quiver on top of it and propped her bow against it. Franck brought over two black espressos.

"How's it going?"

"Me, or *Diana and Acteon*?"

"Both."

"Well, van Roon says that *Diana*'s done – the steps are all there, so all that's left to do is master them. And this." She gently tapped the tapering wooden shaft which stood between them. It was as tall as her.

"I've seen Clara shoot it. She's pretty good," observed Franck.

Lisa shot him a wry look.

"You too, huh? Van Roon thinks she'd make a better Diana than me. Serge never stops patting her head – although if she doesn't know what's behind that, she's pretty naive. And now you. What is it exactly about Clara that's got you all so excited?"

"Hey, all I commented about was her ability with a bow. You don't rate her as a dancer?"

Lisa sighed and drained her coffee.

"She's a *première danseuse*. She's been with the Ballet for eleven years. Of course she's a good dancer. And she'd be a terrific Diana – van Roon's right. She has the wildness in her that he's put at the centre of the ballet. But you don't become an *étoile* because one role fits you like a glove. You have to be up to every role in the repertoire, and Clara's not got the range. Not yet." She paused, slowly squeezing her now-empty plastic cup, quietly crushing it. "Anyhow, nobody likes to have a younger dancer breathing down her neck."

Franck raised a hand in protest.

"Come on, Lisa, you're all of ... what?"

"Thirty-one."

"And Clara?"

"Twenty-six."

"Five years – that scarcely puts you in different generations."

"Tell me this, captain. In five years time, how old will you be?"

"Forty-three."

"And what'll you be doing?"

He shrugged.

"This, or something very much like it. I ought to have inched up the ranks a bit." Or maybe not. Statistically, with over twelve years' active service, he ought to have been named *commandant* by now, and certainly would have been if the Corsican incident had not occurred. Still, captain was not so bad – enough authority to get things done, but not enough to be forced to delegate and wait for others to do it for you. "I might be in a different service." One way or another – either his former masters in national security would have him back, or his attachment to the Brigade Criminelle would finally be declared permanent. "But, on the whole, not a lot will have changed."

"In five years' time, I'll be looking at the end of my career as a dancer. I'll be wondering how much time I've got left – two years, three if I'm lucky, four if I'm in really good shape. Every time I go onstage I'll be telling myself to savour it as much as I can, to store away the memory, to live the moment as intensely as possible. Time moves more quickly in some professions than in others. The five years which separate me from Clara are an eternity. And that means I will relinquish nothing to her."

"When did you become an *étoile*, Lisa?"

"Four years ago. After dancing Henriette in *Raymonda*. I'd like to see Clara do that – she doesn't have the restraint for the first act."

"So you were a year older than Clara is now."

Lisa gently slapped her right thigh.

"My legs were a year older, but my head and my heart had several years on her."

"Well, it's all a bit academic, isn't it? You're Diana. She's not."

"But she is a better shot than me," conceded Lisa. "For all the good it'll do her."

"Because?"

"She's the hind. She doesn't have a bow. If she had any sense, she'd concentrate on helping me shoot straighter. She's the one running the risks."

"Well, figuratively speaking."

"No, quite literally," insisted Lisa.

She took hold of the notched end of one of the arrows in her quiver and drew it out. She laid it flat on the table and slid a thumb under the middle of the shaft so that she could tap the arrowtip on the flat surface. It made a sharp, ringing noise, thanks to the short, pointed metal sleeve with which it had been fitted.

"Surely that's just for target practice," objected Franck.

"Not any more. Piet has decided we'll use real arrowheads for the performance. His way of upping the stakes – making sure we're utterly focused."

"That's insane – and probably illegal."

"Only if someone gets hurt. Circuses have knife-throwers, after all. They're not all in jail."

"This is the Opera Ballet, not a circus."

She smiled at him.

"So your time with Anne-Laure hasn't been wasted. But there is a difference. In the circus, the audience's attention is focused on the edge of the blades. Ours will never know we're using real arrows."

"So what's the point?"

"We'll know. And our knowledge will translate into our acts and our expressions. We'll be wielding lethal weapons – just like real hunters. That's what the audience will see and sense."

"You approve of this?"

Lisa retrieved the arrow and slid it back into the quiver.

"I'm not a choreographer. I'm just a company member. I dance the steps – whatever they might be. That's what I've been trained to do."

"Does Anne-Laure know about this?" he demanded.

"Anne-Laure knows about everything, whether or not she chooses to own up to it."

*

Franck was late.

It was not entirely his fault. He had forgotten that bags were screened at all the entrances to the Louvre. Only when he had handed over his briefcase to a bored security guard did he realise the mistake he had made. He immediately shifted his eyes to the young woman who sat behind the screen of the airport-style X-ray machine and watched her recoil in her seat as the image of his revolver popped up before her. When she turned in her chair, about to cry out to her colleagues, he already had his ID in his hand, holding it up by his fingertips so that it could be snatched from him and scrutinised.

Nonetheless, it took some anxious muttering and a call to the head of security to allow him through. Behind him, the line of tourists stalled and stirred impatiently, but on the whole took the unexplained halt in progress stoically. It was one of the low-profile but nonetheless depressing side-effects of 2001: kowtowing to security had become instinctive in the travelling masses.

He made a note to himself to stick his revolver into his belt under his jacket next time, since for the moment only bags, not visitors themselves, were being checked. Quite how this was supposed to guarantee everyone's security was beyond him.

He walked on briskly, having entered the Louvre through its subterranean shopping centre, an attraction which he was ashamed to note seemed almost as popular as the museum itself. He deposited his briefcase in a smallish locker room presided over by three eagerly chatting young women who afforded him no more than a passing glance and a rote warning that valuables should not be left in their possession. Since they said nothing about firearms, Franck did not bring the subject up. He glanced at his watch. It was now four forty.

Fortunately, given the crowds swarming about underneath Ming Pei's glass pyramid, van Roon's height made him difficult to miss. He was intimidating one of the members of staff posted inside a circular information booth, asking questions of someone whose daily routine normally consisted of silently handing over museum maps printed in one of a multitude of different languages.

He nodded sternly and stepped back just as Franck reached him.

"Sorry I'm late," said Franck.

"This is France," observed van Roon. "I'm getting used to it."

Although Franck was tempted to justify himself by suggesting that punctuality was an overrated virtue – getting the trains to run on time was Mussolini's sole claim to fame, after all – he held his tongue. He too was secretly of van Roon's opinion, that his fellow citizens could do with a little dose of Northern European rigour on the time-keeping front.

"Fortunately," van Roon continued, "we are in luck. It appears that room 15 is only open two days a week. But today is one of those days."

The room in question was on the first floor of the Denon wing, which meant they had to squeeze their way past the hordes streaming towards the Mona Lisa and the oversized paintings by Gericault, David and Delacroix which towered over their spectators, glorying in their status as national totems.

By the time they had reached the end of the grand gallery that ran the entire length of the museum, they had less competition. There were few instantly recognisable paintings to be found at the furthest end of the Denon wing. The collections here were hung in small rooms which appeared claustrophobic after the grand vistas offered by the galleries which preceded them. Van Roon's towering presence did nothing to counter this impression.

Franck was led down a short flight of stairs and made to turn immediately to his left. Room 15, dedicated to painting in Rome and Bologna in the seventeenth century, held but three visitors.

"We'll start with this one," declared van Roon, pointing towards a medium-sized painting attributed to a certain Francesco Albani.

The painter had chosen to compose his image as if looking out from a dark cave across a body of water kept perpetually in the shade by a screen of trees and towering rocks. Onto this background of subdued, earthy tones he had projected eight light-saturated figures, all of them naked women. One, taller than the others, wore a tiny crescent moon in her hair, and pointed imperiously to the left edge of the painting. The object of her attention was shown fleeing, his cloak whipping out behind him, a young man casting a fearful glance over his shoulder. His hair bore not one ornament, but two – stubby antlers pushing out from his forehead.

Franck turned his head towards van Roon, who stood slightly behind him, to let him know he had taken in the painting. It took him a few seconds to catch the choreographer's attention, which appeared to be lost in the canvas. Van Roon stood stock still, the only movement coming from the yo-yo which rose and fell, with futile regularity, tethered to his right hand.

"OK," prompted Franck.

"Now over here," said van Roon, leading him a few steps to the right.

Yet another Italian – this time going by the name of Giuseppe Cesare. Moving from the Albani to this painting was like zooming in on the action previously depicted. The caves and trees had been pushed to the background, allowing five generously proportioned naked women to dominate the scene. With their feet in shallow water and their flesh reflecting the sun, their attention was focused on an interloper who this time stood right next to them, his eyes mesmerised by the sight of a crescent moon on the head of one of the naked beauties, his hand reaching to his chest as if to still his pounding heart. A young man, he seemed unaware that well-developed antlers had emerged from his curly hair. The two hunting dogs at his feet, however, were not. They stared up at them, their lips curling back in a snarl.

"Behold, in all his glory, Acteon, prince of Thebes," proclaimed van Roon. "A gifted hunter, schooled by a centaur, itself half man and half beast, and therefore one who could explain the nature of both universes. One morning Acteon set out with his young friends and his pack of hunting dogs, his pride and joy. In the first light of day, as the forests stirred with life after the stillness of the night, they struck down everything in their path. When midday came, he finally called a halt, having almost emptied the woods of game, and told his friends to rest before they all returned to Thebes."

"No tree-hugging conservationist, this prince of Thebes," observed Franck.

"Different times, different morals. The forest was everywhere. Men had not yet learned to fell every tree in sight and plant the grains that would allow their number to multiply out of control. This was a world where savagery and civilisation were finely balanced. It was also a world where the sacred had not yet been imprisoned in churches and tamed by man. For while the mortals had enjoyed their sport, so too had the gods. Or more exactly, one particular immortal – Diana, goddess of the hunt."

"And of the moon," added Franck, "which explains her taste in headgear."

"And of the moon," agreed van Roon. "She too had been hunting all morning, and when the sun rose high in the sky she and her nymphs sought out a grotto in a nearby valley famed for its cool, pure water. There her companions undressed her and washed away all trace of her exertions."

"Not a drop of blood in sight," confirmed Franck.

"Then along came Acteon, separated from his friends, and stumbled upon the hidden grotto. Diana's nymphs tried to shield their mistress, as no mortal eye had ever seen her naked form. They were too late, as Acteon had already glimpsed her beauty. Furious, Diana cursed him, transforming him into a stag. He fled, his human consciousness trapped inside a wild beast, unable to speak and reveal his presence. His own dogs spotted him and set off in pursuit, joined by his Theban companions. They soon cornered him and ripped the life from him. And so he died, suffering the fate he had inflicted upon so many other creatures, a sacrifice to Diana's refusal to be sullied by an impure gaze."

"Not a very heartening tale."

"Ballet is at its worse when it strains for the happy-ever-after. At least those who write operas have the courage to wallow in loss and despair."

"So what's your take on the tale?"

"My take? You want me to decipher my ballet? That's the critics' job, captain, not mine."

"I'm not much of a critic, so give me a few pointers. *Diana and Acteon* for idiots, if you like."

"There are several layers, like in most epic tales. There is the reminder that Nature is a savage thing. That man's dominance of it is temporary, and that it can and will have its revenge. Then there is the warning that that while men strut and preen, flexing their muscles and arming themselves with technology, women retain a deeper, more potent power in the form of their beauty and their ability to ensnare the mind."

"Like the Sirens? Impossible not to gaze upon, impossible not to listen to, but fatal to those who did?"

"Very much so," agreed van Roon.

"It all sounds slightly misogynistic, if you don't mind me saying so."

"You can say what you like, captain, but don't forget that you're French, so that much of the responsibility lies with you, not with me. Ever heard the term *vrouwen fataal*? Of course not, because even we Dutch were taught by you lot to call them *femmes fatales*. Not that your countrymen actually invented the concept. The Old Testament beat you to it with Judith, Salomé and Delilah. The Greeks too, with their Amazons and with Artemis – the original Diana – a goddess unseen, and therefore necessarily untouched, by man. A goddess who cast out the pregnant nymph Callisto – one of her own – for having broken her commandment to shun all men. If I'm being misogynistic, then Judith, Salomé, Delilah, Artemis and Diana are all to be condemned as no more than monsters called forth by man's fear of women. But I think you'll find more than a few who would rather celebrate them as instances of woman's irrefutable strength."

Van Roon paused, shrugging. His yo-yo continued, unabated.

"That's what I think, anyway," he continued. "It's not for me to say – I'm just a choreographer, an idle fool who pulls dances out of the air. Let the critics decide what it all means. It'll keep them busy, and a little scandal never does any harm. I'll just say this – classical ballet has always portrayed the ballerina as a creature of the insubstantial air while insisting upon the earthbound robustness of her male partner. Surely I can allow myself to be a little subversive on that front?"

"What about Acteon?"

"What about him?"

"Isn't Serge Morin a strange choice to play a young prince? He's nearly fifty, after all."

"Acteon was a hero to the Thebans. All the other youths of the city looked up to him, admired his skills, followed his example, and yet in the end they looked on and applauded as he was slaughtered."

"Unwittingly," Franck pointed out.

"Perhaps. But who can say what they would have done if Acteon, become a stag, had retained his voice. Would they have held back? Would they nonetheless have turned against the one they once worshipped? The subconscious is a nasty thing, captain, and our admiration is rarely devoid of envy."

"So?"

"So – Serge Morin is the one dancer in the Opera Ballet about whom everyone agrees. He is disciplined, gifted, generous and utterly devoted to his art. He is the reigning role model for the rest of the company. And this, despite his reputation as its resident Casanova – for, like the libidinous Venetian, he is universally admired by the sex he seduces, even by the women he has left for others. And yet – though no one will come out and say it – he is an ageing lion. His physical condition is remarkable, and even today he can dance as well as any of his far younger peers, but his time has to be running out. One day he will stumble and he will be devoured – by the critics, by his colleagues, even by the great matriarch herself, Anne-Laure Favennec. Given which, having him play Acteon is akin to offering a glimpse of the future. And the world of dance – like that of Nature – will prove indifferent to his passing. Performance-based arts care only for the present. Legendary performers from the past are only of use insofar as they inspire new acolytes to step forward and offer up their lives. That is why composers, not musicians, achieve immortality."

"And choreographers, not dancers?"

"I'll let you be the judge of that, if I'm the next one to succumb to our mysterious killer."

"You're too tall to strangle."

Which was not untrue – van Roon's height would pose a problem for an attacker.

"Unless I'm sitting down," he pointed out.

Abkarian had been sitting down.

"Stop spreading yo-yos around, then," suggested Franck.

Van Roon snorted and caught his yo-yo as it rose to meet his right hand. He tossed it to Franck.

"Here. Have one. I like to live dangerously."

*

"It only took you two days."

"Two days for what?"

"Two days to finally get round to calling me."

Franck had not been counting, but it seemed that Noémie Berger had.

"Something reminded me of you," he said.

"Now you're spoiling it. You're supposed to have been thinking about me all the time – or at least from time to time. You're certainly not a silver-tongued seducer, are you Franck?"

"Doesn't sound very practical, a silver tongue. Must knock hell out of your teeth. Has to be cold too – like having an ice cube in your mouth all the time." He had often wondered whether the same thing was true of the metal studs that the young had taken to bolting to their tongues. Next time he arrested someone with one, he would ask them.

"But at least it wouldn't corrode," Noémie pointed out. "An iron tongue – now that would be a nightmare. You'd be spitting rust all day long. So tell me, what made you think of me?"

"I'm in the Louvre. It's full of frames. They all seem to have paintings in them, but if you squint a little, you can block them out."

In actual fact, he was no longer in the galleries, but standing under the pyramid, having just recovered his briefcase. Van Roon had stalked off, no doubt heading back to the Opera.

"Must be a quiet day if you're wandering about a museum. Does this mean you've solved your ballerina case?"

"I'm afraid not."

"How about the Witch Doctor?"

"Same case. Same problem."

"So what are you doing? Looking for inspiration?"

"Something like that."

"Did it work?"

"Well, it inspired me to call you."

He heard her chuckling.

"That's quite good. You're getting better at this."

"If you're free this evening, how about meeting up somewhere?"

"Actually, I'm not."

"Ah, OK. Doesn't matter."

He had said no the last time. Now it was her turn. It was only fair.

"However," she continued, "were you to invite me out to dinner on Saturday I wouldn't say no."

"Why not tomorrow?"

"I'll be keeping a low profile tomorrow. Washing my hair, that sort of thing. Saturday is your best bet."

"OK. Let's do that."

"No, you have to invite me."

"Would you like to go out for dinner on Saturday?"

"I'd love to, Franck."

"How about we meet at Le Nemours – it's a café next to the Comédie Française. I'll reserve a table at a place near there. Nine o'clock?"

"Sounds great. Should I dress up or down?"

Franck paused before answering. The question appeared innocent, but he knew better. He did not want to find himself caught up in some form of sartorial arms race. After all, when Sonia Delemazure had accepted his invitation to the van Roon gala, she had casually mentioned the fact that she would wear something appropriate. Noémie was not a model, but there was no saying what she was capable of.

He had hesitated too long.

"I'll dress up," she announced. "See you there."

Franck slipped his phone back into his jacket.

There was always his funeral suit. It had been dry-cleaned for Sophie Duval.

Friday, 22nd May

Clara Santoni stood on *demi-pointe*, her right leg crossed behind her left, her back straight, her head tipped slightly backwards as it gazed over her left shoulder. Her right arm was thrown out to one side, an unwavering straight line tapering to her extended index finger. Her other arm was held against the side of her body, a longbow grasped in her fist. Slowly, she raised her left arm until it too stood perpendicular to her body. Once it was in position her right arm arced towards the quiver on her back, plucking an arrow out. In a single continuous movement she fitted it to the bowstring and pulled it back to the side of her face. All this was accomplished without a discernable tremor, her weight poised in perfect equilibrium on the ball of her left foot.

When the arrow was released it flew past Piet van Roon, who stood maybe ten paces from her, forming a diagonal with two large cardboard pillars, one before him, one behind him. Van Roon was leaning forwards, left foot in front of his right, one arm crossed in front of his chest, the other extended towards Clara, palm raised. He did not flinch as the arrow passed within a metre of him and thudded into the pillar behind him.

The pillar itself, however, proved less imperturbable. It eased backwards as the arrow punctured it, hesitated for a split-second, and then toppled over. Van Roon, who had been watching it out of the corner of his eye, began to chuckle. Clara did the same, and both abandoned their postures.

"You think you'll be able to keep a straight face on the night?" asked Franck from alongside the door to the rehearsal studio – which was fortunately out of the line of fire.

They were in the Petipa studio, which was the biggest Franck had yet seen. It could have accommodated several dozen dancers manoeuvring in formation. Whereas the Lifar studio had been constructed inside the stone ring built over the auditorium and underneath the Opera's central cupola, the Petipa studio sat directly inside the copper dome itself. It was a space without natural light, as piercing windows in the crown that topped the building was unthinkable. Sixteen spotlights hung from a circular frame suspended from the ceiling to compensate for this fact. Above them a spider's web of beams radiated out from a central point, reinforced by horizontal struts every metre or so, before disappearing into the floor. They were a reminder of the fact that although the Opera House appeared to be a classic stone-built structure, it actually rested upon an iron frame, yet another episode in the city's late nineteenth-century romance with forged beams and rivets which had culminated in the Eiffel Tower.

"On the night these pillars will be trees, and they'll have weights at their base," van Roon explained. "And it won't be me – it'll be Serge, whose many years' experience has left him unflappable."

"It's actually Serge I'm looking for," said Franck.

"He's at the Ballet school," said Clara, coming over and kissing Franck on both cheeks. The company's ballet school, which had occupied cramped quarters in the Opera House for over a century, was now based in a modernist concrete structure in Nanterre in the eastern suburbs. "He's running a workshop for the boys who are getting ready to join the *corps de ballet*."

"He'll be out there all day?"

"He'd better not be," declared van Roon. "He's supposed to be rehearsing with Lisa at five. You have something for him?"

Franck had a stiff paper carrier bag in his right hand. He had decided to release most of the possessions which had been bagged for study during the initial searches of Sophie Duval's apartment. When her parents had collected them the previous day they had asked Franck if he could deliver some of them to Serge Morin. Franck had caught himself just before indicating that he could do the same for anything destined for Lisa Roux. Nothing had been set aside for her. Liliane Duval had not abandoned her crusade for the posthumous possession of her daughter.

There was not much in the paper bag: a set of keys to

Serge's apartment, the scrapbook Sophie had made of his career, a framed photo of them dancing together in *The Nutcracker,* and one of Nureyev, signed in his declining years, presumably included because Serge had known the great man.

"Yes, but I can't hang about, so I'll bring it back tomorrow."

"You could leave it with Anne-Laure's assistant," suggested Clara.

"Or with me," proposed van Roon. "One way or another I'll be sure to get it to him today."

Franck accepted the proposition. The bag would be safe with van Roon. One of the advantages of dealing with the self-absorbed was that they lacked the curiosity to go poking about in other peoples' affairs.

"So what are you two up to?" he asked as he deposited the bag alongside the tall stool from which van Roon normally surveyed the room. "Still working things out? I had heard that *Diana and Acteon* was done."

"Done?" echoed van Roon. "You're mixing up your art forms, captain. This isn't the Louvre, full of paintings and statues in immovable majesty. Such works are done when the tools that shaped them are laid down for the last time. Their form is frozen for all eternity. My sculptures are different. They come alive. We choreographers are all Pygmalions. We provide a vision, a framework, a rhythm, a series of steps that you can even note down if you like, but we mould with living clay. What we create escapes us as soon as it is made. A ballet is never done."

Clara came to Franck's rescue.

"You're right, Franck, the steps are all in place. Piet was just making sure I know how to do them all. Those for Diana, I mean."

"Just in case."

Franck and van Roon uttered the phrase simultaneously, although perhaps not with the same idea in mind.

*

Franck peered down into the pool.

"Someone else can handle this."

"Not as well, though," protested Georges Sternberg.

"Well enough. I've got my hands full with Sophie Duval and Léon Abkarian. I'm not the only homicide investigator in Paris. I'll call the quai des Orfèvres and get someone else sent over."

"Come on, Franck. This is a luxury hotel. They're your speciality."

"Very amusing." Sternberg was not wrong. Two years previously Franck had dealt with killings in the Crillon, the Meurice and the Lutetia. But he was in no hurry to add to his collection. "I'll see you around, Georges. Don't let this get in the way of working on my case."

"It's been days since you brought me any new evidence. I get bored easily. Little wonder I'm driven to multi-tasking."

Franck turned and started walking away.

He would not admit it, but he knew that Sternberg had a point. He had to keep his lab team working, and the Opera Ballet case was stuck in a rut. Sternberg's decision to rush to this crime scene, beating his colleagues and claiming it as his own, was understandable. Particularly as it provided an excuse to dawdle in such elegant surroundings.

The rue du Faubourg Saint-Honoré was the capital's other luxury shopping street. Although avenue Montaigne had the best-known names in *haute couture*, the boutiques on Faubourg Saint-Honoré could boast more distinguished neighbours. While most streets would have been more than happy to claim any one of the American, Canadian or British embassies, Faubourg Saint-Honoré had all three. But its trump card was an even greater prize, for number 55 was the address of the Elysée Palace, the residence of the President of the Republic. As a result the Le Bristol hotel, a mere two hundred metres down the street, was never short of wealthy and powerful guests.

The hotel opened its doors in the 1920s, a decade obsessed with its own modernity, and immediately carved out a lucrative niche catering to the rich and cosmopolitan. It continued to prosper, even during the war, when it was the only luxury hotel in Paris to escape being requisitioned by the Nazis. Since then it had steadily expanded, infiltrating neighbouring plots to add more rooms, suites and facilities. That it had done so without ever endangering its reputation as an institution for the stylish and the select said much for its management's acumen. They had never lost sight of the fact that there was nothing the ultra-rich liked more than the presence of their peers and the absence of everyone else.

One of its most prized features was its swimming pool, perched atop its sixth and highest floor. Designed in the 1980s by the man who built yachts for Aristotle Onassis, it was surrounded by teak decking and a host of nautical touches, including a vast mural at one end which represented the prow of a lake-going vessel bearing long-skirted women and moustached men of a previous century. Enclosed and heated against inclement weather it was nonetheless surrounded by massive sloping windows which allowed those relaxing in or around the pool to gaze out over the capital's celebrated roofscapes. Wooden chairs with comfortable-looking white cushions were neatly arranged in a line alongside the pool. Open-fronted units in dark wood held piles of thick white towels. On the terrace outside, sunbeds were neatly aligned between potted shrubs.

As the skies were clear and bright the surface of the pool sparkled in the available light, endeavouring to entice the handful of figures milling around it to test its depths. None felt particularly inclined to do so, however, as its customary blue was tinged with red and a naked man was floating, face down, in one corner. Short and slightly tubby, the only two distinguishing features he presented for the moment were his thick black hair and a narrow shaft of shining steel which protruded from just beneath his left shoulder. A length of thin rope was attached to the end of it, stretched taut and tied to the handrail of one of the two sets of steps which plunged into the waters of the pool. It looked as if the victim, once impaled, had swum away from his attacker until being pulled up short by the cord and expiring.

As Franck reached the the pool room's door his progress was blocked by an anxious-looking man in an impeccable dark pinstriped suit with a crisply folded handkerchief in the breast pocket. Underneath it he had a waistcoat traversed by the fob chain of a pocket watch. Franck briefly wondered whether he had escaped from the mural at the other end of the room.

"Philippe Fouché," he announced, capturing Franck's hand in his own. "Assistant Director of the hotel."

"Captain Franck Guerin, Brigade Criminelle."

"Welcome to Le Bristol, captain Guerin. I do apologise for the circumstances, but I'd like to assure you that all our personnel will give you every assistance in the course of your enquiry."

"I'm much obliged, but it's not my enquiry," explained Franck. "Another of my colleagues should be arriving very soon to take matters in hand."

There was a splash behind him. Franck glanced over his shoulder to see one of Sternberg's team, stripped to his underwear, hop off the lowest rung of one of the pool ladders and wade, chest-deep, towards the body.

"What on earth is he doing?" asked Fouché.

"I image he's going to turn the victim round. That way we've a better chance of finding out who it is."

Sternberg's technician positioned himself alongside the victim on the opposite side from the shaft which had pierced him. He glanced up at his boss. Sternberg nodded from the side of the pool. The technician knelt down in the water, placed his right hand under the victim's shoulder and stretched his left arm beneath him to clamp it around his far hip. He counted to three before tugging and pushing simultaneously, flipping the body over and causing a small wave to run up to the opposite side of the pool.

The victim's face was Japanese. Franck guessed he was in his late fifties. The head of a harpoon emerged diagonally from the centre of his chest. If he had moved after having been hit, it could not have been for long, as he was probably functioning on a single lung.

"Got many Japanese guests?" asked Franck.

The Assistant Director remained studiously polite in the face of what must have seemed to him a patently foolish question.

"One or two, yes."

"You recognise this one?"

"I'm afraid I do. That's monsieur Toshiro Nakamura. He's been with us for the past three days, staying on the fifth floor I believe."

"A regular customer?"

"Fairly regular. Comes maybe once a year, normally with his wife. Three or four days of dining, shopping, concerts, that sort of thing."

"His wife's here?"

"Not this time."

"When was he found?"

"We shut the pool at half past ten in the evening and reopen it at six in the morning. That's when the body was discovered."

"I take it that means he wasn't in the water at half ten last night?"

"I think someone might have noticed if he was."

"So how did he get in here?"

"The lock's not been forced," Sternberg called over from the side of the pool. "Someone had a passkey – either monsieur Nakamura or whoever shot him."

"What is that thing sticking out of him?" asked Fouché, with evident distaste.

"It comes from this."

Sternberg walked the length of the pool, picking up a long object which had already been bagged.

"It was left at the bottom of the pool. I doubt we'll find many fingerprints on it."

He held it up horizontally before the two of them. It was almost a metre and a half long with an open-grooved black metal stock and a pistol grip set a fifth of the way up from one end.

"It's a speargun," explained Sternberg. "For underwater hunting. See these rubber bands?" He pointed through the polythene bag to a pair of thick black tubular bands attached to the front of the stock. "You insert the spear – or harpoon, if you're more classically minded – into the groove on the top of the stock, where it locks into place. You then pull back the bands and catch them on notches on the spear. When you pull the trigger, the spear is released, the bands pull it forward and it flies out the front. No gunpowder, no explosion, no noise – aside from the fish thrashing about as you haul it back in, which you do thanks to the cord attached to the end of the spear."

"Would it work outside the water?" asked Franck.

"Not as well. The spear's got no feathering to keep it straight. That's the water's job. You could shoot someone at point-blank range on dry land, but if your target's more than a metre away, you'd want to be underwater."

"Looks like the spear itself is about a metre long."

"The bigger the fish you're after, the bigger the spear you want."

"Was he a big fish?" asked Franck, turning to the hotel's Assistant Director.

"Strictly speaking, in his field he was one of the smaller mammals," said Fouché.

"And what field might that have been?"

"He was the head of a Japanese state organisation known as the CRD – the Cetacean Research Directorate."

Franck sneaked a glance at Georges Sternberg. Clearly the name meant nothing to him either. He might know about every weapon under the sun, but there were still some fields of expertise which had evaded him.

"Should I have heard of it?" Franck asked.

"It's got a fairly low profile here in France. I think that's one of the reasons why monsieur Nakamura was so fond of Paris. It was one of the few places he could visit without being troubled by critics of his institution."

"Sounds interesting," prompted Franck. "Tell us more."

"The CRD is a scientific organisation devoted to marine biology and a greater understanding of cetaceans and their proper place in the ecosystem of the seas."

"And what exactly is a cetacean?"

"I'm not a scientist, captain," said Fouché, "but as I understand it, the cetaceans include all the major mammals which live in the sea."

"Like dolphins?" suggested Franck.

"Like whales," said Sternberg. "Come on, Franck. Japan plus whales equals?"

"Trouble."

Fouché raised a finger in polite objection.

"Controversy," he insisted. "The CRD runs the Japanese scientific whaling program. They harvest a modest quantity of whales each year in order to study population structure and the impact of whales on fish stocks. They seek to deepen our understanding of whales from a taxonomic, biological and ecological viewpoint."

"They harvest them, do they? I see you've had more than one conversation with monsieur Nakamura in the past."

"It was important that the hotel understand his particular requirements – a need for discretion, above all else. Which, I'm happy to say, is one of our specialities."

"Was – not is," observed Franck. "If Nakamura thought that no one knew he was staying here, it looks like someone slipped up."

"You're being somewhat hasty in your conclusions, if I may say so," objected Fouché. "It may be that his death had nothing to do with his professional activity."

Franck tried not to laugh, but he did not succeed.

"He was put in a pool and harpooned. As we speak, the world's oceans are probably full of joyfully singing whales."

"You sure you don't want this case, Franck?" asked Sternberg.

"Even if I did, I wouldn't be allowed anywhere near it." Sternberg frowned in puzzlement. Franck enlightened him.

"My arithmetic isn't always reliable, but in this case I suspect that Japan plus whales means you-know-who, and that means the DCRI. I have to put in a call."

He stepped away to a corner of the pool room, pulling out his phone.

"He's calling someone else in the Brigade Criminelle?" asked Fouché.

"I'm afraid not. You'll be dealing with quite a different entity on this one," Sternberg informed him.

Franck's conversation lasted less than five minutes. He came back over to them, walking quickly.

"We might have an hour or two. Let's try to find out as much as we can."

Sternberg nodded, suppressing a smile.

Franck turned to Fouché. "I'd like to talk to the head concierge."

They settled down in a tiny subterranean office. It held a battered wooden desk, a trio of mismatched chairs, an overstuffed filing cabinet, a telephone, a flat screen PC and printer, and a portable clothes rack bearing a number of freshly pressed suits and shirts. Four pairs of brightly polished shoes were slotted underneath it.

The coffee for which the head concierge had called arrived on a silver platter borne by a uniformed waiter. He poured cups for both of them from an art deco pot, informed them that the mini-madeleines offered as an accompaniment had left the pastry-cook's oven no more than ten minutes previously, and left them to their business.

Franck drained his coffee, expecting to be impressed. He was. The head concierge served him another cup.

"So you reckon we've definitively lost monsieur Nakamura's custom?" he asked.

"Unless you know how to raise the dead, it certainly looks like it," said Franck.

"I could get you a table this evening at Ledoyen or Guy Savoy. Or front row balcony seats for the *première* of that new ballet they'll soon be putting on at the Opera. Or a private tour of the Hermès workshops. There's not much a diligent concierge can't do, but I'm afraid to say that raising the dead isn't one of them."

"Not even for five minutes so that he can tell us who got him?"

"Not even that, captain. Sorry to let you down. Is it a real mess up there? I've not had the time to go and have a look."

"Lift out the body, drain the water, give the pool a quick once-over with a sponge, and it'll be as good as new. I doubt any guests'll be getting in today, though."

"So long as the spa next door to the pool stays open – that's what really matters. The swimmers can wait for a day. More coffee?"

Franck had finished his second cup. He accepted another one. Le Bristol's kitchens were proud possessors of three Michelin stars and knew that attention to detail was the only way to keep them. They probably inspected every coffee bean individually before grinding it.

"Tell me about Toshiro Nakamura," invited Franck.

"Very Japanese. Liked things neat and clean and well-organised. Very polite and expected the same in return."

"He normally came with his wife?"

"That's correct. She loved classical concerts, going to the Opera, that sort of thing. A serious woman. Not much fun, if you ask me."

"Any idea why he came on his own this time?"

"I don't think it was planned that way. He flew into Roissy from Sydney. She was to come from Tokyo, but something came up. He told us to cancel all the musical events we had set up for them."

"So what did he do instead? He'd been here, what, three days?"

"That's right. Arrived on Tuesday. Didn't bother us for anything. Left the hotel late morning, dined here in the evening, sometimes went out for a walk afterwards. He was probably quite happy to have Paris to himself for once."

"Nothing suspicious?"

"Depends what counts as suspicious. Now, were I madame Nakamura, I'd have been slightly worried about the young woman he ran into in the bar two nights ago."

"Because?"

"Let's start with the fact that she was young – which madame Nakamura no doubt once was, but not in recent memory."

"What's young in this context?"

"Mid-twenties. Nice long legs, which she wasn't afraid to show. Long blonde hair, too – not so common in Japan, or so I'm told. Certainly caught his eye."

"A professional?"

"No. Not here. Strange things may go on in the suites and rooms, but we won't have women of ill-repute setting up shop in the public areas."

"So what happened?"

"I don't have all the details, since the barman was pretty busy. But it seems she started chatting to him."

"In Japanese?"

"No idea."

"How was Nakamura's French?"

"Non-existent. We dealt with him in English. She probably did too. They had a nice long discussion, quite a few laughs, and then she walked away. According to the barman, Nakamura wasn't the only one to watch her all the way to the door."

"That's it?"

"Not quite. More coffee?"

"No thanks." Even Franck had his limits.

"Yesterday morning Nakamura cancelled his dinner reservation. Came back from his day's meanderings fairly early, around five. Left again around seven-thirty, having changed. Got housekeeping to press a shirt for him. According to them, there wasn't a single crease on it to start with, but he was very insistent. Everything had to be perfect."

"So he had a date. Any idea where?"

"No. I could ask around, see if he was in any of the classy restaurants, but I doubt it. He didn't ask us to make a reservation for him, and he couldn't have got into one on his own at such short notice."

"He was seen coming back?"

"Around midnight. Again, I wasn't there, but I'm told he came in with a young woman. Very elegant, long silky dress, heels."

"Blonde?"

"Of course."

"You think we'll find her tucked up in his bed, having a long lie-in?"

"I doubt it. She left around two this morning."

"She strolled out in full sight of the concierge's lodge?"

"So it seems. We'll have her on camera. There's a lot of well-hidden kit scattered about the public areas. Don't feel obliged to tell the guests, though."

"Not afraid to show her face, then. Not afraid to work alone either. A cool operator, this young woman."

"I don't know about the 'alone' bit. She left with another guest."

"She did?"

"Christophe Moulin. Room 214. Checked in two days ago. Due to leave today. Serious-looking individual. Has breakfast at six in the morning, stays out all day, gets back around eleven in the evening. Architect, I believe. Carries plans about with him in big tubes, that sort of thing."

"I bet he does. Don't suppose anyone ever shook one, to see if anything rattled inside?"

"You've lost me, captain."

"The murder weapon was over a metre long. Not so easy to carry about without attracting attention. I'd be surprised if monsieur Moulin checked out as anticipated this morning."

"I don't know." He reached for the telephone on his desk. "Want me to ...?"

Franck nodded.

The head concierge had a brief talk with the front desk.

“He had arranged for a late checkout. They’re sending someone up to his room.”

“Good. I’m going to go back upstairs. Could you get security to go through the surveillance tapes? If they can print off some stills, that would help.”

“No problem.”

“Look, I have to be upfront with you about this. I won’t be handling this case. Another team will be arriving soon to take over. They’ll ask you all the same questions. Tell them everything you’ve told me. I’ve just one request. Don’t offer them any coffee.”

The head concierge offered a complicit smile.

“A little in-house rivalry, captain?”

“Something like that.”

“Anything interesting?”

Sternberg was in room 508, taking photos. Franck stayed in the doorway.

“He’d been celebrating.”

A bottle of champagne had been opened and left in an ice bucket. Two half-emptied glasses sat nearby on a marble-topped commode. The room’s thick curtains had been drawn.

“But not to bed,” commented Franck. The bedcover had not been disturbed, and was still neatly folded back where the night service had plumped up the pillows and deposited some chocolates.

“What did you find out?” asked Sternberg.

“He came back last night with a young blonde.”

“Well that should make distinguishing their hairs easy enough. I’ll tell the team to get their tweezers out.”

“Looks like they had a drink in his room and then she suggested they go up to the pool for an illicit post-midnight dip. Doesn’t look like they undressed here first.” Franck could see no abandoned clothes.

“Definitely happened upstairs,” said Sternberg. “We’d bagged it all before you arrived. The victim’s clothes had been left on one of the poolside chairs. Rather neatly too, for someone being enticed into the water by a siren."

"Bet you didn't find her clothes though."

"No."

"That's because she walked out in them at two this morning."

"She must have had a very long coat, if she managed to smuggle in a speargun under it."

"Somebody else provided that. Probably the same person who got his hands on a passkey for the pool door."

"Any idea whom?"

"Christophe Moulin. Room 214. You should take a look at his room when you're finished here. He was seen walking out of the hotel in our little mermaid's company in the middle of the night. I doubt he's come back since."

"You boys having fun?"

It was spoken from the corridor. Franck did not have to turn round to recognise the voice. She pushed past him and entered the room, checking on who he was talking to.

Franck took charge of the introductions.

"Georges, this is Catherine Vautrin, head of section – what was it?"

"121," said Catherine, slowly gazing around the room.

"Section 121 of the DCRI."

"His boss," added Catherine.

"My former boss," corrected Franck.

"His employer, then," she said, "if we're being administratively precise."

"It's a pleasure," said Sternberg. "But I have to ask you to step back outside and stop polluting my crime scene."

She did not move.

"This is Georges Sternberg, *ingénieur principal* in the forensic service," explained Franck.

"Quai de l'Horloge?" she asked.

Sternberg nodded.

"Is he any good?" Her question was directed to Franck.

"He's very good."

"OK. Sternberg – you can stay until the scene has been

processed. Afterwards our own experts will take over. As for you Franck, I'll walk you out."

"You been upstairs?" he asked.

"Not yet."

"Let me show you first."

The two of them headed up to the sixth floor, taking the lift at Catherine's insistence. Two of Sternberg's assistants were still there, probing the gaps in the teak slats on the floor. Franck introduced Catherine to Toshiro Nakamura, who was still suspended in the water.

"He looks a little surprised," she commented.

"I think he was expecting a little in-pool sex, not being skewered by a speargun."

"There was a girl?"

"Talk to the head concierge. They've got her on tape coming in with him last night and leaving two hours later. She was here on Wednesday too, laying the bait."

Catherine pulled out a cigarette and lit up.

"Hey!" objected one of the technicians. "Ash. Take it out of here."

"Don't you just hate the way they get proprietary about a crime scene?" she remarked, following Franck as he ushered her out onto the open terrace.

"You made the right call," she said. "The head of Japanese whaling speared and left trussed up in a pool? This has Appoghui Terra written all over it. Given which, you can't be anywhere near it. But I'm disappointed to hear it was a girl. I'd have thought Gabriel would have done it himself."

"I doubt he was far away. When the girl left she wasn't alone. She was accompanied by a guest going by the name of Christophe Moulin."

"Is he on tape too?"

"Yes."

"Has to be Gabriel. He wouldn't have wanted to miss the kill. Had to be there to stare into his victim's eyes."

"I wouldn't be so sure about that. There's nowhere to hide in that pool room. If Nakamura had come in and seen someone else, I doubt he'd have stripped off and jumped in."

"So what's your take?"

"I think Gabriel set it up and made sure the weapon was in position. But the girl will have done the rest. She had to get into the water herself to make sure the shot was accurate. Maybe the speargun was left at the bottom of the pool – she stripped off, dived down, snatched it up, and spoiled Nakamura's erotic dream."

Catherine walked to the edge of the terrace and looked down over the side.

"They could have thrown him over here," she remarked. "Nice big splat for the paparazzi before we could erect any sightscreens."

"Not quite as poetic, though."

"That's true, and we know Gabriel to be a very cultivated man."

"And he likes to be discreet."

"I'm sure the management of Le Bristol will thank him for that. Appoghui Terra might not be publicity-seekers, but they're not above a little image management. Shooting heads of industrial corporations might win you the applause of the anarchists but – fortunately for us – it remains generally frowned upon. Standing up for whales, though, is quite a different matter. It won't transform Gabriel into Gandhi, but more than a few will secretly applaud what he's done. He's a smart man. We should have seen it coming."

"Why didn't we?" asked Franck. "And by 'we' I mean 'you'."

"Because that idiot there in the pool didn't keep us informed of his comings and goings. When I'm finished here I'm going straight to the Japanese embassy and I'm going to give them hell. His blood's on their hands, not ours."

She tossed her cigarette over the railing.

"Still, it means we were right to think that Gabriel was in town. Which means you might want to be a little more cautious with your Opera murders. Not to mention paying a little more attention to Clara Santoni."

"I'll keep it in mind," he said. "You need anything more from me?"

"Yes. Get well clear of this place before the media turns up."

"I'll be only too happy to oblige."

He left her fishing in her bag for a new cigarette.

When he reached the hotel's entrance hall he made a brief detour by the concierge's desk. An unmarked brown envelope lay on its marble surface.

"I believe this is for you, sir," said the head concierge, sliding it towards him.

"Thanks," said Franck.

"My pleasure, sir."

They exchanged winks and Franck walked through the revolving door to the street outside.

He headed down avenue de Marigny to where it met the constant flow of traffic and pedestrians up and down the Champs Elysées. He crossed over and walked round the back of the Petit Palais to find a bench far from the crowds. Claiming one for himself, he immediately slid the contents out of the envelope.

They were printouts from the hotel's surveillance system. They were a little blurry, but were in colour. Toshiro Nakamura was easy to recognise as he crossed the marble floor of the entrance hall, smiling at the young woman by his side. Taller than he was, she wore a long blue dress under a light coat, which was open and floated around her. No speargun there. The small handbag over her shoulder could not have held one either. Her hair was blonde and loose, dropping well past her shoulders, but above all obscuring half her face, particularly as she kept it angled downwards – an easy thing to justify when conversing with someone smaller. Franck hoped that the rest of the surveillance tape could provide better shots, but if she knew what she was doing that was unlikely. He glanced at two prints showing Nakamura on other occasions – always in a suit, always with the forward-leaning slant of a man in a hurry. Franck shuffled them to the back of the pack. The next image showed the entrance to the hotel filled with figures, one of whom was circled. A note in the corner of the sheet declared him to be Christophe Moulin, but Franck knew better.

He set aside the print and turned to the next one. It was date-stamped at five past two that morning. The blonde was back in her coat and dress, and had taken the time to blow-dry her hair. She still kept her face away from the camera's prying eye. Not so her companion, though, who was smiling directly at it. Curly hair, an angular chin, a handsome face and an agile frame. Gabriel Agostini, in all his splendour.

But for once, he did not absorb Franck's attention. It was the mysterious woman who troubled him. Blonde, tall, attractive, with bewitching legs and a graceful silhouette, and above all a steady hand and a shooter's eye.

He could think of at least one person who fitted that description.

*

The arrow sank into the target, almost dead-centre.

Clara Santoni seemed unimpressed by her own performance. She plucked another arrow, nocked it, drew her bow, held her position for an instant, and released it. It terminated its short flight, quivering slightly alongside its predecessor.

Franck had called in at the Opera, only to be told that she had gone off for yet more archery practice, leading him to the Paul Gauguin gym.

"I think you've got the hang of it now," he declared.

He was a few metres behind her. He had slid his revolver into his belt at the back of his trousers, just in case. She was handling a potentially lethal weapon, after all.

"Appearances can be deceptive. I still have problems when standing on point or in mid-leap."

"So why bother with the easy stuff?"

"It's like the five positions – you keep working them until they become instinctive, programmed into your muscle memory."

"How about underwater?" Franck asked.

"Sorry?"

"How's your shooting underwater?"

"My what?"

She looked perplexed, which was only to be expected, be she innocent or guilty.

"Let me try another question – when did you last see your cousin Gabriel?"

She shook her head at him angrily.

"Gabriel Agostini is not part of my life. I don't talk about him and I don't talk to him – not willingly, anyhow."

"And you don't do little errands for him?"

"What's this about?" she demanded.

"Gabriel's in town."

This time she did not react – either the news came as no surprise, or was of no matter to her.

"But not for rest and recreation," he continued. "Appoghui Terra carried out an operation yesterday evening. In rue du Faubourg Saint-Honoré. Le Bristol hotel. Ring any bells?"

"I've heard of Le Bristol. Never set foot in it though."

"So that's not you?" Franck had closed the distance between them. He tendered one of the printouts he'd been given at the hotel. The one that showed Nakamura and his young companion returning from their evening out. Clara frowned at it.

"Who's the Japanese bloke?"

"His name is – was – Toshiro Nakamura. It's the name of the elegant girl hanging on his arm that interests me."

"Well it's not Clara Santoni. I've never seen that man before and, like I said, I've never been to Le Bristol, if that's where this was taken."

"Where were you at midnight yesterday?"

"In bed."

"Alone?"

She sighed.

"Remember our conversation about how being single in Paris wasn't a crime? I get the feeling you've changed your mind since then."

"I'll take that as a 'yes'."

"Yes I was alone."

"And before you got to bed?"

"There was a performance of *Giselle* yesterday. Started at half seven, finished at half ten. I left the Opera at eleven or so. Went straight home."

Which would have made it difficult for her to have dinner with Toshiro Nakamura – assuming that was how he had spent his evening before returning to the hotel. He could just as easily have come to the Opera to watch her perform.

"What about the previous evening, Wednesday? You were performing then?"

"No."

"So where were you? I saw you in the afternoon, when you asked me about the second victim. What did you do after that?"

"Met a friend. We had coffee and a chat. I suggested we go to the cinema to see *Etreintes Brisées*. She couldn't, so I went on my own. Then I went home. I don't lead the most exciting of lives, do I?"

"Exciting or not, you lead a life that's very difficult to corroborate," stated Franck. "I need you to come to the ninth arrondissement commissariat with me."

"What, right now?"

"Yes."

"Why?"

"I need your fingerprints."

"And if I refuse?"

"Why would you? You trust me – you've already told me that."

She twisted her lips and began to unstring her bow.

"Pity it's not reciprocated."

Saturday, 23rd May

"They took everything?"

"Everything," confirmed Georges Sternberg. "Their own team arrived about an hour after you'd left. They took everything we'd bagged. They took our notebooks. They took the memory cards from our cameras. They thanked us politely and told us to piss off. I can't say I was surprised. The case is sure to become a diplomatic issue. Japan is very sensitive about the whole whaling thing. They'll probably send someone to liaise with the investigation. The DCRI is just keeping things neat and tidy – which means keeping us out of it."

"Since when did you count as shabby and disorderly?" protested Franck.

"Since I first made your acquaintance, I suspect. At least as concerns anything touching upon Appoghui Terra. Don't worry. I'm not upset about it. I'd rather work with you than with Catherine Vautrin."

It was not much of a compliment, but Franck scarcely registered it anyway. He was thinking about his visit to the ninth arrondissement commissariat the previous evening.

"The thing is, I fed Clara Santoni's prints into the national database yesterday. I wanted to check them against any suspect traces from Le Bristol."

"What – you think it was a family affair? Gabriel and Clara teaming up together to strike a blow for cetaceans everywhere?"

"Let's put it this way – it's a possibility I'd like to eliminate as soon as possible. But I'd have preferred to do so without feeding Clara to the lions."

"By which I take it you're referring to your former colleagues in national security? We'll make a real policeman out of you yet, Franck."

"Maybe, but right now I've got no alternative but to call Catherine and ask her to check the prints."

"Well, you would have," remarked Sternberg, "if I was the kind of person to do what I'm told when someone kicks me unceremoniously out of my crime scene."

"But you're not?"

"What do you think?"

A broad smile spread across Franck's face. Sternberg followed his example.

"What have you got?"

"I've got the prints I lifted from the champagne bottle and the glasses in Nakamura's room. I'd also taken the time to nip down to room 214 and pick up a few there."

"You've scanned them?"

"Of course. I got the obvious hit – Christophe Moulin was indeed Gabriel Agostini – but you probably hadn't added Santoni's prints to the database when I was doing the analysis. Want me to try again?"

"Only if you're not too busy."

"I've just had a promising investigation taken from my caseload. I can spare the time."

It took a matter of minutes. Sternberg logged onto his workstation, located Clara Santoni's prints, pulled up those he had taken from Le Bristol, and did a direct comparison.

"No matches. Disappointed?"

"To tell the truth, I'm probably relieved."

That way, he could leave the mystery woman to the DCRI. He had enough on his plate.

*

It rang again. For the fourth time.

Franck glanced at the screen. It showed the same name as before. Someone was intent on reaching Serge but did not want to leave a message.

It could be an emergency.

He picked up the iPhone.

"Hello, this is Franck Guerin on Serge Morin's phone. Can I help you?"

"Monsieur Morin? Good morning. It's madame Sampaio. I got your note ..."

"This isn't monsieur Morin," interrupted Franck.

"Ah, it's a wrong number. I'm sorry."

"No, no," insisted Franck, speaking quickly to stop her hanging up. "You've got the right number. It's just that monsieur Morin isn't here right now. Would you like me to get a message to him?"

"And you are?" More than a hint of suspicion.

"My name's Franck Guerin. I'm in monsieur Morin's lodge at the Opera. He's just popped out. I answered his phone because I got the impression your call was urgent."

"It is. He left me a note this morning. I checked with the cleaner. She wasn't in yesterday, and I certainly didn't go up either. Can you tell him that?" Although this came as a flood of words, he managed to catch them all. She had a slight accent, but it was not difficult to decipher. Franck was old enough to recall a time when almost all the concierges in Paris were Portugese. Nowadays they came increasingly from Eastern Europe.

"I will," Franck reassured her.

"And if something's missing," she continued, "tell him I'll go and get the police if he wants."

"I'll make sure he gets the message."

"Good. Thank you for taking the call, and sorry to have disturbed you."

"Not at all. You have a good day madame."

"You too monsieur."

She rang off. Franck put Serge's iPhone back on his dressing table.

It took Serge another ten minutes to return. Franck had to open the lodge door to him, as he had a plastic cup of coffee in each hand and a paper bag clenched in his teeth. He bustled past Franck, handing him one of the coffees as he did so, and opened his mouth to let the bag fall onto his dressing table. Two croissants peeked out from it.

"Sorry it took me so long. I smelled the croissants when passing one of the workshops and used what little charm I have to wheedle two of them. Not that I'm allowed croissants myself, but if you don't tell Anne-Laure I might get away with nibbling at one of them."

"Your secret's safe with me." Franck had tried to convince Serge that it would have been easier for them both to walk to the coffee machine, but that would have deprived Serge of an opportunity to demonstrate his hospitality. As a result, Franck found himself kicking his heels in the *étoile*'s lodge for thirty minutes. He should have known that Serge was unable to walk down a corridor inside the Opera without getting caught up in countless conversations.

"Your phone kept ringing," Franck told him. "I ended up answering it, since it was always the same caller. I thought it might be urgent."

"I bet it was van Roon."

"No. A certain madame Sampaio."

"Ah. My esteemed concierge. She hates talking to machines. Won't ever leave a message. Won't have an answering machine herself."

"So you leave her notes?"

"That's right," said Serge. "That's why she called?"

"Yes. She said something about your cleaner not having been in yesterday, and added that she didn't go up either."

Serge nodded, sipping his coffee.

"OK. Thanks for that."

He tore a piece off one of the croissants and popped it into his mouth.

"She also said that she could call the police for you if anything was missing," added Franck.

"She's worth her weight in gold, madame Sampaio. And if you knew her, you'd know that's a lot of gold."

"Has something happened?" Serge clearly felt no need to pursue the subject, but Franck was not so sure. After all, madame Sampaio had called the police, even if she had not known she was doing so.

"No, no. Nothing to worry about. A little misunderstanding, that's all."

"It seems to me that you wanted to know if she or your

cleaner had been in your apartment in your absence. Sophie was killed in her own apartment. Léon Abkarian was strangled in his own office. If you think there's been an intruder in your place, you have to tell me. Our killer's still out there, Serge."

Serge drained his coffee and laid it down.

"I'm sure it's nothing."

He moved over to one of the armchairs arranged around the lodge's fireplace and sat on its arm.

"There wasn't a performance yesterday, so I'd arranged to go out with my faithful hounds and hunting companions." He caught Franck's frown. "The rest of the male cast from *Diana and Acteon*. I took them out to dinner. We were all supposed to go on to a club afterwards, but I couldn't keep up – they're half my age, don't forget – so I bowed out gracefully just before midnight and headed home. When I got in I had the impression things weren't as I'd left them."

"Normally, when an apartment's been broken into, there's not much doubt to be had. A forced lock or broken window is hard to overlook."

"There was nothing like that. No sign of a break-in."

"So what made you think something was wrong?"

"Like I said, it was only an impression. And I may have been a little drunk. Well, tipsy."

"So what was it?"

"It's difficult to say. I felt my place was too tidy. All the drawers were shut. Books were neatly aligned, that sort of thing."

"Was anything missing?"

"Well, I've got a lot of stuff, so I can't be certain, but I checked the really valuable things and they're all there."

"Can I say something that might sound unkind?"

"Feel free, you won't be the first," joked Serge.

"You're caught up in a murder enquiry. You lost your lover to a killer who's still on the loose. Who's chalked up another victim since then. You're working on a new ballet in a race against the clock. You've got a police officer stalking the corridors of the Opera every day. If ever anyone had the right to feel a little paranoid, it's got to be you."

Serge chuckled at Franck's attempt to be sympathetic and understanding.

"I wouldn't have survived twenty years in this company if I wasn't a little paranoid, so don't feel you have to tiptoe delicately around the notion. Anyhow, that's why I left a note this morning for madame Sampaio, asking if she or the cleaner had been in. Since it turns out that neither of them have been anywhere near my place, I think we should just put it down to my nerves. Or maybe to the excellent cognac I had after dinner."

"I could send a team over to see whether your locks have been tampered with," suggested Franck.

"Now don't you start getting carried away, captain. I'm allowed to lose my cool, but you have to remain calm and steady. Too many people are counting on you, me included. And you underestimate madame Sampaio. She's as vigilant as they come. I can't see anyone getting past her."

"Fair enough. Ask her to keep an extra eye out all the same. Tell her to call you if she sees or hears anything strange. And if she does, let me know immediately."

"OK."

"And if you ever get home and think your door has been tampered with, do the same – phone me, and don't go in."

"Who's being a little paranoid now?" asked Serge. He seemed a little embarassed, both by his own reaction the previous evening, and by Franck's concern. He glanced at his watch. "Anyhow, you must excuse me, I've got to go. I promised I'd do some work with a group of *premiers danseurs*. Stay and finish your croissant."

Franck watched him go with the light-footed step he shared with the company's younger dancers.

At least he now had a concrete example of how little importance the *étoiles* attached to locking the doors of their lodges. But that was not uppermost in his mind.

If someone had indeed entered Serge's apartment only to take nothing, it could suggest that the one thing they were looking for had not been there.

Serge himself.

*

"Why doesn't Serge have an understudy?"

"Are you volunteering, captain? It's a bit late in the day."

Franck had tracked van Roon to the main stage, where he was pacing about, marking chalk circles underfoot.

"You've always kept Clara on the boil in case something happened to your leading woman. Why not the same for Serge?"

"I've kept Clara simmering – to borrow your ever-so-poetic metaphor – because I persist in believing that she would make the best Diana."

"Maybe so, but it also means you have a backup."

"I scarcely need to remind you that I've already lost one *étoile*. Statistically speaking, I can't see me losing Lisa too."

"But if you did, you're covered. But not for Serge."

"Serge is indestructible. Ask your friend the Dance Director how many times in his career he's had to bow out of a performance through illness or injury. The answer is twice – in twenty years as an *étoile*."

"It could still happen, though."

"It's a theoretical risk, but a tiny one. Ballet is a lot harder on ballerinas than their partners – they're the ones on points, they're the ones who have to stretch their limbs to the limit, they're the ones who get thrown about. Male dancers do a lot of propping up and a little showing off. That's why Serge is still dancing at forty-nine. If he was a woman he'd have pulled out years ago. Unless he was Margot Fonteyn, of course – but Margot and Rudolf rewrote the rules to suit themselves. And theirs was a different era. They wouldn't have got away with it today."

Franck had no intention of asking van Roon to expand on his historical reflexions. All he was interested in was the here and now – or, rather, the potential near futures it could lead to.

"You're talking about risks confined to these four walls. What if Serge was knocked down crossing the road? More to the point, what if I was determined to stop this ballet taking place? What if I'd already tried by killing Sophie Duval, only to discover I'd done it too soon and Lisa Roux had popped up to take her place? What if I'd also learned that Clara Santoni was in the wings, straining at the leash to replace Lisa at the slightest mishap? What would be my best move?"

"You're telling me you're about to put an armed guard around Serge? That'll help last-minute preparations no end. You don't think you're losing your grip, captain? There are easier ways to kill a ballet than to assassinate its cast. All you have to do is bribe a few critics. I've never tried it, but I doubt they're that expensive. It would be like bribing a scorpion to sting – it's in their very nature. Any fool can applaud, but only a professional can wield ridicule and scorn to mortal effect."

"Let's hope I'm wrong. But for my theory to be baseless, there would have to be some kind of solution to replace him. So, I ask you again, if something were to happen to Serge, who could take his place?"

Van Roon batted the air in front of him, as if swatting aside Franck's persistent question.

"Me, I suppose."

"You could do it?"

"It's a long time since I danced before an audience, and I'm certainly not as agile or as strong as Serge. But I've probably got the same stamina – I am twelve years younger than he is, don't forget – and I have the singular advantage of knowing the steps better than he does. They are mine, after all."

"What about the shooting? You could handle it?"

"You want a demonstration? Now that you know we're using real arrows?"

"I'll take your word for it."

The thought had not previously occurred to Franck, but it ought to have when he had stumbled upon the pair of them rehearsing the previous day – van Roon as Acteon and Clara Santoni as Diana.

If this was van Roon's dream scenario, then perhaps both Serge and Lisa had something to worry about.

*

Franck pushed open the door, stepped inside, held it open, and extended an arm towards Noémie, inviting her to enter. The host moved towards them, his arms wide, his smile professional.

"Good evening. Welcome to Macéo."

"Guerin. Party of two," announced Franck.

"Delighted to have you. May I take your coats?"

Franck stepped aside so that the host could see to Noémie first. She wasn't wearing a coat, but a burgundy velvet shawl with a filigreed border, large enough to drape from her neck to her thighs. She pushed it back from one shoulder and twisted slightly as she gathered it in her arms before handing it over. It was a smooth, graceful move.

Franck handed over his Marco Chiriotti coat, glad to get it off since it was a fine spring evening. Noémie had already remarked upon its clean, angular lines, raising her eyebrows when he had named the designer. It had done its job.

He now stood in his funeral suit, which he had carefully checked for creases. Since he felt it was probably too sombre for the occasion, he had avoided a tie, and gone for a plain light-blue shirt unbuttoned at the collar. He would not turn any heads, but he looked as if he had made an effort, which was all that mattered.

He was certainly in no danger of upstaging Noémie.

She wore a resplendent red dress. Spaghetti straps held a tight-fitting bodice in place, below which a wide ribbon knotted into a generous bow marked the departure point of seven layers of ruffles set at a slight diagonal in alternating light and dark shades, running out half-way down her thighs. An elaborately worked silver chain sat at the base of her neck and three thin bracelets meshed together on her right wrist. A jewelled clasp in her chestnut hair kept it swept back on either side of her head. Her ears, as Franck noticed for the first time, were not pierced.

She nodded appreciatively.

"Nice place."

It was. The restaurant had high walls, massive windows opposite the entrance looking out onto the rear of the Palais Royal, and a stuccoed ceiling whose decorative garlands and cornices dated from the eighteenth century. The floor was polished oak parquet, whose dark tones were repeated by the wicker-backed chairs, the generously sized round tables, and all the other furnishings. A touch of eccentricity was added by the light fittings, constructed out of branches holding up silver platters. Next to the entrance was a more huddled area with circular leather armchairs gathered around low tables, a place for those without reservations. Not for them.

They were seated with their backs to the windows, placed diagonally at their table so that neither would obscure the other's view of the restaurant and its customers. It was a fairly busy evening, but the tables were well-spaced and the ceiling sufficiently distant for conversations to remain distinct and relatively discreet.

"One of your regular haunts?" asked Noémie.

"Not really," said Franck. It was Georges Sternberg, who worked hard at keeping up-to-date with the capital's restaurant scene, who had suggested the place. Franck had never been there before.

"You keep it for when you really want to impress a girl?" she suggested.

"Something like that."

"I'll let you know if it works."

As far as he could tell, it did.

Noémie engaged in a long and detailed discussion with the restaurant's young and very serious sommelier, displaying a familiarity with vintages and *terroirs* that left Franck far behind. She praised every dish that was placed before her, insisting that he taste everything she ordered, since she judged his choices from the menu far too prudent.

It took them two hours, and a bottle of ten-year-old Cornas, to reach dessert. She toyed luxuriously with a pear which had been roasted in salted butter and served with tiny cubes of a caramel-drenched cake. Franck was cautiously working his way through a compote of fennel and apple, an unlikely combination she had convinced him to try.

She had finally succeeded in getting him to talk about himself. Which meant talking about the DST, an organisation whose initials clearly meant nothing to her.

"You were a spy?"

"No. Spies work abroad. That's the DGSE. I was in national security. We looked after France itself. Counter-espionage, counter-terrorism, that sort of thing."

"Sounds exciting. Was it?"

Franck laid down his spoon.

"I suppose it was. It was non-stop. Always a new mission, always a new threat. It was very ... absorbing."

"So why leave?"

"I didn't. Indeed, strictly speaking, I haven't. I'm still a member of the DST, or the DCRI as it's now called. I'm just on secondment to the Brigade Criminelle."

"Inter-departmental cooperation?"

Franck chuckled. His current situation had lasted long enough for him to see the funny side of it.

"More like being sent to the salt mines of Siberia."

"You screwed up?"

"So they say."

"I won't ask how." She placed her right hand on the exposed flesh that ran from the top of her dress to her collarbone. Something Franck would have liked to have done. "Promise."

"Try searching online. It was in the papers."

"You think you'll ever get back?"

"Probably. That said ..."

He did not complete the sentence. To admit that the Brigade Criminelle was not so bad would feel disloyal to his former self, the one who had clutched the DST to his chest with an unswerving sense of vocation. And anyhow, his police ID said 'Brigade Criminelle (temporary assignment)'. There was no point getting too fond of an entity unable to recognise you as one of its own.

Noémie was watching him expectantly.

"I'll wait and see," he continued. "In the meantime, I'm learning a lot. It may sound strange, but homicide investigations are quite an eye-opener."

"Sure. Murders in Paris must be so much more *chic* than anywhere else."

"You'd be surprised." She could not know it, but she was not far wrong as regarded Franck's last two years.

"So what's the news on Sophie Duval – not to mention the Witch Doctor?"

"There is no news. The investigation continues."

He tried to sound upbeat, but apparently did not succeed.

"You've hit a brick wall?"

"Too many possible hypotheses. Too few clues."

"So what do you do in a case like that?"

"Keep hunting. Keep asking questions. Keep on your toes."

"For weeks on end? No one can stay vigilant that long. That's why sentries relieve each other."

"I work alone. I don't have that luxury."

"Then you have to take a break from time to time."

Franck smiled.

"What's this? It's certainly not work."

"I'm glad to hear it."

They left the restaurant at midnight, quickly catching a taxi on the rue de Richelieu.

When they reached Noémie's apartment building Franck waited to see what she would do.

"I've decided that this officially counts as our second date," she announced.

"If you like."

"In which case I get to do this."

She leant over towards him and kissed him slowly on the

lips.

When she finally released him she turned her attention to the driver, who had been watching them impatiently in his rear mirror.

"Take this man home. He needs to rest."

She opened the passenger door and stepped out, gathering her shawl around her. She slipped her phone from her purse and held it up to the window, pointing to it with her other hand.

"Call it," she mouthed, wordlessly.

And with a wink she was gone.

*

Noémie had not been wrong. Franck did need to rest, but sleep was not coming easily.

He lay on his back in his bed, wondering what the future held. Noémie's current stay in Paris would surely soon be coming to an end. Who was to say what – or, more importantly, who – awaited her in Basel. He tried to recall the names she had programmed into her phone before it tumbled so serendipitously at his feet in the metro eight days ago. One had been her mother, but he had forgotten whether a man's name lurked amongst the few others. He should have written them down, but had trusted them to his memory. Normally a faithful companion, it had been too distracted by his fruitless efforts to explain the deaths of Duval and Abkarian to retain them.

He smiled to himself. Normally he would be lying here thinking about the investigation. Given which, he should not be blaming Noémie for keeping him awake, but thanking her for providing a momentary respite from what was proving a frustratingly intractable case.

He reached out for his phone, which he had deposited on his bedside table. He was half-way through texting a message of thanks when he thought better of it and allowed his thumb to erase all he had painstakingly typed. They had said their farewells for tonight. Anything more would seem excessive, as if he was hounding her. True, it could be said that she had done a little of that at the beginning, but there was a time for everything – a time to chase your prey, and a time to lie and rest in the shade. Poor timing had done for Acteon. He was not going to make the same mistake.

He was about to return his phone to its perch when he noticed that he had missed some calls. They must have been made after nine o'clock, as he had switched his phone to silent mode when he arrived at Le Nemours and spotted Noémie waiting for him inside. He checked to see how many – four in total, and all from the same number, one that his phone had recognised.

Lisa Roux had been trying to reach him. She had left a single message after her last attempt. "We have to talk." He thought about calling her back but decided against it. It was past one in the morning. It could wait until tomorrow.

He had enjoyed his own Saturday night; there was no reason to spoil hers.

Sunday, 24th May

"Will you come to the *première* of *Diana and Acteon*?"

Franck had run into Serge Morin as he came through security at the rear entrance to the Opera. They were wandering the backstage corridors together, Franck having explained to him that he was looking for Lisa Roux. Serge told him that they were both due at a costume fitting at ten thirty, and that he thought she would not be in before then. It was a Sunday, after all, and every ballerina deserved a lie-in. With an idle hour and a half before him, Franck was happy to accept when Serge offered to lend him his lodge.

Serge had just pushed open its door – it was unlocked – when he asked his question.

"You think there are still places available?" replied Franck.

"There'd better not be. We haven't sunk a fortune into commissioning a new ballet from Piet van Roon to have empty seats on opening night. Or on any other night, for that matter. Anne-Laure wanted a fresh new piece to pull in the crowds. She's investing for the long-term."

"Are you telling that me the Ballet is a business like any other?" asked Franck. He was surprised to hear such an analysis from Serge. Then again, he had been in the company long enough to think beyond the daily grind of rehearsals, costumes and performances.

"Not yet, but one day it might be. Just look across the Atlantic. The Met auto-finances over half its costs. At best we cover a third. *Diana and Acteon* is supposed to help us improve that figure."

"Well, I'd like to make my own small contribution, but it'll be difficult if all the places are sold."

"You're assuming the box office controls every seat in the house. That's far from true. There have to be some advantages in being an *étoile*, after all. Would you come as my guest?"

This he had not foreseen. Taken unawares, Franck could only stammer something about not wanting to deprive a true ballet fan of a place.

"You'd be doing me a favour," insisted Serge. "I've got too few tickets and too many friends. I can only make a couple of them happy, which means enduring the silent resentment of the rest. But if I give them to a complete unknown in gratitude for his efforts to protect us from whatever curse it is that has fallen upon the Ballet, then nobody's going to complain."

"I really shouldn't," began Franck.

It was true. He really should not. Receipt of gifts and gratuities from a party of interest in an investigation was an *a priori* justification for an internal enquiry.

"Quite the opposite," stated Serge. "You really should. Isn't *Diana and Acteon* at the heart of what's been happening here? Don't you have to see what the killer has been trying to prevent? Don't you have to understand the crime to solve it?"

It was a good argument. Whether or not van Roon's work really was central to the killings, on paper what Serge had just said would make sense. Given which, nobody could criticise him for taking up his offer. And anyhow, Franck was not without curiosity – if only to see the live archery on stage.

"OK. It's a very kind offer, Serge, and I accept it."

"Great. I'll get the places to you tomorrow or the day after. Will two do?"

"Two's one too many."

"You sure?"

Franck paused. His reply had been instinctive, but his thoughts turned to Noémie Berger.

"Well, if you can get two, that would be good," he said.

Serge winked at him.

"I'm glad to hear it, and I'm sure she'll be too."

"Make sure your aim's good. I don't want to be responsible for someone getting pierced by an arrow."

"I can see that turning a date sour. I'll do my best. But I can't speak for Lisa. She's not quite got the hang of it yet. My advice would be to duck every time she draws her bow."

"I hope the tickets mention that attending the performance can be hazardous for your health."

"There's no great art without sacrifice," pronounced Serge.

"Ask van Roon."

"That's easy for him to say. It's you lot who are being offered up, not him."

"Dancers are but puppets who willingly lay their strings in the choreographer's hands. It's our lot. Seriously, though, it should be a great night. You won't regret coming. It's probably the best piece of work van Roon has ever done – and that's saying something. I couldn't have picked a better swansong."

It was a casually spoken phrase, but it jolted Franck.

"Are you serious?"

Serge nodded. He appeared quite serene.

"It had to happen some day. It'll soon be my fiftieth birthday. Van Roon's given me the opportunity to go out on a high. I'll hang on until the end of the season, of course, and that'll give Anne-Laure all summer to work out who'll step into my shoes next year."

"Why now? I thought you were determined to go on as long as possible?"

"So I was, but recent events have got me thinking. Sophie's death will mean we'll have a new female *étoile* sooner rather than later. Why not add a new male one and rejuvenate the Ballet as a whole?"

"You honestly think it needs that? Is this your idea, or Anne-Laure Favennec's?"

"It has nothing to do with Anne-Laure. If anything, she's likely to tell me that this is no time to remove one of the company's long-standing pillars, with all that's happened."

"She doesn't know?"

"Not yet."

"Won't she try to stop you, then, if she thinks the timing is wrong?"

"She can't. I reached the official retirement age for this company seven years ago. I've carried on because I wanted to, and the Ballet was happy for me to do so. All that's required for me to leave today is for one of us to change our mind. It's my decision."

"When will you tell her?"

"Probably after the *première* of *Diana and Acteon*."

"So Lisa Roux's going to have the privilege of dancing with Serge Morin in his last major role?"

"Now you're just flattering me," objected Serge, "but yes, I suppose you could say that."

Unless somebody was dead-set on contesting her that particular honour.

*

"You look incredible."

Lisa Roux turned slowly in front of the full-sized mirror. At first glimpse she appeared to be wearing little more than a collection of fallen leaves, stray vines and patches of moss. The costume team had started with a semi-transparent bodice made of fine muslin onto which they had stitched sufficient woodland vegetation to hide her breasts. They had then added an unconventional tutu angled at forty-five degrees which masked the upper third of her thighs. It was built of ragged layers of green and earth-coloured tulle, which could separate and shift over each other as she moved. Her legs were left bare, but they had embroidered and extended the ribbons of her shoes to look like tendrils spiralling up her calves. Her hair was caught inside an emerald-studded net from the peak of which emerged a small crescent moon.

Serge Morin, who had just complimented Lisa, stood off to one side in short breeches and a tight-fitting leather jerkin. He smiled broadly when he spotted Franck at the far end of the costume workshop and waved him over.

"What do you think?" Serge asked.

"Very striking," said Franck.

Lisa raised an eyebrow at him.

"That's very diplomatic. Unlike Serge, you're commenting on the costume itself – not on how it makes me look."

"Well, to tell the truth, it makes you look like you're almost human, but not quite – it's kind of scary. It's not how I'm used to seeing you, let's put it that way."

"Well done ladies," said Lisa to the three seamstresses who formed a loose group around her. "Judging by the captain's reaction, you've got it just right." She turned back to Franck. "This is the costume for the first act, when Diana and Acteon find themselves hunting in parallel, chasing the same hind with identical movements. This is the goddess of the hunt, with the emphasis on the hunt. In the second act Diana gathers and reviews her nymphs – that's when you'll see the emphasis on the goddess. But you got here too late to see that one."

"How do you find the balance of the tutu?" asked one of the seamstresses. "Since we were going for a disordered effect, you'll probably find it's weighted more to one side than the other."

"You'll have to test it," said another. "Run and leap and spin in it to make sure it's not throwing you off."

"Yes, you're right," agreed Lisa. "I will. Maybe later on? I'd like to have a chat with the captain first."

"No, no, no," she was told. "Do it now. If things have to be changed, we need to know now. Particularly if we have to change the structure of the thing."

"Do you mind?" Lisa asked Franck.

"We'll look after the captain," said one of the women. "Unless Serge wants to take him for a tour?"

Serge shook his head, slipping off his jerkin and placing it neatly on a hanger. "The captain's been wandering about this place for weeks now. It has no secrets for him. And anyhow, I have to go. The fit is perfect, ladies. As ever, I am eternally indebted to you."

He blew them all a kiss, winked at Franck, and skipped out of the workshop.

"I won't be long," said Lisa.

"Take all the time you need," insisted Franck. "I'm in no hurry."

"You could use the stage," said one of the seamstresses. "There's no performance today, and I don't think anybody's out there. That way you can really put it to the test."

Lisa nodded.

“Good idea. It’ll make a change from watching myself in a mirror every time I move.”

And then she was gone.

Franck looked around for a quiet corner. The workshop was large enough to hold four wide workbenches, all of which were covered by half-completed costumes, paper patterns, scattered pins and bolts of fabric. Sewing machines, steam-powered ironing stations, mobile garment racks and haphazardly positioned full-length mirrors made the place a bit of a labyrinth. He had spotted a vacant seat, unburdened by bits of clothing, when one of the seamstresses pointed to his briefcase.

“You’ve lost the stitching at the bottom corner there,” she observed.

This was not news to Franck. He had already lost several pens through the hole, but figured that his briefcase – like himself – should be allowed to show a few signs of age.

“We can fix that if you like.”

“It’s pretty thick leather,” he warned. “It might not be that easy to sew.”

A disdainful snort was all he got in return.

“Hand it over.”

He did as he was told.

*

Two coffees and one repaired briefcase later, Lisa had still not come back. Franck’s patience did not let him down, but the seamstresses proved less easy-going. They wanted to know if her costume could be deemed finished or not. They eventually despatched Franck to go and find her.

The route to the stage was easy to follow. The corridor widened progressively as he got closer to it and then dropped away from him as he stepped out onto its vast surface.

There was no sign of Lisa. Indeed, there was no sign of anybody. Franck advanced across the surface of the stage, heading towards the subdued light of the auditorium.

“Lisa.”

He said her name loudly, but found himself unable to shout. There was a cathedral-like solemnity to the Opera House seen from this angle. The massed ranks of the seats rose before him like an army of angels arrayed in heaven's strict hierarchy. More to the point, legendary voices had sung from where he was standing. It did not seem right to sully the acoustics of the place.

He now stood centre stage, dwarfed by the grandiose architecture around him and stilled by the volume of air it held imprisoned. Lisa had probably headed back to the costume workshop by a different route, arriving just after he left.

The glinting silver moon in her hair revealed her presence. She was in the main seating area, half-way towards the back of the house, draped languorously, her head resting backwards on the top of her seat. Fatigue must have got the better of her, although the wardrobe team was likely to chide her for dozing off with half her tutu trapped beneath her.

Unsure of whether he ought to wake her, given the pressure that she was under with the rush towards the *première* of *Diana and Acteon*, Franck sat himself down on the edge of the stage. He decided he could wait a little longer. Lisa had to be absolutely exhausted to have fallen asleep in such an awkward posture. Despite the prices charged for them, the ground floor seats were not exceptionally comfortable, and were certainly not designed for the angle she had adopted.

Franck's heart suddenly accelerated. Not knowing how to get from the stage to the floor of the auditorium, he pushed himself forward and fell feet first into the orchestra pit, narrowly missing a clump of music stands. He blundered across it and pulled himself up the other side. As he raced towards the row of seats in which she lay he knew that his haste was pointless, but he did not slow down.

Her eyes were open but, unlike the scattering of tiny gems across her hair, they showed no sparkle. Her lower lip was bleeding from where she had dug her teeth into it. He reached out to touch the side of her neck, avoiding the horizontal bruising with which he was now familiar. She was still warm, but her pulse had been squeezed from her.

Franck stood back and looked wildly around him. No movement in the rows of seats behind and to either side of him. No movement on the stage. No movement inside the costumed body of Lisa Roux.

Her dance had come to an end.

*

Five hours had passed.

Georges Sternberg and his team were now clearing up. This was the second Sunday in a row his two technicians had been called out. They were anxious to get home and salvage something from the weekend. Sternberg showed no such concern, and was preoccupied with making sure everything was properly packed away.

The medical examiner had been and gone, authorising the removal of the body, which had subsequently been carried out. The ninth arrondissement commissariat had sent over a small team to help with interviews. Franck had offered a grim welcome to lieutenant Blanchard and two *gardiens de la paix* before unleashing them upon the Opera House's workforce. Fortunately – or unfortunately, in terms of the wealth of testimony to be harvested – there were less of them than usual since no performance had been scheduled that day.

As for Franck, he had drunk three coffees and weathered a mixture of shock, rage and stunned disbelief on the part of those he had talked to.

Anne-Laure Favennec had crumpled.

Quite literally. She had risen when he forced his way into her office, only to tumble into the nearest chair when he told her. Her head dropped to her hands, hiding her expression, her shoulders trembling slightly. But when she looked up again her face showed no trace of tears.

"Two *étoiles*," she said, speaking very slowly and deliberately. "Two *étoiles* in a month. We can't absorb this.

Somebody is trying to destroy us."

"Paranoia is not going to help."

It sounded curt, but he knew she was tough. She could take it. He sat down opposite her and pulled out the pass he had been issued with at the beginning of the investigation.

"I use this to get in here. I flash it at security at the back of the building and waltz through. Makes me wonder just how secure this place is. Apart from the staff entrance at the rear, how many other ways are there to get into the Opera – specifically the auditorium?"

"There's the scenery entrance, but there's security there too. From the front of house the doors are kept locked all the time, except when a guided tour goes through. There are several tours a day, but they're tightly chaperoned – visitors are counted in and counted out."

"In which case the killer probably has one of these," stated Franck, holding his pass in the air.

"It cannot be a member of the company," Anne-Laure shot back. "It's inconceivable."

"Right now, I'm not interested in what is or is not conceivable. I'm interested in what is physically possible. Anyone who was inside the perimeter of this building this morning could have killed Lisa Roux. Until they can prove that they didn't, everyone's a suspect."

"Not the dancers," Anne-Laure stated bluntly.

"Dancers included."

"Me too?"

"You too," insisted Franck. "Where were you from half ten onwards?"

"Here. There. Everywhere. Doing my job, Franck. Watching over the Ballet."

"Was someone with you all the time?"

"All the time? I walk the corridors, I pop into the rehearsal rooms, I talk to the technicians, I take calls, I listen to the dancers, sometimes I even sit down somewhere quiet and think. I probably dealt with dozens of people over the past few hours. How am I supposed to remember who and where and when?"

"Then you're a suspect," stated Franck.

"So be it. That's your plan, is it, Franck? Accuse the entire company, or however many of us were here today and weren't locked up in a sealed room with reliable witnesses? That'll get you far, and it'll do wonders for morale. I have to present *Giselle* tomorrow evening and I can't do it with a dance troupe you've crushed underfoot."

"Cancel the performance. Doesn't Lisa deserve that?"

"She deserves a lot more than that. She deserves us to dance for her."

Serge Morin had shaken his head, his eyes tired, his mantle of exuberant vitality slipping from him to reveal his age.

The news had reached him before Franck did. Three young dancers were with him in one of the rehearsal rooms. They sat on a bench, huddled up against each other, while he knelt on the floor before them. He was speaking to them in a low, reassuring tone. He made a sign to Franck, asking him to wait outside, and came out to him a few minutes later. The two of them sought refuge in one of the storage rooms used by the costume department. Racks of elaborately stitched dresses took up most of the space. Ghostly tutus hung in the air above them.

"Fear is seeping in," said Serge. "Sophie's death was taken to be an accident, a one-off. Since nobody knew about the potential connection with Abkarian, his murder went unnoticed. But now with Lisa – and right here, in our midst – we're on the verge of panic. This place is a home to the creative, to the sensitive, to the imaginative – you can well imagine what they're starting to think. Isn't there some statement you could make to reassure them?"

"Frankly, they'd be wrong not to be worried. Let's hope it makes them think long and hard about what they might have seen this morning."

"You're going to interview everybody?"

"Yes. Nobody can go until they've talked with an officer."

"You want to do me? Now?"

"Are you up to it?"

Serge looked down at his feet. It took him a few seconds to raise his head again.

"Probably not. Who is? Go ahead."

"Where did you go when you left the costume workshop?"

"I'd promised the boys who make up Acteon's hunting troop to walk through the ensembles with them."

"The dancers you were talking to back there?"

"That's some of them. Turns out that they weren't all free, so I rounded up who I could, worked with them, and then did the same again with another bunch."

"While you were moving about backstage, did you see anything suspicious? Anyone who looked out of place?"

"No, not at all. Then again, I wasn't looking for anything suspicious."

"Yes, but you've been here forever. You know every face in this building – the dancers, the support staff, the maintenance people, the guy who restocks the coffee machine."

"I suppose that's true," he conceded.

"So did you see anyone you didn't recognise?"

"No, I didn't." Serge paused. "That's not good news, is it?"

"Not really."

Piet van Roon had bunched his fists, cursed in what presumably was Dutch, and hammered them repeatedly on the desktop before him.

He had not heard – partly because he was hidden away in a tiny office, and partly because no one had dared to tell him.

"What next?" he demanded. "Will the place burn down on opening night?"

Franck sat across from him, pausing before replying.

"I can see you're very upset. Would you like a tissue?"

Van Roon sighed, glanced around the room, and then leant forward towards Franck.

"I can't help Lisa. She's dead. I can't bring her back. People die. Life goes on. When it's my turn, it'll be the same thing. I have a ballet to stage. I've invested a chunk of my life in it.

The Opera has invested a fortune in it. Dancers have invested months of toil in it."

"None more so than Lisa Roux."

"Not true," objected van Roon. "Sophie Duval did all the groundwork."

"I don't recall you mourning her very convincingly either."

"You forget – I'm not part of this company. I didn't grow up here. I didn't learn my art here. I'm a hired hand, moving from country to country, from ballet to ballet. Lisa, Sophie, Serge, Clara – they're resources put at my disposal. They're not my friends. They're not my flock. If you wish to see a mentor's tears, try Anne-Laure Favennec, but you cannot ask them of me."

"OK, so let me ask you this – where have you been all morning?"

"Here," said van Roon, sweeping his hand over the pile of sketches and notes on the desk before him.

"Since when?"

"I don't know. Nine, maybe. I've been rethinking some of the set design."

"Alone?"

"Do you see anyone else here? More to the point, do you know anyone else who could do this other than me?"

"You didn't consult with anybody? You didn't call in anyone from the set workshops?"

"No. I'm not interested in their explanations about why something I want can't be done, or is too expensive, or is too late. I can't do choreography without a dancer, but I can sketch without a carpenter."

"So no one can vouch for you," stated Franck.

"Vouch for what?"

"That you didn't leave here. That you didn't follow Lisa onto the main stage. That you weren't there when it happened."

"That I didn't do it myself?" continued van Roon scornfully. "Why would I sabotage my own ballet? Why would I create a crisis mere days before the *première*?"

"Why indeed," agreed Franck, in his flattest, most neutral

voice.

Because danger focuses the mind. Because difficulty is to be worshipped. Because a replacement was ready to hand.

Clara Santoni had hidden herself away. Franck found her, sombre and subdued, sitting on the stairs of an emergency exit. She smiled weakly at him.

"Can I join you?"

"I don't think I'm particularly good company right now," she warned him.

"I'd be disappointed if you were."

She moved over to allow him to sit beside her.

"Who told you?"

"Security at the rear entrance."

"You were leaving?"

"No, I was coming back. I tried out my costume bright and early this morning. Afterwards I went out to the gym for some shooting practice. Sort of dawdled coming back. Stopped in at a café. Almost wish I'd never left it."

"You'd have heard, one way or another," Franck pointed out.

"But not coming back. Not coming through the gate with a big smile on my face. Not coming home."

"Coming home?"

She cocked her head to one side, as if listening to the vanishing echo of the words Franck had just repeated.

"This has always been my enchanted palace," she said. "Despite the exhausting schedules, despite the bitching and the in-fighting, despite the aches and the injuries, despite the ridiculous hierarchy, despite it all – this was the only place I ever wanted to be. A little girl's dream with costumes, music, lights, applause, the sense of being part of history, of belonging to a family that includes the great names of the past. This is the centre of my world – the only world I ever wanted to live in."

She swallowed and looked at her feet. Franck waited for her.

"It's like a cloud has come over the sun. A big, black cloud.

And suddenly it's gone cold and there's a sense of menace. Maybe there is worse to come. Maybe things will never be the same again."

"I'm sorry," said Franck. She was no longer thinking about Lisa, but about herself. Her own fears had taken precedence. She was not mourning a fellow dancer. She was mourning a paradise that was perhaps lost forever. He stretched an arm across her shoulder, prepared to forgive her inability to step back from her own concerns. She was twenty-six, after all. Not an age at which the self easily relinquishes its grip.

"And, to tell the truth, I'm not sure I can do it," she added in a low voice, nestling against him.

"Do what?"

"Diana."

Franck's arm stiffened, but he did not move it.

"Piet believes in me," she continued. "He has done since the start. And I know I should trust his judgement – he's notorious for being coldly clinical, after all. But I just don't know. It's a really tough part, and whoever dances it at the *première* will define it for a long time to come. I could make this ballet or I could break it. If I screw it up, I'll carry it around my neck for years."

"And if you don't screw up?" he asked delicately, as if walking on glass.

She leant forward, cupping her hands around her feet.

"If I don't ..."

She made a low whistling sound, like an athlete about to refill her lungs for a determined effort. Her voice took on a new inflexion. A hint of desire and excitement.

"... they'll have to make me an *étoile*."

Monday, 25th May

"Get in."

It was a black Peugeot 607, brand new, long-nosed with slant-eyed headlights. The President had one just like it, except that his folded open at the back so that he could play the reigning monarch and wave at the crowds. Catherine Vautrin, unsurprisingly, preferred to hide herself from their gaze.

Franck did as he was told, walking round to the opposite side of the car and getting in through the rear door. Catherine's driver pulled away before he had succeeded in shutting it behind him.

"Are we in a hurry?" asked Franck.

"Don't want you to be late for work," she said. "The bodies are piling up."

"In which case, you can drop me off on the quai de l'Horloge."

Georges Sternberg's forensic laboratory was on the opposite side of the Ile de la Cité from the offices of the Brigade Criminelle. It took no more than a few minutes to walk there from the quai des Orfèvres, but since he had a chauffeur, he might as well make the most of it.

"I hear that the night sky has become ever more sombre – yet another *étoile* no longer twinkling," observed Catherine.

"It shouldn't bother you. You always preferred the cover of darkness."

"That's true, but I suspect the Opera Ballet doesn't share my tastes. It's all about glittering costumes and dainty limbs caught in spotlights doing impossible things."

"They're not so dainty, actually," interjected Franck. "The *corps de ballet* would put most of your team to shame."

The driver scoffed his disagreement. Catherine glared at him via the rear-view mirror. He shifted down slightly in his seat. He was there to drive. Full stop.

"My point is, that the Ballet needs its *étoiles*. All of them. And now there are two spots to fill."

"I don't think they'd take you, Catherine, you're not tall

enough. And they're very strict about smoking inside the Opera House."

She had a cigarette smouldering in her right hand.

"I'm crushed. But that way there's less competition for the other candidates. So tell me, Franck, how exactly is the birth of a new *étoile* proclaimed?"

Clearly she already knew, but he would play her game anyway.

"After the curtain has come down and the dancer has just put in an extraordinary performance."

"Would the *première* of a challenging new ballet by the leading choreographer of the day count?"

"I thought you weren't following Clara Santoni."

"That doesn't mean I'm not taking an interest."

"I didn't know you were a ballet fan."

"Oh, there are still some things you don't know about me, Franck, and it's probably just as well for you. But, I admit, I'm more interested in *la petite* Clara's genes than in her gyrations."

"You have a theory you want to share with me?"

"I don't see the sylph-like Clara strangling two fellow ballerinas and that old rogue Abkarian."

"Every single dancer in that place packs ten times more muscle than fat," insisted Franck. "Physically, she could do it – no question about it."

"That I don't doubt, but mentally?" She extended her hand and tapped lightly on Franck's forehead, bringing her burning cigarette perilously close to his eye. "Have you ever strangled someone?"

He had not, but it was not inconceivable that Catherine might have at some stage in her murky past.

"Up close and personal," she continued. "It's not easy. Now, her versatile cousin Gabriel – a man of many talents – he's probably done it once or twice."

"Why would Appoghui Terra be going after ballerinas? I don't think they pose a major threat to the future of the planet."

"I don't want to cast aspersions on your idol, but who's to

say Gabriel Agostini doesn't have feet of clay? Are you sure he's above giving his little cousin's career a helping hand? Two helping hands, to be precise, with a thin cord pulled taut between them. He is Corsican, after all, which is just another way of saying Italian – and we know how sacred family is to the Italians."

"You underestimate him. You always did. No matter how hard it is for you to believe, he is a man of principle."

"Sure. You want to know the estimated bodycount for Appoghui Terra for the past year? Twelve. That's one a month, Franck. Regularity must be one of his principles. It's a pity clemency isn't."

"Were any of them unconnected with his ecological crusade?"

"No," she admitted. "But once you've lost all respect for human life, it's hard to police the boundaries."

That was rich. Coming from her.

*

"She fought back."

"How do you know?"

"On the two previous victims the ligature marks were clear and neat. Once the cord was in place it didn't move, other than inwards, biting into the flesh and crushing the windpipe. The rest of the neck wasn't touched. We have finger marks where they tried to pull it off, but that's all."

"Not on Lisa?"

"No. There are friction burns on her neck and quite a bit of torn skin. I'd guess the killer's first attempt failed – he got the cord around her neck but she moved before he could tighten it. Whether she actually got away, or the ligature just slipped across the surface of the skin, it's impossible to say. What's for sure, is that he tried again and succeeded."

"How many loops?"

"In the final, fatal attack there were three, starting right at the base of the neck and ending half-way up."

"Three millimetres wide?"

Georges Sternberg nodded.

"The bulge?"

"Right where you'd expect it to be – a widening of the ligature mark just off-centre on the second loop around the neck. Three and a half centimetres long and six millimetres wide, give or take our margin of error."

"Any other damage to the body?"

"Grazing on the front of the left knee. She may have tried to run and fallen on it. Aside from that, no evidence of any blows. Her costume can tell us a little, though."

"It caught something?" asked Franck. If it could provide some hair, fibres or flakes of skin it could be their first real breakthrough.

"Not as far as we're aware. It's not the smoothest of surfaces, so it's painstaking work. We've taken the tutu to pieces – that's a lot of pieces – and are processing them all. But it's yielded nothing so far."

"So what has it revealed?"

"The bodice was made of a very thin and loosely woven fabric. It got torn around her waist. An uneven rip made by pulling, not cutting. I think he got his arm around her and she twisted out of his grasp. Local stretching of the fabric between his arm and her body was so intense it tore it open."

"So Lisa ran and fought, possibly in that order."

"Whereas Sophie Duval and Léon Abkarian just stood or sat there and let themselves be strangled," observed Sternberg.

"They weren't expecting it. She was."

"Which is not particularly surprising. She knew about the two previous victims. Once she saw a cord, or a yo-yo, or whatever, in the guy's hands, she knew what was coming."

"But what if it was more than that? What if she had worked it out? What if she saw the killer coming towards her and knew that's who he was?"

"If she knew, wouldn't she have told you?" objected Sternberg. "You were there with her right before it happened."

"But we weren't alone. She might not have wanted to voice

her suspicions with others around, just in case she was wrong. Let's face it, she couldn't have found some kind of definitive proof ..."

"Unless she's better at our job than we are."

Franck ignored the interruption.

"... so it was a subject she could only broach in confidence."

"Why didn't she drag you off into a corner as soon as she saw you, then?"

"Because she was in the middle of trying on her costume. And she was told she had to put it through its paces right away, so off she went."

"What, she was killed by the *Diana and Acteon* production schedule?"

In a sense, what Sternberg had just said was true. It was a sobering thought.

"With a little help from someone with two hands," insisted Franck.

"And two yo-yos," interjected Sternberg.

"And a robust cord three millimetres in diameter with a bulge in the middle."

Sternberg let the correction stand, for the moment. He was sticking with his hypothesis until a better one came up.

"Who has an alibi?" he asked.

"Favennec and Morin were the busiest but even they could have sneaked away on their own onto the stage if they'd wanted to. Van Roon admits he was alone all the time. As for Santoni, she was outside the Opera when it happened. At least, that's what she says. All that's sure is that she came back after Lisa's body had been found. There's no way of proving definitively when she left."

"Well, at least you're down to four prime suspects."

Franck snorted.

"You mean I haven't managed to widen the investigation beyond the walls of the Opera. But if narrowing's what you want, I can go one better. Neither Favennec nor Morin could have killed Sophie Duval because they were both at the reception for the American Friends where she was supposed to join them. Neither Favennec nor van Roon could have killed Léon Abkarian because they were at the gala at the Theatre de la Ville. So the only person who could in theory have killed all three is Clara Santoni."

Unless, of course, Catherine Vautrin was right and her cousin had provided a helping hand.

"So why isn't she sitting in an interrogation room right now?" asked Sternberg.

"Just because she could doesn't mean she did. Did nobody ever teach you the difference between a necessary and a sufficient condition?"

"I was a poor student. That's why I ended up cleaning up crime scenes. Manual labour was my only option."

*

It was an indictment of the investigation.

To be in a lodge in the Opera House, doing the same thing, for the same reason, but for a different victim.

It did not feel good.

Franck sat on the chaise longue in Lisa Roux' lodge, wondering where to start and what, indeed, he should be looking for. He gloved up and opened the drawers in her dressing table, emptying them item by item onto its flat surface. Nothing struck his eye.

He moved on to the wardrobe that stood behind the door. A dark blue raincoat, a pair of running shoes, a pair of low-heeled pumps, and a pair of suede ankle boots. Four t-shirts, neatly folded on top of a v-necked cashmere sweater and a hooded grey sweatshirt. Several sets of cotton underwear. Two large towels. A cosmetics bag which contained nothing other than make-up. A folder with assorted papers to do with Ballet business. Her handbag and, stuffed alongside it, a stiff carrier bag that should not have been there.

Franck extracted the thick-walled paper bag. He laid it on its side on top of the chaise longue and slid its contents out, one by one. A framed photo of Sophie and Serge, a set of keys, an autographed photo of Nureyev, and Sophie's scrapbook.

This was the bag that Piet van Roon had promised he would pass on to Serge. Somehow it had ended up in Lisa's possession. That Serge might have given it to her seemed unlikely – he would have taken out his keys, and surely he would have kept the photo of himself dancing with Sophie. It looked like van Roon had not carried out the instructions he had been given.

Franck carefully placed the four items back inside the carrier bag. These he had to keep. He then moved on to Lisa's handbag.

It was not the first time he had gone through a woman's handbag, so he knew what to expect. Loose change, a purse that should have held it, several keys hooked on a ring that ran through the nose of a tiny stuffed bull, a packet of tissues, a mobile phone, a foil sheet of paracetamol tablets, a notebook full of chaotic scribbles, a metro pass, a powder compact, mascara, a tube of lipstick which had lost its cap, a colourful assortment of cards with the contact details of various professionals, two pens, and – once again – some things that should not have been there.

They had been wrapped in tissues, around which she had looped two elastic bands in an attempt to make a tiny package that would hold its contents together. Franck counted three vials of transparent liquid, an unused syringe with a securely capped needle, and two differently shaped pills.

They all looked very familiar.

*

"Remember this?"

Van Roon was sitting on the floor in the Lifar rehearsal studio hunched over a sketchbook balanced on top of his two knees. Given his height and gauntness, he looked like a hungry vulture. He lifted his head, frowned at the large paper bag Franck was holding up, and then turned back to the drawing he had been working on.

"No."

"Three days ago I left it with you and asked you to pass it on to Serge Morin."

Franck advanced as he spoke until he was in front of van Roon. He dropped to his knees so that he could look at him over the top of his sketchbook.

"You're in my light, captain."

"No. I'm in your face. Why didn't you do what I asked?"

Van Roon sighed theatrically and laid his pencil on the floor, raising his eyes to meet Franck's.

"You delegated delivery of the bag to me. I did the same thing. I gave it to Lisa Roux and told her to give it to Serge."

"She didn't."

"That was very bad of her, but I don't think there's much we can do to punish her for it now."

"Do you work on being so cold, or does it just come naturally to you?" demanded Franck.

"Nature or nurture – a vast debate. And if it did come naturally to me – if I had the misfortune to be born borderline autistic or with Asperger's syndrome, wouldn't it be an act of cruelty on your part to constantly remind me of it?"

"Not really. It couldn't hurt your feelings if you didn't have any."

"Good point, captain. But to answer your question, no, I don't endeavour to be cold. I endeavour to be focused. Right now I'm tweaking the costume for Diana. Since we have to make another one – your forensic colleagues having carried off the original – I thought I'd take the opportunity to make a few improvements. Quite why discussing the tardy delivery of a paper bag is more important than this, I cannot see."

"You don't see much outside your own little world, do you?"

"I see you getting increasingly frantic because you can't solve this case and stop the killing."

Touché.

Tuesday, 26th May

"EPO, PFC, growth hormone, a tab of amphetamine and a beta-agonist. Aside from a few missing items, it's exactly what Sophie Duval had."

"Single doses, though," observed Yves de Chaumont. "Isn't that rather surprising?"

They were in the *juge d'instruction*'s office. Almost a week had passed since their last briefing. Plus a corpse. Plus another corpse, if Toshiro Nakamura counted, which Franck was sure he did not, despite the DCRI's theories.

"There was a syringe. Maybe she carried one day's prescription with her at a time."

"And you're sure they were hers?"

"We have prints – just like with Sophie," said Franck. "If you combine the partial prints on the vials you come up with Lisa's right thumb."

"Anyone else's?"

"There's a single partial that could be Abkarian's."

"Could?"

"Apparently there's not enough of it to narrow it to just him, but it certainly could be his."

"Sisters in dance, sisters in crime – is that what you're saying?"

"Except that it wouldn't actually have been a crime to use these substances," added Franck. "But it's a possibility."

"So Lisa Roux' indignant defence of Sophie's reputation against the very notion that she might have been using drugs was also a means to cover herself?"

"Could be."

"So did the coroner find any trace of needle use around her veins? Any of the suspected substances in her blood?"

"No," admitted Franck.

"And yet, if she was carrying her daily dose about with her, that would suggest she was in a phase of intense use – with this new ballet she'd been drafted into coming to a head. What you're saying is that the only thing we can prove is that the dope was in her lodge, not in her body. It sounds an awful lot like a plant."

"If so, she planted it – her fingerprints, her handbag, her lodge."

"Her lodge? Behind a door that was probably never locked?" objected Yves. "But let's stick with the fingerprints for the moment and assume you're right – she did plant it. And let's assume Sophie did the same. But let's also assume that neither of them ever actually used the drugs in question."

"That wouldn't make much sense. Why would they both deliberately stash drugs that they didn't use – drugs that you can't get in your neighbourhood pharmacy – drugs that in all likelihood passed through the hands of Léon Abkarian – drugs that could destroy their careers if found?"

"I don't expect you got involved in much narcotics work in your time with the DST?" asked Yves.

"Well ...," began Franck.

"No," Yves cut in. "I don't want to know. You lot were entirely capable of running heroin into the projects in the suburbs if you thought it would keep them in check. Just answer this – how does a neighbourhood dealer work?"

"Buys in bulk, sells in small quantities, keeps his customers hungry while he keeps them supplied, recruits new ones whenever he can."

"And doesn't touch the stuff himself," Yves added.

"What, you're suggesting that Sophie and Lisa were dealing inside the Opera?"

"A niche market – 150 dancers – but given the demands on them, and their own level of ambition, you could aim for a high recruitment rate. Particularly if you were one of their own, if you'd reached the height of their profession and suggested that you'd got there thanks to what you were pushing."

"Sophie and Lisa didn't have the training to be credible prescribers," insisted Franck. "Only Abkarian did."

"So put yourself in doctor Abkarian's shoes. Sporting bodies are cracking down, reinforcing tests, not hesitating to ban the biggest stars in their fields. Even the Tour de France –

where doping has been an open secret for decades – starts proclaiming that it intends to clean up its act. He needs to find new markets. The world of ballet is above suspicion. No checks are carried out, no questions are asked. But it's a closed world, suspicious of outsiders and largely inaccessible. He'd need somebody on the inside."

"Abkarian providing the goods and the advice, with Sophie and Lisa acting as his saleswomen and go-betweens? Abkarian lying to me when he said Lisa Roux threatened him, and her doing the same when she confirmed it?" Franck was sceptical, but prepared to follow Yves' train of thought. "It would explain the fingerprints – he makes up bulk packets for them, they split them up again for individual customers, whose prints don't figure because what we've found hasn't reached them yet."

"And then all three are killed."

"But why? Some kind of territorial war? We're saying it was a niche market, hard for Abkarian to break into. We now have to imagine someone else doing so as well?"

"Why assume it was the work of a rival supplier? Why not that of someone who wanted to weed them out before they choked the entire institution?"

"A true believer, ready to kill to defend the Ballet," added Franck.

"Sound like anyone you know?"

"Anne-Laure Favennec has alibis for both Duval's and Abkarian's murders. She couldn't have done it."

"Are you sure? Your descriptions of her lead me to believe she's a very determined woman. Look how quickly she set up the bribe for Abkarian, which might have been intended to buy something other than his simple silence."

"What are you suggesting?"

Yves shrugged.

"I don't know, Franck. I'm just saying – where there's a will, there's often a way."

*

"You've met her. You know what she's like."

Serge Morin seemed slightly puzzled at Franck's request to tell him about the real Anne-Laure Favennec.

"I know what she seems to be like," explained Franck. "I know how she wants the public to perceive her. But, beneath all that, who is she?"

Serge let loose a low whistle and sat back in his seat. They were in the Café de la Paix, a stone's throw from the Opera itself. Franck had insisted they come there, ostensibly to get some decent coffee, but really in the hope that Serge would feel more at ease talking about the Ballet's imperious head outside the walls of her domain.

"I'm not sure anyone knows," said Serge. "She may turn out to have been the Ballet's most important Dance Director in living memory. She's enriched the repertoire, she's brought a heightened set of purpose to the company, she's paid great attention to the training and coaching of the young dancers, she's established a trend in corporate sponsorship that'll leave us less susceptible in the future to the ups and downs of public financing, and she's faced down the backstage unions on several occasions. All that in eight years. If she carries on that way for the next seven – assuming she'll retire at sixty-five – then she'll have assured the Ballet's place amongst the greatest companies in the world for some time to come."

"You're not answering my question," objected Franck.

"Actually, I am. If you set out to achieve all that, how much time do you think is left for a private life, a hidden sphere where you can be your true self?"

"Not much, I imagine. But that doesn't mean that the inner person just withers away and disappears."

"Oh, I wouldn't be so sure. When you're onstage in a role – you're in costume, you're made up, you're performing the steps – you're completely caught up in it. You're not thinking about your leaking radiator, or the wedding you've been invited to, or what you might get your mother for her birthday. You're too busy being prince Siegfried or Jean de Brienne or whoever. You don't return to earth until the performance is over. But Anne-Laure is onstage all the time."

"Fair enough," conceded Franck. "But what about before? She was fifty when she was named Director. She'd lived more than half her life by then. More to the point, she'd had a successful career as a dancer. You knew her then, Serge. Who was she?"

Serge toyed with their empty espresso cups for a minute.

"That was a long time ago," he said. "When she was named an *étoile*, I was probably eighteen or nineteen, I'd only been in the *corps de ballet* for a few years. In those days the hierarchy was a lot more rigid. You didn't speak to the elite dancers unless you were spoken to. Things have changed a lot – and for the better – since then. It's funny, actually, because Anne-Laure has constantly pushed the *premiers danseurs* and *étoiles* to help and encourage the *corps de ballet*. But in her time, she was very aloof."

"Any reason why?"

"She was too busy hunting down her own imperfections to have any patience with ours. People used to be scared to dance with her."

"She was very critical?"

"No, she was silently contemptuous, which was worse."

"You didn't like her?"

"I was young, enthusiastic, living my dream, dancing my heart out, ..."

"Not much has changed," observed Franck.

Serge smiled ruefully and shook his head.

"More than you can imagine. More than even I realised, up until recently." He paused, and seemed on the verge of taking the conversation in a quite different direction. He offered Franck a brief glimpse of something melancholy and then caught hold of himself. "Anyhow, given all that, I didn't try very hard to make Anne-Laure like me. She didn't cut a very attractive figure."

"And yet I've seen photos. She was very pretty."

"Well of course! Can you name many unattractive

ballerinas who have risen to the top of their profession? Classical ballet is a fantasy world. Even the villainous bit parts go to the slim and shapely. But – despite my notorious inability to resist female beauty – that's not what I meant. There was something frightening about Anne-Laure. She represented what you might become if you really did hand your soul to Terpsichore."

"Should I know who that is?"

"Our muse. If you know where to look, you can find her on the ceiling of the Grand Foyer."

"How long was Anne-Laure an *étoile*?"

"Eight years. She left when she was thirty-six, much to the relief of some."

"The other dancers?"

"No – the man who held the place she currently occupies. You might have heard of him. A little-known Russian who went by the name of Rudolf Nureyev."

"They didn't get on?"

"That would be something of an understatement. Anne-Laure had been an *étoile* for four years when Nureyev was appointed Dance Director. For most of us, it was as if Apollo himself had descended amongst us."

"For her?"

"She lashed out at him for spending only six months a year in Paris, for touring elsewhere on his own, for delegating many of his duties. By not giving himself unreservedly to the company, she saw him as betraying it. Worst of all, in her eyes, was his insistence on dancing."

"Didn't he dance till the end, Nureyev? Right up till his death?"

"Yes, he did." Serge paused, looking sombre. "It's a hard thing to say of a man who is one of the great ballet legends, but he did himself a disservice by his refusal to bow out. That said, look at me – I'm forty-nine. I'm the same age he was when Anne-Laure was castigating his dancing."

"But she's never had a problem with you," Franck pointed out.

"If I'd ever failed to pull off fifteen *grandes pirouettes* in a row, I'd soon have been shown the door. That's why I'm going to retire before it happens to me."

"You said it yourself, though – she's not going to be happy when she hears about it. You're in better shape than Nureyev was."

"I'm not dying of AIDS, captain. It helps."

"She didn't cut him any slack for that?" asked Franck.

"Of course not. Nureyev denied it for years, but we could all see there was something wrong with him. Even had she known, she wouldn't have cared. Diseases, infirmities, broken hearts and family bereavements – these are your problems, as far as Anne-Laure is concerned. They should not become the Ballet's. Look at the way she dealt with herself. She was still a great dancer at thirty-six. She could have gone on, for a few years at least. She wouldn't even consider it. She decided that she had reached her peak and that she wouldn't inflict her decline upon the company."

"What happened then?"

"She went into management – unlike others I could name, she didn't have any illusions about her abilities as a choreographer. She started with regional dance companies and then moved on to the Ministry of Culture. She was waiting for her chance to take the top job, which finally came in 2001. And that brings us up to now."

It was Franck's turn to play with the cups and spoons on the tabletop.

"I've still not answered your question, have I?" remarked Serge.

"Sometimes the absence of an answer is an answer," concluded Franck. "What you're saying is that Anne-Laure Favennec has never wavered in her progress from neophyte to high priestess. That in the cause of ballet there's no compromise she'll consider, no conflict she'll avoid, and no sacrifice she won't make."

Be it of herself, or of others.

Be they her victims, or her pawns.

*

"How's Clara shaping up under the pressure?"

"She's a very brave young woman. Thankfully, she's also very far-sighted, as is Piet van Roon. She knows the role by heart. All she requires is the courage and the conviction to dance it."

Anne-Laure had recovered well since he last saw her. She was facing down adversity, rallying what remained of her troops around her standard.

He had found her in the Petipa rehearsal studio with what looked to be the lowest, youngest rank of the *corps de ballet*. The *coryphées* – or maybe the *quadrilles* – he had still not quite mastered the terminology. She had been leaning against one of the bars which ran round the room, watching them go through their paces under the direction of an assistant dance master. She was being ostensibly present, neglecting the ringing phone in her office, avoiding her assistant. She was intently communicating the fact that everything would go on as before.

He could not help admiring her performance. If it was sincere, it was heartening. If not, it was still impressive.

She made Franck stand silently by her side for ten minutes before agreeing to follow him. They went into the Nureyev studio, the semi-circular twin of the one van Roon had commandeered for *Diana and Acteon*. They remained standing.

"Will she be named *étoile* when the curtain goes down on the *première*?" asked Franck.

"I see you've learned a little about our traditions. But not enough. Only two people know about such a promotion beforehand – myself and the Director of the Opera. I trust you won't be offended if I tell you it's not a subject I'm prepared to discuss with you."

"You'd be happy to see her slip into Sophie's and Lisa's shoes? Even though they're still warm?"

"That's grotesquely unfair. Clara would gladly hand back

the role of Diana if it would bring Lisa or Sophie back to life."

"Would you want her to?"

"Of course!"

"You'd rather have Sophie and Lisa alive, despite their association with Léon Abkarian, despite the fact that they both brought drugs into this place?"

"Now you're being unfair to Lisa. She might have been Sophie's friend, but she had nothing to do with the drugs or with Abkarian. You saw her reaction when she heard about them – she was so shocked that she refused to believe it."

"You never asked me what I found when I went through Lisa's lodge yesterday," said Franck.

"I'm trying to run a ballet company in the middle of the biggest crisis of its history. I didn't realise I was supposed to oversee your investigation as well."

"Maybe. Or maybe you didn't need to be told."

"I have no idea what you're talking about. Stop dancing around me, Franck. Your footwork is clumsy. It's very irritating."

"The same drugs we found in Sophie's lodge turned up in Lisa's. In smaller quantities, but exactly the same, and there's every reason to believe they too were supplied by Abkarian."

She turned from him, raising her hand to cover her mouth. When she removed it, white marks remained where she had squeezed the blood from her skin.

"I should never have listened to you. After Sophie you told me to hold back, not to launch a crusade. Not to have everyone tested. Not to turn the Opera upside down until I was sure it was clean. And now you're telling me Lisa ..." She took a deep breath. "I have to know how far this goes. I'm going public with it."

It made no sense. Not if she was the killer. If she was behind the deaths of Sophie, Lisa and Abkarian, it was to preserve the company, not to rub its dirty laundry in the public's face.

"Not yet," insisted Franck.

She laughed bitterly.

"I've heard that before, Franck. Two dead *étoiles* ago, to be exact."

"What if I told you neither Lisa nor Sophie ever used the drugs found in their lodges?"

"How can you? I thought they were impossible to detect?" she objected.

"If you time the doses correctly, then they are. But both were training for the *première* of a challenging new ballet while still dancing the rest of the repertoire. They ought to have been in a phase of intensive use if they were doping themselves. All the more so as neither had any reason to expect a blood screening. And yet we found nothing in the autopsies. The odds against both of them timing their doses just right so as to come through an unscheduled test clean are too high."

"So what were they doing with them?"

Franck did not want to say it. He needed to preserve what credibility he could in her eyes. But aside from an outright lie, he had no alternative. Yves' drug-ring hypothesis only made sense when posited as a target for eradication by Anne-Laure or someone like her.

"I don't know."

She slumped against the wall behind her, looking at him as if he was a source of constant disappointment.

"I've heard that before too."

"Give me until the *première*," he requested. "Don't shake things up till then."

She sighed wearily, but eventually nodded.

He extended a hand and she used it to pull herself upright.

"Don't take it personally, but I'll be glad when you're gone, Franck."

"Don't take it personally, but so will I."

*

"Clara, we have a problem."

She was bent double on the floor of a changing room, her brow resting on her knees, her hands curled around her feet.

She was alone.

"I take it you're not talking about the blisters that are forming under both my big toes," she commented, turning her head to one side to look up at Franck.

"No, I'm talking about the fact that you never have an alibi – not for Sophie, not for Abkarian, and not for Lisa."

Before replying she released her feet and slowly raised her back to an upright position, her hands trailing along her legs as she did so.

"That's not true. I told you I was at the gym when Lisa was killed. And I was home on the night Sophie was murdered."

"Telling me you were at the gym is one thing – proving that you were there all the time is another. And sitting at home alone watching a DVD does not count as an alibi."

"Have you asked at the gym?" she challenged him.

"Yes I have. There's a guy who thinks he saw you – assuming you're the tall thin girl with the bow and the pretty face – but he couldn't put a time to it. Look at their system – you wave a card and walk past someone dozing inside a glassed-in cubicle. It scarcely counts as an audit trail."

"So what am I supposed to do? Make something up so that you'll believe I've got nothing to do with any of this?"

"Telling me where you were on the evening of the eighteenth of May would be a good start," suggested Franck. "The night Léon Abkarian died."

Clara went silent. She began to gnaw at her lower lip, her eyes fixed on his. The decision she had to take seemed a weighty one.

"If you insist. But remember it was your idea, OK? I never wanted any of this."

She folded her legs beneath her and then rose into the air.

"Throw me that bag," she instructed, pointing to a sports bag sitting on a nearby bench.

Franck handed it to her. She dug out a pair of jeans and a striped cotton top. She pulled off the leg-warmers she had been wearing, replaced them with the jeans and slipped the top over her leotard. She then extracted a pair of tennis shoes from the bag, put them on, and dug her handbag out of it. She opened a locker, retrieved a light raincoat, and dumped the sports bag in its place.

She turned to face him.

"Let's go."

"Where?"

"I'll tell you when we get there."

"Sounds very mysterious," he joked.

"It is," she said, perfectly seriously.

As they left the Opera she extracted her phone from her bag, texted a message with her thumb, and then turned it off.

"Got a metro pass?" she asked him.

"I'm a Parisian. It's my most important possession."

She led him around the side of the Opera House to the top of the avenue de l'Opéra. Getting to the metro station in the middle of the avenue involved taking an indirect path across rue Auber and the boulevard des Capucines. They found themselves moving in pace with a crowd of tourists, everyone's progress being dictated by the same sets of traffic lights.

Once inside the metro they took line eight, heading south. They changed at La Motte-Picquet for line ten, heading westwards. They did not talk during the journey – or rather, Franck attempted to make conversation but Clara ignored him, sunk in introspection.

They finally got off at Porte d'Auteuil, deep inside the southern half of the sixteenth arrondissement. When they emerged from the metro they found themselves next to the bois de Boulogne, a huge wooded park which formed the western extremity of the city. Clara pulled out her phone and turned it back on.

"This way," she said.

A quiet road led them around the hippodrome d'Auteuil, a horse-racing track which was one of the park's main attractions, along with enclosed flower gardens, a lake with a flotilla of rowboats for hire, and countless facilities for distracting children. The other things for which the bois de Boulogne was notorious were less salutary, particularly its flourishing trade in prostitution. If this was where she had been on the evening Abkarian had been killed, then performance-enhancing drugs might turn out to be the least of the Ballet's problems.

Once they had reached the far end of the hippodrome Clara veered off the road onto a forest path. Franck followed dutifully, now accustomed to their silent progress. A jogger passed them, heading back the way they had come, his hooded sweatshirt unsullied by the slightest trace of sweat. In the sixteenth arrondissement even the joggers had to be decorous.

Clara's mobile phone, still in her hand, buzzed. She looked at the screen and stopped.

"I have to go," she announced.

"What, we've come all this way for nothing?" protested Franck.

"No. You have to stay."

"And do what?"

"Wait."

"For what?"

"For whom," came a new voice, a man's, speaking softly behind him. Franck didn't turn. As the words had reached his ears a cold metallic object had been placed at the back of his neck.

"Walk away, Clara," said the man. "Captain Guerin won't blame you for this."

"On you go," Franck confirmed.

He had recognised the voice. He knew who he was dealing with.

Clara cast a pained and embarrassed look at Franck as she walked past him and his new companion, heading back towards the metro. She did not remind him that she had warned him. Franck appreciated her restraint.

"You're not in any danger, Franck," he was told.

"No, I just have an automatic pistol pointing at the base of my skull, and I'm sure the safety's off."

"Never draw a gun and leave the safety on. If you're not prepared to shoot, then leave it in your holster."

"Or in the deep pouch sewn into the front of your sweatshirt."

"I'd say you've not lost your eye for detail, but you did fail to spot me when I ran past."

"You had your hood up. I couldn't see your face."

"Who runs with a hood up in the bois de Boulogne? This is the sixteenth arrondissement, not some high-rise complex in the suburbs."

"Fair point," conceded Franck. "Next time I'll shoot on sight."

"Where're you keeping your revolver these days?"

"In the briefcase." Franck held his left arm away from his body and twisted his hand so that the lock on his briefcase faced behind him. "Just press down on the brass circle, it'll release the flap."

With his peripheral vision he could see a hand open his briefcase, rummage inside, and pull out his service revolver.

"Thank you."

"What now?"

"Let's go for a walk. It's a lovely afternoon. Off the path, though. We don't want to be scaring the locals. Stay a few paces in front of me. And, Franck, don't go diving behind a tree, OK?"

"I promise. Left or right?"

"Left."

Franck stepped off the left-hand side of the path and walked steadily through the trees, listening to the footsteps behind him.

"We'll stop here," he was told.

"I can turn around?"

"Of course."

Franck turned slowly, keeping his hands a careful distance from his body.

"Hello Franck."

"Hello Gabriel."

Gabriel Agostini was in his mid-thirties, with black curly hair reaching towards his shoulders, a sharp-pointed chin only slightly softened by assiduously cultivated stubble, and dark brown eyes which seemed to drink in all he saw. He boasted an unvarying tan, despite having been on the run for years and therefore – as far as intelligence sources could gather – unable to enjoy the Mediterranean climate of his Corsican homeland.

He was a busy man, head of Appoghui Terra, whose self-proclaimed mission was to dissuade the powerful, be they corporations or individuals, from abusing the planet which had so patiently nurtured them. Its preferred methods of persuasion involved high-velocity rounds and remotely detonated explosives. Gabriel was currently the object of four international arrest warrants, having expanded his sphere of intervention from the island of Corsica to the French mainland and then throughout Europe. There were even rumours that he had recently been behind the execution of the head of a massive Brazilian logging operation. For the moment Appoghui Terra seemed in no hurry to confirm or deny the speculation. Gabriel must have decided that remaining enigmatic served his purpose better.

In the eight years he had been on the active terrorist watchlist, only one person had ever come close to catching him. That near-miss had left Franck a nasty scar on his lower abdomen. It had also cost him his place inside the national security apparatus, leaving him in an isolated office in the quai des Orfèvres, on what was turning into the longest-running temporary assignment in the history of the Brigade Criminelle. Little wonder Gabriel always took care to disarm him on the rare occasions when their paths crossed. Which never happened by accident.

"I'm sorry about this, but I couldn't have you needlessly suspecting Clara. Not so close to the *première* when she has to keep her mind clear and focused."

"I didn't know ballet was so important to you."

"But you did know about the link between Clara and me?"

"I had been told, but I had been hoping it wasn't relevant."

"It's not," Gabriel assured him. "Clara has nothing to do with Appoghui Terra. In fact, she thoroughly disapproves of us."

"Not so much as to denounce you to the police."

Gabriel tutted.

"We're family, Franck. We're Corsicans. It wouldn't be fair to expect that of her."

"So why am I here?"

"So that I can tell you where she was on the evening of Monday the eighteenth of May."

"With you, in other words."

"I'm afraid so. Strictly speaking, I had her kidnapped. I had her snatched around eight and moved her about for a while to make sure she wasn't being followed. We had a chat around ten, and then I had her taken home – in a roundabout fashion, or course. We didn't release her before midnight."

"An alibi furnished by Appoghui Terra – that's one for the books. What was this meeting about?"

"To let her know I was near. Like I said, Franck, we're family. I was already in Paris when the first ballerina was murdered. I couldn't ignore what was going on. You've got to admit, it didn't look good – a dancer strangled for no apparent reason. The Opera suddenly seemed to be a dangerous place. I wanted her to know she had some backup."

"So you've had a protection squad on Clara all this time?"

"If only," said Gabriel wistfully. "We do our best to appear an omnipotent, omnipresent organisation, but Appoghui Terra is no more than a small band of under-resourced amateurs. And we've been very busy recently."

"I heard. Something to do with whales?"

"Something like that. Don't tell me you're involved with the Nakamura case too?"

"Of course not. I'm *persona non grata* as far as concerns anything to do with you. Catherine Vautrin's looking after it. I'd be watching my back, if I were you."

"Ah, Catherine's not half the threat she was when she had you by her side. You're one of the best *flics* in the business"

"Thanks for the compliment, but I wouldn't like to have Abkarian's or Lisa Roux' opinion on that. So what did you do, exactly, for Clara?"

“I tasked somebody from the Nakamura operation to watch over the situation.”

“Not the girl who likes skinny dipping, by any chance?”

A twig cracked off to the left. Franck immediately glanced in its direction. Gabriel did not budge.

A young woman was walking towards them. She wore fishnet tights, shiny knee-high fake leather boots, a tiny skirt, and a cracked leather jacket half-open over naked skin. Her hair was long, an artificial-looking honey blonde. She trailed a shoulder bag just above the ground as she walked. Her eyes were caked with liner, her lips smeared with glossy red, her cheeks unnaturally coloured. All that was missing were oversized attention-grabbing earrings. Maybe she had misplaced them since she looked a little lost, perhaps a little dazed, most probably a little high. Whatever it was, she had strayed some distance from the normal hunting grounds of her profession. Despite which, she did not seem worried at having stumbled across one man holding another at gunpoint.

“I’m a police officer – you need to get out of here,” Franck told her. He did not want her to end up like Acteon, slain for seeing what was meant to be hidden.

She ignored him.

“There are three guys coming through the trees behind me,” she said, keeping her voice down. “They’re moving slowly, but they’ve got rifles. Other units are probably moving in around the perimeter of the woods. It’s time to go.”

“Sorry Franck,” said Gabriel. “It appears your former colleagues have been keeping an eye on Clara too. You should have asked them if they could provide an alibi – it would have been much simpler.”

“Kneel down,” the young woman said, now almost beside him.

Franck dropped to his knees. She pulled his arms behind his back and bound his wrists with self-locking plastic strips. She then pushed him forward and did the same to his ankles. As a final measure she stuffed a wad of cloth into his mouth before sealing his lips with packing tape, which she then wound around his head for good measure.

By the time she had finished Gabriel had disappeared.

"Be good," she whispered in his ear. "They'll find you soon enough."

She wandered on, resuming her shuffling gait. Franck felt sure she would stroll right through whatever cordon the DCRI was frantically putting into place. If they were in luck, Gabriel would simply vanish, leaving them to wonder whether he had tunnelled out of the woods or sprouted wings and flown away. If they were not, he would probably blast his way out, leaving a few bodies in his wake.

Franck managed to roll himself onto his back and settled down to wait.

*

"What's your excuse this time?"

He knew what she meant. After all, he had let Gabriel Agostini get away. Again.

Catherine Vautrin fished out a new cigarette and lit it, waiting for him to reply. She had just emerged from a black windowless van. Those who had the misfortune to share it with her had probably absorbed several years' worth of second-hand smoke in the course of a few hours. That said, the sixty or so known carcinogens she inflicted on her team every day were a minor risk compared to the others to which she exposed them.

"How about, I wasn't expecting him?"

"I warned you that Clara Santoni was part of the clan. You should have been expecting him. He was sure to get involved. That, after all, is how we generally catch his type – keep their extended circle under surveillance for the day they turn up at a celebration, or sneak in for a bedside chat in a hospital, or feel obliged to watch a funeral from what they hope is a safe distance."

"Well, since you were expecting him, what's your excuse?"

She came over and sat beside him on the bonnet of one of the DCRI's unmarked cars.

"You're my excuse. Or at least, you're my watchers' excuse. They've been keeping track of Santoni since we heard about the first Ballet murder. They were always a bit overcautious when you were around, in case you spotted them. I told them not to worry – that you were blind as far as tails were concerned." She patted Franck's knee condescendingly. "But they refused to believe me. When the pair of you left the Opera today, they were too slow and lost you in the metro. It was only when Santoni turned her phone back on that we localised you again. After that it took a little time to get into position, and by then he was gone, having trussed you up like a boar waiting for the spit. Not the kind of behaviour I'd expect from any of my friends."

Franck doubted that Catherine actually had any friends. Then again, she was convinced she did not need any.

"You got closer than you think, then," Franck told her. "Gabriel had a watcher too. A young woman dressed as a prostitute. She spotted your lead team – the snipers – moving into position and warned Gabriel."

She blew out a long stream of smoke, apparently unsurprised that her team had been outsmarted. From previous experience, Franck knew that he had just secured someone a tongue-lashing back at headquarters.

"That's the problem with stealth operations," she observed. "You don't disturb the local fauna so as not to stand out, only to discover that they're anything but innocent bystanders. You can give us her description?"

"Yes, but I doubt it'll help. She made a very convincing low-end prostitute. In real life she's probably as *chic* and *soigné* as any of the locals." He nodded in the direction of the stone-built apartment blocks of the sixteenth which overlooked the fringes of the park.

"Of course it won't help, but you know how much we like piling up data these days. Got to have something to keep the RG boys busy."

"Information sharing is supposed to go both ways. You should have told me the truth about your interest in Clara. All I wanted was proof that she couldn't have committed at least one of the three murders I'm investigating. Looks like I could have got it from you."

"Only for Lisa Roux' death. Clara left the Opera that morning not long after you arrived. She spent a little over an hour in the Paul Gauguin gym playing with her bow and arrows and then sat in a café on rue de Châteaudun before heading back. By the time she got there, the foul deed had been done."

"What about the night of Abkarian's murder?"

"We lost her that evening."

"You know why?"

"I can guess. Her concerned cousin getting in touch, telling her not to worry, singing the praises of captain Franck Guerin of the Brigade Criminelle?"

"Temporary assignment," Franck reminded her. That, after all, was what was marked on his police ID.

She scoffed.

"That's a good one. You'll need to bring Gabriel Agostini's head in on a platter before the DCRI will have you back."

"But why did you lie to me about keeping tabs on Clara? If you'd told me she was in the clear for Lisa Roux this mess today could have been avoided."

"But I didn't want to avoid it, Franck. I wanted another shot at Agostini. Since you're the only goat I've got, I wasn't going to throw away a chance to tether you and lie in wait."

Franck pushed away from the bonnet of the car. He had no desire to continue the conversation.

"You should come to the *première* of *Diana and Acteon.* You'll learn a thing or two about the hunter and the hunted."

Wednesday, 27th May

"That's Elisabeth Platel. Looks like her final performance as an *étoile* in *La Sylphide*."

"And that's you, propping her up," said Franck.

"Oh, she didn't take much propping, Elisabeth. She still doesn't. She runs the Ballet school, and she still slips on her shoes from time to time. She celebrated her fiftieth birthday last month. We did a little *pas de deux* at her party. We're contemporaries after all, even though she made *étoile* long before me. Then again, I always was a slow starter."

"That's not necessarily a bad thing," observed Franck. "Think of the hare and the tortoise. You're still performing, after all."

"I never thought of myself as a tortoise, captain," said Serge Morin, breaking out into a grin, "but you might be right. So what is this? Your dark secret? All along you've been hiding the fact that you're a huge ballet fan?"

"It's not mine. Try another page."

Franck had opened the scrapbook at random before laying it on the dressing table in Serge's lodge. Serge slid the tip of his finger in near the rear cover and lifted back the pile of intervening pages to reveal a new photo.

"Aurélie. *Don Quixote.* Now there's a challenge."

The image showed Aurélie Dupont positioned as if she was diving towards the surface of the stage. She formed a steep diagonal with her legs in the air and her head hovering above the ground. Frozen in time, her arms were thrown wide, her neck bent back, her legs crossed and her feet directed towards the heavens. The only thing keeping her from crashing to the ground was Serge. He bent forward as she angled across him, his arms stretched out to mirror hers, his shoulder providing a support behind which she had hooked one of her legs. The only other point of contact between them was formed by her hip and his left leg, bent beneath her. His right leg stretched out to one side, held ever so slightly aloft with pointed toes.

"What happens if she slips?" asked Franck.

"At best, concussion. At worst, a broken collarbone. And lasting shame for me. Ballerinas trust themselves entirely to their partners. Letting them down is not an option. If you can't guarantee that you'll catch and hold them, come what may, then you shouldn't be onstage."

"2007," said Franck.

"Two years ago? You sure?"

"It's marked."

Franck pointed out where the date was written in the bottom corner of the page, alongside a stick-figure reproduction of the two dancers' poses.

"Well, you can sketch it out, but I wouldn't try to copy that at home, captain. Not without a lot of training."

"Those aren't my notes."

Serge flicked through several more pages.

"Me, me, me. I don't think even I have such an exhaustive record of my career. Not between one set of covers, anyway."

"I tried to give it to you last week. I left it with van Roon, along with some other things. He was supposed to give them to you. Instead they all turned up in Lisa's lodge after she was killed."

"Why did Lisa have them?"

"Because van Roon gave them to her to give to you. For some reason she never got round to doing so. But what worries me is that the evening after I left them with van Roon, your apartment might have been searched."

"I did say it was just an impression I had," Serge reminded him. "I've still not found anything missing, so it's got to have been my imagination playing tricks."

"Maybe nothing was missing because this –" Franck pointed to the open scrapbook. "– wasn't there – wasn't where it was supposed to be."

"What makes you think this is so valuable?" Serge flicked through a few pages. "I still have a few admirers, but I don't think they're that fanatical. And anyhow, if they wanted to, they could probably compile a collection like this on their own. A pile of old ballet magazines and programmes, plus all the stuff you can find on the internet these days, that's all it would take. Isn't that how this one was put together?"

"I imagine so, but I couldn't say for sure."

"So you don't know where it comes from?"

"I know who compiled it. I just don't know how, although I thought I knew why."

"You're being very mysterious, captain. Care to enlighten me?"

Franck shut the book, turned it so that the back cover was facing upwards, and opened it at the very last page. The one with the photo of Serge and Sophie Duval dancing together.

"It was in Sophie's apartment. After her funeral, her parents decided you should have it. Along with these."

Franck retrieved the stiff paper bag he had set alongside his briefcase upon entering Serge's lodge. He extracted the signed photo of Nureyev, the photo of Serge and Sophie in *The Nutcracker*, and the set of keys, laying them alongside the scrapbook.

"You think the killer might have come to my place in search of this?" asked Serge, running a finger down one side of the scrapbook.

Franck nodded.

"But didn't you say it was found in Sophie's apartment? If the killer was after it, wouldn't he have taken it there and then?"

"It was in a small writing desk, in a locked drawer. Maybe he didn't have the time. Maybe he didn't know it existed at that point. Look, I agree, this is all hypothetical, but what I need from you is an answer to a simple question – could the scrapbook mean something I don't understand, or even the two photos?"

Serge shrugged.

"Doesn't sound like a simple question to me, captain."

He propped the framed photos on each side of the open scrapbook and thought for a while.

"All of these concern the Ballet – the Paris Opera Ballet. That's Nureyev when he was Dance Director. That's Sophie and me onstage here. And I don't think I'm wrong –" He slowly turned a dozen or so pages of the scrapbook. "– in saying that everybody in this book is a current or former member of the company. That's the only thing that comes to mind."

"Well," said Franck, not showing any disappointment. "Keep thinking about it, will you?"

"Sure. I'll try going through the book again later on this afternoon if you like. I'll let you know if something comes to me."

"I can't leave it with you."

"Why not?" asked Serge, slightly puzzled. "Weren't you originally supposed to give it to me?"

"It's now evidence. It may be the one thing that explains what's going on here. It has to be in police hands at all times now – what we call the chain of custody."

"I can't even have my keys?"

Franck was placing everything carefully back into the bag.

"I'm afraid not. But don't worry – we won't use them to come crashing in on you."

"Fair enough."

"If anything occurs to you, call me straight away, OK?"

"Straight away," confirmed Serge.

Franck left the lodge with the paper carrier bag held tightly in his left hand.

Clutching at straws.

*

Franck stopped dead when he saw the figure in the centre of the room.

It was Lisa Roux. Exactly as he had last seen her, in her artfully ragged tutu and vine-crossed bodice, a crescent moon perched on her head amongst a constellation of green gems.

She pirouetted once, twice, three times, slightly altering the angle of her arms each time. She was in the middle of her fourth iteration when she saw Franck by the door, stopped her motion, and waved him over.

Now it was no longer Lisa Roux, but Clara Santoni dressed as Lisa had been when she hurried out of the costume workshop to her death.

"Captain," she cried. "I'm so sorry about yesterday."

She could not know what had happened after she had left him in the bois de Boulogne. Nothing had been said about it in any media outlet, and nothing ever would. Franck had no intention of informing her either, and he was prepared to bet that Gabriel would do likewise. Not robbing her of her ignorance was a way of giving her innocence back to her. After all, she had not asked to be born into the Agostini clan.

"There's no need. I understand why you did it and you don't need to worry – there'll be no repercussions."

"That's a relief. Although there was one repercussion I was expecting – that you're now prepared to accept I had nothing to do with doctor Abkarian's death, or the others."

"I do," Franck reassured her.

"Good," she clapped her hands. "Now we can get on with the serious stuff. How do I look?"

He would have said incredible but it would have seemed an ill omen, given that Serge had offered the same compliment to Lisa Roux. Nonetheless, the new costume looked more organic, more a part of her, than the original one, which still lay in pieces in Sternberg's lab.

"Well-camouflaged," he offered, walking towards her.

"I'm glad you think so," she said light-heartedly, "but I'm pretty sure my left nipple's on show."

He hesitated to reply, but then decided that she was right – there was no reason not to banter, even though she was wearing a costume originally designed for a woman who had been murdered.

"Not unless it's green and mossy," he reassured her.

"Well, if I keep this on for much longer, it probably will be. I see you have a present for me."

Franck held out the quiver and bowshaft. He had bumped into a wardrobe assistant who was bringing them to her and had offered to take his place.

"You could have strung it for me," she said. "A big strong man like you. It takes everything I've got to bend that thing."

Her slender arms made her complaint seem credible, but Franck had learned a thing or two about what dancers were capable of over the past weeks. In any case, he had never strung a bow in his life.

"I wouldn't know where to start," he confessed.

"Watch and learn."

She took the quiver, pulled out the four arrows it contained, handed them back to Franck, and then sank her hand into the empty container. It emerged with a hank of thin cord. She passed Franck the quiver and took the bow in return. She stood the bowshaft vertically and knelt down to slip the loop at one end of the bowstring onto the tip which touched the floor.

"This is the tricky bit," she announced.

She wedged the inside of her right foot alongside the bottom tip of the bow. She then pushed the centre of the shaft away with her left hand while pulling the top end down towards her. She did so slowly, her right arm straining as she forced the shaft out of the vertical. Once the bow had taken on a curved shape, she released the centre and brought up her left hand, which still clutched the other end of the bowstring, and looped it in place.

"I'm impressed," said Franck.

"Want to try it? See if you've improved?" she offered.

"Not with those arrows, and not in here. I could go to jail for defacing a historical monument," he said, spinning a finger to indicate the walls around them.

They were in the Foyer de la Dance, a fabled space just behind the main stage – indeed, the iron doors that separated them could be pulled open so as to increase the depth of the performance area and allow the *corps de ballet* to enter the audience's field of vision from what appeared to be the distant heart of the Opera House. Ostensibly a room where dancers could warm up before making their entrance, the Foyer's sumptuous decoration indicated that it was anything but a simple rehearsal room or staging area. Twisting pillars ran up the walls on two sides of the room, harbouring comfortable banquettes between them. A third wall was taken up by a vast mirror, providing the illusion that the Foyer continued on, burrowing endlessly into the building. Everything was golden – the walls, the pillars, the garlanded ceiling, the frames of the circular portraits of eighteenth- and nineteenth-century ballerinas which gazed down from on-high, the chandelier which hung in the centre of the room – and the sharp tip of an ill-shot arrow could too easily score or deface such glistening surfaces. Not to mention the vast paintings by Gustave Boulanger which took pride of place on the walls, representing four archetypes of dance – the mystical spiralling of the devotees of Bacchus, the menacing posturing of those of Mars, the seductive intertwining of those of Venus, and the ceremonial parading of those of Ceres. It was no accident that all portrayed a host of scantily clad and generously proportioned women, since the Foyer's true original purpose was to facilitate encounters between the Opera's ballerinas and their frock-coated admirers. Admission to the Foyer had been a perk reserved for subscribers who purchased a front row seat for a year's worth of performances, plus any others who could worm their way into the good graces of the Opera management. Inside the Foyer's walls they could admire, approach and proposition the members of the *corps de ballet* whose gracious limbs could otherwise only be seen at a distance on the stage. Although puritanical critics decried the Foyer as no more than a decorous brothel, the Opera's ill-paid dancers and rich patrons managed to keep the practice alive until 1935. Fortunately, society had evolved and salaries had risen since then, so Clara Santoni could try out her new costume without having to worry about concupiscent onlookers.

"Pass me an arrow all the same," she said. "I've got to make sure the bow's properly strung."

She motioned with her chin towards the quiver Franck held. He extracted an arrow and passed it to her, feathered end first.

She positioned the bow so that it was facing down towards the floor and fitted the arrow to the string.

"This isn't right," she said, frowning. "It's not been served."

"Sorry?" asked Franck, to whom this meant nothing.

"Look."

Keeping the arrow perpendicular to the bowstring, she moved it up and down. The notch at the end of it slid noiselessly along the thin cord.

"Is it the arrow?" asked Franck. "It shouldn't slip that way? The notch is too wide?"

"No the arrow's fine. But no, it shouldn't slip. There should be enough serving around the string here to make a snug fit for the notch. This one hasn't been served at all."

"You've still lost me."

She removed the arrow and plucked at the mid-point of the bowstring.

"That's the string, OK? It's thin, light, and – most importantly of all – never stretches. That way, when you pull it back –" She did exactly that, causing the ends of the shaft to bend towards her. "– the bow follows, storing all the energy of your pull. When you release it –" Which she did, causing the string to snap forward and the bow to straighten its spine instantaneously. "– the string shoots away from you and punches the arrow through the air. Because the string has no give, none of the energy is wasted in expansion and contraction. Because it's so thin, there's next to no air resistance."

"Where did you learn all this?" Franck asked her. He had the impression he was talking to Georges Sternberg.

"Van Roon gave us all a book on archery techniques when we started working on *Diana*. I think I was the only one to actually read it. Anyhow, the arrow mustn't slide about on the string while you're drawing or releasing. If it did, it wouldn't shoot straight. So to prevent that, the string is served."

"That's where we started," interjected Franck. "But I still don't know what it means."

"Serving is a thin, tough cord that you wind around the mid-point of the bowstring. It thickens it enough so that the notch of the arrow holds fast in place. It also makes it easier to position the arrow correctly, since you can feel by touching where to put it."

"And that's missing here?"

"Yes. Normally there should be a short length of serving already in place right in the middle of the bowstring. I'll have to go and get a spare string that's been properly served."

Franck's mind was racing.

"When you say a short length, how short?"

"I couldn't say. That much."

She raised her hand, thumb and forefinger held apart.

Three and a half centimetres, or thereabouts.

*

"What are you doing? You are aware, I take it, that the *première* is tomorrow?"

Franck was in the armoury, a storage space given over to the Opera's fine collection of fake arms and armour. Row upon row of crested helmets, *papier mâché* breastplates, ceremonial halberds, and toy muskets surrounded him. His attention was elsewhere – in a corner where fourteen bows, unstrung, were propped against a wall bearing a row of pegs at shoulder height. Each individual bow stood alone between two pegs. They were all unstrung. Fourteen empty quivers hung alongside them. Bunches of arrows, bound together by the half-dozen, were piled on a nearby table. Next to them was an open cardboard box.

Franck, wearing transparent plastic gloves, was transferring the loose hank of a bowstring from the box to an evidence bag. He had already filled eleven of them, and only had seven to go.

"We need those," stated Piet van Roon, snatching up one of the bags and tearing into it with his fingernails.

"I'll arrest you for wilfully tampering with evidence if you don't put that down," warned Franck in a low voice.

Van Roon tossed the bag back onto the pile of its fellows.

"You're taking all of them?" he demanded.

"Yes."

"The bows too?"

"No, the bows can stay. As can the quivers and the arrows. So all you have to do is buy some new strings. That shouldn't be a problem."

"We've got twenty-four hours, captain. It took ten days for the archery equipment to arrive after my initial request. The dancers here may be fleet-footed, but the purchasing department is ponderously slow."

But methodical. Franck's first port of call having left Clara Santoni had been the cramped office which housed the Opera's purchasing and financial staff. A polite enquiry and a little patience had allowed him to get his hands on a copy of the original purchase order. That was how he knew that whereas fifteen bows and quivers had been acquired, twenty bowstrings had been ordered to accompany them. He had left Clara with the faulty one and was busy confiscating eighteen others, all of which seemed to have been properly served. That left one unaccounted for.

"Buy them yourself and keep the receipt. I'm sure you'll get reimbursed," suggested Franck. "You don't happen to have a bowstring hidden away on you, do you?"

"You want to search me?"

"I will if you don't answer my question," insisted Franck.

Van Roon turned out his pockets and laid the results on the table for inspection: a mobile phone, a key card from his hotel, a wallet holding several credit cards and a few banknotes, a compact notebook, a single pen, and the inevitable orange yo-yo.

"What exactly are you looking for?" he asked, once Franck had given him the all-clear to recover his possessions.

"One of the bowstrings is missing. Do you remember any of them breaking during rehearsal?"

"It's not easy to break a bowstring. They're designed to absorb a lot of punishment. If anything, the bow should snap first."

"Or the neck," suggested Franck.

Van Roon frowned at him, probably checking that he had not misheard. He then picked up one of the evidence bags and held it before his eyes, almost as if it were a thing of wonder.

"You think this is the murder weapon?"

"It fits the bill. Forensics will tell me more. That's why they're all leaving with me."

"All but one, apparently."

"Here's some free advice – if you see anyone toying with one when I'm gone, give him a wide berth."

Thursday, 28th May

"You're going to be late if you don't leave soon."

Frank nodded distractedly. He was scanning the results of the tests on the eighteen bowstrings confiscated the previous day.

The good news was that they produced ligature marks identical to those found on the victims. To confirm the point, two throttled shop dummies stood not far from where he sat, strings still embedded in the plasticine covering their necks.

The bad news – although he had known it was coming as soon as it became clear that one of the bowstrings purchased by the Ballet was missing – was that none of them was the actual murder weapon. Tiny scraps of Sophie Duval's skin, identified through her DNA, had been found on the serving of one of the strings. A similar trace of Lisa Roux had been detected on another. But as both had undergone archery training while preparing for *Diana and Acteon*, this proved nothing. Notching an arrow to the string would have been enough to leave the traces they had found. More importantly, no sign of Léon Abkarian had been detected.

"Had any ideas about this?" asked Franck, gesturing towards Sophie Duval's scrapbook, which lay in a sealed transparent bag on one of the nearby workbenches.

"Nothing concealed in the binding, nothing written on the backs of the photos. With a little help from Annabelle I've made a list of everyone who features in it. The dates added by hand all seem to be correct and although the stick figure drawings could have been done by a six-year-old they accurately reproduce the postures in the photos. The only thing the scrapbook proves, if you want my daughter's opinion, is that Serge Morin is one of the all-time greats. I can't remember everything she said, but elegance, presence, stamina, and virtuosity were all in there somewhere. It seems you've been hanging about with one of the immortals of the dance world."

"One of its ageing immortals. Don't tell her yet, but Serge will be retiring from the company this summer."

"She'll be surprised. She spent twenty minutes taking me through the photos explaining to me how he'd got better over time. Anyhow, here's the list."

Sternberg picked up a sheet of paper with the names of the dancers in the scrapbook formatted in columns alongside key dates – the year they joined the company, the year they became an *étoile*, the year they stopped performing. He passed it to Franck.

"If these were all dope fiends," he continued, "then the Tour de France is going to look squeaky-clean by comparison. More to the point, most of the people on this list are still active in some way or another – dancing, teaching, choreographing, or managing. None of seem to have suffered any physical ailments which could be linked to previous use of performance-enhancing drugs. If we're still looking for a huge doping-related conspiracy, we're staring at a dead end."

"Is that Annabelle's opinion too?" asked Franck.

"Yes it is. With the accumulated wisdom of her thirteen years on this earth, she told me it was inconceivable that any of the dancers in the scrapbook would do that to themselves."

"She and Anne-Laure Favennec would see eye to eye, then. Maybe I should try to arrange a meeting."

"Are you kidding? Introduce her to someone who'll make her even crazier about ballet? I keep telling her it's time she got interested in other things. Boys, for instance. She's there, by the way."

He nodded towards the list. Franck glanced at it, but could not see the name Annabelle Sternberg anywhere.

"Who's where?"

"Anne-Laure Favennec. *Etoile* in 1979. Gave up in 1987."

"There's a photo of her?"

"Her and Serge, dancing away."

Sternberg extracted the scrapbook from its sealed wrapping and turned to the relevant page. Serge was a familiar figure, but it took Franck a little time to recognise Anne-Laure.

"In which case you're right," admitted Franck. "The conspiracy theory is a dead end. If Anne-Laure's in here, then it's not a list of substance abusers. Which means it's about the forest, not the trees."

"You've lost me."

"The book's not about Serge's partners. It's about Serge."

"You don't say. Fifty-seven photos of Serge Morin and after long and careful thought, captain Guerin, with his accustomed brilliance, realises that Morin is the true subject of the scrapbook. Doesn't explain why the killer wanted to recover it, though, if he really did sneak into Serge's apartment."

"If that ever happened. Serge's always insisted that it was only a feeling he had. There was nothing concrete to back it up."

"That I'm prepared to believe. Have you taken a good look at these?" He recovered a small transparent envelope from a nearby shelf and jangled it in front of Franck. It held the keys to Morin's apartment. "Judging by these, he's got two separate locks on his door, both of which have security keys. Assuming he didn't forget to lock up that morning, it's unlikely anyone could have got through his door without a battering ram."

"It's been a difficult time. His imagination could have got the better of him."

"Or he made it up to make himself look like a potential victim," suggested Sternberg.

"Not his style," objected Franck. "He's not the type to clamour for attention."

"How come his two partners were attacked and he wasn't? Why's he the only one who's above suspicion?"

"Because when Sophie Duval was strangled, he was sipping champagne with several dozen wealthy Americans and a handful of the company's leading dancers."

"Fair point," conceded Sternberg. He tapped his watch. "Now you really do have to go."

Franck reached for the jacket he had hung on the back of a nearby chair.

He was definitely not in the mood for a ballet.

*

She was not difficult to find.

She ought to have been, since it was just after seven and the steps of the Opera House were crowded. But although there were many elegant-looking women milling around in long dresses glimpsed through open coats, only one had a silver crescent in her hair.

"Nice touch," said Franck, striding up to Noémie. He was not quite sure how to greet her, but she showed him the way by kissing him gently on either cheek.

"It came up in an auction in Drouot yesterday. Nineteenth-century jewellery. For some reason, no one was interested, so I snapped it up."

"You'll probably start a craze. Shall we go in?"

She took his arm and allowed him to usher them through the main entrance. Once inside, they stepped out of the flow of spectators so that she could take off her coat. She wore a high-necked black dress. It plunged vertically from her narrow shoulders to her ankles, featuring no sleeves and a tight waist. The cut was almost military in its precision, all angles and straight lines. It flattened her chest and made her seem taller than usual, not to mention a little forbidding. Had Diana been present, she would not have hesitated to welcome Noémie amongst her nymphs.

Having deposited both their coats in the cloakroom and shown their tickets, they began to ascend the grand staircase. It was probably the Opera House's most celebrated feature – a wide, curving procession of steps framed by marble balustrades and overseen by lamp-bearing statues. It rose to the temple-like entrance to the floor of the auditorium before spilling out once more on either side to grant access to the building's upper levels, including the splendid public spaces centred on the Grand Foyer. Surrounded on all four sides by tier upon tier of open balconies, it provided as rich an opportunity for spectacle as the auditorium itself. With its imposing dimensions and extravagant decorative scheme, it obliged every visitor to the Opera to submit to the scrutiny of their peers and prove themselves – by their gait, by their dress – worthy of the building itself.

As they rose, Franck and Noémie's progress was observed from every angle. Franck was under no illusion as to which of them was attracting the most attention.

"You want to take our seats straight away, or go for a drink?" he asked.

"If that's a subtly disguised offer of a glass of champagne, then I'm all for it."

This meant that they did not stop at the first landing and the entrance that led to their seats. Two giant statues stood on either side of it, their limbs cast in bronze, their robes carved from Italian and Swedish marble of different hues. Under their impassive gaze Franck tacked to the left, stretching his arm behind Noémie to guide her with the lightest of touches, and leading her up towards a wide marbled passageway where a bar had been installed between the staircase and the Grand Foyer.

They waited patiently, Noémie gazing appreciatively around her, until they made it to the counter behind which three servers worked with curt efficiency. Franck ordered two glasses of champagne. They were served in clear plastic *flutes*, which failed to make a satisfactory clink as they toasted each other.

The doors to the Grand Foyer were open, a special concession made in recognition of the fact that the evening was to see the *première* of a new work. Like many around them, Franck and Noémie were drawn irresistibly in, lured by its sparkling chandeliers and glinting gold.

"Money well spent," remarked Noémie.

It turned out she was not referring to the original cost of carving and gilding the pillars, installing the lighting, and paying the artist Paul Baudry to spend nine years populating the ceiling with allegorical and mythological scenes. She was talking about the restoration work undertaken five years previously, stripping off a hundred and thirty years of soot and dirt so that they could behold a scene little different from the one which had bedazzled those who attended the Opera's inauguration in 1875.

Franck nodded politely while she talked him through the techniques which had been used to return the place to its initial splendour. It was not that he had no interest in what she was saying – Noémie was no pedant, and simply to watch her face lit up by her enthusiasm was a pleasure in itself – but that a figure was bearing down upon them from the far end of the Foyer.

"I'm sorry," he interrupted, "you'll have to excuse me a minute. I'll be right back."

He stepped away from Noémie and slipped through those milling around them, meeting Sylvie Thomas half-way. The tickets for the *première* might have sold out long ago, but it stood to reason that Lasry Frères would have acquired a block of seats, given their previous investment in Piet van Roon.

"Nice outfit," he remarked, leaning forward to kiss her cheeks. She wore a dark silk top paired with a high-waisted soft leather skirt, both vertically pleated and separated by a studded belt.

"It's not nice. It's stark and powerful and shows that though my twenties might be behind me, I can still pretend they're not. But it looks positively girly alongside what your date's wearing. Who is she?"

"Someone I met recently. She's an art dealer, sort of."

"Who doesn't have a name?"

"Noémie. Noémie Berger."

"She's new," observed Sylvie. "Or you've been keeping her secret."

"Like I said, we've only recently met," insisted Franck, intent on changing the subject. "What about your companion for this evening?"

Sylvie glanced over her shoulder as if unsure of whom he was speaking. Near the gold and black marble fireplace that marked one end of the Grand Foyer, three men in dark suits whom she had abandoned to home in on Franck talked amongst themselves.

"Ah, you mean the distinguished silver-haired gentleman

with the remarkably well-tailored suit, the air of cosmopolitan sophistication, and the almost tangible aura of immeasurable wealth?"

"No, the old guy with the grey hair."

"Jealousy brings out a side of you I rarely get to see, Franck. I rather like it. It makes a nice change from your imperturbable virtue."

"OK, he's in his early fifties and his suit looks brand-new," conceded Franck, "but I don't have your gift for evaluating an individual's net worth at a single glance."

"That's Charles Hance. And if you asked him about his age, he'd probably tell you he's in his prime. As far as his net worth is concerned, that's not exactly true – he's a little over half the man he was three years ago – but in all probability he's the richest man in the Opera tonight. Unless some Middle Eastern princeling is lurking somewhere."

"Charles Hance from the States? The one who provided the money for Léon Abkarian?"

"That's right. An American Friend – just like myself."

"They've come over again? They were already here, what, less than three weeks ago?"

"Maybe you've not heard – crossing the Atlantic no longer means six days on a liner. They have these magnificent machines called jet planes now which can do it in seven hours."

"You're forgetting that I lead a very sheltered life. Still, it's surprising that they've all come back so soon."

"They've not all come back. Hance has come on his own this time – well, with two close friends, but not as part of an American Friends delegation. Lasry Frères invited him over for the *première*. He's a big fan of Serge Morin and is keen to find out what this Clara Santoni is worth. I'm sure he'd be delighted to meet someone who's been spending a lot of time in their company recently. Come on."

She laid a hand on Franck's upper arm and prepared to walk him over to her guests. Franck held his ground.

"I'm with someone, Sylvie. I'm not about to leave her

standing on her own."

"She's a big girl. She'll survive. Some man on the prowl will sidle up and keep her company."

It was Franck's turn to look behind him. Noémie had her head cocked backwards, studying the paintings on the ceiling.

Sylvie tugged lightly on his arm.

"What's the point?" he objected. "You might be an American Friend, but I'm not. I won't understand a word he says."

"You underestimate his linguistic capacities – which, I agree, is hard to do with your average American – but in this case you'll be pleasantly surprised. His accent could use some polishing, and he has not grasped the potential for periphrasis that our beloved tongue offers, but you'll have no difficulty understanding each other. Come on – you owe me and you owe him."

Sylvie was a cunning hoarder of debts, and Franck could not deny that she was due more than a few favours from him. But he bridled at the suggestion that he had some kind of obligation towards Charles Hance.

"How exactly do I owe him?"

"He cooperated fully with your enquiry, did he not? He's the one who revealed the money shuttling between the Ballet and the sporting world's favourite physician."

"He came clean over a suspicious bank transfer. That's not doing a favour – that's clearing his name."

Sylvie raised an admonitory finger and wagged it in front of his nose.

"Now you behave yourself. Come with me. Be polite. And try, hard though it may be, to be charming."

This time Franck allowed her to lead him through the crowd.

"Charles, this is captain Franck Guerin of the Brigade Criminelle."

"It's good to meet you, captain," said Hance in effortless French, extending his hand. "I'm Charles Hance."

"I believe your organisation put up a lot of the money for

Diana and Acteon," said Franck. "You must be keen to see the result."

"My organisation?" echoed Hance, looking puzzled.

"The captain means the American Friends," explained Sylvie.

"Oh, I'm just a trustee. It's not my organisation. I'm not chairman yet." He winked at Franck. "Give me another two years, and when I am I'll make sure your Opera Ballet can afford to commission any choreographer it likes. But you're right about one thing – I'm very keen to see *Diana*. Like every true friend of this place – and that's without the capital 'F' – I'm hoping it's a huge success. The Ballet really needs a triumph to shift attention from the recent unfortunate events. For a while it looked like *Diana and Acteon* was cursed. Tonight's got to change all that."

"The captain here is in charge of the investigation into the Ballet murders," declared Sylvie.

"Really? Now that is interesting. Any promising lines of enquiry?"

"I can't really comment," said Franck, unapologetically.

"Of course you can't," agreed Hance. "But I bet you're the one we have to thank for the fact that Serge Morin and Clara Santoni made it to tonight's performance. You must have been watching over them like a hawk. Round-the-clock protection, that sort of thing?"

Franck decided that the best reply was just a shrug. To deny any praise was due would be to shock Hance with the news that the Brigade Criminelle did not have the means to erect a protective wall around potential future victims, no matter how valuable to the artistic community. And he certainly was not going to explain that malevolent spirits had taken charge of ensuring Clara Santoni's well-being.

"You're a modest man, captain," pronounced Hance. "I like that. Let me just say this – Serge Morin is an international treasure. He's also the last one standing of my generation, as far as dance is concerned. He must have gone through hell for this piece – lose two partners and have to make do at the last minute with one who's not even an *étoile* – so you can be very proud of whatever you've done to help him."

"Based on what I've seen recently, Serge is as tough as they come. He didn't need any help from me."

"You got to know him well?" asked Hance, a note of sudden, almost adolescent, eagerness in his voice.

"I can't say that. But Serge is very open, very down-to-earth, very welcoming. Let's put it this way – he didn't treat me like some kind of alien creature defiling the corridors of the Opera."

"That's great," said Hance, beaming. "Can I ask you a favour, captain?"

"Of course you can," interjected Sylvie. "Can't he, Franck?"

"Look, I don't want to impose, so just tell me if I'm way out of line, OK? I've never really met Serge Morin and I'd really – really – like to get a chance to talk to him. Do you think you could invite him to lunch or dinner on my behalf? I'm in Paris all day tomorrow. He can choose the restaurant – no holds barred. Or breakfast even. I'm staying at the Crillon. We could do it there or anywhere else he likes. You think you could ask him?"

Franck glanced at Sylvie, who was looking at him with narrowed eyes.

"You know," he began, hesitatingly. "We're not actually friends. I've interviewed him and had a few chats, but that's about it. You'd probably be better going through Anne-Laure Favennec. I'm sure she could help. After all, it's not as if you and Serge are complete strangers. Didn't you spend some time together when the American Friends were over, at the welcome reception?"

Franck gestured in the air around them. It had taken place in the very surroundings where they were now standing.

"I'm afraid not," explained Hance. "He was the one person I really wanted to see at that reception, but I didn't get a chance."

"But there's a photo," said Franck, slightly puzzled.

"A photo?"

"On the website," explained Franck. "The American Friends website. You and Serge side by side."

"Ah, that photo. Yes, I've seen it. But believe me, Serge vanished almost as soon as it had been taken. I turned to him to ask a question about *Diana* and he was already gone."

"You didn't hunt him down?" asked Franck, trying for levity. "That's what *Diana*'s all about, after all. You should have followed his scent."

"I would have," insisted Hance. "When I want something, I'm pretty determined, and generally end up getting it. But Serge literally vanished. He was at the reception for maybe half an hour, an hour at the most, and then he was gone. Believe me, I wasn't the only person who was disappointed. A lot of the ladies in the Friends are big fans of Serge. He was badly missed. Hey ... What did I say?"

The question was directed at Sylvie.

Franck had gone, suddenly spinning on his heels and pushing his way through the crowd.

"Let me apologise for him," said Sylvie, stepping in close to Hance. "He's under a lot of stress. Probably terrified something might happen tonight on his watch."

Franck hurried down the grand stairway. He had slipped Noémie her ticket as he hastened past her, telling her not to wait for him. He caught her frown, but not the question she fired back at him as he walked smartly out of the Grand Foyer.

Heading against the flow of incoming spectators, he attracted a lot of hostile glances and was buffeted more than once by those he passed. The murmured protests Franck inspired caught the attention of one of the ushers on the ground floor. He planted himself at the foot of the stairs and blocked Franck's progress, glaring ferociously at him.

Franck whipped out his ID and thrust it into his face, barking, "Police business."

The usher stepped smartly out of his path and Franck pushed his way outside onto the stone steps leading up from the avenue de l'Opéra.

He tugged his phone from inside his jacket and called Georges Sternberg.

"Still at the lab?"

"Where else? We don't all get free invitations to the capital's most select *soirées*."

"Can you get Sophie Duval's scrapbook and bring it here?"

"Where? The Opera?"

"Yes, right now. I'll wait for you out front."

"Couldn't get your hands on a programme? Need something to read before the show starts?"

"Something like that. Can you do it?"

"We're the forensic department, not the express delivery department. What's the rush? Come over after the ballet and pick it up if you like, I'll probably still be here."

"Georges. I need it now."

There was no mistaking his tone. Sternberg stopped playing with him.

"OK. Might take me twenty minutes to get there, though, with the traffic at this time of the evening. I'll take the metro – it'll probably be faster."

"No. Bring the van. And if anyone else is still there, bring them too."

"Why?"

Sternberg might still be asking questions, but Franck could tell he was also moving, gathering things up, not holding out for the answers.

"Bring the keys to Serge Morin's apartment, the ones that were in the bag in Lisa's lodge."

"Why?"

"Once you've dropped the book off I want you to go over there."

"Why?"

"To tear it to pieces."

"Are you sure about this?"

"Yes. And one last thing – I need Annabelle."

"Who?"

"Annabelle. Your daughter."

The Opera steps provided an uninterrupted view down the avenue de l'Opéra to where it ran into the unyielding mass of the Louvre. Napoleon III's carriage could have made the distance – seven hundred stately metres – in ten minutes. Georges Sternberg did it in three, despite the five sets of traffic lights in his way, thanks to the internal combustion engine and a wailing siren.

Franck was waiting by the kerb when he pulled up. One of Sternberg's assistants handed him Sophie's scrapbook through an open window. Sternberg leant across him, the keys to Serge's apartment dangling from his index finger.

"Anything particular we should look for, aside from pills and vials?"

"If you come across any spare bowstrings, bag them too," said Franck.

"How long have we got?"

Franck glanced at his watch.

"They've probably just started. A little over two hours, interval included."

"At that speed we can't be delicate."

"Like I said – tear it to bits."

"We don't have a warrant, Franck."

"Yes you do."

"No we don't."

"Yes you do. What's your name?"

Franck's question was directed at the technician who had pushed himself back in his seat to give Sternberg full access to the window.

"Paul, Paul Galley."

"Paul, you know who I am?"

"Franck Guerin."

"Did you distinctly hear me tell Georges Sternberg that he had a warrant?"

"Yes."

"You remember that for your report if it turns out there's

nothing in the apartment. Got it?"

Paul nodded.

"Any suggestions where to look?" asked Sternberg.

"It can't be that hard. If a ballerina could find them, you can."

Franck was still on the Opera steps when the smokers joined him, signalling the start of the interval.

As they bunched together, offering each other cigarettes, toying with their lighters, communing silently with nicotine, a young girl cut through them, studying faces as she went. She wore jeans, a purple jumper, and a short-cut jacket. She had a large tote bag slung over one shoulder. Her serious demeanour made her look older than thirteen.

Franck waved to her. She came over.

"Thanks for coming, Annabelle."

When he had called her on her mobile, she had told him she was finishing up a ballet class near Daumesnil and could not get to the Opera before eight forty. She had made it with five minutes to spare.

"No problem. Show me the ticket."

Franck held up his ticket for the *première*.

"I think it's a good seat," he said.

"You think? You sat out the first two acts?"

"He did, and it's an excellent seat."

They both looked round. Noémie Berger had joined them.

"Annabelle, this is Noémie Berger," explained Franck. "She's a friend of mine."

"His date, actually," added Noémie, looking archly at Franck.

"How is it – the ballet?" asked Annabelle, unconcerned about the exact nature of the relationship between the two adults she was dealing with.

"Compelling. Beautiful in parts, chilling in others."

"I'm sorry about disappearing," said Franck. "Something's come up."

"With the case?"

"Yes, and I need Annabelle's expert advice."

Noémie raised an eyebrow and shot an admiring glance at Annabelle.

"I hope you're making him pay for this," she said.

"She is," confirmed Franck, depositing his ticket for the *première* in Annabelle's outstretched hand.

"Ah, so you're my date now," observed Noémie.

"Looks like it," confirmed Annabelle. "Nice dress, by the way. Sorry about ..." She gestured at herself. "... but I didn't know I'd be coming."

"Not a problem," insisted Noémie. "Maybe you'd like to join me for a drink before the third act? That way the captain can get on with whatever's so urgent it's worth standing me up for." A smile played on her lips as she said this. Much to Franck's relief.

"Not so fast," said Franck, laying a hand on Annabelle's shoulder. "First of all, you have to show me what you showed your father."

He handed her Sophie's scrapbook.

Franck grabbed his phone. He was sitting on one of the marble steps half-way up the Opera's ceremonial staircase, watched over at a safe distance by two puzzled members of the front-of-house staff. Noémie and Annabelle had left him twenty minutes previously, only just taking their seats before the curtain rose on the second half of the *première*.

"Well?"

He had not bothered to check the name on his mobile's tiny screen. It had to be Sternberg.

"A full house. EPO, PFC, benzedrine, steroids, growth hormone, beta-agonists, iron, syringes, even good old ibuprofen. All in ziplocked bags, just as the doctor ordered."

"How much?"

"Lots. Probably several months' worth."

"Where?"

"A steamer trunk in a corner of his bedroom. An original from the twenties, complete with Cunard stickers."

"Locked?"

"No. Lots of framed photos propped up on it, though – enough to dissuade the idly curious."

But not the determinedly so.

The Emperor's box could not claim the best view in the house. Hung directly over the leading edge of the stage, it provided an awkward perspective. Its occupants could study in detail whatever happened downstage centre or left, but missed most of what took place directly underneath them and had no idea what went on upstage right.

It was, however, the largest and most prominent private box, more than adequate to hold a head of state, plus spouse, plus closest hangers-on, framing them with bronze and marble statues, a triumphal arch, hanging garlands, elaborately worked stone columns and folds of red and gold drapery. Napoleon III, had he ever succeeded in attending a performance at his Opera House, would have sat in majesty above his subjects, a vision to rival that offered by the stage itself.

Anne-Laure Favennec cut a more discrete figure, albeit she occupied the box with no less a sense of entitlement, surrounded by her guard of honour from the Ballet staff.

The third act was coming to an end. Diana was leading her nymphs through the forest in hieratic splendour. A hushed reverence dominated the auditorium. Heads craned forward to catch the delicate footwork on stage.

Franck pushed open the door at the rear of the box.

Several heads swivelled towards him, their brows furrowed and lips pursed in silent admonition. Anne-Laure sat at the very front of the box, her eyes riveted on the stage. Franck pointed towards her and then to himself, but those sitting behind her refused to become accomplices in his heedless interruption of the *première*.

"Anne-Laure!" he hissed, instantly provoking a sibilant chorus of hushes.

"Anne-Laure!" he repeated, still close to a whisper.

This time her head turned, slowly and disdainfully, to

identify the source of the disturbance. Her eyes widened when she recognised him. She waved dismissively, mouthed “after”, and imperiously returned her attention to the stage.

Franck pushed through the rear seats, causing their occupants to recoil, and reached out to grab Anne-Laure’s shoulder. She jumped to her feet and spun round, anger evident on her face but her tongue still silent for the sake of the performance.

“Outside,” said Franck, no longer whispering but trying nonetheless to keep his voice low while suffusing it with a sense of urgency.

He stepped to the back of the box, keeping his eyes on her. She gestured to her companions, commanding them to stay where they were, and inched around the side of the box to join him at the door. She left first and he followed her into the corridor.

“I hope you’ve found another corpse, captain. Anything else won’t justify this.”

“Where can we talk undisturbed?” he asked.

“The library,” she indicated, gesturing down the corridor. “It’ll be empty. After all, everyone’s come to see the ballet, not to listen to a police officer ramble on about his failure to solve a triple murder.”

“Let’s go, then.”

She opened a door to a stairwell and headed upwards, not once glancing back to see if Franck was following.

The Opera library was close at hand, having been installed in what had originally been intended as Napoleon III’s private salon, snugly fitted inside the rotunda on the left-hand side of the building to which only the Imperial carriage was to be admitted. Since the Empire itself had crumbled while the Opera slowly rose from its foundations, the entire rotunda had finally been given over to the institution’s archives and museum. Able to accommodate no more than eighteen readers, the library’s reading room nonetheless did so with a level of style and comfort that recalled its original purpose.

Anne-Laure flicked on the lights and swivelled to face

Franck.

"Be quick, captain. I'd rather not miss the final act, if at all possible."

Franck pulled back a chair from one of the room's generously sized reading tables.

"Sit down," he invited.

Once Anne-Laure had done so he laid Sophie Duval's scrapbook before her.

"What's this?" asked Anne-Laure, tapping its unadorned cover.

"I'm hoping you'll tell me. Take a look."

She leafed through the first dozen pages.

"Is this Serge's? Reminiscences of his career?" She looked up at Franck. "I think he'd rather we watched him live than pore over his past."

"Keep going," instructed Franck.

She picked up again from where she had stopped. She began to name the dancers who featured alongside Serge, to identify the roles he was executing, and to comment on his posture.

She made two more attempts to stop turning the pages, looking up at Franck quizzically, only to be told to keep going. When she had glanced at the final image she closed the book, flipping the rear cover down with a slight thud.

"Well?" demanded Franck.

"Like I said, it's a record of Serge's career, which has proved long and impressive and – assuming you actually saw some of tonight's performance – is still worthy of our admiration. Maybe you can clip a photo from tonight's program and paste it in when you return this to him."

"It's not Serge's."

Anne-Laure shrugged.

"One of his admirers, then. He's not short of them. Maybe one of the many lovers he's chalked up down the years. So what?"

"It belonged to Sophie Duval. She put it together."

Anne-Laure appeared slightly surprised.

"I wouldn't have said Sophie was the groupie type, but we know she fell for him before she – well, you know." She appeared reluctant to sully the evening with any explicit reference to the recent events. "I still don't understand why you've dragged me out here to look at this."

"It's more your field of expertise than mine," said Franck. "But I'll try."

He turned to one of the early pictures.

"1987. Serge was a *premier danseur*. I think you'll recognise his partner."

"It was my last year as an *étoile*," commented Anne-Laure, looking at her earlier self without any apparent nostalgia. "We're doing a *pas de deux* from *Don Quixote*."

The younger Anne-Laure formed a diagonal line, one leg crossed in front of the other, her toes pointed, only one of which was actually in contact with the ground. Her left arm was cocked against her hip, palm aligned with the top of her tutu. Her right arm shot out to the side, parallel to the stage, palm open and erect. Behind her, supporting her weight, was Serge, his right arm beneath her, his hand flat on her lower abdomen. His left arm, stretched out away from her, mirrored her right. His right leg was firmly planted on the stage, a perpendicular pillar aligned with the centre of her torso. His left leg, its weight resting on the ball of the foot, respected the diagonal she had formed.

"OK," said Franck, flicking forward. "What about this? 2007. Serge and Lisa Roux."

"Same *pas de deux*," commented Anne-Laure. "Exact same moment."

"So what's the difference?"

Anne-Laure took control of the scrapbook, moving back and forward between the two images.

"The older costumes are more striking. The scarlet and black works better than the new colour scheme. I should show this to the design team."

"No," intervened Franck. "The difference is that Serge is standing on the ball of his right foot, and his left one is hovering above the stage. Look at his right hand. You can barely see it. His palm is probably flat on her back. He's holding her with his fingers."

"I didn't know you were such a connoisseur," remarked Anne-Laure. "It's unorthodox, I'll grant you that. But it heightens the effect. It's more gracious. It's as if both of them were able to float above the ground."

"Try this one then."

Franck took back the book and quickly found the page he was looking for.

This time Serge and his partner were facing in opposite directions. His partner stood on point, her left leg supporting her weight, her right one raised behind her in a steep line, her right arm hovering above it while her left one traced a delicate curve before her. Serge held the same position, albeit on the ball of his right foot.

"1992. Serge's third year as an *étoile*," said Franck. "Dancing with Marie-Claude Pietragalla."

"She's outstretching him," commented Anne-Laure. "She should have stuck with an *arabesque à la hauteur* – Serge is struggling to push his leg as high as hers. She's got at least twenty degrees on him. I don't imagine anyone will have noticed at the time, but the ensemble is not as harmonious as it should be."

"Good," said Franck. "I'm glad you feel that way. So you'll prefer this one."

He moved forward through the pages to stop at a photo capturing the same movement at a different epoch.

"2008. Serge and Delphine Moussin."

The two dancers formed a perfect mirror image.

"You're right. That is better. They're both holding at a hundred degrees, maybe a hundred and ten. They're flawlessly synchronised."

"Is Serge struggling?"

"If so, he's hiding it well. What are you getting at, Franck?"

"In the *Don Quixote* images you have Serge at forty-seven holding the weight of a ballerina with more ease than at twenty-seven. He has better balance and stronger leg and arm muscles. In the last pair you have Serge at forty-eight with greater flexibility than he possessed sixteen years earlier."

"He's a wonder. It's not for nothing he's a legend inside the company – a role model for all the younger dancers. He's the living proof that hard work, discipline and dedication can keep you going despite the ravages of time."

"That's my point," interrupted Franck. "The ravages of time are nowhere to be seen in this book. The photos it contains show a Serge who miraculously becomes fitter, stronger, and more agile in his forties than he was in his twenties or thirties."

"I doubt that," she objected. "A random collection of images can probably be arranged to give any impression you like. Don't get carried away by a few photos. You said it yourself – this isn't your field of expertise."

"It's not my theory I'm expounding. It's Sophie Duval's. She put this scrapbook together. She pored over it. She analysed every image. Look –." He turned slowly through several pages for her. On each one he pointed out the stick figures Sophie had added alongside the images, the angles she had drawn in, the arrows showing where the points of greatest stress must have been. "Sophie worked it out, not me."

"Worked what out? That Serge has discovered the elixir of youth? That he knows how to stop or even turn back the hands of time?"

"No, Serge didn't discover the magic potion. Léon Abkarian did that. Serge just sought him out and followed his prescriptions with the rigour and discipline for which he is, as you pointed out, justly famed. You want to know where the dope is in the Opera Ballet?" Franck shut the book and slammed the flat of his hand upon it. "It's in here, and it's onstage as we speak."

"Surely there have to be tests – blood, urine, whatever – before you start making this kind of accusation," protested Anne-Laure.

"I'm not accusing him of doping his performance. If that was all he'd done I wouldn't even be here. I'm charging him with murder."

"Serge?"

She was blind to the implications of the information he had just given her. She could not see beyond the Serge Morin who was the mainstay of the company, who taught at its school, who mentored the entire *corps de ballet*, who shook hands and posed for cameras at its corporate functions, the Serge who had dedicated his life to the Opera Ballet.

And who had killed so that it would not be taken from him.

"Sophie realised Serge was using something to artificially boost his physique. She searched his apartment – since they had become lovers, she had his keys – and found his stash of drugs. She stole some as proof and hid them in her lodge here in the Opera. They came from ziplock bags that Abkarian had filled – that's why both their fingerprints were on them. Serge, on the other hand, only took out drugs as and when he required them. Anything he touched, he used. Sophie was probably going to bring the drugs to you – she had made an appointment to see you privately the day after her death – but either she confronted Serge or he found out, and he killed her."

"Serge throttle Sophie with his bare hands?" she objected incredulously. "When they were lovers?"

"Not with his bare hands. With a bowstring taken from the equipment van Roon had introduced for *Diana and Acteon*. And then we found the drugs in Sophie's lodge, which led us to Léon Abkarian. That gave Serge something new to worry about. He wasn't going to gamble his career on Abkarian's standard refusal to reveal anything about his clients, so he intervened. Of course, killing Abkarian meant depriving himself of future supplies. He couldn't go on as before. So he decided to retire at the end of this season."

"Serge retiring? He's said nothing to me."

"He wasn't planning on saying anything until after tonight. He was intent on going out in glory – until Lisa got in the way."

"What about Lisa?" Anne-Laure's refusal to believe him was audibly crumbling.

"Lisa wanted to clear Sophie's name. She kept worrying away at the mystery of her death. Thanks to van Roon, she got her hands on a bag of Sophie's belongings destined for Serge. This scrapbook was amongst them. She looked through it and began to understand what it meant. Since there was a set of keys in the bag she went round to Serge's apartment one evening when he was out with the male cast of *Diana*. She found what Sophie had stumbled across before her – his drug cache. She took some samples, just like Sophie. At first she must have thought that she'd found the explanation for the substances found in Sophie's lodge – nothing more. But then she began to realise the wider implications of her discovery. It took her a little time to overcome her instinctive reluctance to believe that Serge was capable of killing, but eventually she tried to reach me, to tell me before Serge worked out what she was up to. But he was too quick and I was too late."

"This is ..."

Confronted with the inconceivable, Anne-Laure could not finish her phrase.

"This is going to end," stated Franck. "Right now."

Piet van Roon stood apart from the others clustered in the wings.

He had advanced as close as was possible to the stage without being visible to the audience and was studying the performance impassively. When a dancer passed alongside him to enter or exit he offered no encouraging glance or words. His creation had taken on its own independent life. It was escaping him before his very eyes and he observed it with a mixture of anxiety and curiosity.

Franck stepped up beside him. It was the last scene of the final act. Acteon was being pursued by his beloved pack of hounds. Franck had missed the moment when Diana, in the course of an intimate *pas de deux*, had crowned him with a headpiece bearing short, stunted antlers – an echo of the crescent moon that shone on her own brow; the gift of total assimilation with Nature and the universe of the hunt; the gesture that signed his death.

Serge leapt and weaved across the stage while four male dancers followed him, boxed him in, toyed with him. Finally they caught and lifted him, eight hands grasping his stiffened legs to propel him above their heads. Serge froze, his arms raised and wrists crossed above his fatal crown. His eyes were fixed on the distant figure of Clara, who stood haughtily at the tip of a wedge formed by her nymphs, all leaning forward, eager spectators of the massacre. Serge brought his arms down and swept them towards her, an apparent plea for mercy which became a gesture of homage, an offering of himself, an acceptance of his fate.

The four dancers beneath him released their grip. As he fell they bent forward, joining hands over him. When they finally broke formation, Serge was a crumpled figure on the floor. Clara moved towards him on points, arms spread, her nymphs keeping a wary distance. She circled his body in a serious of pirouettes and then slid down on one knee alongside him, extending an arm to place a finger on his upturned forehead. As she reclaimed it, she rose, shifting her weight onto the point of her right foot. She moved slowly into an *arabesque*, her left leg raised high behind her as she curved her head and torso backwards, gazing in fascination at her finger as she brought to the edge of her lips. She paused, savouring the moment, and then darted out her tongue, licking its tip.

The stage went dark, provoking a sudden surge of applause and cheering from the auditorium.

In the dim light filtering from the wings, Franck could see Serge leap to his feet and throw his arms around Clara, who looked dazed. The nymphs and hounds crowded around the pair of them, reaching out to touch and hug them.

Van Roon brought his hands together to produce a single staccato clap.

"Formation," he commanded.

The male and female dancers split. The nymphs lined up behind Clara on one side of the stage, the hounds doing the same behind Serge on the other. Serge repositioned his antler crown to sit level on his head. Clara accepted a bow and quiver from one of her nymphs. All drew themselves up, lifted their heads, and faced forward.

The applause was building in intensity as the audience willed the dancers to reveal themselves once more.

"He doesn't deserve this," muttered Franck, stepping forward.

Van Roon's arm shot out and blocked his path.

"What are you doing?" he hissed.

"Arresting Serge Morin."

"What!"

"That's the man who killed two of your Dianas. I'm not having him glorying in this applause."

Van Roon pulled back, studying Franck with apparent fascination.

"You are sure of this, captain?"

"Unfortunately, yes I am."

"You saw how he danced. He was perfect. Clara too. Whatever he has done elsewhere, he has committed no crime tonight. You cannot go out there. Wait until he comes off."

"No," said Franck bluntly, taking a step forward.

Van Roon grabbed his shoulder.

The stage lights came back on. The noise from the auditorium reached a crescendo.

"Is justice so impatient? Let art have its moment."

"Get your hand off me."

"Where's he going to run?" Van Roon clamped his free hand on Franck's other shoulder. "In five minutes he's yours," he whispered urgently in his ear.

Without turning Franck drove his right elbow into van Roon's abdomen. He gasped, released his grip, and doubled over.

Franck strode purposefully onto the stage. It was bathed in light. Serge and Clara had taken a few steps forward and were bowing.

Franck passed around the formation of nymphs, who pretended to ignore him, although their eyes followed his unexpected progress.

Serge rose from a bow to find Franck at his side. He turned to face him. The broad smile he had just offered to the audience in return for its acclamation disappeared instantly. His eyes narrowed to dark slits and his face tensed in anger.

"You have no right to be here," he spat.

"Neither have you, Serge. Not if it meant killing Sophie Duval, Léon Abkarian and Lisa Roux."

"Walk away. As soon as the curtain drops, I'm yours. But don't interfere with this."

Franck shook his head.

"Serge Morin, you're under arrest for ..."

A snarl broke from Serge. The back of his left hand slammed into the side of Franck's face while his right one dug into the pocket of his breeches. Franck instinctively twisted away from the blow, turning from the audience. Serge instantly stepped behind him, raising his arms over Franck's head and slamming them down on his shoulders. Franck saw something thin flash past his eyes before it was drawn back against his neck, hitting it with the force of a blunt knife blade.

As Franck's fingers scrambled to catch the string, Serge's right hand flew round his neck, positioning a second loop. Franck pushed backwards, hoping to topple him over, but Serge was too strong for him. His feet, long trained to maintain his balance, were securely planted on the stage. He absorbed the force of Franck's struggling body without budging. Franck kicked backwards at Serge's right shin. Serge grunted, but his leg did not waver. This time it was his left hand which circled Franck's head. Three loops were now in place.

In a final effort, Franck pulled up his knees, falling heavily to the stage. But Serge had sensed his movement and fallen with him, only more neatly. Franck found himself with his legs splayed before him while Serge was propped on his knees, with all the leverage he required to resist Franck's desperate attempts to push backwards against him.

Franck's vision was clouded with red. Panic seized him. He was unable to do anything other than claw at his own throat, tearing his skin. His mouth remained desperately open, his nostrils flared, but no air could pass. His brain was shutting down. Consciousness was brutally taking its leave.

Then the pressure eased.

Franck lurched forward, throwing himself away from Serge. He twisted onto his back, pulling the bowstring loose from his neck, gasping.

Serge lay at an angle a pace away from him. The side of his face was flat against the stage. His mouth, too, was open, but all that came from it were hissing and burbling sounds. His eyes strained upwards, urgently seeking to find out what was behind him, what had sprouted in his back, what had pierced his flesh and burst the walls of his lungs.

Franck could see the shaft clearly enough. He could even make out the notch and the feathers aligned around it. But it took his troubled vision a moment to focus on what was beyond it.

Clara Santoni, her bow still raised, her right hand nocking a second arrow, just in case.

It was not required.

*

His phone was ringing.

He tugged it out, stepping back from the kerb, having waved goodbye to Annabelle Sternberg. Noémie was accompanying her home. She had hugged Franck tightly to herself and kissed him forcefully on the lips before joining Sternberg's daughter inside the taxi. It boded well for the future.

Franck expected the call to be from Georges Sternberg, about to give him hell for exposing his daughter to the ballet's unscripted finale.

He was wrong.

"You've had an interesting evening, captain."

It was Gabriel Agostini.

"You were there?" asked Franck.

If so, then he might still be in the immediate vicinity of the Opera House. So, too, might be a team from the DCRI, knowing Catherine Vautrin. If Agostini had come to applaud his cousin, it might yet prove his undoing.

"No. I knew I could count on your old boss to stuff the place with her boys and girls. I hope she enjoyed the show. Next time you see her, remind her she's got me to thank for that."

"So who told you what happened?"

He hated to think that it might have been Clara herself. If her first instinct had been to call Agostini, then she had just condemned herself to a future of constant surveillance.

"I had a friend in the auditorium."

One in an audience of two thousand. Those were good odds in favour of anonymity.

"I'm told it was a triumph," he continued.

"I couldn't say," admitted Franck. "I missed almost all of it."

"Turns out she's quite a shot, my little cousin."

"Hard work and discipline," commented Franck. "The Opera Ballet's creed."

"Or maybe it's just in her genes."

Franck hoped not.

He really hoped not.

Friday, 29th May

"What do you want?"

The question was both wary and aggressive, which was scarcely surprising. The hand-written notice taped to the door of the concierge's lodge declared her afternoon hours to be three thirty to seven thirty. It was nearly eight. By the look she was giving him, Franck suspected he had interrupted her dinner.

"I'm sorry to disturb you, madame," he said in his most apologetic voice, "but I'm here on police business."

This was not true, but it did not stop him pulling out his ID and holding it up in front of his chest.

"Let me see that," she said.

He handed it over and she shut the lodge door. A few minutes later he heard her talking. She had phoned the number on the back of the ID. He was impressed. He just hoped the front desk at the quai des Orfèvres remembered who he was. After two years of temporary assignment to the place, there were still some long-timers who deliberately ignored his existence.

The concierge reappeared, this time with glasses perched on her nose.

"What's so interesting about my building it's brought you lot round?"

"Noémie Berger," said Franck.

She had not returned any of his calls that day. Franck was aware that he had not been at his most chivalrous the previous evening, but she could scarcely deny that there had been mitigating circumstances. From where she was sitting, she had probably been able to see the cloud of red invading his eyes as Serge Morin choked him. And she had not protested when he asked her to see Annabelle Sternberg safely home.

But her silence had now lasted long enough to seem ominous. He had just spent fifteen fruitless minutes trying to reach her on the building's intercom. He hoped she was out, but could not exclude the possibility that she was ignoring him.

Or that something had happened to her. If the concierge did not prove cooperative, he might find himself breaking and entering.

"Sixth floor, on the left," she told him. "It's marked over there – forgot your glasses?"

She was talking about the block of letter boxes which hung on the opposite wall. Each one was marked with a name, a number for the floor, and a letter indicating which side of the landing the person occupied.

Franck had already trailed his fingers inside Noémie's box. It was empty.

"Is she in?" he asked. Night would not fall for another hour and a half, so he had learned nothing from staring up at her windows from the street outside.

"I don't know," she proclaimed indignantly. "I don't clock the tenants in and out. Why don't you go up and find out?"

"I'm about to. I was just wondering if you had a set of keys."

"Shouldn't you have a warrant or a piece of paper to be asking for something like that?"

"I do have a warrant," replied Franck, "otherwise I wouldn't be asking."

He opened his briefcase and began to look inside it, frowning and taking his time. Fortunately, the concierge proved less patient than he was. She scoffed at him, stepped back inside her lodge, and returned with a single key.

"You want to come up with me?" he asked.

"I'm far too busy. And it's not my hours anymore. Drop it off when you come back down."

Franck took the stairs, keeping a slow, steady pace. When he reached the sixth floor he had the choice of two doors. Neither bore a name.

He put his head close to the one on the left. Nothing. He tapped lightly upon it. Nobody answered.

"Noémie?" he called.

Still nothing.

"Noémie!"

Silence.

Franck propped his briefcase against the wall, having first removed his revolver.

He slowly inserted the key into the lock with his left hand. There was no handle, just a large knob in the centre of the door. When the lock clicked he leant against it, holding his revolver across his chest. He had already cocked it.

The door opened onto a small salon, furnished with a two-seater sofa, a dining table with two chairs, a flat-screen TV and a shelf unit which was empty aside from a few books and an unoccupied vase. Two doorways led away from the room, one to a cramped kitchen and the other to a short corridor. He followed the latter to a small bathroom and a bedroom which barely had enough room for a double bed, a wardrobe and a single chest of drawers.

Everything was neat and tidy. In the bathroom the towels were arrayed in orderly fashion. In the kitchen dishes were drying next to the sink and all the pots and pans were hanging in their place. The bed was made, its cover smoothed down and a quilt folded on top of it.

Franck checked the wardrobe. It was almost empty.

But not quite.

A worn leather jacket sagged from a hanger, its surface streaked with cracks and mud. Next to it hung a cheap synthetic skirt scarcely wider than a hand's-breadth. Next along was a long blue silky dress. He checked the label. Lanvin – probably straight from their boutique on rue du Faubourg Saint-Honoré. At the bottom of the wardrobe were a pair of long shiny plastic boots that stood stiffly erect. Next to them were propped a pair of elegant black heels. A large plastic shopping bag lay in the corner. Franck opened it knowing what he would find inside. A blonde wig, its tresses long, and a balled-up pair of fishnet stockings.

Franck closed his eyes and rested his head against the side of the wardrobe, using his forearm to cushion his brow. As ever, if something was too good to be true, it was indeed too good to be true.

So much for Noémie Berger.

He moved back into the salon.

Propped up on the sofa was a parcel the size of a magazine, about five centimetres thick, and wrapped in brown paper. Franck knelt down before it and studied it, looking for any visible wires or trigger devices.

When he felt confident he could touch it, he lifted it carefully and ran his hands slowly over its surface. As he did so the paper, which was not taped down, began to fall off.

He was holding a small landscape painting. It was a view of the Ile de la Cité done in oils, probably from the downstream vantage point offered by the pont des Arts. The colours were dull and it had a slightly grimy look. It did little to hold the eye and certainly could not compete with what surrounded it. Made of dark wood, its frame was carved with a luxuriant, many-stemmed plant whose tendrils met and joined in complex ovals at each corner.

A note, hand-written on a square of thick cream paper, lay on top of the painting.

> Dear Franck,
> Toss the painting if you like – some cack-handed amateur from the fifties, I'd guess – but hang onto the frame. It's genuine Art Nouveau – a testimony to the late nineteenth century's impatience for the twentieth – and is not only particularly elegant, but worth quite a bit.
> Sorry for leading you astray, but though my motives were mixed, my pleasure in your company was not.

She had not signed it. The note was probably her last act in the persona of Noémie Berger. She would now go back to her real name or, more probably, another of her aliases.

But he would remember her as Noémie – as the distraught owner of a cell phone left carelessly at his feet in the metro – rather than as the prostitute who had bound his arms and legs in the bois de Boulogne, or the temptress who had speared Toshiro Nakamura with a harpoon.

He turned the note over. There was one last line.

> You're a good man. Don't think too badly of me.

He would try.

But it would not be easy.

WASP-WAISTED

David Barrie

A young model is found dead in a luxury hotel in Paris. A stunning photo of the scene features on the cover of the country's top-selling scandal sheet. It was delivered before the police found the body. In a city obsessed with images of perfection, the murderer's artistic talents are the object of much admiration.

It's Franck Guerin's first criminal case. Used to the murky world of national security, he has to learn to play by the rules. Not so easy when your only clue is the *ultra-chic* lingerie in which the victim was draped.

The fashion trail takes him into a universe of desire, deceit, beauty and profit. As the victims mount and the images roll in, Franck has to train his eye to spot the killer's signature. Not to mention whoever is collecting photos of him...

The first of the Franck Guerin novels. Original, stylish and tightly plotted, Wasp-Waisted recounts a murder enquiry born of a fatal encounter between fashion, art, business and desire.

www.waspwaisted.com

NIGHT-SCENTED

David Barrie

Isabelle Arbaud, as acerbic as she is ambitious, is determined to provoke a revolution in the elitist world of luxury brands. She has poached her rival's most talented perfumer in order to invent an irresistible scent that will catapult her upstart fashion house to the head of the pack.

Someone out there doesn't want her to succeed. The investors who bankroll her efforts keep dying in circumstances which are, to say the least, suspicious. One is run off an isolated road. Another is found backstage at a show during Fashion Week, a bullet in his head.

Franck Guerin, on temporary assignment to the *Brigade Criminelle*, catches the case. A noxious cocktail of jealous rivalry and ill-concealed contempt awaits him. As other killings follow, however, he begins to wonder whether the real explanation for what is happening lies elsewhere – with an enigmatic homeless man who hovers on the periphery of each crime.

Confronted with multiple suspects, all of whom seem intent on pulling his strings, Franck must tread carefully through an investigation which throws a dark light on the gilded city of Paris.

The second Franck Guerin novel illustrates the author's fine grasp of the social geography of Paris, charting a course from the dizzying luxury of the city's fashion houses to the unseen corners where its homeless use their wits to survive.

www.nightscented.com